# *to* LOVE *a* GOD

⚜

## EVIE KENT

# CONTENTS

*Dedicated to the villains I'll always love.*

*"... And while you are here, you shall rule all that lives and moves and shall have the greatest rights among deathless gods: those who defraud you and do not appease your power with offerings, reverently performing rites and paying fit gifts, shall be punished for evermore."*

Hades to Persephone

**HYMN TO DEMETER**

CONTENT WARNING

Please note that *To Love a God* includes content that may not be suitable for all readers. This is a **dark paranormal romance**. As someone who nervous-sweats over certain dark romance themes, I request that you know your own limits and discontinue reading should something take you beyond your comfort zone.

## TO LOVE A GOD

**A Lily of the Valley Novel**
Evie Kent

I spent my whole life training to become a ballet dancer—a soloist, a star. Today, I'm a toy, a plaything, a distraction...

An offering.

A sacrifice to a caged god, to *the* Norse trickster.

Loki.

Trapped in a cave for the sins of his past, he waits for the end of days. Modern worshippers curry favor with gifts and trinkets, spilled blood—and women like me.

Women who resemble his long-dead wife. We all have that look, you see. I'm supposed to be flattered that I remind him of a goddess in an age gone by.

*Fuck* that.

I'm furious.

The ones who came before me were sweet, docile, compliant—just like her. But I'm not sweet. I'm not docile, and I will never be compliant.

I am resilient. I am determined.
I am—*not*—drawn to him.
I will survive this.
I will survive him.
My name is Nora Olsen, and I will not die here...

# PROLOGUE: OSKAR

The man on the other side of the bars was the Devil.

I knew that.

I had known that since I was a child. All those years, I stared at the black mouth of his cave, knowing, deep down, that something foul resided within the mountain. Now a grown man, I saw the hellfire inside *him*. The rage. The malice. The great capacity for cruelty, the kind that paired well with laughter and screams.

Mama and Papa believed in the old gods. The whole village did, or they would have left the Devil to rot in his hole. I believed...

Well, I believed in *him*.

I believed in what he could do for my people, for the bounty he had gifted us for generations.

But did I worship him like my parents and their parents before?

No.

I feared him.

That was the only way with a villain like Loki—fear. Respect for his power, even muted by an ancient witch's curse. Fear and respect... There was nothing else. No in-between. No civility nor friendship. No compassion. No love.

Not for a thing like him.

"Hello, Oskar."

I stiffened, still unaccustomed to the slithering rasp of a god—a trickster, a half-giant. They sent me today because my family had been his emissary since the beginning. Sons and daughters of the original village jarl all made the trek up to his cave, to the electrified bars erected some twenty feet beyond the gaping mouth. The curse encompassed the whole mountain; even if he broke through the bars, he could never walk free.

The bars weren't for *him*, anyway.

Outside, the roar of a spring storm dulled against the stone, the moss, the scraggly, thorny underbrush that grew across his prison. Rain had hammered us all week, unrelenting, biblical flood-level downpour. It was the kind of storm you felt in your bones, and it dribbled off me now, fat droplets falling from the bottom of my jacket. Each one landed with a distinct *plop* on the cave floor.

Each one made my heart race just a little harder.

I sucked in a stuttering breath when his outline materialized in the shadows, more wild beast than man. Six months had passed since any of us set eyes on him properly, but we all knew he was there—forever *here*, trapped, doomed for eternity.

Good. He deserved an eternity in here.

The god emerged from the darkness like a prowling cat, taller than me by a full head, his flaming red hair tangling over his shoulders, his beard thick and matted. A half-mad gleam twinkled in his green gaze. Shirtless today; I didn't dare look below his jagged collarbones to confirm if he was wearing pants. Disheveled. Unkempt. Forgotten.

Maybe even broken.

"We found one," I remarked, fighting for nerve, for a bit of steel in my spine as I dug my phone out of my jacket. So far, we only had her passport photo and a few blurry screenshots from a security camera, but that was enough. "Our agent at the airport spotted her—recommended the usual hotel. Hans at the front desk suggested the park for sightseeing, take the hiking tours up to the glacier and all that. She's... She's here."

The demon slithered closer to the bars, his movements fluid, graceful.

Unnatural.

I held up my phone, shaking. Even with the brightness turned all the way down, its glare made Loki squint.

"Closer, Oskar," he rumbled, his voice rough—unused. Or possibly because that throat of his was shredded to bloody strips; we'd heard him screaming last week, shaking the mountain, his rage quaking through the village.

Such reach.

What more could he do without the witch's shackles?

Everything.

I didn't dare let him tell me twice, even if his outdated Norwegian was a little muddled sometimes. He did it on purpose—refused to modernize. Papa said he spoke every language in all the worlds, this silver-tongued father of lies. Able to deceive in thousands of dialects. And yet he refused to shirk the accent, the old-fashioned lilt and intonation when he spoke to us.

Fucked with us, more like.

"*Closer,*" he growled. Apparently a foot away wasn't close enough. Swallowing hard, I gave him another two inches, then yelped when his monstrous hand shot out between the bars and snapped around my wrist. Something crunched when he wrenched me closer, bone or cartilage—something that *hurt*, but I bit the insides of my cheeks and stuffed it all down. He had no sympathy, no pity.

No heart.

I dragged my feet, fighting to keep away from the bars, from the live wires coursing through them. The electric shock was a recent addition when Loki's previous guest proved to be *just* slim enough to wriggle through.

Every inch of me trembled as he studied my phone with a cocked head and narrowed eyes. I knew for a fact that he tempered his hold on my arm, that if he so desired, he could break bone with a snap of his fingers. But the threat of physical harm wasn't what made me shake—wasn't what kept me up at night. His presence alone was enough, this primordial being capable of great horrors. Bringer of the apocalypse, catalyst of doom.

Loki's thin lips stretched into a predatory smile, his sunken cheeks and crazed gaze cast in a sickly white glow.

"Bring her to me."

We all knew he would like her—she was just his type. Difficult to find. He had been without one for the last seventy-five years, his tastes so painfully specific that he had rejected twelve candidates *before* this damned soul.

"Yes, yes, my lord," I stammered out. I might not worship with the same reverence as my parents, but I knew where I stood on the food chain. Fear and respect.

Loki released me with a shove, forceful enough to toss me backward. I landed hard on my tailbone, but again swallowed the burst of pain as I scrambled up. He wore the same wolfish grin, but his stare had hollowed, like suddenly he was whole galaxies away.

Or just numb.

I'd be numb after eight hundred years inside a cave.

No sympathy though.

Not for him.

*Never* for him.

Without another word, the Devil retreated into his own personal hell, swallowed by shadows, and his cold laughter followed me all the way down to the village. Even the torrential downpour couldn't wash it away, couldn't scrub me clean of his touch. In my dreams that night, I saw the hellfire in his eyes. I felt the iron grip of those large hands on my throat, twisting the life from my wretched body. I all but tasted his smile, cruel and sharp and barbed with thorns.

And when I woke the following morning in a cold sweat, I pitied her.

I pitied pretty Nora Olsen—and feared for what was to come.

1

# NORA

"Hey, babes, can you take our picture?"

*What happened to your fucking selfie stick?* "Sure, no problem."

Seriously, this bitch had spent the last half hour jamming her knees into the back of my seat, and now she had the *audacity* to tap me on the shoulder and ask for a photo? Ugh. I'd left the city to get away from tourist bullshit, but I guess it was everywhere.

Not that I had a right to be pissy about tourists over here when I was one, just one of the sheep wandering around with the herd, but this Scandinavia trip was supposed to be my opportunity to get away from people in general. After all the heartache and stress of the last year, the endless hours in the company studio working myself to the bone, my health faltering, moving all my stuff out of the apartment I thought I'd share with my soulmate for-fucking-ever, I deserved a bit of peace and quiet.

But. Sure. I could take a picture on this brat's phone.

British, the pair of them. Two teen girls who yammered at an octave only dogs could hear all the way from our bed-and-breakfast in Skog. I'd been able to block them out somewhat with my music for most of the trip, earbuds shoved in *deep*, but as we rolled into the parking lot in front of Fare National Park, our hiking guides already on their feet at the front of the huge bus, my ears hurt and my temper had reached critical mass. One more whiff of nonsense and I would go full New Yorker—*that* was a guarantee.

"Okay," I said, kneeling on my seat and holding the blonde one's enormous rectangle phone sideways to fit them both in. "Smile."

Neither did, but they both managed near-identical duck-lip smirks and fuck-me eyes—which I figured was their generation's version of smiling for the camera. Whatever. I tapped once, twice, three times to give them options, then handed back the phone just as the bus came to an abrupt stop. The jerking motion knocked me into the seat in front of mine, which earned me a withering look from the gray-haired crone and her husband sitting there, the very same pair who had spent the whole ride stinking up the bus with coconut-scented sunscreen.

I popped my sunglasses on my forehead, flashing an apologetic—albeit strained—smile, then grabbed my backpack off the seat beside me. Everyone on the bus was a tourist, people just like me who had fled to western Norway for the fjords, the glaciers, and the raw, natural beauty. This was just day one of my three-month jaunt across Norway, Sweden, and Finland. I'd then head down to Denmark to reconnect with cousins I hadn't spoken to since I was a kid, the last tenuous connection I had to Opa and his memory. Today, a national park awaited me, world heritage status and all, its glacier and ice caves famous, and tomorrow was for kayaking on a lake the color of kyanite gemstones.

Then off to Sognefjord, the *king* of Norway's ancient fjords. From here on out, I had it all organized—every hour of every day, from when I woke up to when I crashed in my hotel bed, belly full of foods I'd never tried and mulled nonalcoholic drinks that would knock me out until morning.

And best of all: I was doing it *solo*.

At least, that was the plan.

Yet I had somehow ended up on a bus with thirty other tourists, off to do a group hike at the suggestion of my bed-and-breakfast front desk clerk. He clearly hadn't been listening when I asked for day-trip recommendations that *didn't* involve a ton of other people—either that or he got a kickback from the company who organized the hikes out to the glacier.

The guy was my age, maybe a little younger, but had already seemed jaded from years of customer service, so... probably both.

Waiting for my fellow sheep to gather up their crap and get the hell off the bus was only mildly less frustrating than it had been waiting for people to deboard the plane in Oslo yesterday. I stood at the edge of the narrow aisle, an elbow propped on the seat in front of me, the British teens already deep into photo edits that we all had to hear about. With my backpack on and jacket zipped up, a rush of heat crept up my neck, adding fuel to the fire that was my mood.

I'd been devastated since Opa died a few weeks before this past Christmas. I'd been fucking fuming since I found out Devlin had been screwing my best friend for six months before that but hadn't had the nerve to break things off with me while I was in mourning. And now, two months later... Now I was sad and angry, and fucking tired, jet lag a cruel bitch I should have expected to get hit with harder. Sad and angry and tired and *hot*. I'd never traveled outside of the US before, rarely ever left Manhattan honestly, all my time devoted to my craft since I was a kid. Before this trip, I had spent ages researching, my ability to concentrate on anything besides the drama in my life totally razor-thin—but at least I'd tried.

And May in Norway was supposed to be temperamental, so I had packed accordingly. This morning, the wind battered my adorable little hotel, whistling so shrilly through the rafters that I almost didn't climb out from under the covers. The floor had been cold. The tiny shared bathroom freezing, the hot water limited. The dining room chilly. I'd layered up, dressed to stay warm for the day outdoors.

Just a few hours later, as the herd *finally* started to filter off the bus, the wind had died, there wasn't a cloud in the sky, and the sun beat down like someone had placed a giant magnifying glass over this particular plot of land. Nowhere else. Just here. With me. Because of course.

Trundling down the steep bus steps, I threw my hair up in a messy bun, then undid my jacket as soon as I separated myself from the rest of the group. A few others were also shedding layers, leaving them on the bus as our guides got us organized. Given how swiftly the weather had turned, I had no intention of leaving anything behind, but I did switch out my thick socks for the thinner ones I'd stuffed in my bag this morning. Without the wool climbing up my calves, my lace-up boots felt a little less secure, but they were designed to protect ankles in these sorts of situations, no matter the sock type—right?

Because a ballet dancer was nothing without the tools of her trade. I had rolled, sprained, and fucked up my ankles in my twenty-four years more times than I cared to admit, and even though I wouldn't be back in my studio—*any* studio—

for at least three months, maybe more depending on my mood and my health after this trip, I refused to put my best assets at risk.

Four-hundred-dollar hiking boots in mahogany brown, never used before an hour ago? Check.

Aside from the lone car parked at the other end of the lot, it appeared we were the only ones headed up to see the glacier today. Our huge fire truck–red tour bus cut through most of the parking spaces anyway, but beyond that stood a treasure trove of natural beauty that I *craved*. After everything, I needed simplicity—leaves and dirt and rocks, steep hills that would make my heart race and my body ache and my mind quiet. I needed silence.

Not that I'd get that with this motley crew. Some had the nerve to talk even while our guides went over safety tips for the climb to the glacier, their instructions followed swiftly by a rough timeline for the day. We would be out there, in the raw, ancient forested mountain range, for about six hours total. Food was included in the price of the tour, and we'd stop every two hours to rest.

Given I usually spent the better part of my days training, sequestered in the studio working on routines, perfecting posture and pointes and lifts and arms, arms, *arms*, two hours was nothing. I probably could have gone the full six without stopping, munching on my trail mix along the way, but everyone around me also seemed to be wearing brand-new hiking boots—which suggested we weren't the keenest outdoorsmen in all the land.

We set off as one, moving like a thunderous clump out of the parking lot, across a grassy field, and then into the forest at the foot of the first hill. The path underfoot was worn and obvious, free of underbrush and roots, brown and trampled while the rest of the landscape was lush and green and dangerously uneven. One guide took the lead, walking way out ahead, while the other situated himself in the middle, warning us all the second we crossed under the canopy to stick to the trail—to not wander off.

Gripping my backpack straps with both hands, I hung back, purposefully pacing myself to create a buffer between me and the six Australians meandering along in front.

Groups like this had always set my teeth on edge in the city—whole crowds shuffling around, blocking the sidewalk, stopping to take photos of nothing. They were a huge inconvenience, packed in tight like tinned sardines. If I spotted a cluster headed up the block, all wearing the same stupid hats and helmed by a guide with a megaphone, I would cut across ten lanes of bumper-to-bumper downtown traffic just to avoid them. No question. As I had planned my Scandinavia trip, I vowed never to be like them.

But on the first day, here I was—one of the sheep.

Today was an anomaly. After arriving in Oslo yesterday and taking the train up to Skog, my goal had been to rest up for the trip ahead. Only I couldn't sit still. I needed the quiet, sure, but sitting alone in a cramped room without any of the familiar comforts of home came with new bullshit, too. Lots of thoughts and feelings that I wasn't ready to deal with yet; enter this hiking tour, a chance to be active, to work myself bloody again so I could collapse in a dreamless sleep tonight. From tomorrow onward, I might have some touristy shit scheduled, but I would never be part of the herd again. Sure, I was a travel novice, but I had navigated Manhattan on my own since I was nine: Norway was cake by comparison.

We were only about an hour in when the trail turned steep. My fellow hikers slowed, the group thinning to accommodate for the terrain, but that did nothing to quell the noise. Honestly, how did they expect to see any wildlife when those fucking teens kept cackling with the guide up at the front—and the gaggle of Australians, all roughly my age, stopped every two seconds to take group photos?

I mean, the last picture had consisted of one buff guy pretending to hump a rock that looked like it had boobs, and I just...

I couldn't.

We weren't supposed to veer off the path, but as soon an offshoot presented itself, I ran.

Well, power walked. I mean, there were maps nailed to trees, huge metal rectangles that highlighted all the paths through the protected park, the colored lines indicating that specific trail's difficulty. The path I'd stumbled on was marked green—beginner-level easy—and took the long way around to reach the glacier.

Two minutes in and the noise of the herd fell away. I stopped and glanced back, the trees bowed over the trail, blocking the relentless sunshine, peace and quiet finally settling around me.

*This* was what I'd wanted.

And this was what I'd take. No people, but still plenty to look at, plenty to distract myself with. Perfect.

I mean, I had signed away my right to sue if something happened to me out here, so the tour guides were off the hook for my decisions...

The innate New Yorker in me knew wandering off the beaten path came with its own set of dangers, but I just couldn't anymore. After a swig of water, my sunglasses firmly in place and my legs pulsing with the familiar energy of *movement*, I carried on alone. Just like I wanted.

I walked another half hour by myself, occasionally hearing my group slightly northwest of me, all of us following the same relative route to the glacier. Every map I passed I checked, scrutinized, made sure I was still on terrain that people knew about—that was deemed safe.

Eventually, the trees thinned and the air cooled. At this elevation, my endurance faltered, my breath came faster, my heart beat harder, and as I perched on a boulder that was somehow all angles, I finally understood the scheduled two-hour pit stops. I was in great shape and suddenly struggling; some of the herd must have been *dying* by now.

Ahead of me, the landscape opened to brush and rocks and the odd wildflower, the snowcapped mountain range gorgeous and just—*there*. Imagine living in this much nature all the time, not a glass skyscraper in sight, the constant battle of wailing cab horns a distant memory.

As I sipped my water and munched on trail mix, my hand eventually drifted to my fanny pack—and then to my phone inside. Old habits died hard, and before I realized it, I had tapped on the Instagram icon and then there I was, on my feed.

No reception though.

I pursed my lips.

Probably for the best. My goal was to cut down on phone time over the next three months, using it only for pictures and the odd email update for the few people I had left in my life who might worry if they didn't hear from me every now and again.

I stared at the white screen as it tried to load, searching out a signal, and a familiar sharp and visceral panic struck out of nowhere. A cold sweat spread across my palms. My mouth went dry. My gut twisted.

Just another reason to get off social media for a few months: no Devlin and Maeve over here in the middle of a reception-less Norwegian national park. They'd had the nerve to post a cuddly, heavily filtered photo of the two of them sharing a fucking ice cream cone *literally* the day after I'd moved my stuff out of me and Dev's old place. That had been the straw that finally broke the camel's back. Insta-block, for both of them, on every platform.

I hadn't done it before because... I dunno, maybe I was a masochist. But I had done it then, just a month ago, *finally* cutting out two of the most important people in my life in under a minute as I sobbed and demolished an entire giant Toblerone bar in a single sitting, alone on the couch in my temporary apartment, all my shit in storage, my life in shambles.

Back then, I'd been broken.

And now...

Well, now I was still a little broken—and furious.

Just the thought of it brought the heat back to my cheeks and the nape of my neck. Rage bulldozed the initial jolt of fear at the possibility of somehow seeing them; it got me moving again, same as it always did. Teeth gritted, I shoved my water and my snack mix into my backpack, then threw that on, struggling a little to get my left arm through the strap for some fucking reason, the tussle loosening my bun and forcing me to fix it.

My feet moved of their own volition, wandering absently down the trail as I fumbled with my fanny pack's zipper, phone in one hand, the other viciously ripping at the little metal clasp. A low whine stretched from one ear to the other as all the old emotions crept back in: outrage, indignation, hurt beyond measure.

What they'd done to me, knowing how hard Opa's death had hit, how it shattered my whole world—

"Fuck them," I grunted, finally wrenching the zipper open, glaring down at the baby blue fabric, deep in a familiar tunnel vision as I nudged bandages and alcohol wipes and my passport aside to make room for my phone.

Not realizing I had drifted too far to the right of the path until it was too late.

Until my foot teetered just enough over the edge that my ankle rolled, even in these stupidly expensive boots. I shrieked as I tipped, phone flying, hands groping at the nearby trees for something to grab hold of—to stop myself.

And *just* missing.

I went down hard, the rugged landscape harsh and unforgiving, full of jagged rocks and thorny brush, the slope of the hill so steep that I just rolled and rolled and rolled. Pain lanced my whole body, but my hips, shoulders, knees, and hands took the brunt of it, catching on rocks, slamming into merciless corners. Something slashed across my cheek, my neck. On one roll, the back of my head slammed into a sapling's trunk; the tree just bowed to the pressure, the weight of the hit, and did nothing to stop my fall.

But it blunted my descent enough that I crashed left instead of straight down the hill. It all happened way too fast for me to panic, for me to do anything or *think* anything beyond making it stop.

And it eventually did.

When my forehead met a boulder that, unlike the little tree, really stood its ground.

Then everything went black.

## 2

## NORA

I came to in a world of pain on a very, *very* hard bed.

At first, as I struggled to lift my eyelids, muddling through brain fog and groaning, I reasoned that because of this rock-hard mattress, I must have somehow made it back to the hotel. The bed there was basically a plank of wood with a thin strip of foam on top, and this felt much the same.

But the smell was off.

Musty. Earthy. *Dirt.* My rented room smelled pine-fresh courtesy of the rustic wood accents and whatever cleaning agent they had used on the floor, the dryer sheet for the linens...

My eyes snapped open. Intricate interlocked stonework soared up on a wall that radiated cold about an inch from my face, the space around me dim, shadowed, but bright enough to suggest sunlight was trying to get in from somewhere.

Everything *hurt*.

*Fuck.*

I sucked in a panicked breath, then shot up on my

elbow—only to cry out when the aches throughout my entire body sharpened.

"Easy, easy..."

I whipped around on the thin mattress, on its crisp white bedding with sheets tucked so tight over me it was like I was in a fucking straitjacket. A dark figure rose from the corner, accompanied by the faint creak of—chair legs shifting over hardwood floor? The dull pain between my eyes intensified, stretching back over the crest of my skull to the base of my spine. I'd hit my head on that fall—a lot. So. *Fuck.*

"Nora, is it?"

Seconds later, curtains hissed across a metal rod and sunshine streamed into the small room. I blinked rapidly, the burst of light an affront to what was probably a mild concussion. My shoulder screamed as I raised a hand to shield my eyes, a flicker of panic tightening in my chest to find the back of my hand covered in red slashes, a cream-colored dressing wrapped around my wrist.

"My name is Oskar." Dragging the chair across the space, a man who appeared maybe a few years older than me, thirty at the most, settled at my bedside with a warm smile. He spoke English with a heavy Norwegian accent, but his proficiency in the language was strong, his words clear—just like everyone I'd met since I arrived, honestly. With slicked-back reddish-blond hair, he had gorgeous caramel eyes and a smattering of dark freckles on his cheeks. Lanky. Strong. Dressed in a Slayer tee with a grey sweater over it, unzipped, and a pair of dark jeans, he looked like... Well, he looked like any ordinary guy in Brooklyn.

"W-What...?" I winced, throat like sandpaper, and accepted the cup of water he offered from the end table at the head of my bed with a weak smile. "Thanks."

Lukewarm was just what I needed, and I downed the whole thing.

"I hope you don't mind—I read your passport, just to identify you," Oskar told me as I tapped the last dribbles of water into my mouth. "So... That's how I know your name."

Fuck *me*, I was exhausted. Already I could have just flopped down and slept for another week, every part of me in pain. Sighing, I slumped against the stony wall instead, still struggling with the sunlight. Definitely concussed.

"Where am I? What happened?"

"You're in a village called Ravndal," Oskar said as he refilled my glass from a half-empty pitcher. "You sort of... uh, stumbled out of the woods all bloody and confused." He chuckled softly, his gaze hovering around my forehead—like he couldn't look me in the eye. "Gave Elmer quite a fright while he was planting his carrots, I'll tell you that."

*Huh.* I resisted taking another sip, watching, waiting for this Oskar guy to meet my eyes, but he busied himself with the monumental task of putting the water jug back on the little wood table, then checked his phone.

"I don't remember any of that," I croaked. Not a damn thing. The hairs on the back of my neck stood as if some unseen fingers brushed across my skin. "I... I fell... At the park—"

"You kept babbling about a glacier." Oskar locked his phone and slipped it back in his sweater pocket with an easy smile, still only looking *just* above my eyeline. "If you were in Fare National Park, then you walked quite a way on that ankle."

Annoyed, I closed my eyes and let out a huff. Of *course* I fucked up my ankle on that fall. Of course. The slightest rotation of my right ankle confirmed it, the pain familiar: sprained. Not the worst sprain I'd ever had after nearly twenty years of dance, but still not great either given the fact I'd been wearing boots that had cost a quarter of my monthly rent.

Boots... Boots I clearly wasn't wearing now. In fact, *all* the clothes I'd put on this morning were gone, replaced by a white gown with a scoop neckline and sleeves to my elbows. It disappeared beneath the starchy linens, but it seemed to go to my knees. Studying the nondescript fabric, my brows furrowed, and a sick twist in my belly had me swallowing down a rush of bile.

"Uh, so—"

"The doctor and his assistant changed you," Oskar told me with an apologetic shrug of one shoulder. "I'm sorry, I know that must be unsettling. You were covered in blood and thorns when you were found, and getting you out to a major hospital would have taken hours, so we set you up here. The village doctor says there's nothing fatal, but you might have a head injury."

"Probably." The explanation didn't exactly make me feel better: strangers had peeled my various layers off, seen me naked, put me in *this*. With no underwear. No bra. Which was just... great. I swallowed hard again, throat marginally better after the water, then walked two fingers across my scalp, twitching at the especially painful areas. "I hit it a few times... I fell down this hill while I was hiking."

The dead center of my forehead exploded with pain when I tentatively nudged at it, sharp enough to bring tears to my eyes. I blinked them back, chin wobbling, and sucked in a shaky breath.

"I'm so sorry, Nora," Oskar said softly, placing a hand on the bed—not my leg, thankfully. "I can't imagine what you're feeling right now."

Panicked. Confused. Hurt. Dead tired.

And relieved that someone had found me, that I didn't wake up facedown in the forest with no idea of how I'd got there or where I was.

*Also* relieved that this guy didn't seem like some backwater psycho. He sounded genuine when he spoke to me, sincere, cautious and gentle like he didn't want to startle me. Our eyes met fleetingly, but he looked away first, smoothing out the bedding like that mattered, like I wouldn't rustle it again with my next movement.

Maybe he was just awkward. Direct eye contact wasn't for everyone. In fact, I made a point to avoid it in the city—if you looked at someone for too long on the subway, they either wanted to fight you or hit on you.

"Thanks, I just..." My shoulders protested the rolling stretches I put them through. "Who are you? Not the doctor, right?"

"No, no," he said with another chuckle. "My family line is, er, head of the village, so to speak. I'm descended from jarls, if you'd believe it. Dad sent me to sit with you so you wouldn't wake up alone."

"Oh." I stilled, fighting back another rush of tears. "That's... nice of you."

Oskar shrugged and shifted about in his chair. "It's no problem for me. I was worried about you... Helped Elmer drive you in from his farm."

"How bad do I look?" Because I felt like absolute garbage.

"I'm sure you've seen better days," he remarked distantly, coming in close for a swift assessment and pointing out my facial injuries. "Cuts here and there. Split lower lip and bruise on your cheek. Looks like you survived a bar fight, really."

I snorted, then winced at the sharp aching flash over the

left side of my rib cage. Probably bruised a few of those guys, too, but at least they weren't broken; I would have felt that with every breath. Six years ago, I'd broken two ribs falling down a flight of subway stairs on the way home from practice, and the pain of *that* was nothing to sneeze at.

The room around us was spartan, with only the bed, the end table, and Oskar's chair for furnishings. The curtains were a nondescript pale blue, and the window was intersected by two white lines. Wood door. Stone walls. Nothing.

"Uh, where's my stuff?"

"We put it in a safe for you," Oskar said as he stabbed a hand through his wispy strawberry blond hair, "in the, er, village town hall—just to keep it secure until you woke up again. I can take you to it. We have a satellite phone there as well if you'd like to call someone. The mobile phone reception out here is, uh, *spotty*, as you can imagine."

"Right. Sure." If Opa had found out about this, he would have been on the next available flight to Oslo from JFK, cane and all. That great Danish bear would have done anything, gone *anywhere*, to fetch me if I was in trouble. But. Not anymore. And nobody else was really waiting to hear from me; all my remaining friends were at the studio every day, exhausted every night, and that meant I was the last thing on their mind. Sadness struck like a flicker of lightning, striking my head and skittering to my toes. It dragged me down, made me feel heavy and lethargic when this vacation was supposed to be an uplifting recharge. Clearing my throat, I brushed my thumbs under my eyes and shook my head. "No one to call, thanks. I just want to get back to my hotel."

"Of course. Whatever you think is best."

Ugh. I'd have to rejig this whole holiday now—at least

for a few weeks while my ankle healed and my brain decided how it wanted to feel. This would be my first official concussion; hopefully it settled over the next few days.

Oskar offered me a sturdy arm to clutch as I hobbled out of the bed, kicking the sheets away with my good leg and putting most of my weight on it once I was upright. The world spun, which came with a rush of nausea and dizziness that had me careening straight into Oskar's lean figure. He braced hard, supporting me as I tested out my sprain, putting most of my weight on my toes.

A little smile tugged at my mouth: what had the doctor thought about my gnarly ballet toes? While I hadn't been in the studio for over a month, my contract with the company put on hold for this season due to personal circumstances, my toes still reflected my life's work, my deepest passion. Cracked nails. Swollen, warped joints. Ankles weren't the only things we dancers destroyed in the quest for perfection.

"I could probably do with something to eat," I noted weakly as we crossed the room.

"I'll have a lunch prepared, not to worry."

What day was it? How many hours had that fall knocked me out? My stomach gurgled, unaccustomed to going more than two without food. There was this absurd notion in pop culture that ballet dancers starved themselves to get down to our peak season weights, but our profession was intensely athletic, both mentally and physically demanding, and if we didn't eat, we didn't perform—it was that simple. Healthy fats and lean protein and lots of both filled my days, and as I shuffled down a brightly lit corridor, Oskar supporting me through every labored step, I knew I'd been without for at least half a day, maybe longer.

I needed something soon if I wanted to stay vertical. No getting around it.

The stonework and dark hardwood carried throughout the rest of the building, which consisted of two separate exam rooms, both empty as we passed by, then a waiting room out front with leather sofas and a check-in desk like any other doctor's office. Empty, though, not another person in sight. Maybe Friday had rolled into Saturday? Maybe they took weekends off?

It could have been the next day, because as soon as we stepped outside, I was met by a glowering sun high in the sky—noon, most likely. I'd gotten to the park around nine for the tour, so it could have been a few hours later, but my stomach wouldn't be *this* miserable if that was the case.

"We go as slow as you like," Oskar told me as we worked our way down the building's front steps.

"Thanks, man, I really appreciate it." And I did. My ankle was a nuisance, but the rest of my injuries made it a nightmare to get around without him. Each step came slow and steady, but we stuck to a polished stone path that cut through the village—the *empty* village, again, not a person in sight. But that being said, it was absolutely breathtaking. Flower boxes sat in every window, overflowing with vibrant spring blooms. The grass outside of the paths was full and lush, stunningly green—greener than I'd seen elsewhere. In fact, the village actually felt warmer, almost like the beginnings of a gorgeous summer rather than the temperamental spring I'd experienced so far.

While I had still yet to see any people, Ravndal's housing situation suggested it ought to be full of them. Beautiful stone lodges with wood or thatched roofs lined the path, looking ancient but feeling like modern luxe chalets, each one two levels—at least—with detached garages. I frowned when I spotted the latest Audi Coupé sitting in one of the paved driveways; why have a luxury car out in the middle of nowhere? It wasn't even an all-terrain model.

Devlin had been such a car freak, always showing me what he wanted, bookmarking car ads online, going into detail about parts, relaying all his grand plans to fix something up someday, his *need* to collect classics...

I fucking hated that I knew the make of that damn car.

Ten houses down from the medical clinic and I was wrecked. Just—collapse on the ground after an eleven-hour studio day *exhausted*. But I pushed on, barefoot and broken, knowing my stuff was sitting somewhere inside that huge building dead ahead, in what Oskar had called the town hall. Three floors tall with stained glass windows, the biggest and brightest flower boxes... Yeah, that looked like the center of a village. Maybe they even had a pool. I mean, if someone had a luxury vehicle all the way out here, a pool wouldn't be out of the ordinary—

A thunderous crash nearly had me jumping out of my skin, the sound of metal hitting stone an assault to my concussion. I shirked away from it with a wince, stumbling into Oskar, the commotion coming from my immediate left.

"Oh, sorry, Nora, I..." He tried to hurry me along, his patient shuffling upgraded to an insistent sidestep. Unfortunately, my body just couldn't keep up, and I risked a glance to the left, hoping to finally see another goddamn human being in this place.

And I found one.

An old woman. At her feet, a huge tin watering can, the winding stone path from her home flooded a shade darker. Hunched, rounded shoulders met a long neck, then a withered face. Wrinkles, deep and set, spiderwebbed around her eyes, her thin mouth. While she had a crown of startling white at her hairline, it faded to grey, then a thick black mane—a stylish old-age ombre.

Her eyes though.

They were mine.

Hazel green.

Dressed in layers, from the flouncy floral blouse to her cotton shrug, down to an ankle-length navy blue skirt, she seemed somehow out of place in all this opulence. Like she didn't *quite* fit—a puzzle piece you really had to jam into its spot.

We stared at one another for a beat, my heart whumping between my ears, before her mouth fell open in a silent scream. Her eyes widened, catching the relentless sunshine, brightening to the yellowish brown that mine did under certain lights. She raised a trembling arm and pointed a crooked, bony finger at me, looking like a horror-movie hag come to life with her soundless but anguished screech, her accusatory point...

"Oh my god—"

"Yes, again, sorry," Oskar muttered hastily, taking me by the shoulder and turning me away from the woman. "I hate to call anyone the village loon, but, you know... It would be accurate."

He urged me along as fast as my busted body could go, and although it killed my neck to look back over my shoulder, I did it. A sinking feeling washed over me as I watched a pair of men usher the woman back into the house, her watering can abandoned, her front door slamming shut with an unnerving sense of finality seconds later.

What. The fuck.

Time to get the hell out of here—stat.

But how?

I nibbled my lower lip, grimacing with every wonky step, hobbling along beside Oskar toward the town hall building with a knot in my gut. Would the hotel send a bus to fetch me? Was there a train out here? How far was I from the park? If I'd walked through the woods with a fucked-up ankle and a concussion, it couldn't be *that* far... I bet Oskar could even drive me back to Skog.

Maybe we'd take the Audi.

He was still holding me—clutching me, more like, his arm snaked around my midback, fingers crushing into my tender ribs. The slight furrow of his brow worried me, but I pushed the feeling down. Growing up in what some might consider a rough city, I'd learned how to navigate every kind of situation. Sometimes, snark and sass and a bit of posturing got you out of trouble. Others, a sweet smile and a bit of submissiveness, just for a minute or two, sped things along.

I could play the part in either scenario, but I was definitely more inclined to the former. Nothing like an alpha female to really put a loser wannabe in his place. Smiling pretty to coddle some asshole's ego just wasn't in my wheelhouse anymore, honestly.

And Oskar hadn't *seemed* like an asshole—until he started hustling me up the steep steps to the town hall, his previous warmth replaced by an unnerving spring frost.

Maybe I *would* make use of that satellite phone after all...

I could call... the hotel.

Yeah.

At least someone else in this country, someone who could realistically *do* something within the hour, would know what had happened to me.

Plan.

A balmy gust of wind cut through the village, lifting my strange hospital gown up to unsafe levels. You know. Considering I was naked underneath. Cheeks hot, I shoved it back down to cover my thighs, stumbling a little on the last step. Oskar let out a harsh breath, and I shot him an apologetic smile—one that he returned, but it was stretched a little too wide.

Right.

Strangely rich village in the middle of the Norwegian wilderness?

Classic horror-movie witch cursing me from the front stoop of her cottage?

Weird, too-wide smile from the guy I thought I could trust?

Check. Check. Check.

Fuckery.

There was definite fuckery afoot.

Time to get the *hell* out of here.

"Uhm, about that phone call," I started as Oskar walked me up to the huge arched main doors. Pine-green wood. Golden-brass knobs. Norse runes carved into the panels. Just the kind of architecture I had been looking forward to photographing. "I think I will call someone, actually... I should let the hotel know what happened, because, you know, they organized the hike, and I'm sure the tour guides are freaking out that I'm gone—"

"Absolutely." Oskar finally let go of me, stepping aside to grab one of the round doorknobs. When he twisted it, what sounded like eight individual locks creaked and thunked into place. "Let me just get the door for you..."

*Okay, smile and nod, smile and nod.*

Willing to see how far firm politeness got me, I thanked

him with a grin and a pat on the arm. Air-conditioning whooshed through the open doorway, and I staggered in on my own, cool tile suddenly underfoot—

Then came to an abrupt halt, the scene ahead knocking the wind right out of me.

A grand foyer made of marble and gold and dark wood. Twin staircases winding up the walls to another floor. The stained glass windows gave the room an amber sheen.

In the center of it all: eight figures in black robes, their hoods up, wearing white masks that completely covered their faces. Leather gloves. Standing in a silent semicircle around a...

Wooden crate.

An *open* wooden crate.

Big enough to hold a person.

Big enough to hold *me*.

My heart plunged into my belly. The brain fog resurged with a vengeance, a painful, shrill whine screeching around my skull. Numb fingers. Sweaty palms. A spike of adrenaline made it hard to think, hard to hear—made me shake.

"What the *fuck*?" I stumbled back into a solid body, and Oskar gripped my arms—hard—as the door clicked shut behind us.

"Nora, I need you to stay calm," he whispered in my ear, walking me into the room, shouldering me forward when I tried to plant my feet. The robed figures stared on blankly, and Oskar locked his arms around me when I jammed both elbows back into him, effectively clamping my arms to my sides.

"I need you to stay calm, Nora," he told me again, slowly but surely marching me onward, "and I need you to get in the box..."

3

# LOKI

Men cut their hair short these days.

They wore it slicked back and tidy, with a little volume over the forehead—like a lover had swooped it away from their face. Yes, yes, just like that.

My eyes narrowed as I scrutinized the look in the mirror. Perfect. Just like all the magazine clippings Freida had dropped off this morning upon my request. I had copied it all exactly, leaving a touch of coarse auburn scruff on my cheeks, my chin, my jawline. Tidied up my brows. *Swooped* my hair. Men's fashions hadn't changed all that much from the early twentieth century, though trousers fit tighter, shirts looked crisper. I stepped back and buttoned the top onyx dot of my creaseless white shirt, the sleeves jerked up to my elbows, and then unbuttoned it, then buttoned it again. Open or closed? All the way up to the base of my throat, or a little more exposed?

Perhaps *she* could decide for me, sidle in close with her elegant fingers, teach me a thing or two about how she liked her men.

And that would be *all* this Nora Olsen would teach me, of course. What else could she possibly offer, this human who looked like *her*? Nothing.

Although... She could attest to my efforts, tell me whether I had missed the mark completely with my new outfit, my haircut, my leather shoes that desperately needed breaking in. Beyond that, the rest of our living space had received a face-lift courtesy of another stack of magazines, my alterations going well beyond my appearance.

All this—accomplished in a day. Funny what a bit of dulled magic and the proper motivation could do for a man.

For a *god*.

After giving myself one last appraisal in the mirror, standing tall, shoulders back, I left the lavatory behind—which was really nothing more than a small room in a vast series of rooms that I had made habitable over the centuries. Its primary function *was* waste elimination, the ceiling low but the opening in the ground dropping deep into the earth below. Hopefully Nora didn't mind it; I hadn't the desire to craft a toilet from scratch, even if they *were* in all the magazine bathroom spreads. I'd added a mirror and a sink, the simplest of appliances. Surely she could make do without a porcelain throne for a few weeks.

Or however long this one lasted.

Hands clasped behind my back, I drifted down the calendar corridor, encased in darkness, past the shadowy bedroom. No windows anywhere, not unless I either made them—I couldn't imagine a duller task—or they were naturally occurring slits in the mountainside.

Up the pair of smooth steps to the right, natural inclines in the stone that had been worn down under my feet these many centuries, and into the main hall. This was my first impression—a chance to really *shine*, to show her what I was capable of even in the depths of this wretched curse.

What other cave had electricity, after all? Where else would you happen upon a totally modern kitchen, complete with marble countertops and stainless-steel appliances? Dual ovens, a plunging farmhouse sink. Details, details, details... I'd always had an eye for them, so fucking critical to my survival in a world of Aesir and Vanir and churlish giants and tricky elves.

This was my masterpiece, the space that always impressed the most.

And, like me, it had to be *perfect*.

I drifted over to the oak dining table, capable of hosting twelve warriors along its benches, and then flipped through the magazines scattered there one last time. Details. *Details*. All perfect, all meticulously studied in the last twenty-four hours. My charcoal notes, scribbled in runes so old no one here could decipher them anymore, denoted what I had found the most interesting. Under this bitch's spell, I struggled to conjure something from nothing, to create with no background knowledge, but when I had a template to work from, I could still craft a few wonders.

Exemplified here, of course. The pristine kitchen to the left, so much cupboard space the editors of this houseware magazine would *shit* with excitement. The table before me, ideal for dinner parties, soon to be filled with a gratuitous spread of the goods stacked high in my new refrigerator; usually I just stored it all underground, kept it cool and fresh the natural way. But the magazines were so particular about fridges that it seemed best to adapt—just this once.

To my immediate right, a seating area I had copied almost item for item from another flimsy pamphlet, studying the glossy pages until my eyes crossed, conjuring late into the night. A rust-red couch able to accommodate three people, twin armchairs in a complementary deep blue, the coffee table with all the realm's nations carved into its top, the script for each city elegant, cursive, far more beautiful than my own writing.

And lights. It had been years since I bothered with artificial light—looking directly into them would have pained me had I not opted for a soft yellow. Little bulbs held together on strings seemed to be popular in the—quote —*modern* interior design spreads, so I'd hung two matching strands over the couch. Plus the floodlight over the sink, the various strings over the cabinets. Like stars, they were, each one powered by my mere existence.

No second-guessing things: I had gone all out for my newest visitor.

Surely the effort wouldn't go unnoticed.

Because it *was* all for her. They were always so frightened when they first arrived, these pretty humans plucked from obscurity to entertain a god in his cage. Having a few modern comforts, in my experience, eased the transition, made them feel a little more comfortable.

Of course, they were never truly at ease until I bedded them—until they learned what I could do without magic, what skills I possessed beyond simple tricks and illusions. Only then were they truly mine.

The corners of my mouth quirked with some difficulty, my lips unaccustomed to the simple act of smiling. They felt out of practice, like the look wasn't natural—forced. Strained. A struggle.

It had just been so long.

I'd been so fucking alone. Nearly seventy-five years had crawled by since the last one—

Echoing footsteps stilled my heart, quieted the creeping

darkness, and with a curt snap, the magazines, my guides to modern humanity, vanished from the long table. I pressed a hand to my chest, an old familiar giddy pleasure skittering through me, sparking the rusted, cobweb-addled gears in my brain.

*Time to switch on, you ancient bastard. Time to live again—just for a little while.*

Despite the energy pounding through every muscle, I took my time, ambled along. Over the centuries, extensive renovations had taken place inside my prison, no rock untouched by my hand. Initially, the mouth to this cave opened to a steep drop-off, the plunge precarious and laden with jagged shards at its base. In time, I had constructed a gentle slope, one that curved along the wall from the main hall up, up, slowly up, right to the barred entryway just inside the cave's mouth. The little landing on my side of the bars, some twenty feet inside the mountain itself, was where the villagers usually deposited my demands—my offerings, my sustenance, my companionship.

Today was no different.

They arrived in their ridiculous ceremonial robes, like I gave a fuck about how they dressed to deliver my latest plaything. Behind those white masks, eyes darted about, most familiar, but two I didn't recognize—the most nervous of the bunch, flicking around as they wheeled my delivery box in. I gave them some space, hands entwined behind my back, watching, unblinking, tension steadily rising off the nine humans the longer they lingered in my tomb.

Always nine.

Again—like I actually gave a *fuck* about their numbers. Apparently, because there were nine realms in our universe, the worshipping simpletons figured all they sacrificed to me had to come in sets of nine as well.

One cloaked figure stood guard at the opening in the bars that stretched from one wall to the other, a cell door constructed two centuries ago when I'd first demanded a pretty face to keep me company. That little doorway meant nothing, open or closed: the ward trapping me inside this infernal mountain stood beyond it. Even if I charged the bars, shoved the nine aside and *killed* them where they stood, it wouldn't matter. Revna's magic would hold me. Keep me. Bind me to this fucking place.

Forever.

Hidden to the world, myself included, the witch's ward cloaked the mountain, muted my godly gifts, yet allowed all others to pass freely.

Sometimes I wondered if its invisibility was a mercy; if I had to *see* it, day in and day out, for eight long centuries, I'd have lost what was left of my mind.

Under my watchful eye, the cloaked humans moved efficiently. This was an offering none of them had participated in during their lifetime, but their fathers or mothers would have instructed them in the proper way. Bring the crate inside. Remove it from the little cart with its squeaky wheels. Arrange it in the sunlight spilling through the cave's mossy mouth—and then get the fuck out.

Nine pairs of feet scampered off as soon as the task was done, the last of the lot slamming the door shut behind them. Seconds later, the bars electrified again, jerking to life with a familiar hum. Still I waited, waited, *waited* until I could no longer hear them, their breathing, their stumbling footsteps—my twenty-first-century acolytes. Only when we were truly alone, I pounced.

Hurrying up the last gentle incline of my self-made ramp, I crossed over to the large wooden crate with barely contained glee. Giddiness finally wrung an authentic smile from my lips, and I smoothed a hand over the polished pine panels, the four corners sharp enough to draw blood.

This moment was my *favorite* of the ritual—the anticipation before I finally set eyes on her. So much possibility. So much potential.

Most of all: someone to share in my miserable solitude.

Unable to stand it a second longer, I ripped the sealed lid clean off, hurling it aside with such ferocity that it shattered to bits of kindling when it hit the cave wall.

Oh.

There she was.

Inside, dressed in the usual slip of white cotton, a fabric that turned sheer in the right light, was my gift. Curled up, slumped over—beaten? I frowned at the brace around her swollen ankle, the bandages around her wrist, then reached inside with a trembling hand to brush the hair from her face. More marks. More cuts and scrapes. Was she a fighter, or did this generation simply not understand what I demanded of them?

A quick clench of my teeth. A flash of fire in my chest.

And then gone.

Replaced with anticipation again. Yes, she appeared battered, her white skin peppered with color, but that was all cosmetic, all fixable. Easily.

Her unconscious body coiled around a loaf of crusty bread—freshly baked, from the smell of it. A few huge bites were missing from its head, crumbs littering the base of the crate, and I leaned an elbow on the wood siding as I swooped her hair behind her ear, smirking.

Hungry thing.

I could take care of that, too.

*You'll want for nothing here... if you're a good little human.*

And they usually were. In the presence of a god, what choice did they have?

I ducked down, and as I slipped my arms around her to hoist her up and out, I caught a whiff of the world. Of trees and earth. Of something floral and sweet in her midnight-black hair. It was—intoxicating. My eyes drifted shut, and I lingered, just taking her in...

Until she sucked down a sharp breath.

My eyes flew open, hungry for that familiar shade, the blessed sheen that I craved—

Only I hadn't time to lose myself in the green I'd expected, the hue that had been all but teased in her photo, because Nora Olsen suddenly slammed the base of her palm into my throat. It smarted a little, the blow forcing a cough out of me, but I reared back more out of surprise than anything. She seized the opportunity to leap from the crate in my absence, but then yelped sharply when she landed on that bandaged ankle. The little—tall, lithe, willowy—human doubled over with a ragged gasp, briefly gripping the side of the crate for support before launching herself at the bars.

A distinct *bzzzzz* erupted as soon as she touched one, jittering up her arm.

"*Fuck*!"

The electric jolt had her in its thrall, briefly pinning her in place as it coursed through her body, before she finally wrenched her hand away and toppled backward. She hit the ground hard, crying out again, and then scrambled back, back, back until she collided with the cave wall.

And I just—watched.

Because.

*Fuck* me, that was new.

And a little exciting.

Absently massaging my throat, I tracked her path from

the crate to the bars to the wall. The little thing had looked like some poor lost bird stuck inside a hall, fluttering around the rafters, slamming into windowpanes as it searched for an out.

Usually they were so *docile* in the box.

They came to me crying, cowering, and I coaxed them out with sweet words and fanciful promises, luring them into my arms with time and care. Precision. I had my speech memorized, a handful of perfect phrases that always won them over. Every time. Without fail.

Well. Actually. Once, a century and a half ago, one of my lovelies had crawled out of the box raring to go, her hands in my hair, her lips to mine. In fact, we'd fucked on the box itself—immediately. They were all told *why* they were brought here, and that one—Lorelei—had known her place from the start.

But that got old fast.

It always did.

Sex was great until it wasn't.

Fun until it wasn't.

Exciting—until it wasn't.

But that was what they thought I desired, above all else, and sometimes I forgot...

Forgot that there was more to companionship than carnality.

Shoved up against the wall, knees to her chest, a sweating, panting, shaking Nora glared at me. Face curtained with thick black waves, she had proven herself to be a treat already—so much more than just the physical similarities to *her*.

"Hello, little human." English. This one was American, even with that Danish family name. I always spoke their native tongue; we had so much stacked against us already. No need to complicate things. Hands in my pockets, I tipped my head to the side, smiling down at her. "You look positively *wretched*."

And truly, she did. Bruises marred her face. Cuts on her hands, her fingers. That disgrace of an ankle, so swollen it was a wonder she could put any weight on it at all.

But that was surface-level nonsense. A bit of dirt and dust on an otherwise perfect specimen, and I had all the time in the world to polish her up, really put my back into the task.

When she said nothing, those quivering lips pressed firmly together, I started toward her. Prowled slowly, steadily, my every step making her shrink and retreat into stone that would never yield, never swallow her up like she wanted—for this was a mountain without mercy. *Best learn it now, little human.*

For all her glowering, her efforts to make herself as small as possible, Nora Olsen was far lovelier than her picture had suggested. Tall—taller than the others, an adequate match for my substantial height. Long limbs, lean but strong, her calves defined, her arms wiry. A lot of force behind that strike to my throat... Athletic.

My smile sharpened. I rather liked that—an agile sacrifice, someone who might finally be able to keep pace with me.

But... Details, details, *details*. The odd brown freckle dotted her flesh, her skin white but sun-kissed. Black hair, thick and wavy and long. Well-groomed, this one, her fingernails neat and uniform. Sharp facial features, her chin pointed, her cheekbones severe enough to hollow out her face. Thick black brows and lashes.

I crouched down in front of her, and she shuffled back, panic flashing across her lovely, lovely eyes. In time, she would get accustomed to my movements, to the fluidity and grace of a god. Head cocked to the side, I studied those *eyes*. Perfection. Just what I wanted—the ideal shade. Green overall, but with bursts of brownish gold around the pupil.

Almost exactly like...

Keen on a closer look, I seized her by the chin and dragged her forward for a bit of scrutiny. Nora whimpered and resisted—no surprise there. Her hands shot up as if to fight me properly, but they stilled and dropped back down to her sides moments later, her eyes everywhere but me. I huffed a soft chuckle, mapping the freckling constellations over the bridge of her nose and across her high cheekbones. No makeup, not even a bit of color on her eyelashes. No gloss on her full, succulent lips. Nothing.

Just raw beauty.

*Lovely.*

Well, except for all these gashes. My eye twitched as I took in the cuts and bruises, and still clutching her by the chin, I used my free hand to heal. It had been some time since I used the gift, but it came back swiftly—the release of gathered blood, the sealing of torn flesh, the smoothing of a bruised brain. I saw to all of it, face first, then drifted meticulously down her body, unfurling her by force to tend to every last wound. She fought me, even though I *knew* she felt instantly better under my care, her pain gone, her injuries vanquished. Nora tugged against my every grasp, ripping her hand away when I was through with it, jerking back against the wall when I'd finished walking my healing fingers across her battered rib cage.

I ended on that ankle, my pièce de résistance. Badly sprained, horribly bruised. Here, I took my time, using both hands to undo her bandages. She winced and twitched, her lovely eyes filled with tears when I poked at the ball of inflammation engulfing the top of her foot all the way to the little bit of bone jutting out at the side.

Must have been rather painful...

Slowly, mouth warped in a wolfish grin, I lowered myself to her foot. This time, she couldn't look away, not when our gazes tangled, and not when I brushed my lips over the injury. Her flesh prickled all the way up her leg, right up to the cotton skirt she had jammed between her thighs to hide herself away. A slight lift of my brow had her flushing, cheeks a brilliant red, the rest of her face deathly white.

Cradling her ankle in both hands, I healed her. The inflammation shriveled, the sprain corrected. No longer would she limp or hobble, no more would she cry out in agony when this foot bore her full weight.

I expected relief, perhaps even a bit of gratitude when I glanced at her again, but was instead met with confusion.

Fine. Fair enough.

After planting a chaste kiss on the top of her foot, I eased up so that we were right in each other's eyeline.

"Forgive me," I rumbled, still cradling her foot, "but I so hate it when they send me broken toys."

Her blushes evaporated at that, her lips thinning, her whole body stiffening before me. Let her be indignant at the insinuation; I had just healed her every ailment—the perfect segue to trust, whether she liked it or not. Smirking, I flexed her foot back and forth to show the depth of my reach, her skin so smooth and her toes...

I paused, frowning down at them.

What the *fuck* was wrong with her toes?

They weren't broken, but...

Well, even the prettiest humans had their flaws.

With a teasing line on the tip of my tongue, I looked into her perfect eyes again. "You know—"

And before I could get the rest of the jest out, Nora fucking Olsen kicked me square in the face.

# 4

## NORA

Something *crunched* under my heel, the impact skittering up my leg, and the psychotic dick in front of me reeled back with a shout. His hand shot to his nose—*hope I broke it, you gorgeous freak*—and I shot to my feet. The cell bars had already proven to be a no go, and I wasn't about to try my luck there again; one intense shock that glued me in place was enough for today, thank you very much.

As I sprinted across the landing, I initially gave my sprained ankle some leeway, limp-running to compensate—but I didn't need to.

He...

He had healed it.

All of it.

The shock made my knees buckle, and I skidded into the cave wall with a ragged gasp, then pushed off it and trundled down the slope leading me deeper into this nightmare. Although it was hard to think—coherently, anyway, my mind racing, thoughts jumbled and melding together into nonsense—I did notice one thing: all the stone in here was so... *smooth*. Unnatural. Sure, water could round out rocks, but not to this scale.

*They said he'd been in here eight hundred years. Plenty of time to round out the edges—*

*No.*

*Not a toy. Not a toy. Notatoynotatoynotatoy—*

*Run!*

The momentum sent me flying off the ramp and into some warped version of an upscale downtown condo. I slowed briefly, eyes wide, chest aching and breath coming fast. Was that a—kitchen? A nicer kitchen than mine had been, at that. A table and bench seating. So big. And a sitting area—open concept was in with cave interior decorators, apparently?

"Fucking *go*, Nora," I hissed, pushing off the balls of my feet and racing for a dark doorway at the far end of the sprawling cavern. Swathed in shadows as soon as I crossed the threshold, I staggered down two shallow—again, *smooth* as fuck—stairs, then slammed into another hard wall. My hands took the brunt of it, then my knees, pain flaring in an otherwise perfectly healed body. After he'd touched me, it was all just... gone. No more headache. No more dizziness. No more nausea or sharpness over my ribs. No more swollen ankle and cheese-grated hands.

What the fuck.

What the fucking *fuck*?

Shaking, I patted along the wall like I was in the most fucked-up haunted house of all time, just waiting for another sicko to jump out of the darkness and scream bloody murder an inch from my face. Twice my hands plunged into nothingness, and as my eyes took their sweet-ass time adjusting to the black, I vaguely made out a pair of rooms just off the main hall—but beyond the fact that they were dark, they lacked any further details. For all I knew, they could have both been chock-full of torture devices designed *just* for me.

"This is a coma dream," I muttered with a shake of my head. "This is a fucking coma dream. It's not real."

Only when I snagged my pinky toe on *something* rock-hard along the wall's base, the blooming pain was very, very real.

Another corridor branched out to my left, this time with a light at the end of it. In fact, the whole arched doorway glowed golden, and I took off running, not stopping, not even slowing when I felt a breath on the back of my neck—not until I made it out of the darkness and into...

A pool room?

No.

None of these were rooms: I was inside a fucking mountain.

You know, in my coma dream.

Because *obviously* I had hit my head during that fall and I was still unconscious.

There was no other explanation.

He...

He wasn't a...

I raked my hands through my hair, taking in the landscape's shift. If this *was* someone's home, then this *would* be the pool room—what with the giant body of water to my right, the surface rustling like it had a current. Probably ice runoff melting from the mountain's cap, a stream that eventually became the modest waterfall that spilled from the ceiling down the far wall and into the pool.

Also in the ceiling, right there in the middle, directly over that stretch of dark sapphire-blue water, was a giant, gaping hole to the outside world. Sunlight slanted in—and it was the most beautiful thing I'd ever seen.

The burst of hope pinwheeling around my chest was both explosive and short-lived. Because... How the fuck was I supposed to reach the hole? Like the first cave I found myself in, this one was also domed, the rocky interior smooth. The walls lacked handholds, and the arched ceiling offered nothing—no grips, no rivets, *nothing* to grab if I tried to somehow swing across to the opening.

*Fuck.*

Shaking, panting, I quickly studied the footpath that stretched on ahead. It wrapped around the mountain lake, carried on past the wall with the trundling waterfall, then met with another dark opening, nothing but black beyond.

Nope. I swallowed hard, all that hope dwindling to nothing. No more darkness. No more shadows.

But I couldn't stay here.

I had to—

"Where are you going, little human?"

The hairs on the back of my neck shot up, and adrenaline spiked so hard and so fast that it felt like my heart was about to burst out of my chest. His voice— smooth as silk, deep and ancient, masculine and richly smoky... It rumbled in my ear, licked a blazing path down my throat. I whirled around with a scream, expecting to find him there with those brilliant green eyes, that smirking mouth, a rugged jawline and a shock of dark auburn hair.

I found nothing instead.

Still alone in this place.

He...

I rubbed at the back of my neck, frantically searching the shadows for that *man*.

Was I losing my mind—or had they told me the truth about him?

No. I refused to believe it. Refused to accept that all the stories were true, that there were—*creatures*—out there from legend and myth, beings that walked this earth who looked like us, sounded like us, *joked* like us... and were anything *but* human.

Something shifted in the shadows, a soaring figure in the depths of the narrow corridor I'd come sprinting out of. *Focus.* There would probably be time for an existential crisis later, right?

I shot off on unsteady footing, following the path around the shimmering blue water, but rather than lose myself in the darkness again, creeping along one step at a time, I pivoted. Took a hard right. The waterfall's stream dusted the wall with spray, but it didn't touch completely. There was an opening back there—rocks leading up to it like misshapen stairs. No time for hesitation, for second-guessing and debating; I climbed confidently on the balls of my feet, my touch featherlight, moving fast so that there wasn't the time to slip.

Six feet up, I scurried into a much smaller inlet than I'd expected, with barely enough space for me to crouch in.

But it was hidden away behind the falls.

Relatively secure.

At least no one could sneak up on me from behind.

The water fell like thunder, a constant wall of white and blue and mist in front of me, drowning out *him* and anything else that would make the hairs on the back of my neck stand up. Heart in my throat, I pushed up against the rocks, bracing anywhere I could, and closed my eyes. Adrenaline was great for fight or flight, but long-term it made me shaky, numb, disoriented, and weak. What little

47

bread I'd scarfed down in the crate had started to swirl inside, threatening to come shooting up the second I let my body relax. For now, it stayed tense, every muscle taut, every synapse in my brain firing on high.

Which, in the end, made my thoughts jumbled and my body shiver.

Not great.

Focusing on the pummeling water, I tried to take a few deep breaths to settle everything. In and out. In. Hold. Out —slow release. Slowly, I willed my muscles to relax *just* enough to get the grit out of my jaw, to settle the stiff ache in my neck.

When I opened my eyes, some of the shakiness had ebbed.

Only it came rushing back when I spotted a huge hand about a foot from my face reaching *through* the waterfall. My scream died in that little inlet, the rock and the thundering falls muting my terror, and I shrank back, eyes wide and heart racing, then swatted and kicked at the intruder.

He latched onto my arm all the same, snapping tight around my bicep like he could *see* me in here. Just as I was about to duck down and bite his wrist, he yanked me out— clear through the falls. Freezing water beat down on my entire body for only a few seconds, but it felt like an eternity as he dragged me through, then held me at an arm's length over the pool.

Sleeves rolled up to his elbows, this *man*—I refused to say his name, even in my own fucking head—dangled me by the arm as one holds a kitten by their scruff. And I squirmed like one, flailing and writhing, dripping wet as he slowly ambled down the rockface back to the path. He held me like I weighed nothing, the corded muscle up his arm tensed but not strained, not even a flicker of effort twitching across his handsome face.

One of my kicks nearly landed, my toes *just* missing his side, and he tossed me onto the ground with a sigh. My shoulder took the brunt of the fall, but I rolled with the momentum, springing back up and charging toward the unexplored darkness at the end of the path, less than graceful on the wet stone. The shadows weren't my first choice, but maybe, somehow, I could lose him in them.

"There's no way out."

His frankness stopped me dead in my tracks, my feet suddenly bolted to the ground. Freezing water dripped off me, splatting like thunder. My hair stuck to my face, my neck, drenched. I stared hard at the corridor's black mouth, hating that in my heart of hearts, I couldn't detect a lie.

"Am I just supposed to believe that?" I demanded, my voice hoarse, quivering. Usually I could bark down random assholes on the street, the catcallers and the slimeballs who told me to suck their dicks—as if that was some enticing invitation. Here, with my back to him, I faltered.

That pissed me off.

And more than that, it terrified me.

"I've spent eight centuries searching, little human," he drawled, his smile back—audible, almost, a huge injection of charm in his words again. Like he thought he was the fucking cat's meow. "There really is no way out."

For *him*, maybe, if I were to believe the story about the witch, about Ragnarok...

But no. No, I wouldn't believe that. There had to be other holes in this mountain. The water filtered out of the lake from *somewhere*.

I'd find them. Every last one. Because there was no way in hell I was going to be a—

My heart sank.

A *victim*.

Kidnapped.

Trafficked.

*Oh my god.*

I staggered forward a few steps, but the realization was a knockout—*the* knockout, a blow straight to the gut. My knees hit the ground first, and I braced, catching myself with one hand before I face-planted onto the stone.

All my life, I'd heard stories about human trafficking in the city—women sold into slavery, taken, beaten, abused. Kidnapped in broad daylight. My parents had prepared me for the bullshit evils of this world, and after they had died, Oma and Opa took over from there. Manhattan was my home, and I'd always considered myself savvy, hyperaware that at any moment, I could become a target.

Another depressing statistic.

And now... It had happened.

I...

Oskar—that piece of human garbage—had told me why I was here, my new purpose. *Companionship.* You didn't need a PhD to interpret the subtext: sex. Why else would a *man* want companionship?

*Trafficked.*

Kidnapped.

Trafficked. Kidnapped.

*Traffickedkidnappedtraffickedkidnappedtrafficked.*

I clutched at my chest as the whine in my ears screeched again, mind racing, those same two words *screaming* at me. My breath came hard and fast, and suddenly I couldn't get enough of it, couldn't suck it down fast enough. Couldn't stop gasping. Couldn't quell the panic.

The edges of my vision shimmered white, and my whole body cramped with a humming, TV-static buzz that made me double over.

*If you don't get your shit together, you're going to pass out.* Somewhere, deep down, I was still there—still the same woman who flipped catcallers the bird and told shitty teenagers to get up on the subway and give their seat to people who needed it. But she was *way* down in there, the voice of reason swiftly overtaken by my body descending into full panic shutdown mode.

Cool hands cupped my face, one on either side, big enough to engulf me, strong enough to lift me back up. Everything else was a blur—except his eyes. Green. Emerald green, specifically, rich and beautiful and glossy like a marble. Around the iris, subtle flecks of golden flames. I didn't want to look, but I also couldn't look *away*, those exquisite eyes magnetic. Like a still forest, like a mountain overrun with soaring pines, there was so much to them—an eternity beneath the surface.

They scared the absolute shit out of me.

But... They intrigued me, too. Excited me. Soothed me.

My body settled under his watchful eye, his hands cradling my face. Crouched in front of me, he waited until my breath evened out, until I could support myself again, easing back on my heels.

"They told me w-who you are," I whispered, unable to force the words out any louder—just in case the rest of the world heard me. "*What* you are."

"Yes?" He tipped his head to the side, those massive hands settling on his bent knees. "Say it, then."

*No.* I shook my head, eyes welling, gut churning. No, I couldn't say it. This wasn't real. He wasn't real.

"Say it," he crooned, this time with a flash of perfectly

white, perfectly straight teeth, his canines unnervingly sharp. His beautiful emeralds seemed to darken, a storm on the horizon, brewing in my silence. "I love to hear you humans say it."

I clapped a hand over my mouth when I gagged, that bread from the crate finally ready to make a reappearance. Another heave earned me a second showing of his teeth, his smile deadly, his gaze dangerous.

"Oh, come now," he rasped, dropping down to follow me when I ducked my chin to my chest. "It's not so bad... Two syllables. That's all."

*Oh god.* I really was going to be sick. Saliva flooded my mouth—the mouth sweats, *fuck*, the mouth sweats—and I swallowed down as hard as I could, trying once more to focus on my breathing. Couldn't he see what this was doing to me? I shook my head again, unable to look at him, unwilling to lose myself in that darkening forest.

"Go on, little human..." He grabbed my wrist and wrenched me closer, his breath hot, his eyes full of accusations. "*Say it.*"

"No—"

The levies broke. I turned away with another painful heave—and emptied what little I had in my gut onto the ground beside us.

# 5

# LOKI

Well, that certainly was... something.

She had been doing *so* well until—this.

Ah, there was that bread from earlier, slimy and undigested, along with a smattering of colorless bile. She had nothing else in her, and that was a problem. I took very good care of my consorts; if they played their part well, they needed to last.

I released her so she could fold over and cough, both hands planted on the ground, long, elegant fingers splayed wide. Her eyes watered more and more with each violent hack, and I stood to put some distance between us.

*The thought of your name makes her violently ill—*

"The lake is fresh water," I said tersely, pressing through despite the wicked whispers bouncing around my skull. "It empties... somewhere. I've yet to fully map it. Can't quite fit through the hole. But it's fresh and clean. So." Nora glanced over her shoulder with a grimace, her perfect eyes bloodshot and wet, and I motioned halfheartedly to the one speck of landscape in here that had never been cruel to me. "Tidy yourself up."

I left her with that, preferring her as the beautiful offering in the white dress, the little lamb sacrificed to the starving wolf—not needing to see her scrub the vomit from around her succulent lips, to splash the cold water over her splotchy cheeks. Moving at a good clip, I took the painfully familiar path back to the main hall and headed straight for the kitchen. Under one of the counters, stacked two rows deep across four shelves, were all the cookbooks I had collected over the centuries. Some had such faded ink, such worn pages, that their only purpose was nostalgia. Others were new, vibrant, with glossy pages and typed text, with images so meticulously crafted that I couldn't imagine a human arranging them.

The newest lot had arrived with the magazines; no sense in feeding a modern woman the tasteless, stodgy dishes of the past. As an homage to my darling Lucille, long gone, home on the Amalfi Coast—probably dead, honestly, it had been so long—I went for an Italian manuscript. Flipped through the pages, scrutinizing names and pictures, before settling on handmade gnocchi with a butter and chive sauce. This one had a photo, the little doughy pillows piled high on a blue-and-white porcelain dish, christened with two sprigs of crossed chives.

Lucille had made a similar dish for me from scratch, kneading her dough, portioning it, boiling it. I remembered every second, the way she danced around the kitchen—which hadn't been anywhere near this fancy over seventy years ago—like she was *home*. It was the only place she had any confidence, my darling Italian mouse. Hopefully she had gone on to marry a man who brought a bit of fire out of her, because fuck knows I certainly couldn't.

Though there *was* an intimidation factor that came with being a god's consort.

While I could recall every step, every flourish of Lucille's expert hands, not bothering to do more than skim the recipe, the photo was all I needed. After planting a bowl of my own—heathered grey, matte porcelain, conjured out of thin air from a magazine this morning—on the counter next to the stove, I got to work. The effort to craft each individual gnocchi elicited a sharpness between my brows, but I endured, accustomed to every kind of pain at this point.

Unfortunately, fashioning food from nothing but a photo took more out of me than building all this furniture had, and by the time I heard tentative little feet pitter-pattering along the calendar corridor, I'd had enough. Out came a pan, a stick of butter, some salt, and—well, fuck, I had no chives. Conjuring a whole chive plant, roots and all, left me breathless, but I hid the weakness from all but myself, as I always did.

No one could know.

That bitch's curse had taken so much from me already.

Bare feet slapped up the polished stone steps, my lamb creeping from the shadows—clean, hopefully. None of them had ever been defiant enough not to see to their personal hygiene, but the realms were full of firsts.

"I've got something going for you," I drawled, sprinkling salt into my bubbling butter, then rotating the sauté pan to mix it in. Her footsteps had fallen silent, *too* silent for my liking, and I found her loitering in the doorway when I glanced back, that white dress only marginally less transparent than it had been freshly doused. Perky breasts. Dark pinkish-brown nipples. Hard to miss, really, given the fabric. But it wasn't like I hadn't seen a pair of tits before. My gaze flickered up her figure, and our eyes met just long enough for me to study her expression as I added, "If you can stomach it."

Slicked black hair tucked behind her ears, she licked her lips and crossed her arms over herself, silent, perusing the main hall without a word. So be it. A harsh snap of my fingers ignited the rest of the hanging lights, not just the ones scattered around the kitchen, and I heard her inhale curtly at the surge of soft yellow.

"Quite a kick you've got there." Such a simple statement, yet it carried the weight of a dozen meanings—first and foremost that her lashing out hadn't sparked my ire. I could handle a few swipes of a kitten's claws. Beyond that, I acknowledged her spirit, and the fact that all this time later, my nose still stung a bit.

Impressive, for a human.

Still she said nothing, but I found her deeper inside the space now, standing at the helm of the great table. Not exactly touching it, but close enough to nudge her hips against the edge.

Did she enjoy my craftsmanship?

*Shall I bend you over that table tonight, little human? Fuck you into the oak? Is that what you desire?*

"So, tell me, Nora Olsen from America," I carried on as I plucked a few strands of chive from the new potted plant next to the sink. She was my first American—first consort from across the world. I'd had an Irish girl once with a scream like a banshee, but usually the village found worthy companions closer to home. "Who am I?"

"Someone who shouldn't exist," she croaked, this time without hesitation. I whirled around, nostrils flared, and she scampered a few paces away, cheeks pale. Her eyebrows then shot up when I chuckled. *Someone who shouldn't exist.* Witty creature, this one. My cackles struck the stone and bounced back to her with an intensity that made her wilt, her shoulders rounding.

"Yes, I suppose so, for this day and age," I mused, spearing my fingers through my cropped hair. "And had I the courage, I would have ended my existence long ago, but here we are."

Nora stared back at me like I had twelve heads, not so much as a flicker of amusement rippling across her features. At the first whiff of butter straddling the line between *perfect* and burnt, I turned back and snatched my pan off the burner, setting it aside for a final round of seasoning.

It had never been so difficult before to woo my companions—to sweep them under my wing. Yes, sometimes they were petrified of me and spent a great deal of time screaming and wailing and hiding under whatever would take them, but *that* I could handle. For I was a chameleon, a villain who *listened* when my old friends and foes dug their heels into their set beliefs, the whole lot preferring the ax to a few precise words. Usually I excelled at comforting a terrified woman, smooth like liquid gold, my voice husky, *desirable*, as I coaxed them into my own personal hell.

Nora was—unreadable—her expression subdued, distant, aloof. Unmoved by my voice, my healing abilities, she had yet to crack even a half-smile.

She required effort, tact.

And that delighted me.

For I had always relished a challenge.

"Drink?" After all, liquor loosened many a tongue—

"Water."

I arched an eyebrow as I spilled the steaming butter sauce over her gnocchi. "In my experience, a good pint of ale calms the nerves."

In fact, I had prepared for that—wine, beer, liquor, every poison available had a place in this kitchen, all cool and waiting for those full lips to indulge in them at her leisure. Nora's eyes dipped to the bowl on the counter, and then she cleared her throat.

"Water."

How dull. "*Fine.* So be it."

My back to her, I rooted through the cupboards, not quite remembering where I had shoved everything earlier, until I happened upon the glassware. She certainly didn't deserve a crystal tumbler, so I grabbed a plain, boring glass for her plain, boring drink, and filled it with fresh, filtered mountain runoff that came streaming from the tap. I then placed that and her gnocchi on the table, only to spot her headed for the ramp, ambling along like she wasn't exactly sure what to do with herself.

"You're here for me, little human," I told her, and she stuttered to a stop a few feet up the incline. I cocked my head, gaze slithering along her muscular calves and up to that ceremonial white gown, mind awash with what I might find beneath it. "The sooner you accept that, the more fun we can have."

She lingered for a long moment, her hesitation drawn out, before stalking up the rest of the ramp without the meal I had slaved over. *Rude.* Petulant creature.

A snarl cut across my lips. I would so thoroughly enjoy her inevitable downfall.

After adding a few more fresh chives to my creation, I grabbed the glass and the bowl, then trailed after her up to the electrified bars. The willowy beauty didn't even acknowledge my presence, her gaze wandering the cell door of her new cage, left to right, up and down, meticulous in the way she searched out the hinges.

*Look all you want, darling. Knowing a thing will never take away its sting.*

Her lower lip trembled suddenly, and she sank to the ground, arranging herself cross-legged in front of the bars. Seeing to her modesty, she tucked the dress here and there to cover all the delectable bits, then threaded her hands into her hair and let her head hang low.

I gave her one moment, then another, then released a long, dramatic, impatient breath. Nora flinched, but she still refused to acknowledge me. She remained steadfast, even when I set her meal beside her on the ground.

But halfway down the ramp, I turned back, rising up on my toes to get a good look at her—and caught her sneak a gnocchi piece from the bowl, ignoring the offered spoon, and pop it in her mouth.

Like clockwork—all of them the same. I smirked, then carried on down alone, quite capable of waiting her out.

I mean, I had all of eternity.

And for one as interesting as her, I *would* wait.

For now, the game was afoot—and just like those who came before, little Nora Olsen was destined to lose.

# 6

# NORA

I stared at those damn bars until I couldn't keep my eyes open anymore. Over the hours, the sun had crept across the sky, out of sight, casting longer and longer shadows through the mouth of the cave. The moss around its edges darkened, until finally it was just *dark*, period, the night here and the air chilly. Ass and feet totally asleep, eyes dry, I blinked hard and scrubbed at my face. How long had I been sitting here?

How much longer could I carry on this fantasy that someone—anyone—would crest the hill, appear in the cave's opening, and rescue me from a god?

And was it naïve to think I would eventually rescue myself?

Sighing, I reached out for the empty glass of water at my side, then flinched when I felt more than the bowl and cup he—*Loki*—had initially left for me. My leftover gnocchi was cold, all my water gone, but at some point over the last indeterminant amount of time, my captor had brought up a plate with a single slice of pepperoni pizza on it, plus a bottle of beer—lite, like I couldn't handle a full brew—and a ridiculously fancy cupcake, whipped topping and everything.

What the actual fuck.

What was his *deal*?

*You're here for me, little human. The sooner you accept that, the more fun we can have.*

Ugh. A shiver cut down my spine; I wasn't sure how he thought *any* of this was supposed to be fun for me, but being forced into sexual slavery just wasn't my idea of a good time.

The guy was gorgeous, but of course he was: he was a fucking god. Hot or not, I wasn't game.

And...

Yeah, no, this wasn't real.

Coma dream, remember?

Stiffly, I pushed up, every joint and muscle protesting. If I'd sat much longer, I would have turned to stone with the way I was feeling, and I instinctively reached out for the nearest metal bar for balance, ready to fall into one of my usual stretching routines—only to stop *just* before I made contact. The hum of the electricity scorching through the barred barricade tickled my palm, and I reared back, heart pounding, to stretch without support.

Below, the living area of this nightmare was empty. No god in sight, lurking in the shadows or otherwise. Good. I'd done my best to ignore him all day, really sinking into the circus music blasting through my skull whenever he loitered in the corner of my eye.

But there wasn't really a need to hover, was there? If he was telling the truth and there *was* no way out of this hellhole, then I was fucked. He would always find me, no matter what dark hole I stuffed myself into.

"God damn it," I muttered, on the cusp of crying again, every nerve frayed. Exhausted, pissed off, terrified, I still couldn't think straight, couldn't formulate a coherent escape plan. I needed food—more than the six gnocchi I'd slowly gobbled up—and sleep.

Like *fuck* I was falling asleep in here though.

But that couch was calling my name from the sitting area, creaseless, without a dent or ass impression to be seen. New. It all looked new, from the sparkling countertops to the untouched wood dining table. Everything born of nature was lived in, worn down, but the furniture, the dishware, anything manmade, had an air of freshness to it that suggested this Loki guy had just installed it.

Just set it all up.

For... me?

No.

That was batshit insane—just like everything else about today.

Batshit or not, the couch looked a helluva lot more comfortable than the ground, and I trudged down the slope toward it, constantly on the lookout for *him*. When I made it, skirted around the ornate coffee table and stood close enough that my knees brushed the couch cushion, I hesitated. If I gave in to the comforts of this place, was I accepting my fate?

I rubbed a crusty bit of sleep from my eye, then the dried drool from the corner of my mouth. Apparently I'd dozed off up there at some point, too drained now to even remember.

No. Sitting on the couch wasn't accepting *anything*. If I wanted to be at my best so that I could logic my way out of this, I needed sleep. Food. Water. Something warmer than this fucking dress.

And if he wanted to play homemaker and cook me a few meals, fill my cup when I asked, maybe even knit me a sweater and a pair of pants, then cool. Loki, the Norse *god*, could do that—but only so I could get the hell out of here, *not* so he could charm his way inside said pants.

Off-limits, psycho. Off. Limits.

"This is nuts." I plopped gracelessly onto the couch, and something twinged angrily in my neck. Perfect. Just *great*. Drained, I slumped deeper into the couch, which had a surprising amount of give in the cushions for smelling so new. As I absently massaged the pain point in my neck, I just stared across the space, over the huge table and into the kitchen setup. Numb.

*This can't be happening.*

Something cruel chuckled inside my head. *Girl... It's happening.*

I closed my eyes briefly, forcing back tears, and when I opened them again, the lights had dimmed. Atmospheric, like one of a million cozy, cute little restaurants in the city. Unsure of what to do with myself—and lacking the energy to do anything productive—I stared until every blink became torture, the struggle to lift my lids harder and harder. Then, begrudgingly, I lay down, stretching the full length of the couch, shuffling about to fix the ache in my lower back.

Fuck *me*, this was comfortable—

"We have a bed, you know."

I stiffened, suddenly wide-awake, and shot up. There he was, lurking in the dark doorway—holding a candle like some fucking romance hero, shirtless and barefoot in a pair of slouchy black pants. Heart racing, I scrambled down to the far end of the couch, and despite the fear, took note of the fact that he was, in fact, ridiculously cut.

Spending almost all my time in the studio, I saw ripped guys on the daily. Ballet dancers were *athletes*—

highly trained, highly skilled, every muscle toned to perfection.

Loki upped the ante and then some with those abs, those pectorals, biceps that the guys I knew would *kill* for. A stupidly sharp V that disappeared down south. Lean and shredded, no bulk, all corded muscle and subtle strength. Not braggy or pretentious, not for show—his definition had purpose.

Like... Like a warrior.

But this was what always happened in all the movies, right? The bad guy was hot as fuck, so of course he had a legion of fangirls.

"It's quite big," he added casually, the candle casting shadows across his handsome face, illuminating those *eyes* as they zeroed in on me. "Very spacious. Plenty of room for—"

"*We* have nothing," I snapped, finally finding my voice again. This time, it didn't waver, didn't break. But the weight of the day was obvious, my grogginess, my sheer exhaustion lessening some of its usual bite. Despite that, I hoped the message landed.

Only the bastard *smiled*, lovely and dangerous in equal measures, and my belly looped, heat fluttering around my chest—one lone butterfly with a broken wing.

"Very well," he purred. "Good night, little human."

I swallowed hard, arms crossed tightly over my unsupported chest. "Okay."

Even though a good twenty feet spanned between us, I heard the whoosh of his breath as he extinguished the candle, and when that flame died, so did every other light in the hall. Panic skyrocketed, the last of my adrenaline kicking into high gear as the room surrendered to an oppressive black. Tensed, curled up in a ball at the end of the couch, I waited for the telltale signs of his approach: footsteps over stone, a looming silhouette that was darker than all the rest.

Nothing.

I sat like that for what felt like hours, until my eyes adjusted to the night, and still I was alone.

Totally wrecked, and after a lot of woozy deliberation, I shifted down onto the cushion, still curled up on my side, eyes wide. Watching. Waiting.

*Commiserating.*

*Oh my god, shut up, brain.*

Even lying down, I figured I was too wired to sleep, my thoughts racing, my heart pounding, my body *begging* for rest.

But sooner or later, my eyes closed for good.

Waiting for me in my dreams were his wolfish grins, his haunting eyes, and his possessive touch on my ankle, my chin, my arm...

And eventually—between my thighs.

---

*Ugh.*

Nothing like sleeping for what felt like an eternity, waking up to sunlight streaming into a fucked-up situation, and still feeling totally destroyed.

At first, my eyelashes refused to part, sleep caked in the corners of my lids, and I rubbed both with a long, loud groan. Everything hurt. *Everything.* My back, my neck, my head—my heart. When I eventually got upright, I found myself alone in the hall, a soft, golden light spilling in from the cave's mouth, the shadows of the bars stretched across the opposite wall.

So much for all of this being a nightmare.

I checked myself over hurriedly, finding my skin unmarked, my dress hitched up around my thighs—but more from the tossing and turning of a shitty sleep than a god's wandering hands. Stiffness sunk its hooks in me as I climbed off the couch, joints popping and cracking when I stretched them out.

Ah, yes, hello, completely full bladder.

Awesome. Was there a toilet anywhere? I mean, if the guy had the sense to add a trendy farmhouse sink into marble countertops, surely there was some bullshit, top-of-the-line toilet *somewhere* in this place.

When no walled-off bathroom presented itself in here, I went exploring as quietly as I could. For the most part, I tiptoed along, arms outstretched, still groggy but slowly perking up to my surroundings. When I padded down the stairs into the dark corridor, I heard gentle snoring to my immediate right inside one of the pitch-black rooms I'd avoided yesterday.

I paused.

Was he—actually asleep?

Apparently I posed that little of a threat.

Good. Let him think that. Let him go into our interactions assuming I was a meek wallflower, honestly. When I finally *really* asserted myself, he'd be in for a shock.

Right now, however, the shock was mine: not a toilet in sight. Anywhere. I made it out to the pool room and back again without spotting the telltale outline in the darkness, and eventually just relieved myself at the far, far end of the lake, squatting like a drunk college chick peeing next to a dumpster after a wild night out. Classy, to the end.

I passed a still-snoozing Loki on the way back to the main hall, my stomach roaring, my heart leaping into my throat when a more obnoxious snore reverberated from the darkness. With a little more pep in my step, I hurried straight for the kitchen. Although the rest of the lights were still off, the fridge lit up when I opened its door, cold and full. Frowning, I checked behind the stainless-steel block, searching for a cord and coming up empty.

How the hell was this thing running without a power source?

Never mind. Not important. I shook my head, then dug out a bag of sliced rye and dumped it on the counter, along with a stick of butter. I'd need something *far* more substantial if I wanted to operate at full capacity, but for now opted for whatever would settle my howling gut.

With two slices in the toaster—which was, again, connected to nothing but still did its job—I rooted through all the cupboards hurriedly, taking stock of the supplies, even grabbing some of the instant dark roast I found on a shelf above the coffee mugs. Maybe forty minutes after I came to on the couch, still kidnapped, still trafficked, I had a halfway decent breakfast on the go: buttered toast, coffee, and a green apple from the fruit basket.

What really caught my eye, however, was the array of knives this god had stocked the kitchen with. Twelve dark wood handles stuck out of a pristine butcher's block situated at the other end of the long countertop, next to a fully stocked spice rack. Those... might come in handy.

Now, where I would hide one of those bad boys on my person was another issue entirely. This dress didn't exactly allow for discretion—

A slight and sudden tug on the ends of my tangled hair, fingers whispering from one side of my back to the other.

I stilled, hands curled over the counter, heart pounding like a drum. Was it just another trick of the mind, or could this guy move like a shadow? Both options made my knees weak and my blood run cold. Steeling my nerves, I spun around—and found him *right* there, towering over me, so impossibly close that I shrank back against the counter and tried not to shrivel into a ball at his feet. Still shirtless, Loki gazed down at me with an unnervingly calm expression, a whole lot taller than my five-eight frame.

The submissive angle went out the window in a heartbeat, and I shoved hard at his chest, needing the space of at least an arm's length. Only his sculpted body had no give, and shoving at him was like shoving at a granite statue: futile.

"You have her eyes," he murmured, his voice raspy this morning, thick and thoughtful. His green stare drifted to the clump of knotted black hanging over my shoulder. "And her hair."

*Fuck this.* If I couldn't fight, then I'd flee. Adrenaline surging, I pushed off the counter and tried to skirt around him, first to the right, then the left when he boxed me in with a hand planted on the cabinets. Teeth gritted, I jammed my shoulder into him in an attempt to just bully my way through, but all that effort died when he snatched me by the chin and thrust me into the counter. My back bowed over the waterfall edge, over the smooth corner and the cool marble surface, and I winced when my head met the upper cupboard with a soft *thunk*.

In that moment, trapped, up on my toes and stuck between a literal rock and a hard *god*, I felt very small—woefully ineffectual.

And those knives were so very, very far away.

But I was a New Yorker, and therefore stubborn by nature. I clawed at his forearm, his wrist, trying in vain to pry his fingers from my face, the tips digging harshly into my jaw.

"I've never seen a more beautiful combination," Loki told me, calm and quiet and distracted, like I wasn't flailing against him, raking my nails uselessly over his flesh. "Your eyes, your hair, that *mouth*. Exquisite. And I must say, I've seen many a combination in my lifetime—"

"Fuck you," I seethed, choking out the insult. "Get off me."

His mouth stretched into a strained smile, his eyes mirthless, nowhere near as playful as he'd been yesterday. "You should be honored a god desires you above all others."

"I feel a lot of things," I fired back, trembling in his grasp, "but definitely not honored, you *sick* bastard."

We stared off for a few dreadfully long beats of my heart, my soul on fire, before he tsked at me with three silky clucks of his tongue and a shake of his head. "Remember this, little human... You don't deserve *me*, my time, or my affections, but circumstance makes it so."

As soon as he released me, I was off like a shot, blitzing toward the arched doorway with zero idea of where to go—but knowing I needed to get the fuck out of here.

And as I scrambled down the steps, on the verge of tears yet again, I heard him crunch into my toast just as the kettle started to scream.

7

NORA

Three days of hiding from and rebuffing Loki's transparent advances later, I was still here.

In a cage.

Inside a mountain.

No one had come for me.

And that was just... *wildly* unacceptable.

Other things too: depressing, crushing, devastating. You know, standard rock-bottom stuff.

Three days later, it was finally time to do something about it. I could only explore the safe parts of the mountain's inner workings for so long. At this point, I had ventured beyond the sapphire lake, taking a flashlight from one of the kitchen cabinets to map whatever else I could reach—mostly huge caverns and steep drops. A stream that seemed to link up with the waterfall. Moss. Not a critter in sight and very few bugs to contend with. Overall, beyond the initial made-up rooms, there was a whole lot of nothing in here. Dark corridors. Shadowy pits. The odd hole in the wall that was either too miniscule to squirm through or too high up to reach. One landing *was* both reachable and spacious enough to fit me, but the drop down the mountain's face on the other side was substantial; there would be no surviving a fall like that.

Finding a way out of this place seemed impossible—just like he'd said.

But then again, Loki also thought a hole in the ground in a near-pitch-black room was an acceptable toilet—and he had supposedly been trapped in here for eight hundred years. His mood wavered, turning on a dime. So, the guy's mental status was... questionable, at best.

Still, he appeared to enjoy *me*, which was also, you know, great.

Fan-fucking-tastic, really.

Three days was about all I planned to take of this nightmare.

As they had the last three nights, the lights dimmed just before bedtime. Loki floated his usual offer of sharing a bed. I flipped him off with my eyes. He disappeared. I sat waiting.

And waiting.

Sitting upright on the couch, adrenaline pounding, my mind focused for the first time in what felt like months. In the real world, tonight's plan would never, ever cross my mind. I was willing to shove and kick my way out of a bad situation, sure, but to physically *maim* someone, to cause irreparable damage...

That wasn't me.

But now it had to be.

I estimated about an hour had crawled by since the lights first dimmed, the various strands around the main hall edging toward total blackout every ten minutes or so like they were on a timer.

*His* timer.

Nothing connected to any outlets in here—no pipes for the running water. Hard as it was to wrap my mind around it, *Loki* seemed to be the one generating all the power.

Which was just all sorts of fucked-up that I refused to get into.

As the lights descended to their final midnight glow, the setting *just* before pure darkness, I shot up and tiptoed across the hall—straight to the butcher's block. While Loki had prepared most of our meals, which I usually wolfed down at the far end of the table, refusing to sit across from him and pointedly moving to the opposite end anytime he tried to join me, I had still familiarized myself with the whole kitchen. Everything. Not *just* the knives, even if they were my main focal point. By now, I could ease the biggest one out of its slot without that telltale hiss of sliding metal.

I'd used it to chop carrots yesterday for my salad, taking the time to adjust to its weight. Kind of an excessive knife for vegetables, but I'd feigned ignorance when Loki called me out on it. Tonight, my hand shook as I wrapped a fist around its mahogany-brown handle. Still wearing this flouncy white dress, places to hide it were slim.

Unless you'd spent nearly all your life with perfect posture, capable of holding just about anything between your shoulder blades when you tried. Eyes locked on the doorway that led out to the bedroom, the bathroom, and the narrow black passage that Loki had dubbed the "calendar corridor" for some reason, I hastily hoisted my dress and shoved my hand up my back, careful to keep the blade facing away from my skin.

It took a few tries; pinching a pencil between my shoulder blades during a rehearsal break while my studio friends giggled was one thing. Even if the item was much smaller, the stakes were low. If the knife slipped out, I risked injury—and exposure. A sweaty palm made the whole process trickier than it needed to be, my muscles strained, my heart thundering so hard it was a wonder it didn't wake him.

But I got it. Eventually, with a lot of patience and precise posture, I clutched the knife's handle between the wings of my shoulders. Doing cartwheels on the inside, I slowly eased my hand out from under my dress, then just stood there for a few beats to make sure it wasn't a fluke. The effort to maintain the posture, to grip a smooth surface between my shoulders, made me shake, but I lasted a good sixty seconds without it falling—and that meant it was go time.

*Fuckfuckfuckfuckfuck.*

Shoving my nerves—and my moral objections to what I was about to do—deep, deep down, I crept carefully from the main hall, then down the little steps into the darkness. Arms out, I fell back on years of balance training, then veered to the right just off the stairs, groping around until I felt the doorway to his sleeping quarters.

"Uh, hello?"

"Hello, little human," Loki rumbled back from the pitch-black depths. My heart bottomed out at his voice alone, three nights worth of steamy, terrifying nightmares about this man pounding through me. I clutched at the wall, waiting, fighting to keep my breath even. His chuckle followed the shifting of what sounded like bed linens, like he was sitting up. "Finally come to share my bed?"

"Oh my god." I forced some snark into my tone, even as my knees knocked and my palms erupted in another wave of cold sweat. "Look, the couch is giving me a weird crick in my neck, so, yeah... I'm... here. But this isn't an invitation to, you know, *touch* me, got it?"

He snorted, the sort of laughter that seemed to accompany genuine amusement. Chuckles were the dangerous ones: they either fell coldly from his lips, not an ounce of sympathy in his eyes, or they purred in the aftermath of some sexual innuendo. Neither situation was a welcome one.

"We'll see, I suppose," he mused, and I managed a long, annoyed exhale from the shadows.

"Okay, well, if there's no guarantee, I'm going back to the couch—"

"*Fine*, you petulant woman," he said. The sound of a hand patting the bed made the hairs on my arms stand up. "Just get in. You're safe. I only fuck the willing."

"Do you ever listen to what comes out of your mouth sometimes?" I gagged, just for good measure. "Like *seriously*, dude."

"I'm afraid my offer expires—"

"Okay, okay," I muttered, stumbling into the darkness, arms out and quivering, the knife's blade hanging like an icicle down my back. "I'm coming. I just... don't know where I'm going."

"Straight ahead." More blanket shuffling, followed by a contented sigh from the lurking god. "Go until you hit the frame. It's a round bed, thin linens. You can't miss it."

I didn't bother to thank him; I hadn't thanked him for anything thus far, and if I started now, he might suspect something was up. Instead, I just shuffled along until I collided hard with a wooden frame, and I let out a hiss as pain flared in my shins. Slowly, I crouched over—no easy feat given I had to keep my back perfectly straight, my shoulders thrust back—and felt along the cushy bed's surface.

Then squealed when my hand landed on a bare, hairy, taut leg.

"Oh my god, sorry, sorry..." The apology was instinctual, my babbling a nervous tic that I'd managed to keep in check thus far. A seductive chuckle filled the room as I scrambled along the outer rim of the bed, keen to put some distance between us at first.

"You're a funny little creature, Nora Olsen."

"Okay," I replied flatly, my standard go-to whenever he said something that might coax me into any kind of conversation, pleasant or otherwise. Leaning heavily on my right arm, I eased down to my elbow, then settled on my side, facing him in the darkness. As soon as I relaxed my shoulders, the knife lilted sideways, its lethal blade resting on my dress and not my spine. Good. Just as I'd hoped.

"Okay, I'm in," I told him, still fighting to keep any intonation out of my words, to sound like this was the world's biggest chore—like I was only here out of necessity. Tensed, I slipped my arm under the paper-thin pillow, propping it up to support my supposedly cricked neck. "So. Good night." I cleared my throat, then hastily added, "And don't fucking touch me."

"So vulgar, you twenty-first-century women."

"Fuck off."

Another snort. "I rather like it, actually."

That lone butterfly with its broken wing limped around in my chest again, and I closed my eyes with a sigh. "Okay."

Could he hear my hammering heart—sense my racing thoughts?

Fuck, I hoped not. I'd never been a religious person before, not with all the shit that had happened in my life, but if gods were real, then I hoped—*prayed*—to whoever

75

might be listening that Loki's powers didn't extend to mindreading and supernatural hearing capabilities. *Please.*

Facing him in the darkness, I concentrated on my breathing. For now, I focused on keeping it even—not too fast, not too slow. Just the rhythm he might expect under these circumstances. The seconds *crawled* by, the two of us lying side by side in the darkness, and I made an effort to shift around on top of the sheets so my future movements wouldn't rouse him.

I played the long-con, timing myself, waiting for what felt like a fucking *eternity* before I started to draw my breaths out longer, adding the odd hitch here and there, like I had finally drifted off to sleep. Whenever I heard movement on his side of the bed, which felt huge now that I had to crawl across it with a knife, I sucked in a deep breath and fluttered my eyes open, just in case he was watching.

An eon later, he started to snore.

Softly. Sweetly, almost, not like Devlin's obnoxious roars every night. My heart lurched at the first gentle rumble, but I waited, kept my deep, shuddering breaths as even and rhythmic as possible.

I needed to confirm he was out.

Every limb was stiff by the time I finally adjusted myself properly, stretching my arm around so I could creep up my dress and retrieve the knife. Carefully, I steered it under my pillow, eyes open and slowly adjusting to the darkness. Without a spec of light anywhere, all I could make out was his outline, his silhouetted profile slightly darker than the space around him. Dozing on his back, Loki seemed to have cushioned his head on his folded arms, leaving himself vulnerable —exposed.

Open to a predator.

I swallowed hard. Was I that predator? Could I actually do this?

*Fuckfuckfuckfuckfuck.* I'd never even been in a fight before. Physical violence was always a last resort, but here I was, gearing up to stab a sleeping god.

No.

*I can't—*

*You want to die here, Nora?* demanded a sharp voice inside me, someone who sounded like me, but in this moment was somehow ten times more confident. *This is life or death. Use the knife and get out.*

Tentatively, my hand curled around the wooden handle, but it took me another whole goddamn year to finally inch closer to him. By then, I was white-knuckling the knife and on the verge of passing out, but my mind was made up, my heart set. Once I started, there was no stopping; hopefully inertia would just carry me through to the end.

*Soft tissue. Don't want the blade stuck in bone.*

The thought made me gag, but I swallowed down the rising sickness as I crept inch by inch to his side. Even in the dark he scared me, so large, so strong—even relaxed, his body's contour caught my eye, attractive in the dips and peaks, defined and toned.

A gorgeous monster.

One I'd see in my nightmares for the rest of my life, probably.

Shaking, I pushed up on my right elbow and gripped the knife for dear life in my left hand. Reared back. Hesitated, the mountain absolutely silent around us—and then plunged the blade straight into his throat.

His eyes shot open immediately, arms flailing, and I shrieked as a wash of piping hot blood spurted out all over my hand and up my arm. He shoved at me, gurgling, and I twisted the blade in deeper. The high-pitched whine between my ears drowned out my screams, everything inside me numb, and after receiving a second coat of blood along my arms, I bailed out. Left the knife in him as he bucked and gasped. Rolled off the bed. Collapsed to my knees as soon as my feet hit the ground. Struggled to get up and stay up. Crashed into the doorway.

Realized I was sobbing.

"He's dead," I cried as I wiped the tears from my cheeks—and smeared them with hot blood instead. Sure, I hadn't confirmed it, but I must have hit something vital. In all the old stories, gods could die. Swords and arrows, hand-to-hand combat with other gods... They weren't infallible, right? These guys had weaknesses, just like us. They bled. Felt pain.

Shaking, I stumbled into the main hall and waved my arms. "He's dead! Let me out! He's *dead*!"

Blood splattered the ground—*gold* blood. Fighting to catch my breath, I gawked down at my hands and found them drowning in gold. It glittered in the faint stretch of moonlight trickling in from the mouth of the cave.

"Fuck, fuck, fuck, *fuck*..." I sprinted for the ramp on legs ready to give out at any second. "Hello? He's *gone*! Let me *out*!"

I made it halfway up the sloped path before I heard my name. Gargled and incoherent as it was, that was *my* name—coming out of *his* mouth. I spun around, eyes wide, knees buckling as Loki staggered into the main hall after me, a hand to his throat, his chest and neck soaked in gold. All the lights came screaming back to life at their brightest setting, and the god stumbled hard into one of the armchairs, glaring up at me with death in his eyes.

"Nora, Nora, Nora, *Nora...*" He bellowed that last one, ripping the knife from his throat and painting anything within reach with flecks of divine blood.

Not dead.

Very not dead.

*Oh my god.*

I clapped a hand over my mouth to muffle my sob, regret and fear sinking like anchors in my gut.

Chilling laughter filled the room, falling from his lips like a landslide. Wet, thick chuckles of varying intensity and pitch thundered up to meet me, and I slumped to the wall for support—no fucking idea what to do now. Almost equally unsteady on his feet, Loki tried to push off the armchair, but quickly faltered, collapsing back into it with his eyes wide and wild, his mouth warped in a thin, haunting smile. Just before the chair could tip over under his weight, he steadied himself, still laughing, still crazed, then grabbed the chair and hurled it clear across the room. It crashed into the kitchen cupboards, the collision wrenching another scream out of me and an explosion of shattered wood.

*Can't stay here. Nowhere to go. No exit.*

He wasn't dead.

I couldn't get through the electric bars up ahead.

No one was coming for me.

*No one can hear you scream, Nora.*

Panicked, I hoofed it down the ramp and detoured around the huge table. Loki lunged after me, but noticeably uncoordinated, incapacitated by the gaping tear in his neck, he tripped over the bench and collapsed onto the tabletop, a surge of gold puddling around him. His mouth twisted in a snarl, and his nails ripped into the oak as he scrambled after me, crawling up the table as I ran for my fucking life.

"I'm sorry!" I shouted just as I staggered down the steps and scuttled around the corner into darkness. The bloody god came crashing after me, but slipped and fell hard on the stairs, gurgling something at me in a Norwegian dialect I couldn't understand.

Nor did I bother to try.

I ran until I couldn't run anymore, until my lungs burned and my legs gave out.

When that moment came, I found the smallest, most inconspicuous crevice around to squeeze myself into.

And waited—shaking, wheezing, crying—to see if I would live to suffer another day in this nightmare.

# 8

## LOKI

She had guts, my little human.

More than any of the others, she had *fire*.

And the uncanny ability to disappear for an entire day without making a sound.

With a bowl of roast venison stew in one hand and a flickering torch in the other, I made my way through the mountain's interior. Almost twenty-four hours had crawled by since Nora had attempted to slit my throat while I slept. In that time, I had healed and sat waiting for her in the great hall, loitering at the head of a table still drenched in my own blood.

And *she* had made herself scarce, holed up like a frightened mouse in the nooks and crannies of my cage—knowing full well that she had made a grave error in judgment.

Fiery creature.

A fighter, through and through.

I slowed at a fork in the tunnel, eyes dancing left and right before I veered to the right. Left was a lot of dark roads to nowhere, steep drop-offs and jagged pits. Nora had tiptoed around everywhere these last four days, but I seriously doubted she found any solace that way.

Not without breaking something.

Right forced me to stoop, however, and I ducked down with a wince, neck aching, throat sore with every swallow. While the attack hadn't killed me—and wouldn't in the future, I hoped she realized now—it had certainly taken me by surprise. None before her had tried to murder me to barter for freedom; the others lacked the stones. Still, while it hadn't ended my life, it hurt. A lot. And it continued to throb long after I had healed it. Deep in concentration, calling on every ounce of power I possessed, I had stitched sinew and flesh back together, one bit at a time, until I was whole again.

And as I plodded along now, hunched, the metal torch occasionally knocking against the wall of the tight passage, I estimated another day before I was at full strength again.

Outside this fucking prison, it would have taken seconds to heal, hours to bounce back. Here, I was... winded. Tired. Little Nora Olsen had delivered a powerful blow, and although I had serious doubts she would try again, I'd have to keep a closer eye on her.

Maybe concoct an actual punishment for any future attempts.

For now, I thought a reward suited her—*us*—better. After all, what a brave thing, to attack a god as she did. Even in the moment, my throat split open, my ichor leaking, I'd found it impressive, perhaps even amusing.

But had we broached the subject back then, I wasn't sure how I would have reacted to her—best she spent the day away while I recovered, while I had the time to really reflect.

Currently, I had an inkling about where she had

burrowed. After checking a few of the more obvious hiding places closer to the main hall, I branched out, walking deeper into the mountain, tuned in to the faint hum of a human's life force. All creatures possessed one, supernatural or not, though in my experience, humanity's was always the weakest.

I found her in a pitch-black corridor, wider and taller than the one I'd just traversed. If she had carried on deeper, she would have happened upon a chamber with a few patchy holes in the ceiling, allowing the sunlight to warm her throughout the spring day. Instead, I could practically hear her teeth chattering within the sliver of a trench that stretched alongside the footpath. When I'd first discovered it centuries ago, it had glittered with gemstones embedded in the stone, treasures hidden by dwarves most likely—the greediest lot who spread caches of riches across Midgard, far from their brethren in Svartalfheim. Now, the trench stood empty...

Until today.

She remained still, silent, always conscious of her self-preservation. I admired that about her, that she didn't give in so easily.

But our game would eventually wear thin, and then I would have to force us into a new one.

"Hello, little human," I rumbled, shouldering my torch as I stood at the cusp of the footpath and peered into the trench. Firelight flickered over the grey stone, illuminating white fabric below, her black hair and lean legs. She lay facedown, hands over her head, cowering. "You can come out now... I've brought you something to eat."

Still she didn't move, didn't react. Playing dead. I smirked; how droll.

Sighing, I leaned in and poked her ass with the butt of

my torch, which made her whimper and tighten up, her body curling in on itself as much as possible.

"You know, I'm starting to lose my newfound respect for your courage," I drawled. Still nothing. "Really, this is getting *dull*. If I wanted to punish you, I could. Easily. So, get up. You need to eat."

Gingerly, Nora's hands lifted off her head, and she peeked up at me through bloodshot eyes. "Why?"

"Because if you waste away, we can't have any *fun*." None of them had ever died on me, and Nora Olsen, with all her spirit, certainly wouldn't be the first.

She shuffled onto her side in the thin stony furrow. "No, why are you...?"

Not tearing her limb from limb? Stabbing *her* in the throat and then ripping the blade clean across? I crouched down, arms perched on my knees, and grinned. "I rather enjoy subverting expectations."

Setting the still-steaming bowl of soup aside, my palm like a stove burner, I carefully positioned the torch so that it leaned over the dip and against the wall, flames licking along the grey slate.

"Come here. Let me help you out."

She ignored my extended hand, instead squirming and wriggling upright, then attempting to clamber out herself—again, *dull*. I gave her a few struggling moments before I grabbed her arm and hauled her the rest of the way up, and the second I released her, she scrambled backward along the path, *barely* missing my perfectly seasoned stew in passing.

"I'm afraid I seldom respond how others want me to," I insisted, as if that answered the question those wide green eyes demanded of me. Finally, she stilled, gulping hard enough that I caught the dip in her swanlike throat—and that wasn't the only thing that caught my eye. Now that she was out, I noted the dust and dirt smeared across her cheeks, her hands, up her legs. Bruises dotted her arms and calves, her knees: the consequences of charging headlong into the black. My cage lacked much of its original rough edges, but rock was rock was rock, no matter how fucking smooth.

Beyond all that, she appeared exhausted. Heavy rings around her eyes. Slumped shoulders.

I certainly couldn't have that.

A haggard companion was no fun to play with.

Exhaling softly, I crept closer—only to have her immediately scurry away again, her dress up to her knees, her chest rising and falling in panicked heaves. My expression hardened, and a curt *snap* of my fingers froze her in place.

"Be still, little human." I put up with her surly attitude because I enjoyed it, because it was so wonderfully *different* from all the others. Eight centuries without a fight, surrounded by mewling worshippers and terrified consorts... It got old. Nora was new. I preferred new, shiny —undamaged.

Although I'd depleted most of my healing energy for the day on myself, I had enough left to wash away her bruises. Taking her firmly by the ankle, I worked my way up, smoothing the gathered blood under her skin, gifting her with a rush of energy that brought a vibrancy back to her eyes, the golden green catching in the torchlight. After I'd mended her flesh, I saw to her dress; one touch and it was clean again.

There. Much better.

Far more pleasing to the eye.

While she busied herself with her limbs, examining each one as if I hadn't already demonstrated my godly capabilities before, I grabbed the bowl of stew and shoved it into her hands. "*Eat.*"

Nora sagged under the weight, her arms trembling as she raised it to her mouth and slurped down a gulp. Her tongue swept across her lips, pink and teasing, and I sat back on my heels, content to watch her relish my handiwork. From what I'd noted thus far, she preferred salt and aggressive seasoning, which once again gave me something *new* to strive for in the monotony of my life.

"Why?" she asked again after she'd gulped down half the bowl, having now moved on to fishing out the venison chunks with her fingers. I arched an eyebrow, my silence forcing her to look up at me a few times, embellishing the question with her expressions—the furrowing of her brow, the hollowing of her cheeks, the nervous gnawing at her lip.

"Why am I not furious with you?"

Face flushed, she nodded slowly. I pursed my lips, watching her pick through her first meal of the day, and then pushed back the mirth, the biting humor that always, always, *always* rubbed everyone the wrong way.

"Well, I can hardly blame you," I remarked, my tone serious—possibly verging on depressing. I let it show, let it briefly ooze out of me, and this little creature could take it however she saw fit. "We're both prisoners here." Her eyes snapped to mine, and I shrugged one shoulder. "Aren't we? Captives together. You're mine, and I'm—"

"Hers," Nora said swiftly, catching me off guard. "The one who looked like me... The one you... The witch?"

The *witch*? I chuckled coldly, Ravna's vile face flashing before my eyes. Trust the villagers to have only told Nora of that pest. Did she think I loved *her*?

"No, little human, you look *nothing* like that shrew."

She chewed a hunk of venison slowly, pocketing it in

her cheek as she said, "The witch put you in here as a punishment... for starting the apocalypse."

Hearing it now, centuries later, a crime I could *hardly* be held responsible for, still set my teeth on edge. My lips twitched, and I looked back to the torch, to the fire flicking at the stone. "Hmm. Apparently."

"But there's never been an apocalypse."

I faced her again, my latest consort, my feisty companion. Looked her up and down. So young—but *strong*, resilient in the face of all this. A trait to be admired in her.

In all humans.

Another humorless chuckle escaped me as her face blurred, replaced by a broken Heimdallr at my side, a lifeless Sigyn in my arms. Fresh ocean spray on my cheeks as I helmed the great ship *Naglfar*, an army of giants at my back, the godly brethren who so despised me on the horizon. Blood. Blood. *So* much blood. My children, dead and hunted—

"The world has ended many times before," I murmured, and the color drained from her cheeks, "but never solely by my hand. If you remember one thing here, little human, remember that. We are *all* responsible for the end of days..."

Me no more than the others, no matter what the ancient scripts had to say about it.

I mean, *really*. Everyone's a fucking critic.

No longer in the mood to play, I stood, scowling, and left Nora with the stew, the torch.

"Scream if you get lost," I called back to her, my boots clomping noisily down the path, before disappearing into the shadows...

Into a past I would give my life to forget.

# 9

# NORA

"Look at that... Not a feather in sight." After discarding the plastic wrap, Loki dropped the raw whole chicken on his favorite quartz cutting board with a shake of his head. "Honestly, do you modern humans actually *do* anything for your food? This thing doesn't even come with a head. Nor those clawed little feet. I remember a time when—"

"I want to know about her," I interjected, my voice loud and firm enough to stop a Loki-rant in its tracks. It didn't surprise me in the slightest that this guy was a pro at ambling off into tangents: he loved the sound of his own voice and had been alone in here for hundreds of years—which meant he probably did ranting tirades all the time. Gotta keep that silky, husky, purring voice in working order, right? Gotta seduce the sex slaves somehow.

Still, after a ridiculously long week in here with him, I'd learned to cut him off and change the subject. Otherwise he would just *go*, eventually drifting into another language, talking about shit I wouldn't understand anyway.

The god stilled, pinching a raw chicken leg in each

hand, and then glanced over his shoulder at me. "Oh, do you?"

Seated on one of the dining benches, always sure to keep the huge table between us, I nodded. "I do."

This *her* was the reason I was here, and that meant I had a right to all the dirty details. Loki seemed to have fond memories of her, his expression either softening or twisting sinfully whenever she popped into our conversations, few and far between as they were.

"Yes, well—" Loki went back to the chicken. "—I'd like to shove you to your knees and fuck that pretty mouth of yours... We all want things."

I stiffened, and my belly looped and squeezed pleasantly at his frankness—at the *thought* of him doing that. Because the guy was a smokeshow, eye candy to the nth degree. Stunning. But like always, the flutter of interest immediately flatlined to dread. Loki had spent the last week feeding me innuendos and flirtations, so much so that it was painfully apparent what he wanted. Not like it wasn't clear from the second I clocked him in the throat on that first day, but he had upped his game and made his position *obvious*. I couldn't pretend it wasn't happening anymore, couldn't ignore it or play the comment off.

But I tried. Fuck, did I ever try.

While he'd spent the last seven days painting a vivid picture of all the wicked things he wanted to do to me, with me, on me, I had used the time to get the lay of the land. For the most part, I had the mountain's interior mapped out, though occasionally I still lost my way in some of the more winding tunnels. What I tracked now was our routine—and, more specifically, the comings and goings of the *other* humans in this valley.

Groceries were delivered on Sundays. Loki placed the

order on Saturday—somehow, maybe telepathically for all I knew—and then the food showed up in a crate the following morning. Just like me. Yesterday, bright and early Sunday morning, a group of eight men had hauled the box up to the cave, while another stood guard, holding me at gunpoint as they loaded the delivery into our cell.

At the time, I'd wanted to laugh *and* cry. I mean, there was no way out, but these assholes thought I was stupid enough to try my luck against all of them, a loaded gun, and a god who couldn't die.

That was how fucking little they thought of me.

Beyond that, Loki cooked three square meals a day. He swam in the lake—and so did I, but at different times or I was getting the fuck out of there. We shared his bed, but I had a fortified pillow wall between us, something he thought was just *so* amusing. In the darkness of that room was a whole goddamn library of worn books he had collected over the years; I'd been reading a few of the English texts to kill the time, to block him out, but even a reader like me could only struggle through so many dry history books before needing something else to occupy their mind.

And, frankly, I almost wished I could just talk to the only other person in here. Really. I did. He had called us *both* prisoners in this scenario, which at the time had been fucking laughable. But the more I'd thought about it, the more I realized it was true—to an extent. There was no escape for him either. Once he was finished with me, whenever that time came, he was still stuck in here for the rest of his very long life.

While my fate after him remained undetermined, I seriously doubted Oskar and those other assholes just let Loki's ladies go on living their best lives back home.

I generally tried *very* hard not to think about that.

About that woman with my eyes, my hair, screaming soundlessly at me in the village that first day.

So, yes, the fact that Loki acknowledged the similarity in our circumstances, that we were both captives—it changed things for me. Made me see him in a different light. Not all that much, mind you, because while we might have been stuck here together, we were far from equal.

Nothing reminded me of that more than the fact that the kitchen appliances were humming along without a power cord, feeding off *him* and nothing else.

Therefore, I needed to even things up.

And information was power.

"Okay, proposition," I said, tucking one leg under me as I stared at his bare back, his rippling shoulders, his lightly freckled flesh—at the long ugly lines stretching from top to bottom, the faded scars reminiscent of a whip's lash. "If you tell me about her, I'll let you touch my boob. One boob. Left or right—totally your choice. Over the clothes."

Loki burst out laughing as he meandered down the counter to the knife block, his head thrown back, his mouth open for big, belly-bursting howls that made my cheeks burn.

"Okay, it's not *that* funny." My boobs were smallish, which had worked out great for me over my dance career, but no other guy had laughed before. "I take that as a no, then? What, did all the others give up the whole cow on night one?"

Kind of a crude analogy, but I was operating under the impression that there had been plenty before me who gave him approximately zero trouble and no attitude. I seemed to strike Loki as an enigma, and I planned to work that angle to my advantage for as long as possible.

Men were all the same: they fucking loved the chase.

"If not the first night, then the second," the god mused as he considered his knife choice, hesitating between two handles. "They all knew their place and their purpose."

I bit the insides of my cheeks to keep from snapping at him, rolling my eyes instead. After all, my snark needed limits; outright aggression would get me nowhere. But *seriously*. Anytime we started to vibe together, he usually ruined it with some stupid comment—something to put me back in my place. Something fucked-up and unnecessary. Because we *could* get along. Loki had it in him to be charming and conversational. In fact, it was easy to put two and two together: with his good looks, his wit, his healing touch, I wasn't even a little surprised that women from the past, from a time when my gender had no agency in the world, would give themselves over without much of a fight. I didn't blame them or look down on them.

I understood.

If I had less of a backbone, I probably would have done the same thing.

"But, I have to say," he carried on, whirling around and pointing a knife at me—*the* knife, the exact one I'd buried in his throat only a few days ago, "*you* are by far the most entertaining."

Fear spider-walked down my back, made my heart beat just a little harder. I masked it as best I could, even as I felt the visceral chill inside me, the color bleeding out of my cheeks. That knife. It would have been poetic if he used it to kill me, to cut me up into little bitty pieces. At no point did I trust him not to retaliate for that night, no matter what he said.

He knew it. I knew it. And we both knew that he was

pointing it at me now, even if he *did* plan to break down that whole chicken with it, so I wouldn't forget what I had done.

How I'd failed.

I licked my lips and forced a prickly smile. "Okay. I'll take that as a compliment."

"As you should." Back to me again, black slacks hung low on his hips, his perky ass outlined even in the loose material, he started to partition the chicken, slicing the blade clean through the thigh joint. "But be aware, my little human, that this game of yours has an expiration date."

Fear hardened to dread in my gut, and with his back to me and no reflective surfaces around for him to watch me in, I let it show on my face. Another point to Loki: I *couldn't* snark him off forever. My attitude—and whatever he liked about it—would eventually lose its sparkle, and then I would either have to switch up my tactics... or forfeit the game. The creature before me was breathtaking in his own right, handsome and ancient, all-knowing and unknowable. Hot as fuck. But I couldn't do it. I couldn't just *be* his sex toy.

I had more self-respect than that.

What was more: as soon as he had me, the chase was over. Just like he would one day grow tired of my smart mouth, he would then grow tired of *me*, my body, everything. And where would that leave me? I had no fucking idea how to get out of this mountain, let alone escape the psycho humans in the village who fed the beast— who clearly profited from what limited power Loki had at his disposal.

"Yeah, well..." I rolled my shoulders back, then stood. "I guess everything expires, huh?"

"Everything but me," Loki drawled as he tossed a perfectly excised chicken breast onto the cutting board, the wet *plop* followed by one of his chuckles, the kind that was more batshit insane cackling than anything.

*Yikes.*

*Glad you make yourself laugh, my man.*

Taking that as my cue to get the hell out of his way, I power walked from the main hall straight to the lake for my predinner swim, mind awash with all the crap I had to solve if I ever wanted to breathe free air again in this lifetime.

All the while begrudgingly pushing my curiosity about *her* to the very bottom of the list.

For now.

## 10

## LOKI

"Look, if this turns out to be some fucked-up version of strip poker—"

"It is not," I said smoothly, sliding onto the bench with a pair of shot glasses in hand and a frowning, hands-on-her-hips Nora glaring at me from the other side of the table. *Strip poker.* That certainly sounded like something we ought to play—but not tonight. "The game is Fact or Fiction." I set one glass in front of me, then the other across the table, presumably where she would eventually settle if she stopped being such a boring little thing. "Truth or Falsehood. We each make a statement about the other. If the statement you make about me is correct, I take a shot. If it is false, *you* take a shot. Simple."

"Uh-huh."

"At no point are you required to remove a single item of clothing."

"Right."

I gestured to the spread between us, to the various bowls of potato chips and buttery popcorn, then lifted an expectant eyebrow and flashed what humans today had

95

dubbed a, quote, *shit-eater* grin. Nora had been with me for fourteen long days, and still I knew very little about her besides her name, her origins in America, and the fact that she was a surly, fiery, defiant creature. I craved more—more details, more information, more history—and like everything else, she wouldn't surrender it easily.

Several days ago, before the most recent food delivery, I had innocently asked about what humans her age did for fun. That eventually led me to party food, and she had rattled off options—chips, popcorn, dip, beer, pizza, and liquor shots—without realizing I had catalogued each one to craft some *mood* of tonight's game.

And now here she was, scanning the table full of salty treats, the shot glasses. Her hands left her hips, and she slowly crossed her arms, that suspicious expression faltering and understanding slowly dawning.

*Yes, yes, I listen when you speak, little one.*

"Okay, so, how do you win?" she asked quietly, her dark, thick brows knitted. My grin sharpened.

"How do *I* win?" Cracking open the vodka bottle to my right, an assortment of other potent elixirs lined up neatly at the table's edge, I held her gaze as I filled each of our shot glasses. "I win everything, pet. The question is, how do *you*—"

Nora threw her hands up, then turned on the spot. "I'm out."

"All right, all right, all right, settle down, you ridiculous woman." I capped the vodka with a sigh, its acrid scent threatening to overtake the aggressive melted-butter odor wafting out from the popcorn bowl to my left. "You see, I think we *both* win, as we'll walk away tonight knowing just a bit more about each other."

She wrinkled her nose down at me, quiet for a moment, possibly even contemplative, until: "Gross."

*Fuck*, why did I love it when she was mean? I hummed in agreement, drumming my fingers on the table. "Hmm. A little, yes. It's really just a conversation thinly disguised as a drinking game." My eyes dipped to the spot on the bench directly across from me. "Sit down."

Nora wet her full bottom lip, the flick of her tongue such a fucking tease, then nudged at the bench with her knee. "Fine, but I'm not drinking. You can take that shot yourself."

Of course. All of this would be so much smoother, far more straightforward, if she would just let a few pints of ale lower her inhibitions. But alas, that was the challenge.

"Oh, *boring*," I growled, snatching a few pieces of popcorn and hurling them at her as she marched down the table and around to the fridge. Predictable, her refusal to imbibe, but that didn't mean I'd let her get away with it unscathed. "Boring, boring, *boring*."

"Do we have any mango juice left?" she asked, totally unfazed by my response—and for some reason that gave me a strangely sick thrill. It would wear off, fade away, lose its charm in time, but for now, her defiance made me a touch hard. How *delicious* it would be to finally break her.

"Check the door."

That was her favorite—mango juice. I'd noted that she drank it the fastest, in the biggest glasses, and made sure new cartons of the stuff came with every food haul. Anything to soften that prickly exterior, one thorn at a time.

She returned a few moments later, jug in hand, and climbed onto the bench. Her full shot glass still sat between us, and she looked down at it for a beat, then pinned me with a raised-brow stare that had me snorting. Really, the

EVIE KENT

balls on this woman. The *audacity*. Had I been a less lenient god, a man hell-bent on crushing the female spirit, she would have been well and truly fucked.

Two weeks in, one would think her boldness had become taxing—*dull*. After all, I was just dying to bed her, to fuck her raw and hear her scream, to drink in her pleasure, *make* her bend to my will, my prowess...

But no. The game was still fresh.

Besides, two weeks was nothing to an immortal. A blink of the eye. A flicker of candlelight in the bleak darkness of eternity.

One hand locked tight around the juice carton's handle, Nora used the other to tuck her hair behind her ear. Someday soon, I'd wrap those black waves around my fist. I tipped my head to the side, grinning again, and then chuckled when she nudged the shot glass across the table next to mine.

"*Fine*," I muttered, snatching it up and shooting it back, barely tasting its burn as the liquid spilled down my throat and coated my insides. I then slid it back to her, and the same sick thrill twisted in my chest when she filled the glass with mango juice—and didn't wipe the rim. Look at that. One sip and we had practically *kissed*.

"So, who starts?" she asked, both hands coiled around her drink. I gestured to her with a flutter of my lashes.

"Ladies first, of course."

Her cheeks hollowed—like she was gnawing at them, one of her many habits I'd noted in the last fourteen days. She bit down on the insides of her cheeks when she was either nervous or thinking; I had yet to decipher the nuances between the pair, but I would. I had the fucking time.

"Your name is Loki."

I blinked back at her, stunned and *immensely* disappointed with what had just come out of her mouth. "W-what?"

Nora shrugged. "You heard me."

"That—"

"Is my first fact," she finished for me, the cocky creature. She mirrored my shit-eater grin from earlier, then fluttered her long black eyelashes impishly.

Petulant, bratty, smug little—

*At least she's playing the game.*

Sighing, I took my first official shot, then refilled it to the top as I muttered, "Loki Laufeyjarson, technically, but I suppose I'll allow it."

Nora rolled her eyes, big and dramatic, all for show, and tapped at the side of her glass with one perfectly round nail. I fixed her with a hard look for a moment, then cleared my throat.

"Your work—your profession—is dependent on your beauty."

"Ugh, *boo.*" Her face screwed with incredulous laughter, and she nodded to my glass. "Fiction. *Drink.*"

Had I so poorly misread her? No. A fetching vixen like this one *had* to get by on her looks.

"You're lying," I said, words tinged with a growl that had her settling somewhat.

"Drink or don't play." Her eyes followed my glass as I raised it to my lips and tossed back its contents. "And I'm not lying."

"You know, if it's fiction, you have to clarify *why* it's fiction," I insisted, the vodka bottle's narrow mouth clinking against my shot glass on the next refill. Nora smirked, enjoying this far, far too much for my liking. The point of playing a game was to turn the tide in *my* favor, not hers.

"Oh, is that in the official rule book?" She looked left, then right, then back to me. "You got one lying around somewhere?"

My lips thinned, the air stilling around us, and as if sensing she had poked the bear one too many times, she exhaled sharply and fidgeted with her hair again, pointedly avoiding my gaze.

"I'm a ballet dancer," she told me flatly. "Everyone thinks they know us, but we're athletes. We train hard, and if you can't hack it, you don't make the company. I fought for my place in New York, beat out a ton of other dancers. You can make anyone *pretty* with the right makeup, good hair, a beautiful costume, but if you can't keep up, you're out. It's grueling work—it's *everything* to me, and I didn't get it because of how I look." She cracked her knuckles noisily, scowling down at the table before finally meeting my eyes. "I'm a soloist in my company—*first* soloist. I'm not, like, the lead. My goal was to get to principal in the next few seasons, but I dance complicated roles too. Usually I'm in the studio all day... I've been on a sabbatical for a while."

A dancer. An *athlete*. That came as a surprise, but perhaps that explained her exceptional physique. While I knew very little about the craft of ballet, I'd ask for reference materials from the villagers during the next delivery; it was my understanding that their crops were the best in the country this year. They could pay me back with books on Nora's profession.

"I take it you miss it, then?" Her passion was obvious from the way she spoke about it, and I quite liked that. Desire. Drive. Dedication. In one question, I had learned so much more about her than I had in two weeks of study.

"Yeah, I'm pissed that circumstances got in the way," she muttered as she nibbled on a single piece of popcorn. "I worked my whole life to get to where I was, and then... bullshit happened."

*And it's not fair.*

The unspoken sentiment echoed uncomfortably close to my own narrative.

Shaking her head, Nora sat up straighter and pinned me with another smug look, like she had a *fact* at the ready, another excuse to make me drink.

Maybe *she* wanted to get *me* drunk.

This girl was full of surprises, after all.

"You started the Norse apocalypse," she stated. "Ragnarok."

Ah, *yes*. I had been waiting for that one. "Fiction."

Dumbfounded, she blinked back at me. "What?"

"Fiction. Drink."

"You are *literally* in prison for this—"

My cool chuckle had her pressing her lips together, and I reached across the table to poke her shot glass toward her. "Yes, of course, because all men behind bars are *guilty*."

Nora frowned for a beat, then downed her juice in one gulp.

"I suppose I tend to be associated with its beginning," I mused as she poured herself another glass. "It was foretold that I would only escape bondage in that first cave when Ragnarok—"

"Oh my god, *wait*." She slapped the juice carton down. "You've been locked up in a cave before? This has happened to you *twice*?"

"Do you want to hear the story or not," I crooned, eyes narrowed, and Nora held up her hands innocently before shoving one in the chip bowl. "Now then. It was foretold that I would only escape that first sentence at the end of the

Aesir's reign, that I would remain bound and chained in my
sons' entrails—"

"What the actual fuck," she muttered before shoving a
curled chip into her mouth with a grimace. I showed her a
flash of teeth, skimming right over the horrors of smelling
my own sons' bowels in the chains that bound me to that
fucking rock.

"Yes, times were a little harsher a thousand years ago,
but that was the way in all the realms." I rubbed at a splash
of vodka on the table, smearing it away. "Modern humans
are so *soft*."

"Off topic."

I held up a finger to concede her point. "Yes. Agreed.
Anyway, there are *three* signs, three instances, that were
said to bring about the apocalypse. First—the murder of
Baldur, the most beloved of the gods. I... played a slight part
in that."

Nora stared at me from across the table, expression
riddled with disbelief as she chewed her recent mouthful
like a cow chewed its cud. Clearly she didn't believe that my
part in his death was *slight*—and I suppose I didn't either.
The sun god had died by my orchestration. No getting
around it. I had lived all my life insisting I hadn't dealt the
death blow, that my hands were *clean*.

But my hands were as bloody as all the rest.

"Second," I pressed on, counting them off with my
fingers, "is that there would be three long years of winter.
No summers between—just bleak days and bitter, cold
nights. Brothers would turn against brothers. Warfare,
famine, and strife would erupt in the human realm as we
gods teetered on the brink of conflict ourselves, with the
giants, with each other." I hoisted a third finger. "Lastly, a
great darkness would rise when the wolves of the world

consumed the sun. Then the roosters would visit the giants, the Aesir, and the land of the dead, crowing for war, the final battle—the *doom*."

Nora blinked back at me again, still slowly chewing, her cheeks sunken when she wasn't. *Thinking*. "Right."

"I suppose I broke the first seal, if you will, by ensuring Baldur's demise," I admitted tentatively. Upon hearing the prophecy for the end of days, his mother, Queen Frigg, had insisted all the creatures and plants of this world swear fealty to Baldur, promising to never harm her favorite son.

But she had missed mistletoe, the smallest of them all—forgotten it as the others always forgot *me*. Back then, I so delighted in proving Odin and his ilk wrong, so loved shining a beacon on their failings.

Hurled unknowingly by his blind twin at my suggestion, a single dart of mistletoe had been Baldur's undoing.

And then—well, it was too late to stop it. Fuming, my blood brother Odin All-father condemned me to the first cave, to lay bound to a stone by my sons' guts as a snake dripped venom onto my forehead for eternity.

"*Centuries* later," I stressed, my point on the horizon, "Ragnarok occurred. So, really—"

"So, really, it's fact and fiction," Nora argued, wiping her salty fingers on her sleeve. I opened and closed my mouth a few times, both impressed and mildly annoyed by her deduction.

"I simply played a small role—"

"Fact *and* fiction," she said with a nod to my glass. "Drink."

I felt the liquor's burn this time, scorching down my throat and adding to the inferno brewing in my belly. Yet as I went for the bourbon, in need of a new taste in my mouth, there was this strange buoyancy that accompanied my movements. Nora was the first consort I had ever shared my story with, the first one who seemed interested in knowing the full history—such as it was, anyway. That time in the world was muddled, written records destroyed, most of the participants dead and rotted, ash on the ground and blood on my hands. To the best of my knowledge, a few of the lesser goddesses survived the doom, but of course none ever came looking for me.

That *witch*, an acolyte of Freya—I was the only one important enough left to blame when the dust finally started to settle, my wounds substantial courtesy Heimdallr's blade. Ravna had gotten the better of me, promising to tend to me as I lay dying, but instead trapping me *here* as punishment for her mistress's death.

No matter. She was dead now, at the very least. *Someone* had butchered her—even if it was just the ravages of time.

"The last man you loved," I started, my eyes narrowed as they swept keenly over Nora. When she stiffened, her cheeks pink, I had my answer—my distraction, something vastly more fun to pick at than the brutality of the past. "The last man you loved broke your heart."

"Fact," she admitted hoarsely before shooting back her juice. "I thought I was going to marry him, but, you know, so did my best friend."

My eyebrows shot up, and she shook her head, full lips in a thin line.

"Maeve... She thought... They'd been fucking for almost a year before I found out. Thought they were soulmates and all that bullshit."

"Ah." When she glanced up shyly, I flicked my gaze to the battalion of booze lined up at the end of the table.

*Drown your sorrows, girl.* Nora shook her head, but for a moment she appeared at least slightly tempted. Shrugging, I rotated my shot glass in a slow circle. "His loss."

"Whatever," she muttered, brushing a thumb under her eye before tipping her head back with a sigh. "They seem happy together, so, you know, maybe they are soulmates. At least I didn't marry him."

"Would you like me to fuck with him?"

Her head rolled forward, and she dug into the side of her neck with her thumb. "What?"

"I'm not sure my reach extends all the way to America, but I can *try*—"

"No," she said hurriedly, eyes wide. "No, it's fine."

My mouth spread into a hollow grin. "Coward."

Nora stopped massaging the dip between her neck and shoulders, fire flaring in her eyes and in her cheeks. Hands in fists, she stuffed them under the table and looked me dead in the eye. "You loved *her*—the woman I look like. You miss her."

A lump settled in my throat, hard and thick and resilient. Although I saw hints of my former wife in all the women the villagers brought me, I tried so fucking hard not to think of her, not to picture her face in theirs. If I could help it, I preferred not to address her at all, for she was soft and sweet, unflinchingly loyal, shackled to a monster all the other gods mocked.

Dead at the hands of a giant—after centuries of tending to her half-giant husband. In the great war, for all my posturing, I'd ended up backing the side that butchered her.

Nora was the first determined to know *her*, too. The first to hear my story, the first to prod at the one memory I truly cherished.

Before the bloodshed, that is—the few pleasant memories before the doom.

I clenched my jaw briefly, then picked up my full-to-the-brim shot glass. "That's *two*."

"Two what?"

"Two facts," I said tersely before throwing back the amber liquid. Its bite burned harsher than the vodka, and still I went back for more—*needing* it, the promise of a dreamless sleep and a hazy mind. For I had once loved her *and* I still missed her. "You... Your favorite juice is mango."

The little human's expression faltered; we both knew that was a weak one. Perhaps she realized she had struck a nerve, as her throat dipped sharply with a gulp, and Nora slurped her drink without a word.

But then she came back swinging.

"*She* died in Ragnarok."

Scowling, I tossed back my drink with one hand and snatched up the bourbon bottle with the other. "My wife was murdered, yes, defending the shackled remnants of what was once our family homestead."

Nora blanched, but I ignored the implications of it, the suggestion of some internal conflict brewing inside—because she had continued to *push*. Many of my old kin liked to *push*, eventually realizing that I could only be pushed so far before I retaliated tenfold.

"You're alone in this world," I sneered. "No family, few friends."

That was a given as well: the villagers wouldn't have selected her, even if her appearance was the closest of all of them, the loveliest, the most *beautiful* I had seen in centuries—not if she had an army of loved ones who would search for her if she vanished. An easy win for me, an obvious fact, and I relished her pinched expression, the dart of color in her cheeks. Discussing Sigyn hurt, remembering her battered corpse *hurt*, knowing that I wasn't there to save her *hurt*, and it was only fair to return the favor.

Nora refilled her empty shot glass with a trembling hand, glowering across the table at me. "You feel guilty for *her* death."

My first response was to scream *fiction* in her face and laugh while she drank, but I hesitated, the word clawing up my throat and dying on the tip of my tongue. Because it wasn't fiction. I *did* feel guilty—always had. Hadn't been there to defend her. So occupied in the war, didn't consider the marauders. Wrongly estimated old enemies seeking revenge. *Fucking fool—*

So I drank, swallowing down the bourbon with a grimace, my own bitterness making the drink foul.

"What was her name, Loki?" Nora asked—softly, sweetly. She sensed vulnerability in me and had seized it, but as I uncapped the bourbon bottle, I realized I couldn't fault her. Couldn't blame her. Curiosity was a familiar bedfellow of mine, too.

And...

This was the first time she had said my name in conversation. *Loki.* Out loud. Not a part of this game, not an easy fact to give her a leg up on me. Without malice or hate. It came so... naturally. I choked a little on this unprompted shot; when was the last time *anyone* had said my name without fear?

Without *wanting* something from me in return?

I licked my lips, studying her, one eye narrowed. She wanted something, too, but not the usual—not riches or good health or luck.

Only clarity.

Understanding.

I coughed, stabbing a fist at my chest as the liquor swirled down to my gut. When I was through, the old familiar lump was gone—all because Nora had finally said my name?

No. *That's absurd, you old fuck.*

"Her name was Sigyn," I rasped, struggling for words—like I had just stumbled forth from a month of solitude. "She stayed with me in the first cave. Protected me. Cared for me. Loved me unconditionally—as no one had before, and no one has again. She was devoted to her duty... and she died a gruesome death. Alone."

Nora nibbled her lower lip for a moment, and I frowned when her fingers twitched toward me.

"I'm sorry," she murmured before retracting her hand and hiding it under the table again. I cocked my head to the side, hardening to stone before her, steel in my words and up my spine.

"Why?" I demanded, my tone unnecessarily cruel. "Did *you* disembowel her?"

"Because that's what people say, don't they?" She stared back, unmoved by my attempt to rattle her, even as her eyes turned glossy, the swell of emotion glittering like diamonds under the artificial lights. "It's just what people say when you lose everything, like that somehow makes it better."

Ah. Another fact gleaned from words unsaid. I continued to harden against her, to sprout thorns like I always did. Weakness was unacceptable—so I would pick at her instead, peel off *her* scabs and watch the wound weep. "You're orphaned... recently."

"Fiction," Nora snapped, her softness hollow now, that flash of empathy gone. "Drink. I was orphaned a long time ago, but..." She swallowed hard again as I drank, her eyes on the table, and she swiped both hands under them with a sniff. "But Opa died this past December."

"And how—"

"You're lonely in here," she bit out, raising her voice above mine. I smirked.

"Well, *that's* an obvious one." My laughter sounded forced, even to my own ears, and my usual thin-lipped grin didn't reach my eyes. The second bourbon shot in under a minute made my vision swim, and I blinked hard to bring Nora's glaring expression into a single image rather than the double I was currently seeing.

"Your grandfather died a horrible death."

She spit out a bitter laugh of her own, at no point reaching for her glass as she said, "Is there any other kind?"

"Yes. Some deaths are quiet and dignified." Not many in my experience, but I had witnessed enough over the stretch of my existence to know it was possible. Nora sniffed again, harder this time, and rolled her shoulders back.

"Drink."

I missed the shot glass when I went for it, my hand snapping around nothing. "*Liar.*"

"It was quiet and fucking dignified," she hissed, eyes teary again. "The stroke didn't fully kill him... *I* stopped his heart at the hospital when I signed the order—and he went *quietly.* Drink your fucking scotch."

"Technically it's bourbon—"

"Fuck you." She stabbed her hands through her obsidian mane, trembling. "You want to break the curse around this mountain." Before I could get anything out, she shoved the bottle at me. "Fucking *drink.*"

"Yes, well, another rather obvious one, eh?" The amber liquid spilled over the top of the glass as I poured a fresh shot, and she wrinkled her nose when I licked the puddle off the table. I then sat up with a sharp smile, bourbon dribbling down my chin. "I've tracked that witch's line through the years—matrilineally, of course. She's spawned hundreds of witches, and one of *them* could break this curse. Not that they ever would..."

As far as they were concerned, I was a beast who belonged in a cage. Who in their right mind would ever set me free?

"You don't drink," I crooned, tapping at the juice carton with one finger—harder than I meant to, the plastic jug nearly toppling over the side of the table until Nora caught it. Shaking her head, she threw back her shot, and I struggled to focus on her as the edges of my vision blurred. "Why?"

"I ask a question now," she muttered, her glass still empty, and I snatched the jug, ripped off the topper, and spilled more than enough juice into it.

"No, tell me *why*, little human," I ordered, suddenly desperate for an answer, "because it doesn't strike me as a *choice*, more like a moral obligation."

Tears cut down her cheeks, falling hot and heavy, and Nora threw her hands up. "Okay, I'm done."

"No, no," I growled as she stood, far steadier on her feet than I would have been, "the game isn't over."

"Yeah, it is," she muttered, wiping at her face as she climbed off the bench.

I slapped my palms to the table, the force knocking over my next shot and making her jump. "The game isn't over until I *say* it's over."

For some reason, I *needed* to know—now, more than ever—why she refused a drop of liquor. The others been such good little darlings, so sweet and pliant, so willing... so *tediously* similar. But even they had accepted a glass of wine or mead or ale at my request, hastily gulping it down and watching me through glazed-over stares that had made me so fucking furious at the time. I certainly didn't desire a glazed-over Nora, glossy eyes that couldn't focus, a tongue that couldn't hurl those foul words, call me names, be so *mean*, but before the night was through, I needed a fucking answer.

Only she ignored me, arms crossed, shoulders slumped as she blitzed for the doorway—off to hide again, probably for hours. Hours alone, *Loki*. All alone again. Always alone.

Snarling, I shot up and cleared everything clean off the table in a single sweep, bowls of chips and popcorn, countless bottles of alcohol all crashing to the ground. Calamitous, my temper tantrums. *So childish.* Sometimes they shook the mountain; tonight, this one made Nora shriek and stumble into the wall as she staggered around.

"I gave you the horrors of my past, Nora Olsen," I bellowed, pointing a shaky finger at her, the other hand planted on the table to steady myself. Compromised after all those shots taken in such rapid succession, I had divulged far more in this game than I'd intended. And it had started as just that: a game. I'd wanted basic details on my consort, tidbits to use against her later—but only to make her blush or laugh or soften. Yet Nora had gone straight for the fucking jugular, pushing for details on Sigyn when I so clearly preferred those memories stay dead and buried. I dreamed of her enough, her swollen face, her exposed bowels, her bloody thighs, her broken body. For all her prying, I would take a new memory in Sigyn's stead—one from Nora's past, something gruesome, whatever made her weep. "You owe me that same courtesy."

The color drained from her face, but her jaw hardened, her eyes narrowed, and she pushed off the wall with a scoff.

"I am living the horrors of your *present*, you fucking asshole!" Nora shouted back, our rising voices charging forth like two braying armies, colliding hard and tangling, thickening the air. More tears fell down her hollowed cheeks, her eyes bloodshot. "Cut me a little slack."

And with that, she was gone, disappearing into the shadows. I lurched to the right, but my feet immediately tangled over one another, and I plopped back on the bench with the realization that, ah, yes, I *was* rather drunk. Terrible tolerance these days, for I seldom drank alone.

Not this century, anyway.

Blinking the blur away, I scanned the mess around me, the shattered glass and scattered snacks. Typical. *Always fuck it up, don't you, Laufeyjarson? Always ruin the night—*

One bottle hadn't broken, but rather bounced off the stone and rolled under the table. Without an ounce of grace, I retrieved it, swaying in my seat, and cracked open the seal. Tossed the cap aside. Gulped it all down in a single go.

The room swam when I hurled the empty over my shoulder.

My anger had vanished at some point, perhaps in the absence of my consort, the desolate loneliness creeping back in.

And in its place—emptiness.

Forever hollow.

Always alone.

My eyes blinked in uneven beats until they finally refused to open again, and after fighting it for as long as I could, I face-planted onto the table, dead to the world.

# NORA

Three weeks inside this fucking cave and I—

*Thwack.*

A playing card hit me square in the forehead, corner first, and then fluttered down onto my one-hour-deep game of solitaire. Sighing, biting hard on the insides of my cheeks, I picked it up—oh, look at that, queen of hearts. How fucking *obvious*. Refusing to give the toddler across the coffee table a smidgen of attention when he had been acting like an absolute child all goddamn day, I tossed the card aside, then picked another up from my stack. Eight of clubs. Could that fit somewhere in my rows—

"Play with me, little human."

"It's solitaire," I muttered, then flinched when another card smacked me in the forehead. Fire raged in my chest, and I looked up, huffing my hair out of my face. "The name implies that it isn't a two-person game."

Shirtless, gorgeous, Loki tipped his head to the side, sprawled out on the floor like some Roman emperor. "Well, let's play a different game, then."

"No," I said flatly, shifting between cheeks to get some

feeling back in my ass. I'd been sitting here, on the floor, for ages, pointedly ignoring him and his request to play our thousandth game of cards.

Three weeks in, we had played every two-person game imaginable.

None had devolved into the screaming match of Fact or Fiction, which we had gone out of our way *not* to discuss in the aftermath. I played cards because when we were competing against each other, Loki hit on me less. So far, he had beat me at nearly every game, that calculating mind above and beyond the capabilities of mine, but I didn't care about that. Cards were safe. Easy. I taught him a few from my high school days, he showed me a handful from centuries ago—it was a bonding experience I hadn't expected going into this, and when he had something to concentrate on that wasn't *me*, or about how best to get in my pants, he was tolerable.

More than tolerable.

Charming, even—and not in a sleezy, creepy, let-me-play-with-your-hair-because-it-reminds-me-of-my-dead-wife sort of way. He laughed more freely, shared pieces of his past more willingly; the guy had serious gambling issues whenever elves entered the equation, apparently. Since that night where we had both divulged more than either of us probably meant to, his playful side had grown on me. I'd... warmed to him. A little.

I mean, come on.

A hot god who can *cook* and occasionally let me win at cards?

What more could a girl ask for?

But he was still moody, unpredictable. Sometimes I walked into the main hall and found him just sitting at the table and staring at nothing—but I could tell from the tightness around his mouth, the rigidity of his shoulders, the white knuckles of his fists, that he was *pissed*. Seething. Alone, inside his head, just fucking *enraged*.

Those days I steered clear of him until he found me with a new game in mind, or a recipe he wanted an opinion on. Safe topics. Non-pervy, gropey, leering instances where we could, fleetingly, get along.

Still. None of that changed the fact that it had been three weeks. Three *fucking* weeks in here with no end in sight.

And I was starting to get antsy. Anxious. Cooped up and confined. Even a little claustrophobic some days.

How Loki had managed *eight* centuries in here—eight hundred years, 292,000 days—was beyond me.

He should have been *way* more fucked-up.

Mood swings and tantrums were to be expected after this long in solitary, but that didn't make them any more tolerable on my end. Today, when I had turned down his game suggestion for solitaire after dinner, he had collapsed across the coffee table in a full-blown pout.

And now he was flinging cards from *his* deck at me because I wasn't paying him enough attention.

Fucking *seriously*.

I needed a break.

Only every break I took was the same. Dark corridors and unclimbable walls, freezing mountain runoff in a lake to nowhere, cavernous pits that promised death if I bothered exploring.

There was no break—not from him, not from the solitude, not from the anxiety of being trapped in here.

Kidnapped. Trafficked.

He called me his consort—like a fancy title made it *better*.

Another card struck, this time in the middle of my chin. "Nora, Nora, Nora..."

Loki only deigned to say my name when he was annoyed with me—or when he wanted to be a fucking nuisance. There was rarely an in-between, and the rest of the time it was all *little human* this, and *little human* that. To a primordial being, half-giant, half-god, I figured I was a little human, something infinitely smaller and less powerful, which meant I still had no clue if the name, in his mind, was supposed to be degrading or affectionate in its own warped way.

I didn't like it.

But I didn't like it when he said my actual name either.

"Oh my god." I grabbed the king of spades and flung it over the side of the coffee table. "S*top.* Find something else to do."

"Boring, boring, boring," he warbled back before slamming his full deck on the table.

"Yeah, well, this isn't boring for me yet, so go away."

Out of the corner of my eye, I spotted those elegant, dangerous fingers stroke the top of his deck, then snatch a card and flick it at me. The three of diamonds hit me at the dip of my throat, a little harder than the last few, and I hissed out an irritable breath, finally looking up at him again. Already I had started to shake, so much pent-up feeling pulsing inside me that it didn't take much anymore.

Head resting on his shoulder, neck long and exposed, unscarred from my attack weeks ago, Loki smiled. It was one of his more attractive expressions, a smolder that I felt between my thighs—because I was a living, breathing, heterosexual woman, *not* because it was Loki, trickster god of lies, who was smiling at me. *Anyone* who looked like him would make me blush.

But it was Loki, trickster god of lies, who drove me up the fucking wall when he didn't get his way, and I wasn't sure how much more I could take without cracking.

"I know something we can do to pass the time," he rasped, his brilliant green eyes roving my face, hitting every point a card had landed in the last half-hour, then plunging to my throat. "It's a new game, one we haven't played yet... Just for the two of us—"

"For fuck's sake," I grumbled, my face on fire as I set down my deck and braced myself on the coffee table. Over the last week or so, the lone butterfly in my chest with its broken wing had acquired a friend—totally unwelcome, of course. The two of them liked to flitter about whenever Loki looked at me like that, like he wanted to fuck me, or eat me, or *both*.

Whatever was going on inside that twisted head of his, I wanted no part in it, but as I stood, I had no idea what else I could do tonight to waste away the hours. Walk around? Swim? Try desperately to sleep? A storm had battered the mountain all day and had yet to show any signs of slowing; maybe that would lull me to sleep, even if my heart pounded and my belly somersaulted when he gave me that fucking look.

With one foot asleep, I limped around the coffee table, once again pointedly ignoring the god leering at me—and then yelped when his hand snapped at my ankle. It coiled all the way around, his skin cool to the touch, his grip tight as a shackle, and I stumbled forward, catching myself on the armchair. Panic fired on every cylinder, fight or flight taking over, and since I couldn't fly away, I had to fight.

Only he didn't give me the chance to twist out of his hold, to kick back, to flail and scream and stomp. One hard yank toward him and I was down, crashing to the ground with a grunt, my hands and elbows taking the brunt of the fall. I tried to shoot up, hands scrambling over the smooth stone, dress hitched up around my thighs, but he was just—stronger. More powerful. Loki dragged me toward him with ease, sprawled on his back, head tipped up and gaze pinned squarely on me.

"Loki, *stop!*" I cried, wishing I had just agreed to play fucking cards with him. His touch might have been cool, his skin frost-kissed, but it ignited a fire in me that scorched up my leg and lost itself between my thighs, in my core. The pair of butterflies in my chest slammed into each other in their haste, shooting about, careening into the cage around my heart—all this lovely imagery for what was probably a panic attack. Great.

"No," the god drawled, yanking me to him a few inches at a time. He dodged my kick with ease and then hauled me a full foot toward him and his cruel smile. "You keep losing, little human, all our games... I think you deserve a win."

"No, s-stop," I whined, nails raking across the ground as I scrambled in the opposite direction, my efforts futile. My calves collided with his shoulders first, then my knees, and I squealed when he let go of my ankle—only to grab my hips and arrange me like I was light as a feather, a doll for his amusement.

His plaything.

I'd never felt more the part than right this moment, as he steered me over his face—and locked an arm around my waist.

Legs forced open, knees on either side of his head, he had a perfect view of *everything* I'd been hiding away under this stupid white dress. The fire in my gut exploded, sparks catching throughout my body, the worst of it flaming across my face.

The arm snaked around my hips trapped me in place, immoveable even when I pinched and hit and twisted out the little auburn hairs. Distracted with that, I'd all but forgotten about his *other* hand, free to rove wherever it wished, and suddenly it wished to shoot right up my dress. I squeaked at the first contact of his palm over my belly, squirming and wriggling over his face, over his laughing mouth that tickled my thighs with every breath. Goose bumps ripped across my skin, my nipples pebbling almost painfully when his hand brushed up my torso and between the valley of my breasts.

Fear and excitement bled together inside me, a sickening combination that made my heart race and my mind hazy.

And my pussy... wet.

*Ohgodohgodohgodohgodohgod—no.*

"Let me go," I whispered, my words strained, panicked as I slapped at his arms and wriggled uselessly against him. "Loki, stop, just let me go—"

"No," he growled back, his mouth brushing my thigh. Dark desire dripped from that one word, powerful enough to make me shiver. Heat flared inside me again, the fire burning brighter, more dangerous, threatening to consume every part of me.

This was wrong.

Wrong to be turned on by a man—a god—*forcing* me to...

I squirmed harder, then let out a frustrated scream that bounced off the walls and slammed back into us like the cruelest taunt. *No one can hear you. No one is coming to get you.*

His tongue swept the length of my sex, hot as the fire burning inside me, and I whimpered at my body's response

—the surge of need, like his mouth was the key, the fucking password to my pleasure. Little lights flickered to life in my mind's eye, like the start-up of some massive computer, all from a single flick of his tongue. The fairy lights around us dimmed, but still I fought him.

I just... I had to *fight*.

Loki plucked at my nipples, one then the other, making them harder beneath my dress, and I grabbed at his wrist through the fabric.

"S-stop," I hissed. "You can't—"

My protests died when his silver tongue found my clit, swirling around it, flicking across it, playing me like I was *made* for him. The hand under my dress shot up, skimming my chest, fingers delving into the hollow of my throat like he wanted to bruise me before they coiled around my neck. Snug as a collar, a choke chain that would tighten in my struggles but loosen in my surrender, his hand took hold of me confidently. Gripped firm. Steered me forward *just* enough to spread my thighs farther, put a little arch in my lower back, open me up for him like a flower in bloom.

And then he had me. Simple as that. Licked me, nibbled at my thighs, *fucked* me with his tongue until I was a panting, whimpering mess on top of him. I still fought, but pleasure sapped the strength from my limbs, made me weak in my core. He held firm, refusing me even a breath of movement, his grasp unyielding. I could only adjust myself if he did it for me, and he seemed to like me just where I was, straddling his face so that he could plunder me at his leisure.

I *hated* it—hated him, hated the way my body responded to his touch. The physical attraction had always been there, but I shouldn't melt against his mouth, shouldn't wiggle and twitch with pleasure, shouldn't have to fight this hard to *not* ride his fucking face all the way to an orgasm that would have me seeing stars.

Because that was where this was headed. Despite my best efforts to think of something—literally *anything*—else, Loki brought me back to him time and time again. He knew just how to torment me, where to lick softly, where to apply the pressure. Even his rough hold on my hips thrilled my traitorous body, his hand collared around my neck more exciting than five years of mediocre sex with Devlin.

"F-fuck you," I seethed, only I wasn't sure who I was really cursing—him for forcing me into this compromising position, or me for loving the sweet heat swelling between my thighs. Teetering on the brink of oblivion, I gave it one last go, one last pathetic attempt at resisting *everything* he was doing to me. But I couldn't focus, couldn't center my mind enough to think past this. Every single one of my muscles tightened like strings pulled taut. My vision blurred to black as I clenched my eyes shut, gritted my teeth, clung to his arms instead of slapping at them.

And then the strings snapped under the pressure.

I came with a humiliating screech, my body jerking against his mouth, his attentions squarely on my clit. His hungry little groan reverberated against me, and that spurred another rush of pleasure, the fires inside gone nuclear.

That was the best—

I'd never had such a—

*Fuck.*

The orgasm sunk its hooks in the more he licked me, dragging out the intensity for longer than I'd ever experienced before. I could usually manage a climax with Devlin, though they were few and far between with us, and I *always* got off by myself. But as I splintered apart under

Loki's harsh caress, it was almost like I had never truly climaxed before in my whole goddamn *life*. Like this was the first time, the best time, and it had ruined me for anyone who *wasn't* the god with his hand wrapped around my throat.

He shoved me deep into the black, not stopping until pleasure became pain, until he had milked a few blazing aftershocks of ecstasy out of me. Shaking, I sobbed out something incoherent, and finally his grip loosened. Coated in a sheen of sweat, I collapsed forward when he let me go— only after a sharp nip at my inner thigh, a bite hard enough to leave a bruise.

I crawled off him a destroyed woman, weak-kneed and boneless, the embers still sparking in my core. Panting, shivering, unable to form an intelligent thought if I tried, I scrambled over into a seated position, then hastily shoved my hand between my thighs, bundling my dress there—like that actually mattered anymore.

And Loki simply watched me, stretched out on his side like a cat in a sunbeam, smirking, evidence of the deed smeared around his mouth and chin.

I wanted to scream at him, call him every awful name under the sun.

I slapped him instead.

Hard.

Right across the face, the crack of skin to skin echoing through the hall.

And it fucking *hurt*. Pain blazed up my arm, right down to the bone, like I'd slapped a statue and not a flesh-and-blood man.

But I swallowed the ache, furious at the both of us, embarrassed beyond measure, then stood and scampered the fuck out of there, off to hide away again—somewhere dark and quiet, far from him, to collect the shards of my dignity shattered by his mouth.

Because from the way he looked at me, the wolfish glint in his eyes, the dangerous twist of his lips, if I stayed a minute longer, I'd be fucked.

Literally.

And—I might not fight it as hard as I would have an hour ago.

1 2

LOKI

I loved sex.

*Loved* it.

Women, men, orgies, bound and gagged, soft and sweet, any hole, in my standard form or something else entirely—I just loved fucking. Always had.

And it was yet another piece of my life that that *bitch* had stolen from me when she cast the ward around this mountain, sealing a broken, bloodied, *weak* god inside for the rest of his days. Sex and shapeshifting—gone. At the very least, the villagers had found me after about a century, which meant *eventually* one of my favorite things returned. The rest would have to wait until oblivion, when the realm cracked in two, when the mountain splintered, and then maybe, just maybe, I might walk free.

Or I would be stuck even deeper, forced even farther underground, but it was an eventuality I preferred not to dwell on.

With my consorts, I could fuck again.

And after tasting Nora last night, I *would* fuck again. The game was over, my patience up. She could still be surly to me, as mean as she liked, but I'd have her now—again and again, in every position possible. Here, there, and everywhere.

From the way she had screamed through a climax, spilled her desire all over my hungry mouth, she would have me too. Despise the situation, loathe my teasing, *hate* this mountain—she could do all that and more, but Nora Olsen desired *me*.

That was all I needed to push forth, to set aside the cards and the food and the courtship rituals unspoken between us—it was done. Over. Complete. It had dragged on long enough, three agonizing weeks without so much as a glimpse beneath that sacrificial gown. We had crossed a great many barriers last night, and I intended to forge ahead with *tenacity*, drag us both kicking and screaming into the ferocious darkness on the horizon.

I mean. What the fuck else did I have to do with my time?

The first game might be over, but the second had only just begun—and already it was far more interesting.

She had spent the night elsewhere, out of our bed and deep in the mountain, which I could hardly begrudge her. Were I a gentleman, I would already have had breakfast going, coffee brewing, eggs sizzling in the pan, and a cold glass of mango juice waiting in her usual place at the table. Instead, I leaned back against it, arms crossed, partially seated on the oak's edge, and watched the dark doorway like a hawk. An hour had passed since her usual rising time, but I had already proven to be a patient god. I could wait all day for her, but I would fucking *wait*.

Another hour crept by before she surfaced, her hair wet and slicked down her neck from a swim, her flesh dry. When we'd parted ways, she had left me flushed and sweaty, evidence of our latest game smeared across the both of us. Now, Nora was clean, pristine—virginal in white. I cocked my head to the side, appraising her swiftly from top to bottom, the corners of my mouth kicking up when she paused on the top step—stumbled to a halt, more like, when she undoubtedly realized she couldn't avoid me forever.

Her tongue swept across her full lips hurriedly as her gaze darted about. To her credit, she didn't blush bright crimson under my relentless stare, but she fidgeted nervously, some of her confidence shattered.

Then, to my surprise, she stood a few inches taller, her posture perfect as always, and breezed into the main hall like nothing had happened. I bit back a laugh; something had *very* much happened, and she refused to so much as glance toward the scene of the crime.

My little consort flashed a strained smile in passing, saying nothing about the empty kitchen, the clean counters, the cold stove, and instead marched straight for the refrigerator.

"What do you want for breakfast?" she asked lightly, popping open the door and perusing the icebox's innards like she had never seen it before—like it was *so* bloody fascinating. I studied every minute detail of her over my shoulder, wondering if she intended to feed *me* this morning, our roles suddenly reversed.

No. The creature was just making polite conversation, something else to distance us from what had happened.

And I couldn't allow that.

Wouldn't allow that—not when her embarrassment so delighted me.

That was why she'd slapped me, after all. A futile attempt, yes, but fueled by humiliation over the fact that she had succumbed at last.

That she had *liked* every little thing I'd done to her.

*I can read you like a fucking book, girl.*

"You, little human." She stopped rummaging through the shelves and shot up, her head snapping in my direction, eyebrows creeping up her forehead. I pushed off the table. "I'd like to eat *you*."

With a shaky breath, Nora slammed the refrigerator door shut just as the color finally plumed in her cheeks, and I prowled around the table toward her.

"I'm afraid, after last night, my tastes have become rather singular."

She shook her head and backed away; didn't she know that just piqued a predator's interest? Nothing more thrilling than the chase to us higher-order beasts. But after the pleasure I'd gifted her with last night, she ought to be running *to* me, not from—straight into my arms for another round, for fuck's *sake*.

"You..." She shook her head again, arms crossed, shoulders hunched. "*You...*"

"Yes, *me*." I stalked toward her retreating figure, my far larger steps dwarfing her shuffling, closing the distance between us fast enough to make her blanche. "What is it, little one? Am I not handsome enough?" My hands flew to my shirt, wrenching it over my head and tossing it away. Let her see me—let her witness what she so staunchly denied herself. "Am I not beautiful enough for you?"

Annoyance prickled in my chest that she still resisted me, even now, but then I also quite enjoyed it too. Obviously I had no fucking clue what I *actually* wanted, but what else was new?

I hastily unbuckled my trousers and shoved them down my thighs, kicking them off with a snarl and a flash of teeth. Bare before her, I stood tall and proud, my body that of a *god*, what all humans lusted after—what women craved and men coveted. And still she refused me, turning in place and offering me her back instead.

"What do you *want* from me?" I demanded, on the prowl again, my prey the loveliest I'd ever tasted. "Do you prefer to fuck your men?"

Nora swiveled around, eyes wide, jaw dropped, and I flashed a cruel grin. At least I always knew how to get her attention—shock was such a useful tool.

"Shall I be rougher?" I hastened my pace, encroaching on her swiftly, and she matched my every step with several of her own, unwittingly steering herself toward the wall of the ramp. "Gentler? Do you fantasize about being forced? Shall I grow tits and a cunt for you? Is that preferable?" When her back collided with the stone, I pounced, trapping her in place with a hand on either side of her head, my body dominating hers, my hardening cock nudged up against the white cotton. Nora turned her head away, breathing hard, and I wrenched her back to me with a forceful hand on her chin. "Tell me what you *want*!"

And I would fucking give it to her, the stubborn thing— or she could just let me go on guessing. Either way, I would have her.

I. would. *have*. her.

Heat flared between us, bodies molded together. Tremble as she did, chest rising and falling with panicked breaths, she met my eyes defiantly, never cowering, never folding. She stared back with hellfire blazing behind those perfect greens, a forest engulfed in flames, and I had never wanted her more.

And so, at long last I made desire reality. Still gripping her firmly by the chin, I swooped down to claim her mouth for my own—only for Nora to slap at my arm and try in vain to squirm free, tucking her chin into my palm. I forced her back up, the fire in her eyes raging in my chest, and caught her lips in a hard kiss that had her gasping. Her lashes fluttered, like she was fighting to keep her eyes open, and she smacked at my arms, my sides, then kicked my shin with her little foot, her warped toes.

Alas—her moan was her undoing. Exhaling a gentle, minty breath from her nostrils, scented like the toothpaste the villagers had provided her weeks ago, Nora uttered the faintest of sounds, her mouth softening somewhat against mine. I responded with a growl, pushing in firmer, my hand twining into her damp hair and tipping her head back to accept me. The movement nudged her lips apart, but it was *her* tongue that sought out mine first, darting into my mouth and flicking at me. Fleetingly. Teasingly. When I chased, a predator entranced, she snapped at my lips—hard—and raked her nails up my neck.

Not gentler, then. She was fire—and I would give it to her, be the fuel to her flames.

Our kiss turned fierce fast, aggressive, the pair of us dueling for control. Nora gave as good as she got, arching up against me and twisting her fingers harshly into my hair. She was exquisite—delicious, ferocious, all that I had imagined she would be in these last three weeks. As always, my little human did *not* disappoint.

Cock at full mast, I skimmed my hands down her lean body, over curves and valleys that I'd only sampled last night. With her mouth fully open to me, tongues clashing, Nora squealed when my hands smoothed the sensitive undersides of her thighs, and I chuckled darkly into our kiss. Gripping tight, I wrenched her legs apart and hoisted her up. For the first time, she towered over me, the shift in our angles giving her the high ground. She kissed harder, fought fiercer, biting at my lips, my tongue, writhing against me, ripping at my hair when my cock nudged her core.

Until those cruel hands found my chin, cupped my jawline—and she *shoved*. With all her might, Nora pushed me away, gasping, trembling, tears suddenly streaking down her cheeks.

"I'm a person," she cried hoarsely, her eyes bloodshot and her lip bleeding, "not a *toy* for you to play with while you pass the time in your prison cell!"

Did she realize what dangerous ground she trod—to stop a predator on the cusp of his kill? I flashed my teeth at her, panting, glaring.

Ever so slightly shaking.

Humans had always been the playthings of the gods. In every pantheon, every era, every realm, humans existed for *our* amusement.

But I kept that to myself, instead swiping my thumb over her swollen lower lip, wiping away the bright red droplet—then licking at it, the flick of my tongue making Nora jerk her head back into the stone. Her eyes widened. Her nostrils flared. After a brief moment of incredulous shock, she reacted, snapping like the tigress who'd just had her tail pulled by a vexing monkey.

She hit me. Slapped me—hard, again—across my face. Even in such close proximity, she lashed out, set her own boundaries with her strikes that fell like mist against my cheeks.

And I let her snarl and bare her fangs, flail against my naked body, hiss and scratch—because I so loved her fury. Intoxicating, her fire, after centuries of meek lovers and quiet companions. *Exciting*.

I allowed her a few really good smacks before I reminded her that I *wasn't* the monkey and she wasn't the tiger. *I* was the apex predator, so far beyond her that she was but a fly buzzing around my face. Without a word, I snatched her wrists and shoved them back against the wall, pinning them next to her head. Nora's lips thinned as she bucked against me, only to still a second later, face bright red when she no doubt felt the ardent insistency of my cock nudged up between her thighs. Her dress had parted, allowing me a taste of her heat, her slickness, but I wouldn't push in. Not yet. Not now.

I'd fuck her within an inch of her sanity—but not today. The time wasn't right after... *this*.

So I kissed her instead. Captured her lips and *devoured* her like one of the ancient pillagers of this land—a warrior taking what he wanted, when he wanted, as he wanted. She screamed into my mouth when our lips parted, teeth gnashing, tongue stabbing, her eyes wide and accusatory as they glowered into mine.

But she rocked her hips against me, bucked and ground down, her heels digging hard into the small of my back. Her body betrayed her—time and time again, it would side with *me*. Let her heart and her mind think what they wished, fight as they wished; I'd have her one way or another.

I'd make her disloyal body *sing*.

Pain suddenly spiked in my lower lip, poignant enough to make me hiss and retreat. I reared back, blinking rapidly, stunned to feel ichor weeping from the wound.

She had made me bleed. *Again.*

My tongue darted out to taste, to confirm, and I scowled. Her blood had such a delicious metallic tinge to it, whereas mine tasted much like the apples that had blessed my kind with immortality long ago. Fascinated by the fact that once more she had wounded me, I set her down and dabbed at my lip, not caring that she shoved off the wall and kicked me on the way out.

Gold stained my fingertips. Pain throbbed across my lips. *Fuck*, how this little creature made me *feel*.

After almost a century of numbness, of blinding rage and haunting lows, she breathed such life into me with her fire...

I simply couldn't let her go. The thought of waking up each morning without her and her unpredictability, her beauty, her foul mouth—it made my chest tight.

"I'm sorry, little firebird."

She stopped immediately, hands at her sides in fists, her hair ruffled. The new name would have caught her attention, a step up from *little human*. For she was a firebird —*my* firebird, bold and brave, fearless to make a god bleed twice.

I leaned against the stone wall, shoulder bearing the brunt of my weight, and then let my head *thunk* hard against it as I studied her. "I'm afraid I can't let you fly away home yet."

Nora whipped around, brows furrowed, full mouth arced in a frown, her confusion lovely. I swallowed, the lump in my throat stubborn as ever, then forced a half-smile, all my previous *oomph* fading at the realization that I, Loki Laufeyjarson, trickster, god of lies and shapeshifting, father of Fenrir and Hel, needed her now.

Needed this little human, this raging firebird, just to get through the days in here.

"And I *am* sorry for that," I added softly. She would keep me on my toes, remind me of the man I was before I'd been sealed alive inside my own tomb. It was selfish to hold her just for *that*—indulgent and cruel.

That had never mattered to me before.

And it shouldn't matter now.

It *didn't* matter now—regardless of the strange ache in my chest, how it sharpened at the thought of keeping her forever.

Nora stared at me for a long moment, her expression unreadable, her mind undoubtedly filtering through everything—the underlying motivations of my apology, the new name, what it meant to her and her long-term captivity alongside the beast. When she finally looked down, I expected her to turn on the spot and stalk off; she was rather adept at dramatic walkouts. Instead, she veered to her left, past the table and into the kitchen area, straight to the kettle. She grabbed it stiffly, popped it open, then shoved it under the faucet. Seconds later, the hiss of running water filled the main hall. A few beats after that and she had the coffee brewing—then the eggs out, along with the stack of raw pork strips. *Bacon.*

She got to work on breakfast as her belly growled, loud enough that I heard it all the way over here, and mine responded in kind. Pushing off the wall, I strolled toward her, noting the way she tensed with each passing step, then scooped my trousers off the ground and slipped them back on. No need to shove a half-flaccid cock in her face, after all.

Not only that, but I'd quickly learned the sputter of bacon grease was rather dangerous to any bits of exposed skin in its path.

Briefly, I stood in front of the refrigerator, watching her work, watching her shake ever so slightly in front of the stove, her jaw clenched and her movements stilted. I then dug out her mango juice and set it on the table, along with our plates and glasses and cutlery.

Sat on the bench in my usual spot, waiting. Smiled briefly when she served me a cooked, salty, sizzling, fried breakfast. Poured her a glass of juice. Got up to fetch the cream and sugar for her coffee. Settled in across from her at the table.

Then we ate in silence, accompanied by the clatter of forks and knives on porcelain, just as the first *boom* of thunder, a storm rolling across the outside world.

A storm brewing inside *me*, my mind splintering apart just as lightning splits the sky—over her, what she suddenly meant to my survival, my *sanity*. My consort. My little human.

My firebird.

# 13

## NORA

One month.

One month in here and I was starting to lose it.

Ever since *firebird* came into play, I'd worked hard to keep my distance from Loki, exploring parts of the mountain I had been too afraid to before, swimming more, *demanding* a toilet and a bath so I could hide away in the tub for ages like I did at home. Only back then, I used my tiny bathtub to nurse my aching joints and bones and muscles, totally wrecked from an eleven-, sometimes twelve-hour days at the studio.

Here, I was restless, but my body seldom hurt. And if it did, there was Loki with his magical touch to heal me. He had done so with my lips after we'd kissed for the first time, touching each with one finger, his intense stare scaring me—exciting me, too, yet another reason I had kept my distance.

The guy could *kiss*.

He could do a hell of a lot more than that.

And... As the days went on, the walls closing in, the loneliness had really started to make itself at home inside me. Sex offered intimacy, closeness, comfort. With Devlin,

135

sometimes it had felt like a chore, something to just knock out of the way before we went to bed. I'd be exhausted from a day of dancing, or even a performance, but he wanted it, and to keep the peace, I would give it.

Our sex was just okay. Occasionally good, rarely great.

Loki had been great and we hadn't even done the fucking deed.

One month in, I *got* it—why he wanted to screw all his kidnapped women. It passed the time. It was a fantastic distraction from your feelings, both inside and out. Nothing triggered a wave of feel-good hormones like a stellar orgasm, and for just a few fleeting moments, you weren't completely alone in here.

I understood.

I almost *wanted* it—but no. *Fuck* no. If I gave in completely, the game was up. I was done. He'd send me away, sick of being abused and hit, and then those psycho freaks out there would put me in a house and keep me forever.

No.

Fuck no.

I blinked the lake back into focus. Having long since dried off after my evening swim, I had just been staring at it, numb and lonely, empty on the inside. The last month had proven that I had fire raging in my soul, possessed a resilience that surprised even *me*. But I was getting tired. And bored. And suffocated.

Depressed. I'd been clinically depressed before—after my parents, and probably after everything that had happened in the last six months with Opa's passing and Devlin's betrayal. Maybe the darkness was back. Maybe it would be here to stay this time.

Just as I toed at the shimmering blue surface, music

erupted from the main hall, loud enough that it carried through the calendar corridor and hit me like a ton of bricks. Was that—Elvis? I retracted my foot from the water, arms crossed, and turned toward the familiar croon. We had given up on cards for about two weeks now—so apparently the god I was stuck with had moved on to music.

Tricky bastard.

*Obviously* that was speaking my language as a dancer.

I had to give it to him: the guy was trying. In fact, I'd never had a man work so hard to fuck me before—and this one was a god who thought he was better than me, point-blank, because I was human and he wasn't.

Swallowing thickly, I glanced over my shoulder, passed the waterfall to the arched opening on the other side of this cavern. Even in the dark, I knew the winding pathways by now, could navigate them alone with a growing confidence. But I had already walked them today—and if I wanted to *keep* walking them each day, pretending they hadn't lost their novelty, I shouldn't do it more than once.

So I shuffled toward the music. Through the calendar corridor, the name still a total wash on me, past the updated bathroom and our shared bedroom with the wall of pillows firmly in place dividing the bed. Up the polished stone steps. Into the doorway of the main hall, where I stopped. Seated on the couch, Loki had a record player I'd never seen before arranged on the coffee table, out of which warbled an exceptional recording of "Jailhouse Rock."

The corners of my mouth flicked up. How fitting—a song about partying in prison. Was that an invitation?

I scanned his relaxed posture, knees spread wide, arms stretched out along the back of the couch as if this was just a casual evening spent listening to the record player. Shirtless again, like he had been all week, at least he was wearing pants. A chill spider-walked down my spine; his body, in all its naked glory, had been burned into my mind's eye and liked to pop up in my dreams, all that muscle, the raw *power* in every limb.

A huge cock.

Like. Bigger than I'd ever seen, even when it was limp.

Intimidating, kind of, a hog of that size.

Eyes on the spinning disc, Loki raised a full bottle of whiskey to his lips and chugged back at least two shots' worth. Then, after wiping his gorgeous mouth with the back of his hand, his gaze slid to me, and he straightened, retracting his long limbs as if to make some room, his expression suggesting that he had *just* realized I was even there.

I rolled my eyes. Sure. Like he hadn't known I was standing here—he could sense me a mile away, but *sure*, let's pretend I'd actually surprised him.

"Hello, firebird."

I fidgeted with my hair, most of it dry by now, a few damp patches at the base of my skull occupying my fingers as that *name* hit me. Firebird—better than *little human*, and a thousand times more preferable to him purring my actual name. It was complimentary, at the very least, and some part of me wondered if he chose it because he appreciated my fight.

Because he... *liked* me being an asshole? Probably not: Loki didn't strike me as a masochist, but what the fuck did I even know about him.

"Where did that come from?" I asked with a jut of my chin toward the record player. Loki studied it for a moment with a—rare, kind of unsettling—soft smile.

"There's a lot you don't see in our bedchamber," he

mused before taking another swig of whiskey. "Come on, then... You're a dancer. Show me your moves."

Arms crossed, tapping my one finger on my bicep, I strolled into the hall, right up to the armchair—ignoring the spot in front of the coffee table where he'd given me the best fucking orgasm of my life.

"What," I started, forcing some New York attitude into my words, like I wasn't just a dark cloud floating around the passages in our mountain prison, "you want me to get up on the table and dance for you?"

Loki shrugged, circling the bottle's mouth with his finger. I shook my head and scoffed.

"Fuck you."

The god chuckled, then downed another shot. "Just a thought." He crossed one leg over the other, ankle resting on his knee, feet bare. "What else do we have to do? Plan to stare at the water all night again, eh?"

Embarrassment ripened in my cheeks, punctuated by a flash of *anger* that made my eyes water. If it wasn't for him, I wouldn't be forced to pick between this and staring wistfully into a motherfucking lake all night, would I?

"Teach me something, firebird," he insisted, scooting to the edge of the couch, bottle dangling loosely from one hand. Already his breath smelled of booze, yet his eyes possessed an unnerving *focus* that told me a slowly-nursed quart of whiskey was nothing to a creature like him. He cocked his head to the side. "Show me your passion."

My heart skipped a beat at the thought, at the way his gaze seemed to scorch right through me, past the outer layers, all the walls I had to constantly erect around myself in here—right down to the marrow. Another bout of rage flared when my belly looped pleasantly, my sex tingling with interest. I *hated* that my body responded to him over basically nothing—that I was attracted to him, and not just for his looks.

Most of all, I hated that the misery I was in, the darkness closing in on all sides, was because of him, because of *his* circumstances.

And I absolutely fucking despised that suddenly I realized I couldn't do this sober anymore.

Teeth gritted, I stalked around the coffee table and wrenched the whiskey from his hand, hesitated for a few seconds, then brought it to my lips and tossed my head back.

Oh *fuck*, that *burned*. I doubled over, coughing as searing hot, acrid liquid sizzled down my throat and exploded inside me like a nuclear bomb. A glass of champagne was all I had allowed myself in the past—the smart thing to do would have been gentle baby steps from there, maybe a beer or a cider, but here I was, throwing caution to the wind and going in for my second chug.

It hurt just as much this time, the burn not even a little dulled, but I pushed through, my eyes watering, my nose threatening to run. I'd watched friends use alcohol to disconnect from life's problems since I was a teenager; I was allowed one goddamn night to do the same, right? After all, they had always seemed to have a *fantastic* time when they were shitfaced, always bouncing around, giggly as hell, smiling like it was the best night of their lives.

And then there had been sober me, in for the ride but also out of the loop.

No more.

"Yes," Loki said with a barking sort of laugh, "*finally*. Join in on the fun, firebird."

I kept chugging until my stomach somersaulted—and not in the fun way, but in the *I'm two seconds out from puking* way. When I finally ripped the bottle from my lips, the world was black; I'd closed my eyes at some point, and the main hall swam when I opened them again, everything just a little off-kilter already. Coughing, I slammed the whiskey onto the coffee table next to the record player, and as Elvis moved on to "Heartbreak Hotel," I felt both wobbly on my feet and totally disassociated from the fact that I was a prisoner inside a mountain with a god.

Wow.

I should have started drinking on night one.

"Get up, then," I ordered, staggering into the open space between the sitting area and the dining table. "I'll teach you how to bop and rock 'n' roll, Loki, my man."

The god snorted as he stood, and I swallowed hard, my insides on fire, my eyes stinging with tears—but my mind a beautiful hazy blend of nothingness and footwork. Yeesh, whiskey hit so fast.

*Fast, fast, fast, just like the car.*

Pressing a hand to my forehead, I grimaced, clinging hard to the nothingness, to the footwork for classic swing. Over the years, many of my ballet friends and I had taught classes to young dancers as guest instructors. I could teach competently, patient and thorough in my direction, in my precision for every posture, every angle of a dancer's foot, the delicate fanning of their fingers.

But I refused to give him ballet. Ballet was *mine*—he couldn't have it.

So, I fell back on swing dance routines that were bound to throw him for a loop with their frantic footwork and swinging hips and gyrating legs.

Only Loki picked it up after one or two demonstrations of the moves, a perfect student, light on his feet with exceptional rhythm. He held me like a partner was supposed to, never veering too low on my hips, never accidentally brushing by my chest—which, unsupported, bounced *so* much that I found myself missing the restrictive sports bras I'd been wearing since I was thirteen.

The whiskey made me shaky on my feet—but it also made me laugh more at his bullshit, made my movements exaggerated and free. Made me willing to fall into his arms, leap and jump, fling myself at him with full expectations that he would catch me, lift me, swing me around and over his shoulders like we had been dancing together for years.

Just a couple of kids at the dance hall in the height of the fifties swing era, Elvis blaring on the record player and liquor thrumming through my veins.

"Look at *you*, firebird," Loki proclaimed as he spun me out, our feet mirroring each other with perfect triple-step and kick motions. He hadn't stopped smiling since all this started, probably because I was drinking at long last and infinitely more malleable. Nicer, too, with almost three-fourths of a bottle of booze in me. "Letting loose, having *fun*... Where has this side of you been?"

"Hey, I can be fun without being, you know, plastered," I argued—slurred—as I tugged my hand away and spun out, knees wobbling and room spinning. *Never been drunk before. Never, never, never—just like him, so drunk.* I staggered around the god with a flourish, swiping the nearly empty whiskey off the table. Sweat stained my forehead, the back of my neck. I hadn't worked this hard, danced this much, in almost two months.

"This side of me just *never* comes out," I admitted with a sloppy shrug, the jerky movement knocking me off-balance and into the table. And I did. not. give. a. fuck. Was this why people got wasted? The zero fucks given? Hungry for more, I devoured the last of the fire water, then threw the bottle in the general direction of the doorway. Only the glass didn't shatter—just clunked and bounced and eventually rolled out of sight. I swiped a hand over my whiskey-stained mouth, grinning, staring him down even as the world around me went full topsy-turvy. "You wanna know why?"

Loki's face blurred in and out of focus, finally sharpening with a few good blinks—and from the look of it, he was loving every fucking second of this new, drunk-off-her-face Nora. Classic dude.

"Yes," he purred, still shimmying and shaking to the king, his steps *perfect*. The best student I'd ever had. "Tell me every lurid detail, firebird."

"Well, as you know, I never drink," I remarked, my heart suddenly *pounding*, my mouth too dry, my chest on fire, "because a drunk driver killed my parents." Loki's movements slowed, and a flood of bile shot up my throat. I swallowed hard, smiling a smile that didn't reach my eyes, a little shaky as I carried on. "Yeah, he left the bar, fucked-up, way too drunk to drive, got in his car, and then hit *my* parents head-on. They were on a d-date night. I was with Oma and Opa—they'd just had a nice dinner, and he fucking hit them with his god-goddamn car. They died instantly in the crash. Alcohol limit was way, way over."

I pushed off the table, adding a few stiff flings of my arms to the beat, "Don't Be Cruel" wailing out of the record player.

"Everyone was surprised he was even conscious, he was so fucking wrecked. I was eight and a half." The room swam again, but not from the booze. Anger blurred my vision, stung behind my eyes—anger and grief and loss—and I smeared the damp up my face, over my temples and into my hair, hands trembling. "I vowed then never to drink, because fuck the stuff that took my two favorite people away from me—that ruined my life."

Try as I might, I couldn't *stop* the tears. Couldn't blink them back, sniffle them all up, so I just let them careen down my cheeks, even as my lips stretched into a manic grin that could finally give Loki's a run for its money.

"But here I am, shitfaced for the first time," I sneered, eyes narrowed at him, our surroundings just hazy darkness, a breathtaking god front and center. "You brought me to that low, Loki. *You* and this fucking place made me break m-my vow and drink."

I lurched toward him, toward the perfect student who had stopped dancing midroutine.

"And I feel awesome." I hurled the words at him, hoping they struck just as sharply as a slap—harder, because he could withstand so much more. "So fucking *fantastic*. So *fun*. How about you? How do you feel knowing that's what you do to me—make me do the thing I promised I would never..."

*Whoa.* The room literally spun this time, and I planted my feet, squared my shoulders, falling back on a lifetime of grounding myself for some sense of stability. Chin folded into my chest, I pressed a hand to my forehead and willed the mountain to settle. When it finally did, I lifted my head up, my eyes suddenly heavy—and my heart hard as steel.

"*You* make me drink," I forced out, totally unaware of what the fuck was coming out of my mouth at this point, functioning on autopilot, on *feeling*, "because I fucking *hate* you."

I hated what he did to me—that I was here for him, that I had been kidnapped and trafficked for *him*.

Hated that despite it all, I still wanted him. Still wished he would throw me onto the table and *fuck* me into forgetting everything. Craved his touch now more than ever, because he knew just what he was doing, how to make the world melt away through pleasure.

And, yeah, I hated him for that, but right now, I hated myself more. Hated my body's *need*, hated that I had given up and drunk a shit-ton of whiskey. Hated that my inhibitions had dwindled to nothing—that one month in here had broken me.

Even if I'd been sober, I probably wouldn't have been able to decipher the storm of emotion ripping across Loki's face. But I'd caught his attention, that much was clear, and I was treading a very, very, *very* thin line if the grit of his jaw and the twitch in his cheek had anything to say about it.

But fuck it.

He wanted this—*me*. Let him have me, then.

"What do you think?" I demanded, staggering toward him but veering away at the last second, going nowhere, my back to the kitchen. "Come on, *firebird*. Tell me how that makes you *feel*."

The passive-aggressive tone and fluttering of my lashes sealed my fate; Loki snapped. He charged after me with strides I could never match, and somehow my drunk ass managed to not trip over my own two feet as I scrambled backward—all the way to the fridge, which I hit hard, first my back, then my head. But whiskey numbed the pain, and suddenly I understood a whole hell of a lot more about people in general, about why they drank this stuff. Tragedy's bite was softer in a whiskey haze.

Only tonight, Loki wasn't drunk. No games to have him throwing back shot after shot after shot, his eyes cloudy and his mood dangerous. He hunted me with a narrowed gaze, his steps precise and focused, until he too met the fridge—but with his hands, which slammed against the stainless steel on either side of my head. I flinched when his fist came next, his lips lifted in a snarl, his green eyes hard as he pounded it against the innocent appliance. A slight roll of my head told me he had dented it, cracked the surface like it was nothing.

He could do that to me—easily. Crack my bones like *they* were nothing.

Which was...

Hot.

I bit down on my cheeks, hating myself, hating that his anger sparked something gross inside me, that seeing him *emote* was a goddamn turn-on. Looming over me, seething, scowling, he was vulnerable. So often, this god was impenetrable, always had the upper hand. Here, now, my anger had struck a chord; I'd maybe even hurt him. Insulted him. Spat in the face of whatever relationship he had thought was brewing between us.

Well...

*Fuck* his idea of our relationship. My hands fell to his chest, solid as stone, unyielding when I shoved.

*Fuck* this place. My fingers crept up his sculpted body, over his shoulders, to his throat, the underside of his chin.

*Fuck* everyone out there. I dragged my nails through the stubble along his jaw, my hips arcing toward his like he had his own fucking gravitational pull.

And most of all, *fuck* him. I hooked an arm around his neck and kissed him, hard and furious, slamming my lips to his with the cry of a wounded—but still fighting to the last breath—animal.

Loki kissed me back like he wasn't being careful anymore, thrusting me up against the fridge, his fingers stabbing through my hair and wrenching my head back. He tasted like the whiskey's burn, and I felt it slithering down my throat and pooling in my gut, igniting between my thighs. Lust and hate. *Passion.* I'd never felt it before—not like this, not even on stage, and definitely not with Devlin.

Not my finest moment.

I was sloppy and all over the place, rough, scratching at him, hungry for a taste of golden blood, starving for *his* suffering to match mine. So I bit him as hard as I could, snagging his thin lower lip and chomping down. This wasn't just a kiss—with Loki, it never was. It was a fucking battle, and if I could make him bleed, then I'd won *something* in here.

He reared back with a snarl, his lip swollen but the flesh unbroken, and I clapped my hands down on his heaving chest, both of us panting, gasping for air. Locked my arms at the elbows. Shaking. Here but not. *Guilty,* suddenly, for throwing all my efforts this past month out the window for a bottle of booze and a hot guy. *God.*

A throb of sadness extinguished the flames inside me, and my chin wobbled as I fought back the next flood of tears.

"*Fuck* you, Loki," I hissed, my words thick and heavy—like my heart. Like *everything.* I needed to get out of here, but there was nowhere to go. Not bothering to wait for a retort, I ducked around him and blitzed for the doorway. It wasn't safe to wander around a pool of water with my veins more whiskey than blood, but fuck it. I had to move. Had to—

One strong arm snapped around my waist just before I reached the steps, and I lurched forward with a squeak.

"Fuck me? Fuck *you,* firebird," Loki growled in my ear, locking me in place like a bear trap for my entire body. I squirmed against him, wriggled and kicked out, smacked at his arm around my waist—all for nothing. Like always. He just held tighter, wrenched me closer to him, my ass tucked neatly against his hips, his cock insistent and *there*. Apparently rage got him off, too. Frightening, the two of us together. His teeth caught my ear, his free hand gathering my hair and throwing it over my one shoulder, opening me up to him in a way that felt so fucking intimate that it made me whimper.

"Let go—"

"You've been here a *month* and you're coming apart at the seams," he fumed, mouth hot as it ripped along the column of my throat and clamped down on my shoulder. The pain bloomed bright, everything else fuzzy, and I kicked back but missed him by a mile. The god gave me a little shake, jostling me about, then stilled me with a harsh hand in my hair and a knee shoved between both of mine. "Do you even deserve your new title? Where the fuck is my *firebird?*"

Furious and empty and *drunk*, I gave him all the fire I had. I fought. I screamed my throat raw, yanked his hair, kicked his shins, scraped my nails up his bare arm. And nothing. His grip never loosened, his bite never softened, and soon enough his free—dangerous—hand found its way under my dress, skimming up my thighs without an ounce of kindness. I wriggled and squirmed, trying to force him off, yank him out with both hands, then scrambled for something to anchor myself on.

The doorway.

I curved my fingers over the stone just as he slipped one of his own between my folds, rubbing me with a rough exhale against my neck. The first stroke had me shaking, burning up from the inside out—because he found me wet. I knew it. He knew it.

He *had* me.

I could just ride it out—or keep on fighting.

And I had already given up once today.

I pushed back—chose to fight when all I wanted to do was fly.

Useless, every effort.

He was steel. He was a hurricane. He was this fucking mountain and then some, immoveable and cold. But so, so, *so* good with his fingers. Loki had me trembling in no time, shivering with pleasure as he played me with long, elegant fingers. Thumb on my clit, occasionally a finger or two thrust inside me, stroking me, *fucking* me like he had wanted to from that first day.

And eventually I let him. I folded—*again*. I gave in to the burn, to the cozy nothingness, to a head empty of thoughts and a body that felt *good* after all this time. Even before him, I hadn't felt good in so fucking long.

Knees buckled, hands weakly grasping at the doorway, the only thing keeping me from collapsing into a puddle on the ground was him. My sole support system—if I just let him. If I just gave in. Loki worked me harder, eventually tormenting my body with both hands, his teeth on my throat —one hand for my clit, the other pumping three fingers in and out of me. Too much. Too *much*. I gritted my teeth and clenched my eyes shut, as if that would muffle my sobs.

As if that would stop it.

I should have realized by now: nothing could stop it.

Nothing—and no one—could stop *him*.

This month had shattered me, but tonight, Loki put me back together, all my muscles taut, pleasure drowning out the whiskey, so *he* could splinter me apart by his own hands.

And when I broke this time, I did so with a scream, a smile, and his name on my lips...

## 14

## LOKI

Nora might have been a ridiculous drunk, quick to succumb to the bottle and emotional beyond measure, but she made the most delightful noises when she came. All the others —*all* of them—had always been so quiet and dignified, demure, like their pleasure wasn't *really* happening at all and everything about our fucking had been for me.

So dull.

She was anything *but* dull, no matter how she made me feel, how she played on my emotions, my temper.

Thrilling to the last, my firebird.

As her body sagged in my arms, trembling through the aftershocks of whatever made her shriek my name as she had, I slowly released her, mindful that she didn't face-plant onto the ground. After all, she was compromised: drunk on whiskey and pleasure, she could very easily knock herself out if she wasn't careful.

But not yet.

The night wasn't over.

Far from it.

Better on her footing now than some ten minutes prior,

she shuffled forth and collapsed against the arched opening at the helm of the steps, gasping, panting, shoving her hands through her hair. Cheeks flushed a delicious red, she refused to look at me, acknowledge me, so much as glance my way—but I didn't need that from her anymore. The game was *done*, dead and buried. Time to move on to the next one, firebird, where we would both be victorious with every fucking round.

I prowled after her, brain switched off for the first time in eons, fueled by primal instinct alone as I went for her dress. So fragile, the white cotton, so pliant in my hands. It was all she had, and I was cautious not to tear it as I spun her around and yanked the fabric up her body and over her head, then tossed it aside. After tonight, I'd insist the villagers bring her something better to wear—whatever made her most comfortable.

Tonight, however, she'd wear nothing at all—and she had no say in the matter.

Although I'd thought it impossible, my cock hardened further at the sight of her, straining against my trousers. Staticky black hair met perfect shoulders, sharp collarbones, small but full breasts with brownish-pink nipples. Besides the odd dark dot here and there, her skin was unmarred, the only freckles across the bridge of her nose like a constellation. Long limbs. Narrow hips. An ass that mirrored her breasts—perky and taut and *perfect.*

She was exquisite, my firebird, in body *and* mind.

Nora swiped at me when I swooped in, but her open-palm slap hadn't been a deterrent before and it certainly wasn't now. Without even flinching, I ducked down and scooped her up, threw her over my shoulder, relishing her soft mewling protests as I strode down the steps and into the black. The darkness had been an unwelcome constant in my life for eight fucking centuries; I could see in it just fine, navigate it with my eyes opened or closed—but I would always crave the light, the warm caress of fire and the fleeting wisps of golden sunshine. Nora struggled in here. She still wandered the mountain's passages with her arms outstretched, her steps cautious yet slowly becoming confident.

She struggled most in the bedroom, the darkest of the made-up rooms; at least the bathroom had a mirror that occasionally reflected the light. Here in the pitch-black, she whimpered when I tossed her onto the bed. Naked and beautiful, she rolled onto her side, pushed up, groped the linens for the circular wooden bedframe that always guided her to *her* side. Lips hitched in a snarl, I lashed out, yanking her ridiculous pillow wall off and hurling it into the silent abyss around us.

Next came my trousers, the hiss of the zipper stilling her, making her breath catch. Had I not felt the slickness between her thighs, *felt* her cunt dance around my fingers when she came, I would have held back—possibly just tasted her tonight, *licking* her until dawn, whether she liked it or not. But Nora desired me. Hated me too, apparently, but she craved my touch just as I *needed* the companionship of her body.

My cock fell like a lead weight once free, springing forth, solid and lusting, and I kicked my trousers off my ankle with a scowl, eyes fixed on *the* perfect prey. She squirmed up the bed on her belly, and I crawled after her, dragging my mouth from the crook of her ass up the delicate swell of her lower back, tracing her spine with my tongue and teeth to the base of her skull. Little bumps erupted across her flesh, and she shivered beneath me, her hands twisting in the blankets.

I'd fantasized about how I would first take her, but it had never been anything like this—never organic, flowing from one movement to the next, not a thought in my mind of where to go from here. I coiled an arm around her hips, then hauled her onto her knees, ass up for me, and Nora planted a hand on the wall, shocking me when she arched her lower back, opening for me like a flower in bloom. *Fuck.* I hissed, cupping my hand over her ass, gripping hard as I nipped at her ticklish sides harsh enough to leave marks. Evidence—of her surrender, my dominion.

Of *us.*

Fire lapped at my insides, bright blue and violent, threatening to burn me alive, consume me whole. Desire. It had been far, far too long since I *truly* desired one of my consorts, lusted after them beyond the basic need for release. And because of that, I would take my time with her.

Fuck her until dawn. Feed her a feast to refuel, then carry on fucking her well into the night.

Taking her firmly by the hips, I nudged against her slick heat, against a cunt still dripping wet for me. Nora jerked out of reach—or, at the very least, *tried* to, one final attempt at maintaining our status quo. Smirking, I wrapped my arm back around her, capturing her, trapping her in place like a rabbit snare, then slowly thrust into the inferno between her thighs. She moaned, unfurling for me with every inch, smacking at the wall once, twice, three times with a hoarse whimper.

*Fuck,* she was tight enough to make me see stars, and while that primal thing inside me, the beast who longed to devour every part of her, demanded I just *go,* fuck her into the bed with no remorse, I took my time. Painful as it was, I filled her slowly, knowing that I was likely far larger than she was accustomed to. Teeth gritted, I sank into her bit by bit—until finally I was *home*. For a few precious moments, buried to the hilt, I was a man again, not a prisoner, not an animal confined in a cage for all its miserable life.

*Alive.*

Nora made me feel alive—with her smart mouth and her fiery cunt.

She wriggled in my grasp, squirming, fighting, arching her hips—grinding back into me. I inhaled sharply, pleasure exploding behind my eyelids like a show of pristine oriental fireworks. Magnificent, the displays I'd seen but once in my life. And would never see again.

Except when I was inside her.

The thought broke me, dragged me away from the considerate lover to a monster who *took*. I bucked against her, retreated only slightly before driving back home, the last semblance of control waning—gone. One hand seized her hip, the other planted firmly on the wall, and I *had* her as harshly as I wished, thrusting, pulling out completely and slamming into her, fucking her as I'd imagined that first day. Savagely. Brutally. *Making* her mine.

She withstood me, much to my surprise.

And it shouldn't have.

This was a firebird who had made a god bleed twice; she could endure, and she did so beautifully. One hand still on the wall, Nora ground back, rocking to meet my hips, knees spread wide for balance. Yes, she moaned and whimpered, cried out incoherently, tried in vain to pry my fingers from her hip, but she took, too, her body proving just as greedy as mine. Just as hungry.

Her hand shot back, swiping at my chest with nails that had proven their worth, their fury still seared up my neck. Teeth gritted, I twisted out of reach and pounded hard, driving her into the bed to a symphony of breathy groans and cries.

*You make me drink, because I fucking hate you.*

Clear as day, her voice rattled around my skull like she had said it again, spat it out at me with all her drunk venom. Why had it stung so much before? Annoyance flared in my chest—both at myself for letting a human's emotions affect me, then at *her* for being so fucking influential without even realizing it. She had such power over me, this human, my consort, my *plaything*.

None of them had ever had power over me before. None of them had ever made me work, made me feel. She was like fucking *air* in the way I needed her, and that drove me mad.

"Tell me again," I urged, tone cruel, hips fierce as they slammed against her over and over. "Tell me how you *hate* me. Go on, firebird. Do it. Say it again."

Nora buried her face in the blankets, one arm thrown protectively over her head, the other still planted to ensure she didn't knock into the wall with every vicious thrust.

"*Do* it." Why did it matter? What did *I*, a god, blood brother of Odin, father of monsters, have to prove here? That she—this orphan, this dancer, this slip of a girl—had no real influence over me? Pathetic. *Always so pathetic.* I twined my fingers through her hair, then steered her upright so she had to prop herself up on her elbows, gentler with her black waves than I was with the rest of her body.

"I h-hate you," she gritted out, her words punctuated with every thrust. My smile turned vicious, my heart bitter, and I fucked her harder.

"You want to know one of *my* secrets?" I slipped my arm around her chest and yanked her to me, slowing briefly from ravenous to concentrated, grinding against her ass, toying with her sensitive little clit, my mouth to her ear. Nora blinked hurriedly, her cheeks a deep plum, her nipples harder than diamonds, bouncing—*trembling*—with every ragged breath. My tongue flicked at her earlobe, a wretched secret dangling from its tip—something I had never told anyone. Not my wives. Not my sons. Not my blood brother. "*I* hate me, too."

With every fiber of my being, I *despised* all that I was, all that I had done, all that had transpired by my design. Death, destruction, heartbreak, loneliness. Everything. *All your fucking fault, Laufeyjarson.*

I let her go, nudged her back down to the bed with a hand between her shoulder blades, then resumed my previous pace. Usually when I fucked them, I could forget; Nora brought it all to the surface somehow, and a sick part of me admired that about her. Lesser men would have pounded into her as a punishment, ravaged her body to put her in her place, but it wasn't her fault.

She didn't realize the sway she had over me...

What a sharp tongue and an untamable spirit did to me.

So I fucked her with her pleasure in mind, eventually hoisting her hips to access her clit again, grinding into her until she shattered in my arms. She came with another shriek, breathier this time, strained, fisting at the blankets and bucking against me like a wild thing. Her body danced around my cock, her inner walls shuddering through a climax that made her curse under her breath, made her spit fire and swing at me.

On the brink myself, I eased out of her, intent on switching positions so that I could look into her eyes for the next release.

Only out of nowhere, as soon as we disconnected, she

rolled off the bed and blitzed out of the room with a speed that surprised me.

Then thrilled me.

Did she really think she could bed a god for, what, fifteen minutes—and then it would be *over*?

That I would only make her shriek twice tonight in unearthly pleasure?

Smirking, I clambered off the bed, self-loathing temporarily forgotten, and set off to reclaim my prize.

## 15

## NORA

I had no idea sex could feel like *that*.

So... So...

*Good.*

Phenomenal.

Mind-blowing.

Just... fan-fucking-tastic.

It never had before, and it probably never would again; Loki had ruined me for mortal men, and that just made everything worse.

Because my body *desperately* wanted to get back in that bed with him, let him do whatever he wanted to me so long as it always felt like *that*. But my head screamed, *Girl, get the fuck out while you can.* And my heart...

My heart was a disaster, drunk on whiskey and Loki, a riddle beyond understanding in my current state.

*No time to think.*

*Just run.*

He knew the insides of this hellhole better than me, but if I could just evade him long enough, maybe the message would sink in. What that message was—unclear. *I want you, but I hate you and everything you stand for, but please just do that thing with your hips and fingers again—*

Ugh. With a shaky hand to my forehead, I stumbled down the calendar corridor, away from the bedroom, past the bathroom. Although my feet were still way less coordinated than I was used to, my mind had cleared up a little—from the whiskey, at least. Coherent thoughts and sentences and logic trickled through the drunk fog, but everything else was a mess. *I* was a mess—

A familiar silhouette loomed at the end of the tunnel, blocking the light, naked and proud, his face cast in shadows. I yelped; Loki could move swift and silent as a shadow, but never like this. Staggering to a halt, I stumbled back around, but then there he was *again*, a darker outline than the black around him, backlit by the lights from the main foyer. Behind me. Two of him. One had to be fake, right?

I whirled around, struck by a sudden wave of dizziness, and planted a hand on the wall to steady myself. The one guarding the door to the waterfall and lake—*he* couldn't be real. Or...?

"Fucking *hell*, you goddamn prick," I growled, lunging toward the shadowy version of the god who had just pounded me through another one of the best orgasms of my life. Then stopping. Then spinning back and staggering toward the other. One real. One fake. One had to be—

For the first time all month, light blasted through the calendar corridor. My heart leapt into my throat at the onslaught of bright white, and while it threw me off-balance, I craned my head up, mouth hanging open at the dozens of strings stretched taut across the ceiling, dotted with tiny bulbs like starlight.

Then...

"Oh my god..." I pressed a hand to my mouth, eyes watering. There, engraved in the walls, were countless little tick marks, deep notches that had to stand for all the days he had been stuck inside this place. Thousands of them, everywhere, with no order, no strike-through at five—all around me. On both walls. On the ceiling behind the strings of light. At the foot of the steps by the main hall, he had started slicing into the floor, a good dozen stretching toward the bedroom—toward the real Loki's feet.

I'd always thought the calendar corridor was such a fucking dumb name...

Now I got it.

And it broke my stupid drunk heart.

Swallowing hard, I forced my stiff legs to move a few paces closer to the end of the corridor, the constant crash of the waterfall growing louder, until an arm like steel snaked around my waist and yanked me back. I collided with a wall of muscle, lightly perspired, the heat of sex rising off him and bringing with it a distinctly masculine odor that made my mouth water. This time, I went without a fuss, too wrapped up in the burst of light and the depressing number of carved lines that I just couldn't...

Like a fist to the gut, it took the breath right out of me. Eight centuries was so hard to conceptualize—until now. Until it was just *there*, visual as hell, a reminder that he had been a caged animal for a very, very long time.

Taking me firmly by the arms, Loki yanked me around and steered me into the wall, my back and shoulders protesting the too-solid surface as soon as we touched. Closing in, towering over me, it was easier to really take him in. Effort kissed his pink cheeks, his shiny forehead, and he smelled like the air *right* before the sky broke and battered the earth with a storm—*the* storm to end all storms, the kind that reminded us nature would always win. It wasn't a scent I could put a name to, but more of a feeling, his eyes dark and heavy, fixed so wholly on mine that I just wanted to sink to the floor and curl up in a ball.

But at the same time, I never wanted him to *stop* looking at me like that, like I was the center of his whole fucking universe—like there was nobody else but me. No one had ever looked at me like that, intense, totally one hundred percent *present*, as if they weren't thinking of what they needed to make for breakfast tomorrow, or when to pick up groceries, or did they need a haircut.

Both scenarios, the feared and the desired, made me melt.

Angry red lines stretched up his neck, across his chest, and he let me touch them tentatively, just a whisper over his skin. I'd done that. I'd hurt him again, marked him up. No golden blood this time, but I wasn't completely powerless— just like he wasn't totally indestructible.

When he'd had enough of my cautious exploration, Loki ducked down and hoisted me up, settling between my thighs. Without a word, eyes fixated on my swollen lips now, he speared me with his cock, filled me with one swift, brutal thrust that made my eyes roll back into my head. Exhaling a stuttering breath, I endured the spark of pleasure *and* the subtle dart of pain. My arm wove around his neck like it had a mind of its own, and while lifted up, I could reach the ceiling, thread my hand through the light strings, brace myself for what I knew would be a hell of a ride.

Only he started slow this time, pumping in and out, stretching me with a shaft I thought I'd never be able to take. Far bigger than I was used to—a few inches above average, and I let him in, clenched around him, gingerly rocked my hips back and forth to chase the delightful tickle in my core.

The tenderness didn't last; I expected nothing less after what had happened in the bedroom. Loki was a savage lover, working us both up to a frenzied pace that had him pounding me into the wall, his smiling mouth sucking and nibbling and licking at my neck and shoulders. He fucked hard. He fucked fast. He hit *all* the right spots without guidance...

Devlin had never been able to manage this pace, this frantic rhythm that made my pussy sing like a world-class soprano. He always fizzled out *just* before I could really get going, whereas tonight, on the crest of my *third* orgasm, Loki showed no signs of slowing.

Just one of the many, many differences between a man and a god, apparently.

Try as I might, I couldn't rock my hips up to meet him anymore, couldn't twist and wriggle the way I usually did to drive my own pleasure; the ferocity of his body was impossible to match. I kept my arm around his neck instead, clinging to him for dear life, my fingers working into his surprisingly soft hair. Every thrust of his hips caught my clit, the collision setting off little sparks of sharp pleasure inside, like flint crashing together to start a fire. Slowly, darkness crept into the edges of my vision, everything around us fading away until it was just Loki and me, the violence of our union, the symphony of my cries and his harsh groans echoing through the corridor, filling this whole fucking mountain...

"Oh, *fuck!*" My third climax detonated like a nuclear bomb, slamming into me and *exploding* through my every cell. The shock waves plumed up and out, bringing with them a delicious heat that flared brightest in my chest and my cheeks. Wildfire scorched under my skin, spreading fast and furious, the pleasure pinwheeling around inside different than the last two orgasms—sharper, more poignant. Maybe I was just sobering up, or maybe every climax with a god was like a fucking snowflake.

This one hit the hardest, but like all impossible highs, it was followed by a swift and vicious low. Pain crept into my hips, my lower back, my thighs. The world around us sparked, all of it in such finite detail that I squinted. Too bright. Too much. Sure, it was grey and black and white, but even *that* was overwhelming for me.

Sadness struck like a dagger to the heart, sorrow bursting the dams inside—flooding through me, extinguishing every last ember. As Loki dragged a sharp openmouthed kiss up my neck, I shuddered and snapped my lips shut, muffling a sob.

Was this what alcohol did to you? Fucked with your emotions, amplified everything you *didn't* want to feel? Because, hot damn, I had enough sadness and sorrow in my day-to-day existence—I didn't need a whole tidal wave of it now out of nowhere.

Warmth cut down my cheeks, and as Loki's merciless pace tapered to a slow grind, I realized I was crying. A lot. He straightened, his cheeks dark, his forehead shiny, his eyes *alive*—and he frowned when the sorrow exploded out my mouth in a stuttering wail. Humiliated, I wiped at my cheeks, still chasing my breath, a dull ache rising between my thighs.

"Is this it?" I hiccupped and smeared my nose across my forearm, a total disaster, the furthest thing from sexy as I blubbered—as panic closed an icy fist around my heart, squeezing tighter and tighter with every ragged breath. "Are you done with me now?"

For the first time all month, Loki's whole expression softened. No cruelty. No sneer. No rage. He brushed my hands aside, effortlessly steadying my sagging frame to the wall with his body, and then wiped at my cheeks. Gently. Tender touches, featherlight and thoughtful. As his breath warmed my lips, his forehead found mine, and he cupped my chin, holding it for a moment before kissing the tip of my nose.

Then he laughed.

Kissed me deeply, sharply, in a way that made my toes curl and my breath catch. Made those two idiot butterflies in my chest dance.

And as Loki carried me back to the bedroom without a word, I figured that was answer enough.

# 16

## NORA

Oh.

Oh shit.

*Oooooooooooooooooooooooooooooooooooohfuck.*

Mouth sweats. So many mouth sweats.

I peeled my eyes open, only to be met with a throbbing headache and a gut two seconds away from emptying everything I'd ever eaten right onto the bed. It certainly didn't help that Loki's two-ton arm had, at some point, flung itself over my waist while we slept. The god snored on softly behind me as a cold sweat rippled across my skin from head to toe.

Swallowing hard, I yanked the covers off, shoved his arm away, and pushed upright—only for the room to spin. Who would have thought a pitch-black room could *spin*, but somehow I saw it bleeding to the right, my head topsy-turvy again. I was just sober as hell this time. Oh fuck. Oh *fuck.*

Sweaty, shaky, weak, I scrambled out of bed, grasping into the dark, but my legs gave way as soon as I was on my own two feet. Knees buckled. Thighs *screamed*. I collapsed to the floor with a soundless wail, pain knotted in every muscle. Reaching back with a trembling hand, I gripped the wood bedframe in an attempt to find my footing.

We'd had a *lot* of sex in this room over the last however many hours, and it didn't surprise me one fucking bit that I couldn't stand in the aftermath. Not at all. Loki's snore snagged in his throat, and the linens rustled as he rolled in my absence. The guy was insatiable; no way the women who gave it up on night one lasted longer than a week in here without literally falling apart.

And the whiskey was just insult to injury. *Oh.* I swallowed down a surge of bile, and as I struggled to stand, the next wave was actual vomit. *Oh fuck me.*

Twelve-hour rehearsals kicked the shit out of dancers. We spent a lot of our free time icing injuries or soaking in a hot bath to calm our raging muscles—and that was with our bodies primed for that kind of abuse. Show season was a nightmare, and you came out of it exhausted and exhilarated, the thrill of performing for a paying crowd more than enough to carry you through the physical toll.

But I'd never felt like this.

As I limped out of the bedroom and took a sharp right down the corridor to the bathroom, I felt like I'd been hit by a fucking bus. *Everything* hurt. My head. My stomach. My poor, battered pussy. Thighs, arms, calves. All of it ached, burned, throbbed—I couldn't even stand upright or I'd burst into tears.

Somehow, I made it to the toilet, collapsing onto it and shoving up the lid *just* in time for me to hurl my guts out. Never had a hangover before—not from alcohol, anyway. Grief, rehearsal, having your heart torn in two by the man you thought you loved and your supposed best friend: the feelings of dealing with all that bullshit combined simulated what I had imagined a liquor hangover might feel like. This was worse. So. Much. Worse.

Hugging the porcelain bowl, I puked until it was just dry heaving nothingness, my abdominals working overtime to squeeze out every last drop of poison. Never again. *Never* again. As I slumped against the wall, a cruel little voice at the back of my mind sneered that Mom and Dad would have been so disappointed in me for breaking my vow...

But my parents had been cool as fuck.

They would have understood—the circumstances I found myself in, the overwhelming sadness that had followed me around since Opa died...

I was allowed to mess up. Everyone I loved had always taught me mistakes happened. Acknowledge them, learn from them, grow as a person.

If I survived the night, I guess I'd have to grow as a person. *Ugh.* Like I had the energy or the emotional capacity for that.

I sat there for ages, stuck between the toilet and the wall, naked and hurting and dry heaving. By the time it finally ended, exhaustion had set in. I needed about a gallon of water to feel even remotely human again, and then a full year of sleep. After rinsing my mouth in the sink and splashing some cold water on my face, I shuffled and whimpered my way to the main hall an inch at a time. Full granny posture engaged, my shoulders rounded, my arms curled into my chest—the slightest wobble of my breasts with each step fucking *hurt.*

Apparently fantastic sex had consequences. Who knew?

By the time I hauled myself up the two steps from the calendar corridor to the main hall, tears streaked down my cheeks with no signs of stopping. I broke apart in the doorway, sniffling and shivering—sniveling, really, just an absolute disaster. But I'd never been in this much pain before...

And in the dim glow of the kitchen, the strings of lights over the couch shimmering faintly, I finally understood why.

I was purple, bruised from top to bottom. His fingerprints marred my arms, my chest, probably my neck. My thighs had taken the worst of it, black and blue and ugly, glaring even in the soft light. No wonder it hurt to move—to even *breathe*. A sob caught in my throat, and I shambled deeper into the hall, headed for the kitchen cabinets. I tried to hold it in—didn't want to wake him, didn't want to *look* at him right now after what he had done to me. Mind-blowing sex didn't cancel out... *this*.

The exhaustion had worked its way into my bones by the time I reached the counter. Unable to raise my arm above my head to open the cabinet and grab a glass, I just folded over and cried into my hands. How long would it take to heal from this? Weeks. One night of incredible pleasure for weeks and weeks and *weeks* of agony.

Eventually, I managed to snag a glass, then dragged myself down the counter to the sink. Filled it, my arm shaking, barely able to withstand the weight of a cup of water. Only I couldn't bring it to my lips—could barely stand.

So. Much. Pain.

And as I slumped onto the counter again, trying to even out my breathing—like fuck would I hyperventilate and pass out here—I wondered just where I would convalesce. Because we'd had sex. A *lot* of sex. And that was what Loki had wanted from the beginning—a good fuck. *Would* he send me back to those village psychos now? He'd never answered my question, never even hinted at a reply.

Would they stick me with that screaming old woman? The one who had looked like me in all the ways that counted—she must have been the last one. Loki's former *companion*. Kidnapped and trafficked and fucked, then discarded.

My lower lip wobbled, and I pressed a hand to my eyes as the tears flowed harder, hot and wet, slicking over my palm.

"Nora?"

*Oh fuck.* Difficult as it was, I pushed up, leaned back on my elbows and swallowed the twinge of pain as they dug into the harsh countertop. Loki stood in the doorway, cast in an array of shadows and flattering light, naked and semi-erect, because of *course* he was ready to go again. I held out a hand when he stepped into the main hall, my lips trembling.

"Please go away," I rasped, my throat thick yet sandpapery, every word a chore. "Please, I can't take any more."

My body might have been in shambles, but adrenaline spiked the second he crossed into the room. I couldn't outrun him now, couldn't dart around him and make a break for one of my usual hiding places. Stuck. Trapped. *Fucked.*

Loki approached me with a frown, his green eyes slowly roving my body. When I flinched back, hand still up and shaking, he slowed, his steps suddenly cautious, one at a time.

Like I was a frightened fawn he'd happened upon in the woods.

"Please, *no—*"

"I'm sorry."

I blinked back at him, his words an outright shock. An apology? *Really?* I'd only heard it once before, and back then, I had taken him at his word. Here, it was hard not to, his expression unreadable, his brows knitted. The god closed in on me, then helped me straighten up with a hand on my elbow. I whimpered and jerked out of his grasp, the sudden movement hurting way more than his touch.

"In my enthusiasm... Sometimes I forget," he murmured, mapping my bruises with one finger. It ghosted over my flesh, there but not—just enough to make the angry welts and splotches prickle preemptively. Loki shook his head, sighing. "The first time... I..."

Wow. This *was* an apology. I swallowed hard, fighting the urge to collapse onto the floor. My legs couldn't take the weight of the rest of me anymore, my back muscles on fire. Even a shift in my stance brought on a world of hurt. Fat, heavy tears cut down my cheeks, dribbled off my chin, plopped on the ground.

Loki's eyes finally flashed up to mine. "Sometimes I forget how fragile you are."

"I'm not fragile," I fired back. My voice might have cracked, every fiber inside blown to pieces, but I still had a backbone. I wasn't fragile. I wasn't made of glass. I was *human*—and he was a dick for forgetting that.

"No..." Loki's smirk had an affectionate tinge to it, and he swiped my hand, holding it gently between us. "No, not fragile... You're a firebird."

He dropped to his knees so suddenly that a whoosh of cool air brushed my face, ruffled my hair. Zeroed in on the most painful part of me, the darkest bruises along my inner thighs, he curved his long fingers around the backs of my knees, and panic lanced through my chest like lightning.

"Don't touch me—"

"Hush now." No matter how soft and tender he said it, that was still a command—an order. As much as it pained me, I kneed him in the chest and tried to squirm around him, but Loki caught me—*easily*—and held me in place with nothing but his fingertips on my legs. Agony shot through every limb, and I clutched back at the counter with a sob, defeated once again.

Just as he had too many times before, Loki healed me with nothing but a caress. He worked slowly, meticulously moving across the landscape of my body with furrowed brows and a tight mouth. Starting with the worst of the bruises, he stroked the tender flesh—and the blood dissipated, like the trauma had never happened. Bit by bit, he fixed me from the bottom up, and by the time he had corrected my too-plump lower lip, I felt like a million bucks.

Like I'd slept for a week straight. Not hungry, not thirsty—satiated in every way. Alert. Aware. Mobile.

This man could save the world. With nothing more than a bit of godly influence, he gave those villagers long lives, healthy children, flourishing crops—wealth beyond measure. All in exchange for *me*. And with me, he had eliminated weeks of painful healing in minutes.

There was so much good he could do out there.

I mean, muted by that curse, he was operating on power save mode. If he was at one hundred percent, could he fix the human world with a snap of his fingers?

That was why I didn't immediately sprint off as soon as I was well enough, didn't cuss him out for hurting me, kick him and scream in his face before burrowing into the mountain for the rest of the night. I just stood there, whole and functional again, wondering what he could do in the grand scheme of things.

And then remembering that it didn't matter. Saving the world—a pipe dream. He was trapped in here forever, me right along with him. No sense of putting on the rose-colored glasses yet.

My healed lower lip quivered at the thought.

"Do you feel better?" Loki asked, his fingers whispering along my jaw, down my throat. Eyes closed, I nodded.

"Yes."

"Good."

My eyes snapped open when his lips found the dip in my throat, his mouth slowly drifting down my body.

"Never again," he whispered against my skin. Goose bumps prickled over my arms, my legs, my nipples pebbling under his attention. "I promise... Never again."

"Loki, stop—" I trailed off in a moan when his tongue delved between my folds, flicking over my clit. Pleasure bloomed in my belly, warm and hazy—not like a fire this time, but like a sauna after a horrendous day of practice, every muscle instantly relaxing in the humidity. That was Loki for me: as soon as he licked me, kissed me, *touched* me, I was a fucking goner. Pathetic, to be so wrapped around a man's finger, but there I was, thighs spreading enough for him to nudge between. He hoisted me onto his shoulders with a soft growl, the sound primal, possessive, sparking a sharper pleasure inside me, and I wove my fingers into his hair, hanging on for balance.

Loki was a lover unmatched, unparalleled by anyone I'd been with in the past. It was like he just... *knew* me, knew what I wanted, what I needed. And right now, I needed tender and gentle—something more lovemaking than fucking. Fucking had been great, all nails and teeth and the frantic, violent collision of our bodies. But that was done for tonight; I couldn't take any more of that.

He licked me tenderly but thoroughly, even his hands cradling my ass gentle. No more bruises. No more pain—not the physical kind, anyway.

In time, my hips started to rock against him, worked *with* him to bring me to the brink of oblivion. Eyes clenched shut, mouth open and needy little moans falling from my lips, I plunged into the black smiling again, my eighth climax in the last however many hours seeping like liquid gold.

He set me down when I stopped writhing against his mouth. Only then did I realize how tight I'd been twisting his hair, yanking at it in a daze, and I loosened my stiff fingers, then groped at the counter behind me for support.

Loki rose like a soaring tidal wave, tall as this mountain and grinning—and for once the twist of his mouth was neither patronizing nor assholeish. He was just a man, smirking at a woman who he'd made climax all over his face. I flushed painfully at the wetness around his mouth, which he wiped away in front of me like he wanted—maybe needed—me to watch. To see. To acknowledge.

Okay. So maybe a *little* assholeish.

But without an ounce of douchebaggery, he grabbed my glass, dumped the contents, refilled it, then handed it back to me when I found my footing again. Cold water. Just what I needed, my body glistening, the nape of my neck hot, my chest a furnace. I gulped down a mouthful, then stiffened when he took my hand. Loosely. Not urgently, not possessively. His fingers twined with mine as both of us watched them furl.

He stepped away, this god of unrelenting pleasure, and at first I didn't follow. I held my ground, clutching my water in one hand, *barely* holding his in the other. Loki stopped. Waited. Glanced back at me with a neutral yet cozy look

EVIE KENT

that made me weak in the knees and roused those stupid butterflies again. So, I took one step after him, then another, and another, until finally we padded out of the main hall together and into the bedroom. Unlike every other time I stumbled around in the dark, searching for the bed and hoping I wouldn't stub my toe *again*, Loki walked me over to my side. He took my drink, tugged back the covers, helped me in, and tucked the blankets up to my shoulders.

"It's here," he murmured, his gravelly whisper followed by the *clink* of glass on stone. He guided my hand down to the cup and let go when my fingertips tapped the rim.

And then he was off, disappearing from my side and reappearing on his. The slightly too-hard mattress dipped when he climbed onto it, and for once, there was no leer, no little comment about the two of us in bed together. He climbed in and under, silent except for his occasional breath and the shuffling of his body beneath the blankets.

Space.

He was giving me space after—everything.

And as I lay there in the pitch-blackness, arm hanging over the bed, hand next to my glass, back to him, I realized...

I didn't want space. I wanted a solid, masculine body big-spooning mine, just for tonight, for comfort and reassurance and a whole bunch of other bullshit reasons that I would scoff at in the morning.

But I forced myself to be still. Not to engage. Stay in one position. Don't talk. Don't roll over. Eventually, I drifted off all by myself.

Alone... and lonely.

17

LOKI

A dozen blueberry pancakes. Three types of bacon—smoked, cured, and maple. Scrambled and poached eggs. Hollandaise sauce. Toasted cinnamon bread in the basket, coffee on the go, diced fruit, and a giant jug of mango juice.

The consort of a god deserved nothing but the best after a night of ravenous fucking.

*Finally.*

My firebird had been everything I'd hoped she would be and more. Passionate. Fiery. Most of all, she was herself. Not disconnected from the moment. Not meek or frightened. Willing. Beautiful. Well worth the wait.

And she deserved something special, something more than healed bruises and a burst of energy, the elimination of her hangover... Something better than the feast before me, even. What, precisely, I would gift her with was still percolating around my brain, but given enough time, it would make itself known.

Maybe a set of ballet shoes.

The thought made my lips twitch up. *Yes.* She would enjoy that, wouldn't she?

If she ever dragged herself out of bed, of course. I had been rather loud during the preparation of breakfast, knocking pans and clacking silverware—because I refused to have today turn into one of those *days* where she slipped away and hid in the mountain. We had connected last night. We deserved some time together in peace, eating and talking and deciding where to take this next.

Preferably back to the bedroom, but I was open to suggestions.

When she appeared in the doorway, wearing her white gown because she had nothing else, I knew what to gift her with in the meantime: a new wardrobe. No longer the sacrificial lamb, she could have whatever she wanted. If she pointed it out to me in a book or magazine, I could even craft it from scratch; the villagers could fetch everything else—anything she desired, no matter the price.

I straightened up in her presence, reaching for the mango juice to pour her a fresh glass. Bright-eyed and pink-cheeked, Nora lingered in the doorway, staring at the spread with her arms crossed. Toes curled, too, like she didn't want to set foot in the main hall.

"Good morning..." Let her be her usual fussy self. It hardly bothered me—not when I knew how to make her *sing*. I gestured to the plates and bowls and bread baskets. "Just a little something I whipped up."

"Are you tipping me in breakfast food?" she asked, eyebrows rising when I snorted.

"After last night, I think *you* should be tipping *me*, but—"

"You need to chill," Nora muttered as she cautiously sauntered into the space, headed for the table but not in a hurry. "You were fine. Adequate."

She really was the loveliest distraction from the horrors

inside my own head. Feisty and sarcastic, bold and brash—I wanted to keep her forever, if only her human life extended that long. Smirking, I popped my chin on my fist, elbow on the table, and let out a luxurious sigh.

"Only adequate? Well, I'll have to try harder, then." Her cheeks darkened when I looked her up and down, a sudden and powerful possessive ache in my chest that I hadn't felt in centuries. "Any notes, firebird?"

Swooping her loose hair behind her ears, she climbed onto the bench across from me, settling into her usual place with a shrug. "I dunno... Don't be so needy? Have some dignity, man."

"You truly are the most ridiculous woman," I remarked as she sampled her mango juice, the glass hiding a small, albeit telling smile. "We'll produce a scale and you can rank me next time... Critique my form."

Nora rolled her eyes and licked the juice remnants from her lips. I so wished I hadn't healed them—wished I could see them all swollen and brutalized in the harsh light of day. In fact, nothing about her appearance suggested anything out of the ordinary had happened last night. Not a shred of evidence remained: no bruises, no handprints, no bags under her eyes from the lack of sleep. A rather selfish thread inside me demanded I leave her next time, ravish her thoroughly and heal her the following day, after I'd had the chance to take it all in.

But that would be rather cruel.

And I *had* promised—never again. I'd be gentler in the future, more cognizant of her human limitations, even when she looked so delectably divine.

The kettle shrieked suddenly, dragging me out of my stupor, my lazy perusal of her unblemished form. Nora shifted uncomfortably under my scrutiny, then let out a sharp breath when I stood to fetch the boiling water. After filling a mug for each of us, leaving her to flavor hers however she saw fit this morning, I was back at the table and loading up my plate, meat-heavy and indulgent from the start.

Yet Nora just sat there, both hands wrapped around her glass of juice, her eyes unfocused as she stared at the pancakes. I allowed her a few long moments of *that*, then cleared my throat.

"*Eat*," I prompted, nudging the pancake plate toward her. "You've earned it."

"Gross," she muttered with a shake of her head, then reached for the cinnamon-swirl toasted bread in its wicker basket. I had heard that response many times over since Nora had graced me with her surly presence—*ugh*, gross— but this time it lacked the usual snark. Strange. Given what had transpired last night, all of it, from the drunk declarations to the rough sex to the tender apologies after, I'd mentally prepared for a few different versions of Nora this morning. Shy. Quiet. Subdued. Angry. Relaxed. Who could predict *anything* with this creature?

But this was... unexpected. And yes, that was *expected* with her, only she seemed fine—just heavily distracted.

"What is it?"

She had the courage to look me in the eye without flinching, holding my gaze briefly before dropping it down to her plate. At no point did she go for the toast, and I rolled my eyes, because this was *boring*.

"Tell me, firebird." I poked her shin under the table, which made her jump and flush pink again. "I promise my ego isn't quite so fragile that any real concerns you have—"

"I'm thinking," she said loudly, pointedly speaking over me and tapping her fingernail on the side of her glass, "about what's going to happen when you *don't* want to fuck me anymore."

Frowning, I snatched a sliver of bacon, then crunched down on it. "Why?"

"Uh..." She looked up at me expectantly, like I should just *know*. When I stared back and shrugged, Nora scoffed. "Well, why not?"

"Because when our time is up, you go home." Simple as that, really. As much as I used my consorts for my own selfish desires, kept them here to break up the tormenting monotony, I was always jealous of them when it came time to leave. *Always*. Preferring not to think about that, about my pathetic personal failings, I scooped a forkful of scrambled eggs in my mouth, then reached for the saltshaker to season it more to my liking while my other hand went for my piping hot coffee. After a noisy slurp, I set everything back down on the table to find Nora still staring at me—like my statement just wasn't enough.

"Right, so, my companions have never been with me for more than a month—maybe six weeks. You and I have only *just* begun the fun, but the time *will* come for us to part ways." It always did. Hardly fair to trap a pretty songbird inside a cage for all its short life. "The villagers will arrange transportation for you. We'll kiss goodbye at the gate. I'll tell you not to miss me too much, and then... off to live the rest of your life without the pleasure of my company."

Without this *place*. Without shackles and darkness— only memories. More good than bad, or so I foolishly hoped.

Nora blinked once, twice, then burst out laughing as I had never heard before. Whole body jiggling, eyes watering, forehead crinkling, *howling* laughter exploded all over me— grated on me. With a hand over her mouth, she seemed to struggle to contain herself, while I failed to see what the fuck was so funny.

"*What?*"

"Y-you think..." She wiped away the tears as her giggles slowly fizzled. "Oh my god, you think they let us *leave*? Just go back to our lives after a sexcation with a *god*? Are you for fucking real?"

While sexcation was a completely foreign term to me, I could deduce its meaning. Fixing her with an unimpressed look, heat gathering at the nape of my neck as she continued tittering to herself, I snapped up another piece of bacon, which immediately crumbled into pieces between my fingers.

"That's what I told them to do—"

"You know, for a smart guy, you really are dumb," Nora told me, finally grabbing her toast and taking a huge bite out of it. She shook her head, chuckling and chewing, then started to fill her plate. Anger flashed at the thought of her possibly knowing something *I* didn't about this whole situation.

"What makes you think—"

"When that Oskar asshole was walking me to the town hall, where they had the fucking *box* waiting—" She flicked her eyes my way, accusation in every syllable. "—there was this woman who looked like me."

I wiped my greasy fingers with my thumb, then nudged my plate aside and threaded my hands together on the table; she had my full attention, even as annoyance warmed my ears, a quiet but pitchy whine stretching from one side of my skull to the other.

"She was way older," Nora mused, plopping a spoonful of scrambled eggs onto her plate, followed by two pancakes, "but same hair, bright eyes... We probably had a similar build when she was my age. And she was just out there, watering her plants, until she saw me." A few strawberry halves joined the steadily growing heap of food. "She saw me, and she just... froze. Dropped her watering can. Pointed at me. Did this horrible silent scream thing... I had nightmares about it the first week, the look on her face, like she *knew* where I was going, what I was in for. Then two men grabbed her and dragged her into the house."

That... couldn't be right.

It had to be a villager that she had seen, not...

*Lucille.*

My gut twisted, and the intuition that had steered me left and right throughout my very long life told me to believe her—trust her.

But no. *No.* Not Lucille. She had been so sweet and pliant, only ever chatty like Nora when it came time to go home to Italy. *Then* she had told me all about her village, her life there, her friends and family and goats, her ancestral olive groves...

In an age gone by, when *my* villagers had first started bringing me human consorts, I had issued a very clear directive to the jarl: they all go home after. They were not my slaves, nor were they to be kept and acquired by the locals. These women—they were special. Different. Elevated above their fucking peers.

I had been so clear—

"The world doesn't know the supernatural exists," Nora remarked after a dainty sip of her juice, motioning to me with her chin, "and you're proof that it does. *You* are proof that those assholes out there aren't brilliant, or miracle farmers, or genius stock guys who breed these high-IQ kids —it's all *you*. They're cheating the system because they have a god who gives them everything so long as they feed him and buy him whatever he asks for. They lucked into this life, and if you think they're going to let some *whore*—" We both seemed to bristle at the word, her voice catching and my chest tightening. "—ruin that for them by telling the world what's going on, you're fucking deluded."

My mouth dried and my appetite vanished.

Could I really have been so stupid, so naïve? I was a *god*, and my acolytes were to obey my every word.

But I could hardly go around checking on them. My influence stretched far. I blessed them with the basics left at my disposal. In return, they fetched me anything I desired.

Had they played me for a fool all these centuries?

Had I become complacent *and* miserable, a shell of my former self in every way imaginable?

I pushed my plate away, scowling at the oak.

"Syrup?"

Not bothering to look up, I hooked a finger through the handle on the glass bottle and passed it over to her. Nora took it without a word, but seconds later there was the little *pop* of the jar opening, followed by the telltale scent of sugary, sticky maple.

If Lucille was still in the village, manhandled and contained, what had happened to all the others? Imprisoned for all their lives—just like me?

I had *never* wanted that for them, desperate as I was to keep all my pretty birds just so I wouldn't be so fucking *alone*.

And all this time in their absence, I had been terribly alone, horribly lonely—and they had been, what, just down the hill in the village?

My coffee mug cracked as my eyes narrowed. Across the table, Nora inhaled sharply.

I would root out the truth in all this.

They couldn't have fooled me all these years...

No.

Conflict soured in my belly, clouded my ever-working mind.

*No one tricks a trickster.*

During the next food delivery, I would find my answers —one way or another.

And whether the unfortunate messenger lived to tell the others that I knew...

Well, that was still to be decided.

## NORA

Lightning split a black, miserable sky.

*Crack-boom.* Thunder answered, shaking the mountain down to its foundations. My skin prickled with another rush of goose bumps, and I tugged my knees in tighter to my chest as a fresh gust of cold wind ripped through the little nook I'd recently discovered. Forty-six days inside this place and I thought I had found everything there was to find—but not so.

Way, *way* into the mountain, the wall sloped up, its surface nowhere near as smooth as the well-traveled paths closer to our living quarters. The first time I'd stumbled onto it, sunlight screamed through, illuminating the corridor and turning the darkness golden. Up I'd climbed, frantic, only to discover like every little wormhole in here, the fall out the other side would kill me. Hundreds of feet stood between the nook's sharp edge and the ground below, the mountain's face slanting inward. Dangerous, even for experienced climbers—especially without a rope and hooks and whatever the fuck else those daredevils used.

Even Loki had deemed it impossible for me to tackle

without the right gear and years of experience. We hadn't touched back on what we had chatted about at the breakfast table after I'd finally given in to him, but he entertained the idea of my escape without a snarl or a sneer these days. All the sex probably had something to do with it, but whatever. Killer orgasms and a god who gave me his honest opinion on whether a fall would break every bone in my body? I'd take it.

A wall of rain had steadily hammered us all day, sucking all the June heat out of the air and replacing it with a summer chill that made me shiver in my jeans and T-shirt. Apparently giving in to panty-melting sex meant I could finally ditch that dress; the week after our first time, a whole new wardrobe had shown up alongside the food delivery in a crate all its own. I'd picked out what I liked, what made the most sense for the environment. Loki had demanded a demonstration—a fashion show, because what the hell else did we have to do?

I'd agreed on the stipulation that *he* try on the clothes I didn't want. Tit for tat.

And he did.

Because he was a good sport—and probably because there was no one else around to judge him, to make him feel ridiculous when he acted like a fool for me.

To his credit, he had really committed to the part. I mean. The guy could rock a leather miniskirt, even with thighs like tree trunks and a dick an inch away from poking out the bottom.

*That* had been a fun day.

One of the few that we had, both of us weighed down by this place—him more than me, but I was catching up fast and we both knew it.

Another streak of lightning slashed the sky, stretching

across the horizon and scattering violently in a dozen different directions. Thunder followed immediately after, the storm on top of us. Over the roar of rain, I heard it: a soft throat clear to my left.

Loki had found me.

I'd been here since lunch, watching the storm. Since we'd first consummated whatever the fuck we were—consort and god—it had taken him less and less time to come looking for me when I went wandering.

And not because I couldn't wander, but because he seemed to... *need* my company.

Deep down, when sadness spiked and sharpened in my own chest, I probably needed his company in here, too.

Seconds later, his head popped up in the nook's opening, followed by his handsome—albeit somewhat dour —face. Wordlessly, Loki climbed in, cramped and ducked low. While I could kneel comfortably without knocking my head, the nook was less accommodating for a man who was half-giant. But he made it work, shifting about with a frown until he eventually mirrored my posture: knees up, arms wrapped around them, dressed in all black on the other end of the eight-foot gap in the mountainside.

While he studied the raging storm, the wind ruffled his cropped, dark auburn hair, lightning catching in his ever-changing gaze, I studied him. Definitely a sad day, his shoulders slumped—and not because of the space issue—and his mouth in a thin line.

I knew the feeling well, the flat affect of depression, the numbness that swelled inside until you felt like you were just going to *pop*.

"Do gods make the rain?" I asked, throat thick after hours of silence. Loki's eyes flitted my way briefly, then back

186

out to the wall of grey rain, droplets splattering the first few feet of stone inside the nook. A gust of wind brought them deeper, and I tucked my chin into my crossed arms, bracing against it.

"Not always," he croaked back, using his shoulder to wipe the rainwater from his cheek. "But some can."

Batshit insane to think about, what these creatures could do. How they could influence every little thing we knew in this world, all the stuff we chalked up to science and nature. Yeah, it rained because of, you know, *reasons*, but the idea of a lone figure snapping his fingers and *boom*, downpour, still boggled my mind.

"So..." I wiggled side to side to get the blood flowing through my ass cheeks again, stiff and uncomfortable but in no hurry to get out of here anytime soon. "The curse mutes your powers?"

Loki's gaze swept across the landscape hungrily, mapping every detail. "Hmm. Yes."

Even crazier to consider all that he possessed outside of this mountain. He already had so much *ability* at his disposal in here, gifts leaps and bounds beyond my own. Despite the muzzle, Loki was so fucking *powerful*; now that we were having regular sex and he showed no signs of kicking me out anytime soon, I could accept that the power was hot as hell.

Beyond healing me and creating objects out of thin air just by looking at them once in a picture, he had done *so* much for the villagers over the centuries. I'd rooted around the topic during pillow talk one night, demanding to know them—my real enemy—as best I could. What had started as a poor, backwater community had become a thriving force in the country, in the *world*. Their produce was considered the best Norway had to offer, and they grew it deep in the forest, in land no one had thought useable. Their lumber exports were prized and coveted. Their kids got into all the best universities, advancing deep into politics and influential spheres—all because Loki willed it, gifted them with luck and opportunity. These guys had gotten rich and powerful off him...

And it just didn't seem right.

Trapped in here, he wasn't exactly drowning in worshippers. He didn't *choose* them; it was circumstantial, their codependent relationship, and it was sick.

Like showing off a beautiful tiger for a paying crowd, then raking in the profits while this wild thing lived in a squalid cage.

It was bullshit.

And it made me *hate* them so much more than I already did.

"Which one do you miss the most?" He had mentioned something about changing forms once—that was probably a handy power to have in your back pocket.

Loki stared out into the storm for a beat, then leaned over and extended a finger at the nook's opening. My eyes widened when his fingertip suddenly bent backward, the nail going from pink to white like it had met a formidable barrier.

"I miss free air." He withdrew, folding in on himself, and let his head *thunk* back against the stone. "I miss going where I please, when I please... Traveling between realms on a whim, scaling Yggdrasil with my own two hands—"

"Scaling *what*?"

"The world tree," Loki muttered as he glowered at his finger, flexing it up and down, his nail pinkish again. "All the nine realms rest upon its branches. It connects this world to the next and beyond... I miss that most of all. I would give it all away, all my power, to walk out of here and roam again."

I nibbled my lower lip, heart sinking—aching—for him. Definitely a sad day, that raging storm a black mirror for both of us. We fought a lot less lately, and I had a theory it was because we understood each other a bit better. Sure, sex bonded two people if they let it. Broke down barriers, upped the intimacy. Made you vulnerable. But if the villagers were *keeping* consorts against his wishes, Loki couldn't just kick me out. It wasn't really about *me*, but more the fact that they weren't listening to him—weren't following orders. I was stuck here, *really* stuck, just like him.

Trapped. Lonely. Forgotten as the rest of the world carried on without us.

Acknowledging *that*, this horribly depressing experience we shared, bonded us more than awesome sex ever could.

Swallowing hard, I tipped forward and crawled across the nook. As soon as I settled beside him, my back nestling into the stone, rooting out a comfortable position, Loki stretched his long legs, arms limp on his lap.

"You shouldn't wish that," I told him softly, adjusting my snug faded jeans, the rips purposeful to the design at the knees and near my hips. The bland white tee, loose and scoop-neck, stood in sharp contrast to his rigid black button-down.

"And why not?" He grinned as lightning snared in his eyes again, all of it seeming hollow.

"Because if you ever got out, your powers could do *so* much for the world. Don't give them away. They really are a gift—"

"And who would want me?" he mused, chuckling coolly

with a sidelong glance. "Who would desire *Loki* as their savior? Stories have made me the villain—evil."

I shrugged, unfazed by that tone, the one he used to bait me when *he* was feeling insecure. "I dunno... It's been a while." Distantly, a hundred feet down, ancient pines bent to the will of the storm. "You can always change the narrative."

I mean, could he cure cancer? His healing abilities alone were enough to make him a globally-worshipped deity —with the right PR backing him, maybe. Not that he had an obligation to fix humanity, even if he *did* somehow get out of here. Loki had spent all this miserable time tending to a bunch of village assholes who were just using him. He missed free air. If he got out, I'd expect him to wander again. A lot had changed in eight hundred years, and he didn't exist just to be mankind's shepherd.

Still. He could do so much for us.

We had never discussed other supernatural creatures— if they existed today, what they were capable of doing. But if they were around and possessed even a tenth of Loki's muted power, maybe they could pick up the slack for a while.

Another gust of wind dragged in the rain, and I crouched behind Loki, using him as my god-shield against the elements. Peering down at me, expression unreadable, he took the brunt of the cold and the wet, turning his back on the outside world to create a wider barrier. When the breeze died down, thunder shaking the mountain again, he wiped the damp from my cheeks, then ghosted a lone finger over my lips, plucking at the bottom, and down to my chin, along my jaw, over my pulse until he reached the hollow of my throat.

I swallowed hard, still unsure how to react when the

full weight of his attention rested squarely on me. His eyes traced the lines of my face, lingering on my lips, then plunged to my neck, to his finger resting in the sizeable dip. If he applied even a little pressure, it was like a ton of bricks crushing my windpipe; he had done it before.

And I'd liked it more than I should have.

Nibbling my lower lip, I wrapped a hand around his finger, easing it away from my throat, then pushed up to kiss him. I had fought this so hard—for weeks and weeks, I had denied both of us intimacy and companionship. *Connection.* My fears had been totally valid, especially after seeing Loki's reaction to just the *idea* that the villagers didn't send his consorts on their merry way when he was done with them... But that was still one long month of descending into darkness totally alone.

At least now, just for a little while, we could be something more than two people stuck inside a fucking mountain. Two prisoners trapped together. Two miserable captives who wondered if they would eventually die in these stony corridors, rot away and turn to dust.

I smoothed my hand up his cheek, across a sharp jawline and coarse auburn scuff, and Loki leaned into me with a low rumble. His lips parted just as he snaked an arm around my back, drawing me into him, and we fell into a disturbingly familiar rhythm, mouths moving together, the kiss deep and slow.

Excitement sparked in my belly, scorching southbound without delay, when his tongue flicked at mine, teasing and playful, the flames even brighter when his teeth caught my lower lip. His touch thrilled me, but the feeling stemmed from something deeper than a skilled hand and a mouth that kissed me so *thoroughly* I felt him in my marrow.

Unfortunately, it was a feeling I still couldn't put a name to.

His fingers found my jeans, plucking open the button and yanking down the zipper, and I climbed onto his lap with a gasp, some of our usual hurried franticness seeping into what had been—briefly—a tender moment. Pleasure bloomed between my thighs when I ground down, his cock thick and hard, positively raring to go. My arms coiled around his neck, our breaths rising, our bodies rocking—

And then I smoked the back of my head on the nook's ceiling.

"Owwww," I whined into his mouth, crouching down and rubbing at the spot that ached. Loki's hands soon joined mine, our lips a breath apart—his crooked affectionately—and he shooed the pain away with a simple touch. Straddling his thighs, I leaned back and shook my head. "This is *not* a conducive space for fucking."

"Nonsense," Loki purred, dragging me flush against him and sneaking a hand under my shirt, teasing my back with his nails. "*Anywhere* is conducive for fucking—if you're creative enough."

And as always, Loki was a goddamn fountain of creativity. Even in the tight space, we somehow made it work, shuffling about, shifting, maneuvering our bodies even with his generously tented pants.

Which was another issue entirely: that white dress I'd worn for the first month sucked, but it was way more quickie-friendly than skintight jeans.

Clumsily, I eventually managed to kick them off and down the slope, no panties, no bra—because of course Loki wasn't thinking about either when he put in a clothing request. Aching for him, for the closeness, I crawled onto the sprawled-out god, who lay waiting, lazily stroking himself as his eyes roved my body unchecked, and he claimed me with a single thrust.

On his back, Loki took the mountain's bite all unto himself—no bruised shoulders or hips for me this time, even if he always healed me when all was said and done. Stretched and full, nipples poking through my flimsy tee, I sank down with a sigh and buried my face in his neck, let him pillow his head on my folded arms.

I had started to find comfort in his smell—in the scent of a *man*, all primal energy and the rough, raw wilderness that I dreamed about each night. What I smelled like to him was still a mystery; I bathed each day, had the odd deodorant stick show up when I pressed him for it, but Loki had a way of breathing me in that was so fucking *hot*... Clearly he enjoyed it, whatever it was.

We rocked together as the storm hammered the mountain, as lightning flashed bright and angry inside the nook and thunder rattled in our bones. On my knees, arms under his head, I closed my eyes and ground down, going with the easy flow for once instead of biting kisses and punishing caresses and Loki's glorious hips pummeling me into whatever surface I found at my back—or at my front, bent over and moaning. With one arm wrapped tight around my waist, *almost* like a hug, Loki threaded his other hand into my hair and bucked up to meet my writhing body. We sought out mutual satisfaction, tension rippling through our limbs, breaths catching and hitching and whooshing across one another's skin.

Muddled into the rising pleasure, the fire burning bright in my core, a strange twist of *feeling* took root inside me again. Affection, maybe. Appreciation—possibly. But I had to keep it straight in my head and in my heart: whatever it was had to come from *this*. Comfort, closeness, companionship... Loki and I found that in sex, not in each other. It was all circumstantial, making the best out of this fucked-up situation—no longer fighting it, just working as one to not feel so goddamn depressed all the time.

But it was tough to keep it straight, especially when he kissed me, cupped my chin, and smiled. I'd never wanted a fuckbuddy for this exact reason: sex and feelings were just too easily intertwined.

In New York, I always had the option to walk away if it ever got too messy.

Not here.

Not with him.

I came with a shiver and a moan, burrowing into his neck as *three* butterflies—the other two had found a friend, the bastards—soared in my chest, beating their wings to the pulse of my climax. Loki tipped into oblivion shortly after, thrusting harder, gripping me tighter, twisting my hair as his hips shuddered and his gorgeous body tensed.

The rain hit like a cold shower seconds later, billowing into the nook and dowsing us both. I managed a weak laugh, taking most of the wet this time, but Loki had me dry and clean in seconds. His hand went for my thighs, as if to heal the dull ache throbbing between them, but I pushed it away with a shake of my head. *No. Not this time.*

A part of me enjoyed the pain—if only because it reminded me of what had just happened, that I wasn't here alone, and that if I needed him, Loki was *the* best distraction around.

We drifted apart in a strangely cozy silence, each settling on either side of the nook again. Me half naked and quickly covered in goose bumps, him rumpled and flushed and distant, eyes on the horizon.

Our legs outstretched toward each other.

Feet an inch apart.

And the storm showing no signs of lifting anytime soon.

# 19

## LOKI

"My lord, you realize if she can access the internet, she *could* call for help..."

Hands clasped behind my back, I tipped my head to the side and stared down little Oskar Jakobson—all grown up and as patronizing as his forebearers—and his waning father through the electrified bars of my cage. Honestly. These two really did think I was the simplest fucking creature on the planet, didn't they? First, they kept this magnificent modern invention far, far away from me, and then there was the small matter of carrying on the tradition of completely disregarding my wishes for the last few centuries...

No longer.

I asked for their presence outside of the usual delivery so that I could get them alone, without the prying eyes and ears of the men who handled the food shipment crates. Here, I would find real answers.

"Of course I will monitor her actions," I said pleasantly, my smile barbed. "She will not alert anyone to her situation. After all, I can, how did she put it, *kill* the Wi-Fi anytime I choose."

"Yes, but—"

"Do you doubt my integrity? My *sincerity*?"

Jakob Jakobson—the family had lost all sense of name originality until his wife popped out Oskar—flushed bright pink, and my grin sharpened. Naturally, they *should* question all that, for I was Loki Laufeyjarson, the father of lies.

After glancing at his father, Oskar's cheeks turned the same shade of pink, a near perfect mirror of his old man in just about every way.

"No, no, my lord, never," Jakob stammered, his voice gravelly, harsh after decades of smoking, the scent of it ripe on his clothes, in his hair, on his fingertips. "We will acquire a top-of-the-line laptop for you and your mistress by tomorrow morning, as you wish."

It had better be the best fucking model out there; Nora would know if it wasn't. "Good."

"Is there anything else?" Jakob had grown crinkled as of late, the decay of human aging evident around his thin mouth, his small eyes. In another decade or so, he would be gone, leaving Oskar in charge of this village—in charge of *me*. My eyes narrowed at the thought, but my smile remained.

"No."

The pair bowed and started to back away. I let them slink *almost* to the mouth of the cave before I perked up and snapped my fingers.

"Oh, *yes*," I crooned. "One little thing."

Father and son returned to my gate within seconds, practically tripping over themselves to not keep me waiting. Fuckers. They likely laughed at my misfortune the second they were out of earshot. I bit the insides of my cheeks, rage churning in my gut, then relaxed everything with a soft breath.

"When I'm through with my consorts, what becomes of them?"

Oskar hurriedly looked to his father, less skilled at masking his emotions than the old man, who continued to stare *just* over my left shoulder. I waited, let the silence drag on, until finally those aging eyes dared flick to mine, and I arched an eyebrow.

"The *truth*, Jakobson."

"Well..." The old human scratched at the back of his neck, his salt-and-pepper hair trimmed and neat, his facial hair much the same. Handsome in his golden years, but fading now, his son stepping into his prime. What a strange experience it must be—to watch your successor bloom as you withered away.

Yet despite the wrinkling skin, Jakob's bright blue eyes were keen, calculating, and I anticipated a bald-faced lie.

"We house them here." Honesty. How unfortunate for him. Jakob cleared his throat, cheeks colored again, his knee-length shorts and that hideous buttoned floral T-shirt suddenly seeming too heavy for him as a bead of sweat slid from his hairline to his temple, then down the side of his face. "We give them a home in the paradise you created for us, my lord."

The fire in my gut exploded. "I was *very* clear with the first jarl... They are to return home when I am through with them."

Humans were right to fear the quiet before the storm, the moment that the forest fell deadly still. All the color in Oskar and Jakob's faces vanished, leaving both men a deathly white at the shift in my tone. Gone was the playfulness, replaced with a calm swift and sharp as a dagger. Jakob smoothed a trembling hand down the front of his ridiculous shirt, then approached the bars without his son. Behind me, porcelain plates clinked together and water hissed from the tap; Nora had opted to wash the dishes by hand tonight, in need of something to occupy her time with, and I had let her, knowing it would do her no good to hear any part of this conversation.

"Respectfully, Lord Loki," Jakob started, eyes darting about before dropping submissively to the ground, "this is a better home than most of these women have ever known—"

"Strange," I said curtly. "I don't recall ever asking for your opinion on the matter. I gave a direct command to my *flock*, and now I'm to learn that it was not obeyed? That for centuries you and your family have ignored me?"

"No, of course not, but—"

With a simple wave of my hand, Oskar's right shinbone snapped in two. The man collapsed with a harsh, agonizing screech, his lower leg split at the injury site, one half still connected to his knee, the other deviating sharply to the left. Panicked, Jakob raced to his son's side and collapsed on the cave floor beside him, hands skimming the break that would send shards of bone into the boy's bloodstream—a break that I would *not* heal.

"Now that I have your attention," I hissed, wrapping my hands around the bars, the electric bite no more than a fucking tickle. Jakob lifted his gaze to me, flushed again, no doubt spiraling into fear and rage at what I'd done to his son —what I could do to *all* of them. Oskar, meanwhile, had rolled onto his side, curled into a ball, and hid his sobs behind his arms. My lips quirked into a thin smile once more, unbothered by the display. "You will do as instructed. Remember, Jakob Jakobson, son of Jakob, son of Liam, son of Askel, son of Halfdan, son of *Gorm...* I am caged, but my reach is *far*."

"Yes, my lord," Jakob whispered. The pair waited for something further, tensed, but a dismissive flutter of my hand sent them scampering off, Jakob dragging his boy out of the cave and into the free air.

I watched them go, fuming.

Because I knew even with that display, they would ignore me. Coddle me. Appease me with another girl, fancier technology—whatever they could find to keep me docile and distracted. Nora had been right—so *fucking* right. The villagers of Ravndal had dubbed me the fool for centuries, and they would continue to do so long after today if I wasn't careful.

Nora could never leave this place. Never return to America. Never dance again on a stage.

Never be free.

Seething, I stalked away from the electrified bars and deeper into my prison, my infernal torment, desperate for a good distraction—or there was no telling what this rage would make me do.

That scream spelled bad news—even if it made me feel just a *little* vindicated.

Not that I wanted anyone hurt, but fuck Oskar for what he did to me, shoving me into a wooden box as I fought and cried and begged...

Just the memory of his face, the last thing I saw before they sealed me in with a loaf of bread and an explanation that had sounded so batshit crazy at the time, made me tight. Teeth gritted, I slammed the tap to the left, culling the flow of water, and set my recently washed glass on the drying rack. On a scale of zero to ten, my love for doing dishes by hand ranked somewhere in the negative fifties, but at least it was something to *do*. Grabbing a towel, I dried my hands distractedly as I turned around and spotted Loki storming down the ramp.

I swallowed hard, taking him in. Statuesque and brooding, everything about him hard as ice—handsome beyond compare, even in a simple pair of slacks and a loose long-sleeved shirt scrunched up to his elbows, his feet bare. It was easy to imagine him at the helm of a ship, his plain clothes transformed to armor and leather, leading an army into battle against his fellow gods, but I preferred *not* to think about that side of him. Somehow it was just easier to imagine him as my sarcastic roommate, my hot fuckbuddy— my gorgeous cellmate. Depressed and lonely, just like me.

But from the twist of his lips, something about that conversation had gone wrong. Very wrong.

No laptop? I'd figured the request was a stretch, but Loki had a way with words—and technically, these villagers were supposed to fetch him whatever the hell he wanted without question.

Fear skittered up my arms and knotted in my chest, blending with an uncomfortable—and very unwelcome— pulse of interest between my thighs. He had never looked so furious before, his cheeks dabbed with a faint flush, his eyes stormy and very, very faraway.

Furious and *hot*.

He stalked toward the kitchen with long, powerful strides, maneuvering effortlessly around the furniture, not slowing until he was within a few feet of me. Without meaning to, I scrambled down the counter to put some space between us. The god stilled and blinked back to the moment, a flash of recognition suggesting he had only just realized I was even here.

I plopped the dish towel on the counter, hands dry but shaking. Curling them to fists, I crossed my arms and leaned a hip against the marble edge, head cocked. "Hey—"

Loki sidled closer, making my heart skip a beat at one of his panther-like movements, so fluid and *fast* that there was no way I could pretend he wasn't a supernatural creature anymore—a god with no equal. Scowling, he looked me up and down, then nudged me aside and turned on the tap again. Seconds later, he had his hands buried in the sudsy water, his head drooped as he rustled soaking dinner plates around in the huge sink.

"Loki, it's fine," I said softly, stepping in to shoulder him out of the way. With that expression, so steely-eyed, everything about him like flint, he probably shouldn't be handling anything breakable right now—and that included me. "I want to do the dishes—"

"Leave me be, firebird," he growled, snatching the dish soap and spurting half the bottle onto the rough sponge I'd been pestering him to replace. "For your own sake."

The warped desire I had for his rough touch and his kisses so deep, so possessive, that it was like he could taste my soul abruptly fizzled out. Sure, Loki had frightened me before, but he'd never warned me off... like he wasn't sure he could stop himself from, what, snapping? This was new.

And terrifying.

I held up my hands and stepped back, then wordlessly scuttled to my usual spot on the other side of the table. The oak bench felt more supportive than ever as I sidled in, a cold sweat on my palms and a nervous flutter in my belly. Me from a month ago would have heeded the warning—got the hell out of dodge, made myself scarce. Instead, I sat there watching him as he washed dishes, his back and shoulders rustling, his movements rough and stilted.

A part of me *really* wanted to know how that conversation went, but self-preservation kicked into high gear and wouldn't let me ask. Burning as they might be, the questions vanished, replaced by a low, pitchy whine between my ears, my heart beating loudly, firmly, against its cage.

Water dribbled across the counter as Loki moved a plate from the sink to the drying rack, shoving it roughly into place alongside everything I'd already washed. I winced before it even happened, knowing the porcelain couldn't take his manhandling like I could. It started with a crack— then a splinter, the plate splitting and shattering into three huge pieces. Mustering up a smile, I was two seconds away from teasing him, about to insist that I take over if we wanted to have anything to eat off tomorrow morning, but the air stilled around us. So did Loki, and so did I, watching him stare down at that plate, his handsome profile shifting from a neutral—albeit annoyed—expression to pure *rage*.

I shrieked when he grabbed the drying rack and hurled it at the backsplash. Everything inside shattered, glass and porcelain exploding across the tile. Shards ricocheted back at him, but Loki was fucking bulletproof, moving straight onto the cabinets and *ripping* them out of the stone. Hurling them away. *Screaming* so that the mountain shook all around us. His rage was volcanic and brutal.

And I finally had enough sense to just get out of the way. My body launched into flight mode, but I had to pivot and duck for cover with a shriek, heart in my throat, when a cabinet flung over my head and slammed into the doorway that led off to the rest of our prison, smashing into dozens of little wooden pieces. Hoping—*praying*, maybe even to him —that Loki's wrath was reserved for the kitchen, I did a one-eighty and beelined for the sitting area. Shoved the couch away from the wall and crawled behind it. Curled into a ball, arms over my head, and waited out the storm.

A thousand years later, it all went quiet. Loki's fury stopped thundering through the mountain and rattling deep into the earth. No more crunching glass or splintering wood. No more silverware clattering to the ground. Just—silence. Fingers cold and numb, I sat up straighter, which triggered a wave of dizziness and panic. My breath came harder, faster, but I still crawled up the back of the couch, using it and the cave wall for support—because my legs sure as fuck couldn't hold me up right now.

All destroyed. Everything. Cabinets torn off, marble in pieces. The fridge at the foot of the ramp. The oven door wedged into the couch. Dust and debris floated around him, this fuming god, who stood there shaking just as visibly as I did. While I fought back a flood of anxiety, breath coming hard and fast, Loki seemed to struggle to catch his, hands limp at his side, head bowed.

He had flipped that huge table. Hurled it clear across the hall so that it stood upright below the landing at the top of the ramp. The benches were on their sides. I gulped; had I had stayed there, sitting and screaming and cowering, would I have been spared? Would he have even noticed me?

I suddenly felt really... small.

Insignificant.

And claustrophobic.

Hit with a rush of heat, I shuffled out from behind the couch, from the two feet of space that had felt so protective a minute ago, now stifling and tight. Only my body didn't want to move; it wanted to hunker down and hide. I pushed it as much as I could before eventually slumping back against the wall.

"Did... Did you ask them about us?" My gut somersaulted, adding nausea to the mix. Great. "About what they do with us?"

Still glaring at the ground, chasing his breath, Loki just nodded. His stony silence post-meltdown said a lot.

"Sucks when people lie to you, huh?" I mused, the feeling painfully familiar, Devlin and Maeve and Oskar all compounding in my brain, a sea of lies waiting for me outside of this mountain. The only one who hadn't bullshitted me—as far as I knew, as far as my instinct allowed me to believe—was the *father* of all lies.

What the fuck had become of my life?

Seriously.

My lower lip wobbled when Loki finally looked up, his eyes soaring to mine. They blazed up my figure like they had an anchor attached, a tether weighing them down, heavy and exhausted and destroyed.

I'd been right.

The villagers didn't let us leave. I could never go home. My fears—all one hundred percent valid.

And there was nothing either of us could do about any of it.

I folded over with a strangled cry, grief and panic tangling together, the combination detonating like a nuclear bomb. The shock wave scorched everything I had left inside, flayed me alive, and I sank to the ground, sobbing.

A light touch to my wrist quieted what could have easily been a full-blown panic attack. My head shot up, eyes swimming with hot tears, cheeks wet, nose stuffed, and Loki wrapped an arm around my shoulders. Without hesitation or waiting for an invite, I just climbed into his lap—knowing that I weighed nothing to him, that my shuffling and rearranging, my curling up and bawling into his chest felt like *nothing*. Seconds after I settled, shuddering against him, he snaked both arms around me, one coiled tight around my waist while the other hand threaded into my hair.

"I won't let them have you, firebird," he murmured against my forehead, his lips cold, his breath hot, his words a promise that tattooed itself across my skin. "I swear it. You *will* go home, as I always intended."

Numbly, I nodded—because I believed him, this *god*,

the only constant in my world right now who understood. Maybe I was a fucking idiot to fall for it, to accept whatever he had to say on blind faith, but what else could I do? Fight?

I wasn't sure I had any fight left.

But I also wasn't going to spend the rest of my life in this cave or that fucking village. I was *not* going to die here.

So, I let him hold me. I fisted my hands into his shirt and clung to him.

All the while wondering, now that everybody was on the same page, now that the truth was out there...

Where the hell did that leave *me*?

Mountain runoff sluiced down my back in cold, heavy tracks, and I staggered to a halt in the bedroom doorway. "Oh my god, is that...?"

I had never seen light in our little sleep-fucking den before, and only one thing out there could cast Loki's divine features in such a sickly white glow.

It was finally here.

*Ohmygodohmygodohmygod.* Modern technology. Proof that the rest of the world existed—that I hadn't *always* been here and everything that came before was a lie.

Wrapped in nothing but a towel, I ran squealing into the room, then— "*Fuck*," when I smoked my knee on the bedframe.

"Honestly," Loki muttered, brows furrowed, squinted eyes fixed on the too-bright laptop screen. "You'd think every time you walk in here is the first time—"

"Shut up and gimme." I plopped down next to him on his side of the bed, our hips together, and threaded my arm under his to snatch the device away. "This... You did it. You *got* it."

"Was there ever any doubt?" he crooned, leaning back on his elbows. "I seem to have turned it on and completed the initial setup."

All without a power cord. Again. I smoothed my fingers greedily over the brand-new keys. So unlike my laptop back home—none of the letters worn off, no dust collecting under the space bar, the screen *not* splattered with toothpaste droplets from that one time I pulled my electric toothbrush out of my mouth while watching a show, the whirling head still going and spraying everything in a two-foot radius with spit and paste. So. Beautiful.

"Did you have a good swim, firebird?" Loki murmured, walking his fingers up my back—hard over the towel-covered bits, soft over my bare skin. My nipples pebbled and my arms prickled with goose bumps.

"Hmm, yeah," I said distractedly. After last night's epic meltdown, Loki and I had spent a lot of time just sitting there in silence, me mulling over my depressing future inside this fucking mountain and him ruminating over the fact that his worshippers had been lying to him for centuries. This morning, when I had padded out for breakfast, all puffy-eyed and miserable, I'd found the kitchen fully restored like nothing had happened, not a piece out of place. Loki had even seemed to be in a slightly better mood, and a part of me now wondered if it was because of *this*, the special delivery that must have arrived before I woke.

Had he been trying to set it up for me while I'd taken my morning swim?

Five butterflies flitted around my chest now, steadily growing in numbers, smitten with whatever gesture Loki did that could be construed as *sweet*. My head knew better. This god wasn't sweet: he was just trying to survive in as comfortable, peaceful a setting as possible. Picking fights with each other—because we were bored, frustrated, sad, lonely—just made a bad situation a thousand times worse.

"Did they acquire us a good model?"

"Honestly, I don't know much about computers," I told him, clicking on the internet icon and squealing when a window popped up and holy *fuck we're connected.* "But it looks new. The keys are clacky, and it's fast."

"Excellent." Loki sat up, jostling me as he curved an arm around my waist, his hand planted on the bed next to my hip. "Let's investigate a way out of here, shall we? I did what I could to connect to the, er, interweb."

"Yeah, you're fucking amazing," I whispered, typing whatever random shit came to mind in the search engine— New York City, The School of American Ballet, my favorite pizza place a block away from my old apartment, that one bar that stole my fake ID when I was seventeen... *Not* Devlin McDervish. "Seriously. I don't know how you do it."

"A lot of concentration."

A quick glance over showed the pinch of his brows, the twitch in his eye, the thinning of his lips. Seriously though. He *was* amazing. The butterflies in my chest flapped harder, and I leaned in to kiss his cheek. Loki blinked down at me, stiffening, and I shrugged at the unspoken question dangling between us, my lips tingling from his cool skin, the coarse grate of his scruff.

"Thank you." And I meant it—from the bottom of my heart. "This is going to make life in here a lot easier for me."

"Good." He studied me for a beat, all those little tells of intense focus never once faltering, the internet a full five bars. "I'm glad. Now..." Loki rolled his shoulders back, both of us brushing off the tender moment like it too had never happened. "Shall we research Ravndal? Perhaps locate a map of the surrounding—"

"Oh my god, *no*." Heart in my throat, I snapped the laptop shut, extinguishing its full brightness. A familiar black blanketed the room, and Loki cleared his throat awkwardly beside me.

"So—"

"No, it's just..." I took a deep breath, mentally ticking off all the things we would have to do to this laptop first. Firewalls and malware detectors and whatever else the tech geek articles suggested to keep this thing safe. "Those assholes probably put so much stuff on here to keep track of our searches, maybe even the keystrokes. It's doable." Not that I knew *how*, my expertise leaning more toward the precise body mechanics of a perfect fouetté rather than computer security. "We can't let on that we're trying to find an escape for me."

Last night, he had promised that he wouldn't let them have me—that he would find a way *home*. At the time, I had been so overwhelmed with the truth finally landing, all my suspicions confirmed, that I hadn't had time to really digest his promise. This morning, in the cool light of day, Loki's vow made me melt.

He actually *cared* what happened to me outside of this place, what would become of me when I finally left.

A shame that after all this time, he couldn't eventually leave alongside me. Eight hundred years had to warrant a parole hearing, right?

"They can track our movements on the line?"

I bit back a grin; he could learn the proper slang later.

"Probably," I told him with a huff. "I mean... You're a god, sure, but you're basically just a prisoner. Unlike *me*, you're a high-value captive, right? They'll do what they can to keep tabs on you, maybe even hack the webcam so they can watch us in here—"

"*What*?"

"Okay, simmer down." Even in the darkness, I felt his rage, volcanic again and seconds away from imploding. No need to trash yet another room, especially one where I couldn't take cover in. I patted his thigh, the limb thick and sturdy, more muscular than any male dancer I'd seen—like steel when I'd sank my teeth into it the other night before wrapping my lips around his cock. "We can cover the webcam with a piece of tape or something, then we need to figure out what to search that won't come across as a red flag if they see it. We can do this. We..." I pursed my lips, rethinking that. "*You* can outsmart them."

"Agreed." Another long beat of silence stretched between us, until Loki's fingers found my damp hair, swooping it aside to expose my neck. "Are you so eager to leave me, firebird?"

My belly looped at the softness of his words, each one touched by a whiff of vulnerability. It tugged at my heartstrings, his tone, but I forcefully reminded myself that, again, it wasn't about *me*; I would be broken too if my only companion in seventy-plus years was itching to bail.

Clearing my throat, I stood and readjusted my towel, tugging it up to cover as much of myself as I could. "It's not about you... anymore." I waited for a chuckle, both of us highly aware that the start of this—*us*—had been combative at best. When he stayed quiet, the distant echoes of the waterfall almost answering for him, I fidgeted, heat pluming in my cheeks. "You... You know that, right?"

"Of course," he said, firmer this time—but still sad. Still lonely, both of us lost in the dark. My fingers twitched toward him, as if to sweep through *his* hair for once, but I dug them into my towel and stepped away.

"Okay, well, let me get dried off and get cleaned up." Somewhere far away from him so we could both regroup after whatever the fuck had just happened in the last thirty seconds. "And then when I'm done... Loki, god of mischief, I would very much like to introduce you to the planet Earth of today through the wonders of the world wide web."

# LOKI

Midgard had changed since the days I walked it.

Aggressively.

Perhaps for the better, perhaps not—that remained to be seen.

Good or bad, I had spent the last four days consuming all I could through a brightly lit screen. The new nations. The global wars. The shifting political dynamics—very few kings and jarls nowadays. Far more democratic leadership, far more rebellion in the streets. Social media was a treasure trove of insight into modern-day humanity. *Videos*, moving pictures with sound and color, were a fucking treat. Nora had taken the time to show me her old life—photos of her friends, her family, her dance studio. Two days ago, we'd sat together in bed and watched *hours* of ballet, just for her.

And for me. To hear the joy in her voice, see it shimmer in her eyes, in the authentic lift of her lips and the nonstop babbling explanations about every move, every leap, every turn, every frock...

It was endearing.

Made me smile.

Made me... content.

The internet was a marvelous creation akin to my long-forgotten gifts—the ability to see beyond this world, to detect lies from truths, to reach into a human's mind and sift through their past. Odin would have been *furious*, for he had lost his eye for this sort of knowledge, for the ability to search up anything and everything, to find the answers —*detailed* explanations—in seconds.

It lifted my spirits.

And it infuriated me beyond compare.

For it had been kept from me for decades, all this "smart" technology that humans like Nora took for granted. Jakob and his ilk had hoarded knowledge, kept it for themselves, while I gifted them with luck and fortune and favorable weather. In return, they offered me old books and quail eggs for my fucking breakfast. Cloth and trinkets. Consorts like Nora were the only gifts of *real* value my pathetic acolytes had ever given me. Her companionship trumped the wonders of the internet—barely, mind you, but I wasn't about to tell her that.

Little Nora, my firebird... So excited about the laptop, so keen to show me television shows and New York City and old photos of her parents. So vibrant after weeks of collapsing in on herself anytime we *weren't* fucking. For the last four days, she had seen to all the cooking, unable to pry me away from the laptop—yet never far herself.

But this morning, she had crawled out of our bed in a familiar grey fog. Her eyes hollow. Her smile forced. It had returned, the desolate misery that I knew so well, my constant bedfellow in this wretched mountain. Understandable. Something new and shiny could only distract for so long before this place crushed your happiness to dust.

So, on the afternoon of the fifth day, I finally closed the laptop. It died immediately on my lap, hot and heavy, the little fan whirring slower and slower until it stopped. No longer forced to fuel it from my own reserves, my concentration waned—and a wave of exhaustion hit. So much learning. So much focus. I hadn't felt this drained in years, and I let my arms slump to my sides, my head flop back against the wall, alone in the bedroom, sprawled out on the bed. Eyes rimmed with bags, I flicked them down at the laptop, itching to open it and dive back in.

Strange, this sudden addiction to technology. I'd always had a thirst for knowledge, but having such unfettered access from my own bed certainly upped the ante.

But I would see to Nora instead. Her mood necessitated companionship—because there was always the risk I might lose her. If she collapsed too far in on herself, a star imploding before my eyes, no one and nothing would bring her back.

And how terrible—to lose such ferocity, to watch my firebird die.

That being said, for her own sake, I *did* want her to leave this place, return to her Manhattan borough, take to the stage again. Dance her little heart out before a crowd of adoring onlookers. She had the charisma for it, the body, the agility, the all-consuming passion. It seemed a shame to lock her away in here forever.

Yet I craved her company just a little while longer.

The thought of her leaving me hit harder than it had for any of my previous consorts, and not just because I would once again be so painfully alone... but because *Nora* would be gone. A very distinct, crucial difference. It wasn't my pain that I feared, but her absence.

Another strange addiction—not for information, but for

*her*, a slip of a girl who put me in my place with nothing but a raised eyebrow and a pursed mouth.

With a heavy sigh, I pushed the laptop off my thighs and rolled out of bed. Stiff all over, I emerged from the bedroom like some hideous cave troll, eyes tired, an irritating ache in my skull. Scrubbing at my face, I sauntered into the main hall—and immediately found her at our prison's gated mouth. I stretched my limbs with every step, twisting this way and that on my amble up the ramp, not stopping until I was by her side, slightly more alert at the sight of her delectable calves, a hint of thigh exposed beneath the hem of her pinstriped summer dress. White with pale blue lines, it possessed a shapelessness that I despised, but Nora had insisted it was comfortable.

I mean, if she wanted to be *comfortable*, why wear anything at all?

Not acknowledging me, Nora chucked a stone through the bars, frowning when it hit the ground, bounced a few paces, then rolled to a stop.

"Firebird..." My gaze swept over her hair trundling down her back, that black mane thick and luscious after so many dips in our private pool. "Have you nothing better to do?"

To emphasize my point, I snapped an arm around her waist and yanked her to me. She collided against my chest with a soft giggle, a sound that turned to an indignant squeak when my teeth grazed her neck. Little bumps erupted down her arms, up her throat, and she squirmed out of my grasp with a subdued smile, poking me hard in the gut after my lazy attempt to keep her.

"I just..." She plucked another pebble from the ground. "I wanted to see if I could see it."

Hands threaded behind my back, I crouched down to

her level and squinted, all for show, all to make her mouth stretch wider. "See what?"

"The curse," Nora remarked, tossing the stone through the bars. "The wall that stops you."

"No, I'm afraid you can't." We both watched the pebble bounce and bounce and *bounce*, then skitter into the shadows of the fading afternoon sunlight. "I can't either."

Which was fucking infuriating some days, unable to see the walls of my own bloody tomb.

But I could feel it. *Oh*, yes, how I could *feel* it, hard as Thor's hammer, strong and steadfast as young Vidar, dripping with magic like Freyja. It was there, and I had stopped testing its might long ago.

Nora tossed another stone, distractedly this time, defeatedly maybe, and when she veered too close to the electrified bars, I lashed out like a viper, coiling around her wrist and tearing her back.

"Careful, firebird."

Her eyes dropped to where we touched, to my hand snapped tight around her delicate, bony wrist. Possessive, my hold, like I had the right to touch and take however I pleased.

Because I did.

"Can we break it?"

I released her, slowly peeling finger after finger from her flesh. "The ward?"

Her arm dropped to her side, hand flexing in and out of a loose fist, her cheeks pink. "Yeah."

My snort had her blush sharpening in color, and she planted a fist on her hip as I smirked down at her steadily narrowing eyes. "Do you think I'd still be here if I knew the answer to that?"

"No, I mean... All magic has to have an undo button,

right?" She had grown far less reactive to me—to my tone, my words, my looks, my moods. I rather liked it, having someone in my life who didn't react to my every impulse, who allowed me some social leeway when others had staunchly refused.

"Curses like this one have a signature," I insisted, hands in my pants pockets as I faced the bars, perusing their very existence with disdain. "The witch who cast it and her daughters after would be the only ones capable of undoing it... It's a very specific lock, I'm afraid, and it needs the *exact* right key."

Nora shifted in the corner of my eye, facing the bars alongside me, the pair of us a unified front. Silent for a moment, she rocked side to side, from one leg to the other, hips swaying. "Maybe that exact right key is on Facebook."

I exhaled a dismissive chuckle. "Don't get my hopes up, firebird."

Tucked away in a little rocky crevice, an attempt made with moss and a transported spiderweb to hide it, a dull red light blinked down at us. The laptop wasn't my first true brush with modern technology, but I had never been privy to the eye my *worshippers* kept at the front gate, nor had I ever bothered to understand the mechanics until now. A mistake on my part—just another in a long line of fuckups. Gnawing at the inside of my cheek, rage sparking in my gut, I sidled closer to Nora again, enveloping her willowy figure with mine. She fit so perfectly, her back to my chest, her shoulder blades like sparrow wings, her neck like a swan.

Best of all, she smelled like *life*. Like a world that had aged eight centuries without me, tempting and sumptuous, *beckoning* me to explore every inch just as I had with her. More literally, my firebird had a faintly floral aroma from the deodorant she used—jasmine, according to the label—combined with the fresh clean scent of the mountain spring.

Exquisite.

She shivered when my mouth found her neck again, her hair nudged aside by my chin, her flesh claimed with the first graze of my teeth.

"Have you noticed them?" I rasped, burning the inquiry up her throat, dragging my parted lips to the base of her ear. "The eyes watching from the shadows?"

Nora's breath hitched, and her brilliant greens flitted about, searching.

"No, no, don't be so *obvious*, firebird," I rumbled as I wove one hand down her figure, over her bony hips, her strong thigh. The other delved up, crushing the shapeless cotton fabric between her breasts. Up, up, up her elegant neck until I could really grab hold of her chin, stilling her, parting her full lips ever so slightly. My mouth continued to work her flesh, teasing and tormenting, threatening to spill her bright red blood all over my teeth. My hand delved lower, hoisting up her dress, slipping between her thighs. All for show. All for the fucking *camera*.

Let them think my focus was her, always her, and not them.

In the meantime, I guided her chin *just* far enough to the right for her to—

"Oh my god," she murmured, her lower back arched, that perfect ass tucked snugly against me, my cock a sudden and undeniable rod between her cheeks. "Is that...?"

"If it wasn't there, I would just break the bars and set you free," I told her—promised her. I would, after all, let her fly away home. Not yet. But one day. When she couldn't suffer my life a second longer, I'd shoo her back to the real world and tack on luck, fortune, and health... If my reach extended all the way to New York, of course. "But they're watching. Always watching. They'll catch you, little firebird, and put you back in your cage. Maybe even clip your wings." The thought elicited a snarl deep inside me. Down the ramp, dishes rattled and the lights flickered. "I can't allow that."

Nora stopped writhing against me, her body going slack. The reminder that there was no escape—I'd fucked this up. My intention had been to distract her, to boost her mood, and all I'd done was make things worse.

*Classic Loki.*

My cheek twitched, centuries of shame and blame from the other gods burning in my chest, making my throat tight.

*Made it worse for both of you now. Don't let her see. Don't let her see what a fuckup you are—*

Fortunately, I was rather adept at stuffing it all away, deep, deep down where no one ever dared look—my long-entrenched self-loathing. With a forced grin and a semi-erect cock, I spun Nora around and scooped her up, relishing her surprised squeal as I tossed her over my shoulder.

"Come along," I urged, one hand creeping up her thigh, my thumb probing her damp cleft. "I think I've had enough of the internet for today."

Nora wriggled and squirmed as I stroked her, those dancer's hands whispering down my back and grabbing at my shirt.

"Oh yeah?" she said with a laugh, sounding much more herself again. "Does that mean you haven't found the porn yet?"

I slowed my descent down the ramp, racking my vast mental library for the term and coming up short. "The... porn?"

Another giggle, the sound accompanied by a wiggling of her little toes, broken and busted nails healing now that she wasn't forced to wear those torturous pointe shoes every day.

"Oh, Loki." Nora patted my backside as we drifted toward the bedroom. "Do I have a treat for you..."

# 23

# NORA

Three months.

I had been inside this fucking mountain for *three* goddamn months.

May. June. July. Two days until August. Every day, I added another line to the floor of the calendar corridor; Loki had whipped up some chalk out of thin air when we'd realized I wasn't strong enough to make permanent ticks in the stone like he did. Plus, it hardly seemed fair. In theory, my time here was temporary. His was forever. He deserved to dig into the mountain, scar it up, *hurt* this place like it hurt him.

Ninety days.

Ninety *fucking* days and I was losing it.

And that was why I had started to accept the odd cocktail. No more whiskey binges for me—I couldn't take the hangovers or the guilt, but Loki proved himself to be a baller bartender, mixing a shot into my favorite mocktail creations whenever I had an especially hard night.

If I was stuck in here without him, I'd die. Every day, I found myself looking at him when he wasn't looking at me, wondering how the fuck he had survived this long, how he made it through the long patches of solitude between consorts. As a god, he possessed a strength none of us mere mortals could touch. He knew it. I knew it. All the assholes in the village knew it. But what he didn't know, maybe what he refused to acknowledge, was that he had an inner strength, too, this fire burning that kept the all-consuming darkness at bay.

I had come to admire that about him.

He was a survivor.

And he knew how to make me laugh even when I absolutely, one hundred percent did *not* want to.

"I said *third* position," I bayed at him, swirling my French Sparkle—mango nectar, a splash of raspberry vodka, a touch of champagne, then a sliced mango over the tumbler's rim—and pointing at his feet. "What the fuck is *that?*"

Standing on the oak table like it was our very own stage, Loki looked down at his feet, then threw his hands up. "It's third position, firebird. Don't question it—"

"That's fourth if I've ever seen it," I shot back, hopping off the coffee table and padding over to fix his positioning. "Look. Look at how far apart your feet are. Third position is heels together."

Similar to first position, third required perfectly straight legs. I slapped at his calves, reminding him to take the bend out of his knees, then nudged his bare feet back so that his ankles lined up. Feet lined up. Ankles together. Straight legs. *Perfect* third position.

"There," I said after another sip of my cocktail, the mango dominant and the alcohol a faint afterburn. "That is third position."

Loki stared down at his feet again, then tapped the tabletop with his toes. "Do little children really do this?"

"Uh, yeah..." I sauntered back with a grin, the expression feeling a little less hollow now than it had an hour ago before we started all this. "Like, five-year-olds do this. There's a reason they're called the basic positions."

And he had them down pat, all five positions. Just like our swing dance lesson, back when he'd forced me through the first *real* orgasm of my life and I'd then slapped him as hard as I could, Loki picked everything up in seconds. But for me, he played dumb. He gave me *just* enough to nitpick at. As usual, I knew it and he knew it, but we pretended not to—pretended this was *real*, like we were ordinary roommates who flirted and fucked to pass the time, not an all-knowing deity and his human consort who both vividly understood the reality of their situation.

"Okay..." After another sip of cold mango deliciousness, I set my glass on the coffee table and clapped my hands together. Loki lifted his eyebrows at me before slugging back the rest of his bourbon. Thankfully, neither of us had ever gotten as drunk as we had on our worst respective nights—that Fact or Fiction drinking game was now a hard limit. "Let's move on to arm positions."

"Oh, firebird," Loki said, sighing and moaning out each syllable like a petulant child. He set his crystal tumbler at the end of the table. "I'd *much* rather watch you dance."

He then climbed off, bypassing the bench entirely with those long, strong legs of his, eyes fixed squarely on me. Bearing the brunt of a god's interest was enough to make anyone weak in the knees. These days, I could handle it— spine straight, chin up, knees locked—like he wasn't gazing straight through to my soul, but the butterflies in my chest, their flock multiplied tenfold, were such suckers for his intensity.

"Go on," he purred with a slight nod toward the dark doorway. "Fetch your shoes."

Three weeks ago, I'd found them just before I climbed into bed. At first, I had no idea what the fuck was on my pillow, stuck in the dark and exhausted from surviving another day... And then I smelled it—the blend of leather and silk. And then I *felt* them, hard and unbroken, shoes that had never touched a dancer's feet. New and shiny, just for me.

Loki had sat through hours and hours and *hours* of filmed performances, some from my company, most from the Bolshoi crowd. He could easily conjure things so long as he had a good picture to work off—and I had known right away, as I clutched a pair of soft pink pointe shoes to my chest, that he had conjured them for *me*.

Of course, seconds later I burst into tears. Sobbing, I'd staggered from the bedroom to the main hall, where I found him on the couch, surfing the web. Shoving the laptop aside, I collapsed into his arms and just hugged him with every ounce of strength I possessed. Wailed into his neck. Thanked him profusely.

They weren't *my* pointe shoes. They weren't worn in and familiar, contorted to the grooves of my feet, both hardened and softened by countless hours in the studio and on stage.

But I loved them all the same.

I loved them even more after I broke them. Carved up the soles for traction. Beautiful, pristine shoes could be a dancer's downfall; you had to completely rely on them. To dance, they needed to become an extension of you, just another piece of your body. Shiny and new did nothing for a performer—they were just art at that point. Over the last few weeks, whenever I was feeling especially down, I made Loki's gift ugly, cracking, cutting, snipping them until they were *mine*.

"No," I muttered, tucking my hair behind my ears, not really in the mood to perform for anyone. I hadn't danced in the shoes yet. Tried them on, yes. Flexed my feet. Tested the strength of the solid tips. But to actually go through the motions of routines I knew better than I knew myself... "No, it's fine. I don't—"

"Go on." Loki closed the distance between us in three long strides, effortless, more graceful than any dancer I knew. "For me."

As I drew a breath to argue, he caught me by the chin, rough enough to make my heart race. My lashes fluttered, and Loki tipped his head to the side, that fucking smile telling me we both knew he had me.

"I want to watch you dance," he rumbled.

And that was officially the sexiest thing any man had ever said to me. Devlin used to attend my opening night performances, but we never really discussed the show after —not in the same detail we did for his beloved classic cars, anyway.

"We don't have any of my music," I insisted weakly, feeling a slight wobble in my knees when his grin sharpened and his grip hardened. "Or good floor to dance on—"

"I'll take care of that." Loki looked more pointedly to the door, the message clear. "Fetch them." He squeezed hard, forcing my lips apart, jerking me a few inches into his personal bubble, my feet scrambling to keep up. "*Now.*"

Ugh. Why did I find him so fucking hot when he got all bossy?

And why, after all this time, hadn't a bossy, demanding, *rough* Loki lost its shine? Why did it still get me all riled up?

"Fine," I sneered, twisting my chin out of his grasp and shooting him an over-the-top scowl, "but you're getting Dance of the Sugar Plum Fairy, and you'll *like* it."

Loki crossed his arms with a snort. "Will I? Fairies are assholes."

I stared up at him for a beat, then shook my head and waved him off. Right. Obviously if gods were a thing, fairies were, too—discussion for another day.

Because at no point would I let my divine fuckbuddy sully my memory of the Sugar Plum Fairy. Although I had never performed one of *the* most complex principal roles on stage, I'd been an understudy last December when we performed *The Nutcracker* for night after night of sold-out halls. Even though I was officially listed as Dewdrop on the playbill, I had spent countless hours learning the Sugar Plum Fairy's routine on the off chance that Aubrey—two years my senior at the academy and an exceptional principal dancer—couldn't perform.

I'd never danced it for anyone but my company. Never needed to don the elaborate costume or wear the fairy's crown. Aubrey had nailed every performance from our first night to the last.

A strange giddiness fluttered in my chest as I scampered toward the bedroom, my feet already getting into character for the delicate, dainty footwork of the Sugar Plum Fairy. Ideally, she floated across the stage, effortless, like her pointe shoes never touched the ground.

Her routine hadn't crossed my mind in months, yet now, as I dug Loki's present out from under my pillow, every step flashed across my mind's eye. Muscle memory kicked in, my shoulders rolling into their proper *perfect* posture, my fingers ballerina-graceful as they coiled around my shoes. Energy thrummed through me from top to bottom, my lips twitching into a performer's smile—the one we wore that said no, our feet *weren't* killing us, that dancing on our tiptoes was fucking painless.

When I returned to the main hall, I discovered Loki had been busy in my absence: the huge oak table and its benches had been pushed farther into the kitchen area, all tucked away, the space open. To my right, the armchairs were now stored neatly against the cave wall next to the couch, the coffee table positioned alongside them. So much room to roam, for one coupé jeté after another after another. There were many in her dance...

Giddiness exploded inside, making my legs tremble with every step and my arms quiver with preperformance energy.

"What the fuck happened to your shoes?" Loki growled, staring down at them with a mildly horrified expression as he settled on the table's edge, bourbon in hand. I tapped a finger against the slashed bottoms, grinning.

"I made them mine."

That seemed to satisfy him; as I headed for the couch to lace up, Loki refilled his drink, all the while wearing this little smile that I don't think he meant for me to see, so soft and subtle—and human, in a strange way.

Once I had my shoes on, laced as tightly as I could, I fell into my usual stretching routine for my feet, flexing them, arching them, warming up my hamstrings. After months of no dancing, even before I'd left for Norway, my life back home in shambles, I couldn't just jump into the fairy's routine. I'd pull something—*everything*, more like—and I wouldn't be able to let Loki fix me. If you were a dancer, pain was part of the job. One of my mentors always said that if you woke up in the morning without pain, you were no longer a dancer.

I had been physically pain-free under Loki's care.

Nothing he could do for my mental health, apparently, but my body—it had never felt this good. The ballet studio had been my second home since I was a kid, the barre an old friend. All these months without the usual aches and pains... I wasn't a dancer anymore.

Until this very moment.

Until he asked me.

Pushed me.

"I should stretch," I said distractedly, hunched over, pushing each foot to its limit and beyond for a set count. "You know, just to be safe."

"Then stretch."

My eyes flicked up, and I found Loki watching me from the huge oak tabletop, seated on it, a full drink in hand. Voice tinged with darkness, his gaze was shrouded, its color like the boughs of the oldest pines in the deepest part of the forest, where sunlight died before it hit the ground. Swallowing thickly, I did my best to ignore him, ignore the intensity again, the way he watched me go through my routine without saying a word.

But he tracked me, my every movement studied and catalogued as a predator does its prey.

Just to get it over with, I could have skipped a few steps —but if there was anything in my life that made me thorough, that made *me* intense as fuck, it was ballet. For ballet, I did nothing half-assed. Stretching dragged on for a full forty-five minutes, and still Loki said nothing, just watched and drank and smirked when our eyes met. Whenever I could block him out, I sank into the familiarity of the routine, my body welcoming the twist and pull of every muscle, the methodical loosening and relaxing and strengthening of joints.

When I eventually finished, a small, miniscule part of me felt like a dancer again, coated in a thin layer of perspiration, my jean knee-length cutoffs and slightly too-small Van Halen tee nowhere near conducive for bodywork. But there was the ache, the twinge that told me I was ready to *work*.

Eyes closed, I let everything hang loose for a few beats, willing my heart rate to slow, indulging in the soreness. *I've missed you.*

"Are you finished?" Loki was standing when I opened my eyes again, having closed the distance between us by half. After I nodded, he summoned me with a crooked finger. "Good. Come here, then, and shut your eyes."

Confusion spider-walked down my spine, a dull reminder that with Loki, nothing was ever straightforward. Hesitating, I smoothed my hair away from my face, ready to give my left tit for an elastic to lop it up on top of my head. Another beckoning of his finger, his eyes slightly narrowed this time, set me in motion, and I kept going until we were almost on top of each other.

"Close your eyes," he murmured, a little reminder that made me frown.

"What are you—"

"Just do it, firebird."

Sighing, I obliged, then flinched when his cool fingers smoothed along my jaw, across my cheeks, not stopping their slow, lazy journey until they reached my hairline.

"Let me in, firebird..." Loki's whisper slithered seductively around the depths of my skull, and I stiffened with a sharp breath. Darkness reigned behind my lids, but at the sound of *him* inside my head, a soft glow suddenly

EVIE KENT

flickered, faint as candlelight. His touch faded, as did the sounds of the mountain—water dripping, wind screaming through distant corridors. Warmth bloomed in my chest, melting lower as he crooned, "Take me home. Show me your studio. Let me see it—every detail."

I swallowed hard, then did my best to picture my old studio. It wasn't difficult; I used to spend more time there than I did at my apartment. The sprawling space, so bright with a full wall of floor-to-ceiling windows. The opposite was rough exposed red brick with a mounted wood barre that stretched its full length. Light laminate floors designed to look like shiny birch planks. An enormous mirror along the left wall, always spotless. An expensive black piano next to the door. Airy and bright, my studio, with rustic touches and brick that I occasionally scraped my knuckles on.

"Open your eyes," Loki urged, his voice hoarse as it licked along the crown of my skull, then *dripped* down my spine. I almost didn't want to leave this headspace, remembering my studio, his voice so fucking delicious, but I did—because I wanted to be the Sugar Plum Fairy, and if he—

"Oh my *god*." When I opened my eyes, blinking hard, lashes fluttering, I was there. In my old studio. All around me—golden sunlight slanted in through the huge windows, so bright and vivid that I *felt* their warmth. I stepped around Loki, gobbling it all up in a panic, like if I blinked again, it would disappear.

It didn't.

It was still there—the mirror, the piano, the birch floor, the barre, and the brick.

"This..." *Can't be real. Can't be happening.* My chest rose and fell in hard, fast beats, and I pressed my hand to it, willing it to slow.

"Don't overthink it," Loki drawled, and I whirled around to find him in the studio with me, this stranger in my safe place. "We're here—just for you." He crossed his arms, grinning, then lilted to the left and leaned against the barre, his shoulder to the brick. "Show me. Dance for me, little fairy. You have a *ravenous* audience."

Fuck *me*, did he ever know how to make a ballerina feel wanted.

My cheeks burned crimson, and I padded over to the starting point on the far side of the studio in my beat-up but unbroken pointe shoes. Loki rotated on the spot, following me with a gaze that certainly felt ravenous, but his stance suggested he had to put his full weight on the barre—like he needed it for support. It groaned in protest when he shifted in place, the usually solid wood dipped and warped.

Same, barre. Same.

Positioning myself in the far corner, I settled into a B-plus pose: resting on one leg, while the other stretched back, toes to the floor, with a slight bend in the knee. Arms out and down, gracefully at my sides, fingers light as air. But I couldn't move. Couldn't start. Not without a song so familiar that even non-ballet fanatics knew it.

"Can you..." I licked my lips, unsure if this was asking too much. "Can you make the music?"

"If you can think it," Loki remarked. He swept his hand through his hair, as if totally at ease here, only this time his hand noticeably shook. And his expression seemed pinched, like he had the whole world on his shoulders. My Atlas.

This... was a lot of effort for him.

Closing my eyes, I thought of the first few tinkling notes to "Dance of the Sugar Plum Fairy."

"Let me hear it, firebird," he urged, his voice in my head

again, softer this time, wavering slightly. I cracked open one eye.

"This is the most incredible thing you've ever done, Loki." Transporting me somewhere else, somewhere far, far away from the fucking mountain—amazing. He truly was a god, not just in name or birthright, but in status and power, too. "Seriously."

His throat bobbed. "Just play me the music."

Sometimes he reveled in compliments, but he tended to shy away from the authentic ones, those that spoke to his character and not just his skills in the bedroom.

Eyes clenched shut again, I went through the melody as best I could, remembering it first on the piano, then with the whole orchestra. The subtleties. The bells. The light and delicate feel of it.

And then there it was, tinkling through invisible speakers, filling the studio. At first, I just wanted to sit down and enjoy it, but there was no telling the toll this took on Loki—so I moved. I dropped down to my entrance pose, then glided into my pointe work, tiptoeing onto the makeshift stage, embodying the Sugar Plum Fairy as best I could. In the scene, she was there to show her status, to prove she belonged with her prince—she needed to float. She needed to be effortless.

Up on my toes, floating, flying through movements and positions and postures I'd left behind in New York... I was free.

I was a dancer again, and nothing else mattered.

Crisp and light pas de bourrées. Fingers and eyes and smile working as one, giving my audience a proper show— like I *was* his fairy, Loki my prince, and I so adored dancing for him. Reaching arabesques, my hips tight, pushing into the posture even as they protested.

Despite the odd wobble, I remembered the routine well, forever ingrained in my mind after hours of rehearsal with Aubrey and our mentors. I glided around the space, becoming the fairy, until the final never-ending piqué manages that used to haunt my dreams—tight, fast turns that carried the ballerina around the whole stage, gaze stabilized but body *whipping* around in place. Step onto a straight leg, the other up and forward, folded perfectly, arms out and then in so close for speed and precision and movement.

The most difficult part of the routine.

The one that used to leave me breathless and dizzy until I *finally* conquered it.

All the way around the stage, spinning and gliding and spinning and tiptoeing and a little jump and all the way around—

I collided hard with Loki's solid frame near my final mark, where I would pose, elegantly, looking royal from head to toe. Graceful hands. A humble smile. Breathing slow and steady even as my heart hammered behind my ribs.

Loki stopped that. Stepped in the way. I grabbed at his chest as the music tapered off, steadying myself, panting, exhausted and exhilarated.

And...

And as I lifted my eyes to his, maybe, just maybe...

A little smitten.

Enamored, possibly, with the god who had asked me to dance, given me these shoes, promised he would never hand me over to *them*.

Yes, I was stuck here because of him, because of his loneliness, his selfishness, his refusal to admit that humans weren't playthings for the divine, but in that moment, it didn't matter. For a few precious seconds, he was the man who had given me all *this*, watched me hungrily as I teetered and pitter-pattered around my old studio like I well and truly *mattered*.

I gripped his shirt and stood up on my pointes, then dragged him closer, his mouth crashing to mine. He gave in without a fight, falling obediently into a kiss that started as all our kisses did: rough and frantic, intense, lips colliding like the crack of thunder and instantly parting— as if neither of us could get enough. But unlike all the others, this kiss softened almost just as fast, me easing back to flat feet, Loki following with a possessive hand stretched over my lower back. His eyes closed first, mine shortly after, and our mouths moved as one. Slowly. Deeply.

As soon as I cupped his face, something shifted between us. The air grew heavy. The butterflies in my chest exploded, thousands of them beating their wings in some sick celebration that had me smiling against his lips.

*Romantic.*

Our kisses had never felt romantic before. Violent, yes. Abrasive? Definitely. Domineering and lip-bruising. Only occasionally intimate. But this was like curling up together on a cushy couch, rain hammering the nearby window, everything dark and cozy and complete. It was the first time you truly *looked* at this other human being who fucked you and laughed with you and carried all the groceries for you— and realized they were your *person*, and the world just wasn't right without them.

And that scared the absolute shit out of me.

To suddenly feel so deeply for someone—for *Loki*, of all the creatures in the goddamn universe.

To feel so raw... and know that one day, I would leave

him forever. I *would*. I'd get out of here, with or without him.

A rush of tears prickled behind my closed lids, and I retreated with a sharp breath, my chest aching as if someone had shoved a whole load of glass shards into it. My eyes fluttered open...

And we were back.

*Here.*

My studio was gone, all the light and airy replaced with an oppressive grey that made my wounded heart sink. My hands slid down Loki's neck, then his chest, as I glanced around with watery eyes. This place was so fucking depressing. So closed in, even if the main hall was over a hundred feet tall. It was confined and dark, ever-present, a constant reminder that we were stuck, fucked over by my own species—that humans were keeping us here, that *humans* would never let me go home. The stony floors, walls, and ceiling. The catalogue furniture. The stainless-steel appliances that ran without wires or outlets.

I bit the insides of my cheeks, catching a sob halfway up my throat and holding firm to the point of pain.

Loki hadn't moved, his hands on my hips now, his face so beautifully relaxed; it was the first time I'd ever seen him look like this, and that made me hurt even more. When his eyes finally opened, slowly, like he couldn't stand to do it, his gaze first settled on my face, then slowly lifted to the depressing landscape around us.

"Sorry," he whispered roughly, hands raking up my figure like he was mapping my every curve. "I'll get it back in a—"

"*No.*" I twisted out of his grasp, bereft without him but unable to return to a fantasy *knowing* it was just a fantasy. Wishful thinking. Nothing but our imagination and a pinch of godly magic. "No." Tears careened down my cheeks, and I shook my head, backing away from him in my pointe shoes, my body aching from the fairy's dance. "No, if it's not real, I don't want it."

The muscles along Loki's strong jaw rippled, like he'd bit down, clenched hard, and he caught me before I could get much farther. His hands found my face, engulfed it, and I stiffened, gasped, a protest ready to go—terrified that he might drag me back to the studio whether I liked it or not.

But he just brushed my tears away, drying my cheeks with his thumbs. Swallowing thickly, the lump in my throat refused to budge as I grabbed his wrists and closed in on him until our bodies collided. *Real.* He was real—and I wanted that. Needed it.

Needed *him.*

Loki Laufeyjarson, in all his raw beauty, his fury, his mood and tantrums and jokes and leers and pensive quiet.

Only I...

"I have to get out of here," I whispered shakily, fighting to hold his gaze as I felt him slipping away from me, his ancient greens clouded over. "I can't be in this fucking place anymore."

He said nothing, his expression distant, and I stood up on my toes, supported by my shoes, and grabbed hold of his face—shook it hard enough to bring him back to the present.

"Loki, *we* have to get out of here."

And I meant it. Impossible as it might be, *he* needed to get the fuck out of this mountain even more than I did. Eight hundred years—three months. Our situations were nowhere near comparable, even if my lifespan was infinitely shorter.

Loki's eye twitched, and he gave a little headshake. "I doomed my own kind, firebird. I belong—"

"You played a part in the beginning, yes," I argued, a fire sparking in my gut, its flames sparking up my throat and pulverizing that fucking lump. "You did, and you deserved to be punished for manipulating some blind guy into accidentally murdering his brother. It was a really shitty thing to do, never mind kick-starting the fucking apocalypse." Look at me—lecturing a god. "But *they* did the other two things that made Ragnarok a reality, and eight hundred years is enough. You're eligible for parole, Loki. *Take* it."

The storm clouds in his eyes darkened. "And *how* would I do that?"

"I don't know." Really. I had no clue how to get *myself* out of here, let alone breach an impenetrable magic wall. "We'll figure it out. We'll find a way… somehow."

The sentiment didn't exactly bolster much confidence—in either of us, probably—but if I was getting out of here, we ought to fight for him, too. Yes, we might fail. *Yes*, this could end in heartbreak. But we had to try.

He had so much potential to offer the world.

And he had suffered enough in here.

Loki shook his head more vehemently this time, avoiding my gaze, roving the main hall as if he *hadn't* memorized every detail in the last eight hundred years. Gnawing at the inside of my cheek, I gave him a few seconds before I pushed up again, my mouth hungry for his, desperate to show him that I was serious.

Only when we kissed, we flatlined. Immediately. Loki made no effort to kiss me back, the romantic spark from earlier fizzled to ash. Eyes open, the god took me by the shoulders and pushed me away, harsh enough to knock me over if he hadn't held tight.

"*No,*" he rasped, expression unreadable. My brows

knitted, hurt and rejection twisting in my belly, and I crossed my arms—like that alone would protect my heart.

"What?"

"If it's not real..." He finally looked me dead in the eye, primordial and all-powerful and so fucking *fierce* that it made my knees buckle. "Then I don't want it anymore."

Confusion ripped through the panic, the hurt, and I just stood there as he strode off, disappearing into the mountain without another word.

Couldn't he feel it—how *real* that kiss had been in the studio?

We'd kissed countless times before. Screwed regularly. Cuddled on bad days and kept each other company on the good ones.

But *now*, when clarity had hit me like a fucking freight train, he couldn't feel that it was *real*?

I undid my shoes with shaky fingers, tossed them aside —and ran barefoot into the oppressive darkness after him.

## 24

## LOKI

*Pathetic. Weak. Useless. Lower than dirt...*

After three months together, I couldn't let her go.

But knowing what this place did to her, I couldn't let her stay either.

Not after I'd developed... *feelings.*

At this point, it wasn't just the desire for fiery companionship that drove me to her—it was more. I needed *her*, not just anyone. Nora Olsen. Her beauty, her wit, her passion. Watching her dance had cemented that into my tormented mind, bringing together thoughts I had battled for weeks.

Thoughts I had locked away alongside *feelings* that shouldn't be there, should never touch my heart. Feelings for a *human*, rooted and coarse, nestled into my bones. I had never feared loss before, yet I feared the loss of her—and not just when we eventually discovered Nora's way out of here, something that still eluded me for all my talk, but also the loss of *her* in, what, eighty years? Eventually Nora Olsen would leave me, temporarily or forever, and it was better—wiser—to cut the tether *now* than then, when my heart couldn't stand it, when I would destroy whole worlds just for her.

You know.

From inside this fucking mountain.

That kiss inside her studio, inside our bonded minds, had shattered me.

Because it was so fucking sweet, so perfect, so *intimate*...

No one had ever kissed me like that before. Not Sigyn. Not Angrboða. Not any of my past consorts—and none of those to come, surely. That kiss had sparked longing, desire, need, which was nothing out of the ordinary for us. Fucking her was nothing new. Nora had become my fine wine, my golden apple, and I craved her taste. But this time, there was a strange kindling in my chest for something *more*. To protect her. To cultivate *us*. To entwine and grow roots as one.

Pathetic.

*Weak*, a god succumbing to the whims of a mortal.

But I had always been pathetic, always been weak. Hiding behind tricks, behind cruel jokes and pranks that went too far. Taking the rejection of the Aesir to heart, letting it affect me, hurt me, rile me up so that when I lashed out, *I* was the one to suffer in the end.

Weakness had been in my nature for so long—but Nora made me weaker than all the rest.

She made me feel deeper than all the rest.

She made me... *yearn*.

Yet she desperately needed to escape this hellhole, go home, don her *own* pointe shoes again for an adoring crowd consisting of more than one lonely god, and I, a smitten fool, would do whatever I could to give that to her.

So, I couldn't feel anymore.

Couldn't take root in her.

Needed... space. Break the romantic connection growing, strengthening, hardening between us, the cord tying her to me turning to steel as the days crept by. Go back to just fucking her, teasing her, riling her up, using her to vent my frustrations as I did to all who dared drift into my orbit. Become the whiny child again who enjoyed plucking the wings off flies: a god with no regard for the lives of human beings.

It would hurt her.

Make me *ache*.

But in the end, it would be better for both of us—or, at the very least, better than wherever we were headed now.

*If it's not real, then I don't want it anymore.*

I had taken her words and flung them back, almost perfectly, because I sensed she would take it and run. Nora couldn't possibly feel for me as I did for her; humans paled in comparison to their godly counterparts. Their emotions were fleeting, their relationships stunted by mortality. My firebird had made a physical connection with me, but I was just her security blanket, something to keep her warm and safe, to provide comfort on the long, lonely nights. She didn't—*love*—me.

Not that I loved her.

But...

If I hinted at it, I knew that would scare her off, make her backpedal fast.

And with space between us, I could whittle down my feelings to shells of their former selves.

Encompassed in the bitter chill of mountain run off, the thundering waterfall reduced to a dull roar, I gazed into the murky depths of my lake. Facedown in the water, I floated there, spread-eagle and staring, capable of holding my breath for almost an hour if necessary. This prison of mine offered countless hiding places, but Nora had discovered them all these last three months, and my body—my mind, my heart—had needed a good splash of cold water to get out of the moment.

Pathetic, weak, *and* dramatic, wearing my clothes, floating back-up in the middle of the lake.

But alas. Here I was. And here I would stay until my racing heart settled, until the water washed away the remnants of that kiss, until I was numb again.

A disruption in the calm lake's surface erupted to my right, the splash, the intense impact, hinting at one of Nora's famous cannonballs; she had never learned how to dive and rebuked my offer to teach her. Seconds later, familiar hands found my back, my shoulders, ineffectual in their efforts to yank me upright. I exhaled, bubbles pluming from my nose, the bleak darkness of the lake going in and out of focus, then shot up—if only to quell her frantic scrabbling, not because I *needed* the breath.

I gasped anyway—*dramatic fucker*—and dragged the same old thick, heavy air into my lungs, soaked to the bone and in no mood to change that.

Nora bobbed in the water next to me, black hair slicked down her neck and fanning around her, those bony shoulders bare—oh hello, tits, good evening, dusky-rose nipples. Naked. She'd had the sense to strip down before she dove in, her clothes in a messy pile at the water's edge. Eyes wide and searching, a touch fearful—did she think I'd tried to drown myself? Something inside me balked at that, for I'd already told her I lacked the conviction to end my own life.

I kicked my legs in slow, even beats, effortlessly floating in front of her, a sneer on the tip of my tongue, a few forced words prepared to scare her off for the night. Before I could get them out, Nora grabbed my face and sunk her little claws in. I jolted, water splashing up between us.

"What are you—"

"Shut up, Loki," she growled, scrambling up my body, scaling me, using me to support her in the middle of a lake I so rarely ventured into with another. Nora's fingers twined through my hair, ripping my head back, her eyes no longer wide and panicked but totally and utterly consumed by flame. "Just... shut the fuck up."

Her kiss was brutal, nothing like our last, her lips a desperate punishment meant to brand me. Little did she realize, my mouth had been scarred long ago—but until this moment, I'd thought nothing could top that, when Odin All-father had sewn my lips shut for orchestrating the death of his son. My blood brother had silenced me for centuries, the twine thick and steadfast, the needle scarring my flesh as no blade ever had.

And then here was Nora and her fucking kiss, her mouth so firm, so strangely powerful, intoxicating in its control over me. She was nothing in the grand scheme of the universe, yet she possessed me as though she were the almighty. Our mouths parted, tongues tangled, teeth gnashed. No whiff of romance. No hint of sweetness. Yet intimacy shone brighter than the dawn, *connection* humming between us.

I kissed her back because I was weak, pathetic, wrapped around my firebird's little finger without ever realizing the walls had been closing in.

But we couldn't—

It had to stop.

I cupped her chin as I tore my mouth away, holding her in place even when she tried to follow me, chase me, hands in my hair *wrenching* me back to her. Treading water, bruising her jaw while my other arm snaked around her naked body, I shook my head.

"Firebird, stop this—"

"It's real, you fucking idiot," she rasped, her voice a perfect match for mine in the moment—strained, wary, uncertain, pained. Nora coiled her hands around my wrist, gently breaking the hold I had on her chin, then cupped my cheeks. My miserable heart skipped a beat. Her breath caught in her throat. "It's real, so just... shut up."

Her lips found mine again, claimed them most ardently, and I let her. Fire blazed between us, scorching down my body as she wrapped herself around me, kissed me like she meant it. *No, no, no.* A very stubborn part of me refused to believe it—that any of it was real, that I was *more* to her than the god who pleasured her, comforted her, fed her each and every day. But she tasted so fucking authentic, needy in the way she held me, that same spark from the ballet studio flickering in my chest.

No. She wasn't *needy*—Nora was passion and sincerity. For I, the father of lies, had always been so adept at sniffing out falsehoods, even inside this cage. My mind refused to believe it, but that gut feeling seldom steered me wrong. To her, it was real. To me, it was...

Horrible.

As I kissed her, stabbed a hand into her hair, hiked her up my body, nipped at her lower lip hard enough to make her squeal, I felt the walls closing in around us again. What was real to her resonated in me, yet it damned us both. For now that she was *mine*, I longed to keep her. Only this place suffocated all who dwelled within. The mountain would kill her—and being without her would be a slow, painful death for me. The longer she stayed, the more real it would become for both of us... and the more depressed she would get.

Misery loved company, sure, but I couldn't watch her suffer forever.

Eventually, I would find an out.

And by then, we would be so deep in *real* that parting would be akin to Ragnarok. It would scar us, torment us, possibly even *break* us.

In the end, this was a lose-lose situation, and if I were a stronger man, a better man, I'd put a stop to it now while I had the chance.

No one had ever called me strong before—or *good*, for that matter. So I kissed her back, matching her ferocity and running with it. Overpowering her. Consuming her. Holding tight, keeping her head above water, I kicked us over to the side of the lake and pressed Nora up against the smooth stone at its edge. Pinned there, she writhed against me, gloriously bare, her mouth hungry and her hands brutal in my hair, along my neck. Nails dug into my shoulders. Fingers ripped at my soaked shirt. Together, we wrenched down my trousers, her hands teasing my engorged cock, and when I pushed into her, driving all the way home in a single thrust, my firebird *sang*.

Her moans soared over the roaring water, the trundling falls, and I braced myself as best I could on the stone, toes clutching, hands gripping the dry shoreline. The first rock of my hips had her whimpering, just as the first clench of her cunt had me seeing stars. Nora clung to me so tight, her arms cuffed around my neck, that she choked me; I pumped harder, faster, driving her into the stone with a savagery that should have frightened her.

Should have sent her running.

Nora endured, arching up to meet me, stabbing her

heels into my lower back. She cried my name against my skin, poured all her little noises into my mouth. Her teeth sunk into my shoulder, into the wiry tendon that flickered in my neck. She was ferocious and beautiful. A mere flash in the passage of time, her life fleeting, but somehow in my arms, she felt ancient, eternal...

Mine.

Completely, wholly, thoroughly *mine*.

She came shortly after I stopped pounding into her and ground my hips to her molten center instead, working her inside and out just how I knew she liked. Months ago, she had fought this—oblivion, the pleasurable abyss my touch offered. Now, she chased it, shuddering and trembling, writhing her hips as she crested another climax.

"It's real for me," she hissed, eyes shut, body shaking and on the verge of snapping. "I-is it real for y-you?"

I twisted my fist in her hair, yanked her head back and bared her neck, unable to look her in the eye as I muttered, "Yes, firebird."

"Louder."

"You don't order a god—"

"Louder!" Her voice struck me with the might of a hurricane. Splayed out before me, my sacrificial lamb, Nora proved herself a lioness—not for the first time, most assuredly not for the last...

And that only made me crave her more.

I'd spent centuries with lovers who never challenged me, never defied me. Sweet and meek, loyal and earnest and *quiet*. Docile. Obliging. I had love for them in my own ways; Sigyn had been my closest ally until the end, but perhaps I had never been *in* love before. Not like this. Not until her.

Nora dared to command me. Shamelessly, she set the tone—pushed my boundaries, thrilled me to my core. As much as I dominated her body when we fucked, bent her over tables, tied her to the bed, roughly collared her throat as she came with me laughing in her ear... *She* was in control. *She* let me do it, all that I wanted, all that I *needed* to with her.

No one had ever given me that before.

Trust.

Warped, fucked-up, unfettered trust born from tragedy.

I gritted my teeth, driving into her furiously, mountain runoff splashing around us. Why did the thought of *trust* set me on the edge? The realization nearly made me explode inside her, but I fucked her through another climax that made her eyes roll back in her head.

"*Yes*," I snarled. *Yes*, you relentless creature—it was real to me. And it would destroy us.

Nora smiled, the stretch of her mouth victorious. "Loki, I can't h-hear you—"

"*Yes*, it's real," I bellowed, pumping harder and harder until I shattered. Pleasure hit me like a falling star, and I splintered apart in her arms. Releasing her hair, I buried my face in her neck, shuddering and jerking into her embrace.

And Nora Olsen, my firebird, readily welcomed me home.

In the aftermath, the mountain water cooled me, its chill a constant in my world. But she was warm. And soft. And *mine*.

So I held her just as she held me. I propped her up against the lake's edge, making a mental note in my pleasure-addled brain to heal her as soon as we climbed out. Her back and hips had taken the brunt of brutal lovemaking, our first true union as *lovers*, everything out in the open now.

Through the haze, a wretched, sneering little voice

reminded me that I had damned us to heartache. This could only end badly, whether she ever escaped this awful place or not.

But I just held her closer and breathed her in. Eyes closed, I cradled the back of her head in my hand, and my skin prickled as she dragged a lazy finger up and down my neck. Fear could wait until tomorrow. For the moment, this was real to both of us—and I intended to make the most of it before everything went to shit.

## 25

## NORA

Four months in here. September loomed on the horizon, and there was no end in sight.

Even with the laptop to connect me to the outside world, even with Loki's company, our relationship strengthening, deepening, the longer we relied on each other in here—it wasn't enough. I was drowning every fucking day. Stir-crazy. Bored. Frustrated. Angry. Depressed. Isolated. Solitary confinement was a goddamn death sentence, and Loki had to sit here waiting for a death that would never come. It wasn't fair. None of it. Not the way I felt about him, that I cared for him, ached for him—all the while knowing that this place would eventually break us.

Knowing that my life was fucked from here on out, whether I was stuck inside his cage or not.

And it just...

It hurt.

A lot.

Waking up each morning, even with the varied routines we had in place to keep things fresh, to allow us both some personal space throughout the week before falling back into bed together... Torture. Ongoing torture, day in and day out.

Today was a Wednesday. After marking my little line on the ground in the calendar corridor, I had set off for my midweek hike of the mountain's innards. Loki occasionally accompanied me, but I'd left him with one of his latest hobbies: sourdough bread. He liked to bake it from scratch, nursing the cheesy-vinegar-smelling base throughout the week so that he could whip up an exquisite loaf from scratch. Baking had been considered women's work back in his day, but Loki had done just about everything else in here; confinement certainly expanded one's horizons, especially when there was nothing else to do, when you had literally done everything else under the sun.

So, this morning, I hiked alone, hair damp from my quick dip in the lake after breakfast, thighs aching from last night's bout of punishing, *perfect* sex with a god who played my body like he had a PhD in it. Feet bare, wearing a pair of slouchy olive yoga pants and a shapeless white tee, I padded along the familiar paths, used to the darkness now. Four months later, one hundred and twenty-two days inside, I knew the twists and turns like the back of my hand. I knew what to avoid, what would support me if I felt adventurous enough to climb and inspect the nooks higher up the walls. I knew where the path dropped off and which steep corridors made my thighs burn if I bothered to walk them.

It was always the same, but occasionally there was comfort in routine.

Only life had become much, *much* too routine for my liking.

For Loki's, too.

He kept his shit together better than me, but he also had

way more practice at surviving in here—alone, forgotten, the world spinning on without you.

Had anyone started looking for me yet? Did they even notice I was gone?

My fleeting glimpses of social media suggested not. Everyone had their own lives, their own problems—and I factored into neither.

Stupid Scandinavia trip. I'd told the few friends I considered near and dear these days that I'd be off the grid, mending my broken heart and grieving for Opa. My Danish cousins had insisted I just let them know whenever I was ready to visit; enjoy your trip, see you when we see you. Of course they weren't worried about me... I was off backpacking and living the good life, right?

Teeth gritted, I tried not to think about that, just one of many invasive thoughts that were always such fucking downers if I stayed on them for too long. Instead, I took a tunnel that dipped down and around, bringing me along the base of the mountain, one that would eventually lead me to pools full of black, glittering water that I'd never dipped so much as a toe in. Loki had suggested not to, and even without all the information, who was I to doubt him? But the pools were weirdly pretty, and the air was always cooler down there. Trailing my fingers along the smooth stone wall, I drifted along, in no hurry to get anywhere fast, and then—

"Ow, ow, ow—god fucking *damn* it," I snapped, pain blooming in my pinky toe when it snagged on the little bit of rock that jutted out into the shadowy corridor. This wasn't the first time it'd nearly torn my toe off, and it probably wouldn't be the last; I always underestimated how deep into the tunnel it was situated, so every motherfucking time, it caught me by surprise.

Hopping a few paces forward on one foot, I braced myself on the wall and gripped my screaming toe. It would settle in a few minutes, like always, but I still whipped around to glare at the offending rock—like always...

My heart skipped a beat.

My mouth went dry.

Where there was darkness, suddenly there was *light*. A thin beam of gold sliced across the corridor from the spot that always caught my toe. I gawked down at it, stunned, slowly processing the fact that I'd finally hit that stupid bit of rock hard enough to knock it loose. And behind it, sunshine. An unexplored path to the outside?

Oh my god.

Oh my *god*.

Everything inside me lifted at the thought of finding something *new*.

Heart in my throat, I dropped to my knees and scooted closer. Sure enough, there was the dick rock that had it out for my pinky toe; I hurled it away and crouched lower. The hole was about the size of a grape, but with some cautious—mildly frantic—poking, I parted the crumbling opening just enough to shove an apple through.

Holy shit.

Adrenaline skyrocketed as I got on my belly and peered into the opening with one eye. On the other side, a narrow, low tunnel stretched through the mountain's base—straight to the outside world. From the scattered bones and very faint scent of shit, it must have been an animal den at some point.

But now...

Now it was my way out. The village was on the opposite side of our prison, cameras trained on the main opening. This... Maybe they'd missed this. Its size, its position—maybe they had ignored it completely.

"Holy *shit*," I squealed, ripping at a few more pieces of rock. "Loki!"

If I couldn't burrow my way through, I knew a certain god who would be happy to lend a hand. With his strength, he could open this up from grapefruit-sized to Nora-sized in five minutes flat—guarantee.

"Loki!" I shot up on trembling legs, my palms slick with the old fight-or-flight sweat, struggling to think straight, to process, to plan *anything* beyond getting through that fucking hole. Grinning like a lunatic, I staggered down the corridor that would eventually take me back to the main living space, shouting for Loki as I went. "Come here, come here, come *here!*"

At the distant echo of boots on stone, I rushed back to my salvation, determined not to lose it, an irrational fear churning in my gut—like if I left the hole alone for too long, the mountain would seal itself up.

Loki came racing around the corridor's gentle curve in under a minute—not a bad response time, actually—with a panicked look in his eyes.

"What? What? Are you hurt?" he demanded, slowing from a sprint to a jog to an abrupt halt when he found me crouched on the floor in front of the sunbeam, which I gestured to like I was demonstrating the best *Price is Right* prize of the season. His brows furrowed, and he stabbed a hand through his hair, hair that had grown out since I'd arrived, framing his face in gentle auburn waves. "What... is that?"

"It's a way out," I said, giddy as fuck, adrenaline making me shake. "I just found it... and it's opening the more I pick at it." Difficult as it was, I tried to keep my excitement in check, because while this *looked* like a possible escape, it could end up being just another serving of fuck you from the mountain. "I think I can fit through if I really squish."

Both of Loki's hands snapped in and out of tight fists briefly, my enthusiasm not as infectious as I'd expected, before he squatted down and squinted into the sunlight.

"The village is on the other side, right?" I mused as I jabbed at his arm, unable to help myself. Seriously, he could look a *little* more enthused about my discovery. Instead, he just hummed back at me, a low rumble that could be a yes or a no.

"Well, then maybe they aren't watching this," I carried on, refusing to let his hesitance ruin the first good thing that had happened to either of us in weeks. "It looks like it was an animal den, or something... See all the bones?" I waited for an answer, but Loki just crouched lower and examined the hole in silence. Whatever. "So, maybe *this* could be my escape! Move. Let me see if I can fit..."

I nudged at him, and when he didn't budge, I got down and shouldered him out of the way—or, at the very least, inched him aside as much as he would let me. Sure, he would have to make the opening a lot wider, but I was long and lean, thinner now than I had ever been during peak performance season with the company. With enough scooting and shuffling, I could squeeze through. Burrow my way out. I dug at the opening, clawing off a few more of the thin stony layers.

Then, just as I looked at him and drew a breath, about to ask if he could give me hand, Loki grabbed my arm and hauled me up.

"*No,*" he growled, his grip bruising and his expression unreadable as he dragged me down the corridor—away from salvation. I planted my feet, adrenaline spiking again, but this time it steered me into *fight* territory, somewhere I hadn't been with Loki in months.

"What are you doing?" I tried to twist my arm away when he stopped, indecision ripping across his features. "Are you okay?"

Obviously not, but if I could deescalate this here and now, we could get back to what mattered.

"No, you can't..." His tongue flicked out to wet his lips, eyes on the sunbeam for a long moment before he turned away and shook his head. "You can't, firebird."

"Loki," I snapped, dragging my bare feet, *trying* to make myself as heavy as possible when he started marching me down the corridor again. Not that this tactic had ever worked before or anything, but, you know, it was the thought that counted. "What the fuck? *Stop.*"

But he didn't. Loki towed me from salvation to the waterfall, unmoved by my struggles, dragging me like a flash flood hauled away everything in its path.

"What the hell is happening?" I demanded through gritted teeth, muscles already sore from fighting him. "This is a *good* thing. Can you just *stop*?"

When he finally did a few long strides from the calendar corridor, he spun back so suddenly that I almost crashed into him.

"You can't go, firebird." Loki shook his head again, his fingertips bruising up my forearm. "No. No. I'm not... You..."

Realization struck hard and painful. My eyes widened, and I booted him in the shin, viciously twisting my arm this way and that. "You selfish *asshole*! What, are you just not ready for me to leave yet?"

His jaw clenched, the muscles rippling, and his eyes

seemed to darken as he stared me down. "You're not going through that, that, *den*. No."

"Yeah?" I glared up at him over the tip of my nose. "You gonna stop me?"

He could. Absolutely. Loki had proven time and time again that I was no match for him physically, but that wasn't really the issue. In the last four months, we had shared so much of ourselves with each other. It was *real*. And now he was pulling this *bullshit*? No. No. Unacceptable.

"I don't... want to," he said slowly, *finally* easing up on my arm. Not that it mattered: there were five huge bruises glaring back at us, purple and ugly. I scoffed, used to ignoring pain, to pushing through it until my body finally collapsed.

"But you will, right?"

He swallowed hard, so fucking handsome in his black button-up, his tailored grey slacks, boots that gave him an air of true authority as he stomped about. Fuuuuck, I *loved* when he wore those boots while he screwed me.

I loved when he screwed me—period. But right now, from the twitch in his cheek to the tightness of his mouth, I knew he was about to screw me again, and not in the way that I loved.

"You're not going," he muttered, and before I could argue it, he tightened his hold on me, five individual pain sites *screaming*, and dragged me into the calendar corridor.

"*Loki!*"

"I can't... lose you," he admitted as I grabbed at the etched-up walls, planted my feet, pounded his back with ineffectual fists. Sure, I understood the panic, the fear: if I was gone, he would be alone again. Forgotten. He *hated* this place, hated the loneliness, but so did I.

"We've talked about this," I spat as he lugged me up the

steps into the main hall. "You can't just go back on your promise. You can't." My voice cracked, followed swiftly by the sting of tears. That managed to slow him, but he still didn't let go. "You're better than this."

"No," Loki muttered, shoving me at an armchair like I would just sit in it—like I was one of his other dutiful consorts. "No, firebird, I'm not."

"Bullshit." I steeled myself, refusing to sit, refusing to let him throw me around a second longer. I glared at his handsome profile and stood tall. "Yes, you are. I *know* you are."

"You know *nothing* about me," he thundered in my face, his features furious and broken. The dishes rattled. The cupboards trembled. The lights flickered. But I stood firm.

"That's not true," I told him, proud of how steady I kept my voice, lifting my chin and looking right into his eyes. *You don't scare me anymore, god.*

Loki scratched at his stubble, then finally released me with a shove toward the ramp. He positioned himself squarely between me and the doorway into the rest of the mountain. "You're not leaving through that thing. I'll cave it in if I must."

Hot, angry tears finally spilled down my cheeks, and I let them, refusing to break our locked gazes. "Don't you fucking dare."

"Don't push me, firebird."

"*Fuck* you."

I marched around him, taking a wide berth so that he couldn't just grab me again, when suddenly the lights extinguished. And not just the strings of lights artfully decorating our living space, but *all* light. The appliances died, their constant hum silent, and it was like this petulant god had found a way to blot out the sun.

"You are such a *child*." Arms up, I crept forward in the dark, eyes as wide as possible, only to clip my hip off the corner of the table. Loki said nothing as I hissed and swore, totally camouflaged in the surrounding blackness. Pain bloomed around my midsection, my hip bone taking the brunt of the hit, but I was way too riled up to care. "Turn the fucking lights back on."

Nothing. I gave him the benefit of the doubt, waiting about thirty seconds before scoffing and groping out into the darkness.

"For fuck's sake," I muttered, navigating a room I thought I knew so well totally blind. It took longer than it should have, and I knocked my knee on both the bench seating *and* an armchair, but I made it out without him stopping me. Stumbling down the steps, I veered left into the calendar corridor, the roar of the waterfall guiding me, and skimmed my fingertips along the chipped walls on either side, until—

"Oh *shit*."

Until I tripped over an immoveable object that wasn't usually there. I fell hard, toppling over a seated, hunched Loki, legs tangled around him. Anger dulled the pain in my hands and knees, and I scrambled into a crouch, glaring in his general direction, before reaching out to smack the shit out of a god having a motherfucking *tantrum*...

And found him trembling.

"Hey." Everything in me softened, and I crawled forward slowly, carefully, rearranging his limbs until I could climb into his lap, straddle his hips, and wrap my arms around his neck. His breath fell in fast, short huffs against my throat. Maybe this hadn't been a tantrum at all: maybe it was a panic attack. I closed my eyes and snuggled in closer —because *that* I could understand.

"I know you have to leave," he whispered hoarsely, arms somewhere not around me, my hug unrequited. Still, his nose brushed the curve of my neck, his mouth moving against my skin as he spoke. "I know you *need* to leave. And I did this to myself, to... to *us*, encouraging our bond, but the thought of you going out there, where I can't follow—"

"Stop." I cupped his face, still blind even with my eyes stretched open as far as I could push them. Not that I needed to *see* to see him. I knew his face. The slight dimple in his chin, the rugged jawline, all scruffy and villainous. The slight bump on his nose, as if he'd broken it one too many times. His *eyes*, forever green, wonderfully eternal. As my fingers whispered up his cheeks, as I captured his face firmly, I knew *him*, even in the dark. "Loki, you know that if I'm getting out of here, it's to find that witch's descendant, right?"

His trembling downgraded to the odd shiver, his voice tainted by a frown. "What?"

"Yeah." I grinned, wondering if he could see it, if it was only *me* lost in the black. "You think I'm just gonna go home and forget about you?" If I'd had the chance during the first month, maybe even the second, that would have been my only recourse—the best way to survive. But not now. Not anymore. I chuckled, mimicking *his* patronizing laughter perfectly. "Wow. You're dumber than I thought."

Loki shook his head ever so slightly, still trapped between my palms. "Don't—"

"When I'm out, I'm going to hire someone to find her." I had savings and Opa's inheritance at my disposal. The only holiday bookings I'd made in advance were in Norway; months ago, I'd wanted the freedom to go wherever the urge struck. Yeah, I had plans, but very few had required deposits. Now, with disposable income at my fingertips for the first time *ever*, I had decided after the *real* talk that if I got out, I would put it toward something good. "I mean, you'll need to give me her family's details, but I'll find her, bring her back here, and all together we'll break the curse..." I swallowed hard, throat suddenly thick, the tears from before resurfacing—no longer furious, but hopeful. "And then you'll be free."

Loki sat stiff and still beneath me for a long time, firm between my thighs, so solid, like he had turned to stone and become part of the mountain. Then, with a deep breath, he moved; his hands crept up my calves, over my ass, until they finally settled on my back. At first, the pressure was featherlight and distant, until I nipped his neck, and then he clutched at me, one hand soaring up to the nape of my neck and cupping the back of my head.

"Why?" he croaked, so tentative, so incredulous—as if he just didn't believe me. Given his past, I couldn't blame him if he thought these were all empty promises, that I was just saying what I needed to in order to walk the fuck out of here. And even if he took my promise as genuine, it probably sounded like a pipe dream, something nice to imagine but impossible to do.

Hell, maybe that was the case.

Maybe I was dreaming too big, betting too high on myself.

But I had to try. I couldn't leave him here—not without a fight.

"Loki," I murmured, hands sliding down his neck so that his pulse beat slow and steady against my palms, "you can do so much *good* with your powers. You can help people, make the world better, but above all..." I swallowed hard again, eyes closed as I pressed my forehead to his, our noses nuzzling. "You are *not* an animal. You don't belong in a cage. You've suffered enough. It's... It's *enough*. And I..." When I opened my eyes, thick tears cascaded down my cheeks, four months of emotion coming to a boil and making my heart spill over. "And I will b-be the *last* woman those fucking people kidnap."

He dragged me in for an embrace at last, and I clung tight to him, shaking, gulping down my sobs. Once again, we found comfort in each other, even without the promise of freedom, without a hope for tomorrow. In the safety of one another's arms, we were *home*—just for a little while.

And when the floodgates finally closed, when I beat back the storm, we both settled on the floor together, me curled up on his lap, my head tucked under his chin. Loki wiped at my face with one huge hand, drying my tears in two swipes, while the other played with the ends of my hair. Arms folded to my chest, I breathed him in, the musk of the man I had fought and hated and fallen for all in the confines of this fucking mountain.

"So..." I cleared my throat, words slick with feeling. "How do we do this?"

Loki sighed softly, then brushed his mouth over my temple as he said, "I have a few thoughts."

The thousands of butterflies in my belly soared, and I smiled in the slowly lifting darkness, light trickling back in from all sides. "Of course you do..."

# 26

# LOKI

Hand wrapped tight around her throat, a fleshy noose with no give, I cocked my head to the side with a cruel smirk.

"Does that feel good, firebird?" I missed nothing, gaze blazing across her naked figure, from the ropes knotted around her midsection that trapped her hands behind her back, that twined up and around each breast, onward to the black silk gag between her lips, all the way to her wide, pleasure-addled eyes. Nora whimpered and mumbled something incoherent in response, bouncing with my every brutal thrust. Even as cool September drifted toward cold October, another month under our belts, both our bodies were slick with sweat from ravenous fucking right out in the open.

On top of the dining table this morning, rather than my girl bent over it.

"What was that?" I purred, features twisting into a frown of mock concern. With a hand cupping my ear, I sat up a little, hips settling on the oak again, allowing her a few precious seconds of rest. "I couldn't quite make that out?"

She moaned helplessly, shoulders slumping, breasts the

faintest shade darker in their bindings. This was our first foray into shibari rope binding, and after a lot of internet research, we had kept it rather simple. On top of the ropes around her breasts and her waist, twine twisted around her bent legs as well, forcing them to stay in one position, my firebird forever kneeling—before me with my cock nudging the back of her throat, then on top of me while I toyed lazily with her clit. We had spent the better part of the last hour working her up, ruining her, making her eyes water and her whole body blush.

While I loved the look, there was a purpose behind it: for the last ten minutes, we'd had an audience. Awkward throat clearing and hurried footsteps punctuated our morning fuck, the villagers hauling in our huge weekly delivery in four massive crates. When they'd first arrived, I acknowledged them with a backward glance, but at no point did I stop pounding into her.

Fun as it was, that was the *game*.

No consort had ever been inside this cave as long as Nora Olsen. We had passed the five-month mark, and in order to free her safely by mid-October, before the *real* winter set in, everyone out there needed to think we were still hot and heavy, as my girl phrased it. We were, of course, hot and heavy. Smitten. Infatuated with each other outside of the bedroom. But that was difficult to express, and my worshippers likely assumed I collected girls for sex...

Not love.

Not true connection.

This was the third delivery day they had stumbled upon us in the throes of passion. The ones before hadn't been quite so salacious: the first had been just a heavy groping session, lips locked as we loitered at the electrified gate, like we just couldn't help ourselves while waiting for our order.

The second, meanwhile, had been a quiet, fully clothed fuck on the couch, missionary, my ass out for all to see, Nora's moans rebounding off the walls. She always clung to me, but for the voyeurs, she squeezed extra tight—so they could really *see* it.

"Poor girl," I crooned, my whisper amplified to a dozen different voices of varying pitches—like I was playing with my food before eating it. My words rose like thunder, cracking through the main hall. Near the gate, someone tripped, the distinct sound of some poor bastard's feet tangling and knees hitting the ground making Nora's lips quirk. I bucked into her hard, a reminder that she had a role to play, and she batted her watery lashes down at me, nipples dancing with every heaving breath. I flashed a wolfish grin, one that *did* make her blush. "I rather like you this way... All tied up and nowhere to go."

She responded with a hapless moan, squeezing her eyes shut, and I resumed my punishing pace, one hand on her throat, the other on her hip, each bruising in their own right. I pumped into her, hard and rough and fast, making my firebird bounce and squeal, until the gate clanged closed. Her eyes snapped open, and I slowed, both of us peering up and finding ourselves alone.

Grinning, I pinched her chin and arched up to remove the black silk gag.

"Good girl," I praised as I settled on the table, the oak cool beneath my shoulders. "Are you all right?"

Nora nodded, then croaked out, "Yeah."

Purplish-blue fingerprints marred her throat, her hip, and I made a note to heal them later—unless she told me otherwise. Sometimes she did. Sometimes I caught her studying them in the mirror.

"Shall we investigate our loot?" I asked with a sigh,

jerking my chin toward the ramp. She licked her swollen lips, brutalized a little while ago by my mouth and teeth and cock, and then shrugged.

"I dunno." The minxy tease rocked her hips, milking a sharp spike of pleasure from my core. Ignoring my scowl, she shrugged one shoulder, then fluttered her lashes again, a vision of innocence. "Maybe when we finish?"

I answered with a smile full of teeth and danger, shoving the silk back into her mouth, then grabbing her throat and pounding up into her hard enough to make those tits really bounce.

We had been ordering quite a lot in the recent weeks, our delivery requests doubled in size, sometimes tripled. It had been Nora's idea, something discussed over candlelit dinners, our feet touching beneath the table. Many of the supply requests had been frivolous: paintings, rugs, a brand-new dish set, fresh linens. She'd thought it best to make it seem like she was here for the long haul, adding a woman's touch to my prison—*nesting*, she had called it. Making it feel like a home. It gave off the impression that she intended to stay, and the villagers catching us all over each other, totally fixated on *us* and not them, only compounded that.

They had to be unsuspecting.

The more assumptions they made about *us*, about the silly human girl who had fallen for the wily charms of an immortal trickster, the better.

Half of our supplies we kept, decorating the main hall, warming everything up. The rest I transformed into goods she would need for her escape. Over the last few weeks, we had consumed a number of fictional disaster and horror movies, hiking trips gone wrong, mountain climbs turned fatal, cabins that were pure evil. Conjuring backpacks and hiking boots and first aid kits out of nothing would have taken a lot out of me, but being able to *see* them, I could easily transform a kitschy painting that was *supposed* to hang in our bathroom into something worthwhile.

Thus far, Nora had much of what she would need to suffer through the first breath of a Norwegian winter. Thermal gear—a sleeping bag, fleece-lined leggings, a puffy jacket that made her sweat whenever she wore it around the caves. A GPS device, one that I would fixate on and provide connection to so that she could move through the landscape undetected.

She still needed weaponry to protect herself. Food to sustain her.

But...

That was pretty much it.

My firebird was almost ready to fly away.

It was a thought that threatened to drown me, even now when I was buried balls-deep inside, forcing pleasure and blushes and moans from her with ease. So I focused on that, on the cries she made when she came, on the way her cunt danced along my cock, how her belly shuddered through every pleasurable contraction. I loved to watch her come.

Just as I loved her.

I forced my lips to stay stretched in a patronizing smile as she writhed on top of me, bound and gagged, all the while knowing that in a few weeks she would wriggle through that old den—and leave me. And I'd let her, because she deserved freedom. Her promise to find that fucking bitch's ancestor was sweet, and I suspected Nora would try with all her heart to bring the modern-day witch back here.

In the end, she would fail. It was inevitable—I had *almost* come to terms with it.

What mattered most to me was that when she escaped this place, and she would, Nora Olsen would eventually go on to live a full, happy human life. In sixty, seventy, maybe eighty years, married and bloated with life's experiences, she would die just like she was meant to. The world would keep on turning, and I'd be stuck in here... alone.

Just like *I* was meant to.

I went on fucking her long after her climax, forcing another small one out of her before I shattered apart. Clever little contraption, that metallic coil in her womb. No pregnancies yet. No telling if any of the other consorts, those without access to contraception, had been so fortunate. Had they birthed a demigod out there in that village? Did my lineage live on?

Or did they just kill the monsters in their crib?

More to obsess over, to weigh me down and bury me alive when Nora was finally gone.

After wiping the sweat from my brow, I saw to her bindings. The ropes left lovely marks across her flesh, ones that neither of us saw fit to remove just yet. Her freedom was short-lived, for I replaced the ropes with my arms, drawing her into my lap and cradling her to my chest as we sat in the middle of the dining table to catch our breaths.

"Okay," Nora murmured, cuddling under my chin before peeking over my shoulder at the crates. "Let's go have a look."

I sighed softly and just held tighter when she squirmed.

"In a minute," I whispered, wanting to hold her a little longer.

While I still had the chance.

"I think it's snowing."

A gust of chilly air billowed in through the Nora-sized hole in the mountain's base, and I squinted against the cold. Blackness greeted me at the far end of the den, peppered by tiny white dots and a ground hard as steel. October was basically in a full-tilt sprint toward November, a bitter Norwegian winter on the horizon, and it was either get out now or risk being snowed in.

Although I felt him hovering beside me, crouched low and somber, Loki said nothing. He had been *very* quiet all day, and I understood why, but I wished he could have put on a smile—just for me. Just for us. A part of me wondered if he thought I was doing cartwheels on the inside, so giddy that today was the day I'd finally make a run for it. I mean. I was. I hadn't been able to sleep much last night, just counting down the hours until it was time to *move*. But that didn't mean I wanted to leave him. The thought of going to bed without him tomorrow, wherever I was, cut my heart into tiny pieces, and Loki's silence, his longing looks, his refusal to meet my eye for more than a few seconds all day just crushed those little itty-bitty pieces to dust.

Clearing my throat, I pushed up, sat on my heels, and wiped the grit from my hands. Loki stared down at the opening, mouth in a thin line, and only looked up when I took his hand, threading our fingers together and squeezing.

He was so cold today, but maybe it was just all the flannel. I'd been sweating since I added the *many* layers, but come nightfall—real nightfall, not this sun setting at 4:00 p.m. bullshit—I would appreciate the extra padding. My backpack full of supplies weighed just about as much as I did; Loki had insisted that I carry guns and ammo and knives alongside my food, my thermal tent, and the first aid kits. The GPS tablet he had crafted from a weird artisan vase we forced the villagers to find for us was heavy as fuck, but it would get me *far* away from this place, out to Gamleby—which was about a week's hike away. From there, I'd grab a bus, a train, *something* to Oslo; we had decided the best thing to do was to lose myself in the more populous areas. Rent an Airbnb under a false name using the IDs Loki had made. Hunker down. Make sure no one had followed me.

Loki would stay here and keep up the same insane delivery schedule, ordering like he was ordering for two. We even recorded my voice on the laptop—moaning, laughing, screaming, crying, calling his name. He intended to play it whenever the village assholes popped in, just to keep up the charade. Magically, he could produce my voice, make it whisper through the interior caves, but the thought had seemed to upset him when he proposed it a few weeks back. The recording was just... easier. It required less of him.

Because he had already given so much to me.

After, you know, inadvertently *taking* my whole life away.

But never mind.

"Hey..." I shuffled closer, pressing a hand to the dead center of his chest—just to feel his slow heartbeat, to imprint it on me so I could remember all the times I had fallen asleep to it. Those nights, I could forget. Those nights, there were no nightmares. Loki continued to stare down at the opening, pointedly avoiding me until I forced myself into his eyeline, our gazes locked. "I'm coming back."

His lips flickered into a weak smile, and before I could get another word in, he kissed me. Sweet and deep and *aching*, our mouths melded together, falling into a familiar rhythm that I would miss in my fucking marrow the second I got out of here. His huge hands cupped my face, held me close, and I clutched at his sweater, green like his eyes, hard enough that the stitches groaned.

We had done this already—fucked last night, kissed and whispered sweet nothings in the hazy aftermath until I fell into a fitful, fleeting sleep. But now, it was like neither of us wanted to pull away first, clinging to each other, grabbing and groping and hands in hair. His breath warmed my cheek and his touch set my soul on fire.

And when he *finally* put an end to it, I felt like there was a piece of me missing without him. Even with his forehead pressed to mine, our eyes closed, our breath racing, I felt lesser now that we had stopped—like the end was near and I couldn't resist it anymore. Couldn't think wistfully about this day that was weeks and weeks away, all the while knowing I could crawl into bed with Loki that night, or laugh about something stupid over lunch, or push him off the rocks at the waterfall so that he belly flopped dramatically into the pool.

*Fuck.*

"Be safe, firebird," he croaked, and our eyes fluttered open together. I licked my lips, wondering how soon after this I'd stop tasting him, stop smelling him—campfire smoke and masculine musk and an evergreen forest as old as time.

"Helga Kristianson." That was her name, the witch's ancestor. I knew it by heart, could spell it backward and forward, had *burned* it into my brain. "I'll find her."

Loki had kept tabs on his captor's line for generations, and to summon this one's name, her age, her general location, he would disappear into long, scary trances. Sometimes he stopped breathing, his eyes clouding over, his body stiff as a corpse. He always came back, of course, but my heart still dropped into my gut and out the other side, worried that *this* time I had lost him.

Helga was twenty-one, blonde-haired and brown-eyed, tall and athletic, and lived in southern Norway like her ancestor. That was all I needed to get started, and whatever the fuck I had in my bank account would pay a top-notch private investigator to do the rest.

Loki and I stared at each other, me still in his lap, my hands on his chest, all bundled up in winter duds that were making me sweat. Time seemed to slow around us, until he finally blinked first, then nodded to the opening.

"Go," he ordered, all stiff and distant and cold. I swallowed thickly, hating how he sounded, until his eyes softened, and his mouth brushed over my cheek and up to my ear. "Before either of us change our minds."

Today had been in the works for months. I dreamed about it. We talked about it all the fucking time. I thought I'd be ready...

Only now that it was here, I couldn't move.

I couldn't tear myself away from him.

But I did. I forced my reluctant legs to climb off him, then grabbed my huge backpack and shoved it through the opening. I did so with shaking hands, adrenaline spiking and tunneling my focus to this moment, to the first step. Once my bag was out of reach, when I needed to crawl and shimmy in after it, I shot Loki one last look, squeezed his hand one last time, blinked back a rush of unwelcome tears before sniffing and dropping down on my belly.

It was a tight fit. Even with the added width Loki had torn into the rock, claustrophobia set in almost immediately. Musty air filled my lungs with every breath, and it was slow going the whole way through, pushing my bag ahead of me, then wriggling over stabby rocks, wincing as old bones disintegrated beneath my hands and knees.

Suddenly, the resistance disappeared. My bag flew away from me with one final shove, clearing the tunnel and tumbling into the great outdoors. I tensed, holding my breath, waiting for the explosion of screaming alarms, maybe even gunfire, footsteps falling like bombs as a bunch of village guards descended on my innocent backpack.

But there was... nothing. Nothing but a softly howling wind and the quiet of a cold October evening.

I inched forward, my jacket swooshing over the ground, one final rock deciding to be an extra-stabby dick when it jabbed into my thigh. With a wince, I poked my head out the opening, then gulped down a lungful of free air for the first time in six months. Tears swelled and fell, and this time I let them, shakily sucking in more freezing air, even as it burned my throat. So much colder than inside the mountain —Loki must have regulated the temperature for me, keeping us cozy and comfortable all this time.

Shivering, I wriggled the rest of the way out, then pushed upright, rising to my full height, blinking into the darkness of the outside world—and then immediately collapsing onto my knees. Mountain rock sloped down ahead of me, ambling along until it met a dense, dark pine forest. A light dusting of white coated the slate; my backpack had already started a collection of snowflakes, some of the fatter ones holding their shape.

Holy shit.

Holy *fuck*.

Outside.

Freedom.

It had *happened*.

Mouth dry, throat sandpapery, palms sweaty, I ripped into my backpack and dug out my hat, my gloves, and my night-vision goggles. Loki had crafted the latter after we spent a whole week binging classic and modern spy movies, cataloguing any equipment that might be useful for my hike. After shoving my gloves into my jacket pockets, I popped the goggles on, tightened the strap, and flicked the little button at the side. The world blended into shades of green, little details popping out at me—scraggly moss along the mountain's face, the individual trunks and branches at the tree line. Tiny, smeared footprints in the snow some twenty feet away, something dark and furry scurrying up and into a hole in Loki's prison.

*Loki.*

With a shuddering breath, I scrambled back to the den's opening. He was there, waiting for me, peering through the Nora-sized hole with a grim smile.

"Fly away, little firebird."

*Fuck*, that hurt more than I cared to admit. I braced on the jagged exterior, wondering if he could see me staring right into his eyes through these ridiculous spy goggles. "I'll see you soon. I promise."

I meant it. I really did.

Loki just nodded—like he didn't believe me, like he never had.

In that moment, I wanted to tell him that I loved him. *That* was why I'd be back here, why I was so determined to return to this hellhole. I fucking *loved* him with all my heart, for all that he had done for me, for the person he had made me, for the strength and perseverance I'd learned I had in his company.

But I choked.

Throat too dry, a lump settled squarely in its middle and blocked the words.

My lower lip trembled. When I came back here with Helga, when we broke the curse and Loki finally walked out of this fucking cage, I'd tell him. Scream it from the mountaintops. Whisper it while he slept. *I love you.*

So rather than muddling through and risk the words sounding forced, I kissed my hand and offered that to him instead.

"Soon," I told him, my voice cracking. "I'm coming back."

"I believe you." No, he didn't—but he would. Loki sighed, the wind suddenly whipping harder through the trees, the elements all around me seeming to echo him. "Now *go*."

After shoving my hands into my gloves, I threw my backpack over my shoulders and bolted down the snow-covered slope. I slipped. I slid. I fell on my ass more than once. But then I was off, Loki's sigh lingering on the breeze, and quickly lost myself in the trees.

Every inch of me on fire.

# NORA

The doorbell's chime launched my heart into my throat. Even at the flood of adrenaline that spurred my body to *run*, I waited, letting the obnoxiously long tune play out to completion. As the final note echoed throughout my Majorstuen studio apartment, I rose from the fold-out couch, smoothed my hands down my checkered sweater, my flannel leggings, and padded over to the door. Hands trembling, I took my time unlocking everything, like I was in no hurry, and then opened the door wearing what I hoped was a breezy smile.

Helga Kristianson smiled back, just as breezy, her cheeks bright red from the chill. February in Norway was the fucking pits: freezing cold, dark all the time, and Oslo was as expensive as Manhattan. But none of that mattered anymore. She was *here*. The Swede PI I'd hired out of Stavanger had done his job and found her shortly after the new year kicked off. *The* Helga Kristianson, the right one, daughter of so-and-so, so-and-so, so-and-so, all the way back to the witch who trapped Loki in that pit for eternity.

"God kveld," I greeted. *Good evening.* I'd had a shitload

of downtime on my hands while the Swede hunted for Helga, acquiring every piece of information possible about the nursing student who attended the University of Oslo full-time—who was apparently single, had worked as a bartender before starting school, and had a vacation cabin *way* up north. In the meantime, I had turned my passable Danish into passable Norwegian, and was pleased to finally use it with someone who wasn't a store clerk, a bank teller, or the doctor I'd seen for the miserable winter cold that plagued me for all of January. "Det er hyggelig å møte deg."

"It's nice to meet you, too," Helga offered as she extended her mittened hand for me to shake, the red woven fabric dusted with snow. She shook her head with a laugh, then hastily yanked her mitten off and gave her bare hand instead. "Your Norwegian is getting very good."

"Takk." *Thanks.* I shook her hand, both of us gripping hard and firm, and bit back my disappointment at not feeling anything out of the ordinary. Helga was the first supernatural being I'd met outside of Loki, and if I hadn't known going into it that she was descended from a powerful line of witches, I would have had absolutely no idea. How many others had I interacted with obliviously over the years? A lot, probably.

Positively beaming, I stepped aside and gestured for her to come in. "It's much warmer in here."

"Oh, *definitely.*"

Sweet, personable—just like she'd been in our chats. When she pulled off her dark blue cap, a long blonde braid fell over her shoulder, my own fishtail plait a near perfect match. I'd stalked all of her social media, obviously; she had a thing for braids, and I figured the more we looked alike, the less ominous I'd appear when I finally dropped my earthshattering request.

Closing the door behind her, I made an effort not to lock it. Oslo had been *way* safer than Manhattan in the four months I'd lived here, but bolting a thousand locks every time I shut a front door was a lifelong habit I'd never shake. Still, I didn't want to scare her off.

As soon as my PI had found her, social media had been my in. We were closeish in age, so my sliding into university Facebook groups and whatnot online had been easy. I mean, her profile was *barely* private, for fuck's sake. I could see all her groups, her likes, her dislikes, without even being her friend. Helga had a thing for cycling, and now that she had her own flat—her words, taken from her ad in one of the English-centric groups—she wanted a stationary bike.

And guess who had one to sell?

In mint condition?

Me.

Well. I had one after I read and replied to her ad, forking over two grand for the best model deliverable with two-day shipping and then slashing the price to practically nothing to entice her. We'd been chatting back and forth over the last week, me laying on the charm thick to establish trust, and after her night class this evening, she had offered to stop by to inspect the merchandise. If she liked what she saw, Helga had promised to come back with a rental truck and buy it.

Hopefully it wouldn't come to that.

Hopefully we could get this sorted out *tonight*.

"This is a cozy place. Great location."

"Hmm? Yeah, it's been awesome for getting to the university," I said, the lie rolling off my tongue, arms crossed as I sauntered in after her. I had chosen one of the more expensive Oslo neighborhoods to establish my home base in, but I'd wanted to be central—whatever made it easier to get

EVIE KENT

Helga here. The studio had served its purpose for the last few months; all Scandinavian-sleek, it was full of hard lines and corners, monochromatic and tiled, with functional furniture and a small TV. As a native New Yorker, I hadn't balked at the rent, and thankfully had had enough in my accounts from Opa's inheritance to pay for the PI, this studio, and then Helga's inevitable fee to break the curse.

After that, it would all be gone, every last cent, but that didn't matter to me—not anymore, not after four months away from him, all those nights spent thinking about the god I loved trapped inside that mountain, miserable and brooding, fearing I would never come back.

"So, here's the bike," I announced, crossing from the front door to the storage closet next to the kitchenette. All it had inside was the bike, which weighed a fucking metric *ton*. Coat unzipped, scarf loosened, Helga hurried over to help me haul it into the main living space.

"Oh, it's *perfect*," she said, her English on point and heavily accented, her eyes bright and eager as they swept over the brand-new exercise bike loaded with all the bells and whistles. She then looked to me, brows knitting. "Are you... sure you want to sell it?"

"Honestly, I thought I'd use it all the time," I insisted, leaning back against the quartz peninsula with a sigh—like I was *so* disappointed with the turn of events. "But it's just collecting dust and taking up space... I realized kind of fast that I don't like cycling as much as I thought. Might get a treadmill instead. More of a runner these days."

*Shut the fuck up, Nora.* I pressed my lips together tightly to stop babbling. The best lie was a simple one—no need to embellish. Helga seemed not to notice, totally enraptured with the bike, crouched down to inspect the gears and the pedals.

"Amazing. It's in such good condition," she murmured, inspecting it with curious hands as her perfect English turned to muttered Norwegian. Right. Helga Kristianson was kind of a weirdo for bikes, but whatever. I let her sink into it for two minutes—one hundred and twenty seconds that I literally counted out in my head—then cleared my throat.

"So..." A cold sweat broke out across my palms, my belly looping. *Here goes nothing.* "Do witches really *need* to exercise? Isn't there, like, a spell to help you stay in shape? I would have thought that'd be a perk, or something..."

I trailed off with a laugh, one that wasn't quite as breezy as my smile at the front door. Helga froze, withdrawing her hands from the underbelly of the bike seat before slowly peering up at me.

"Are you—"

"My name is Nora Olsen," I told her—because what we had discussed over the last week was mostly true, with a few convincing lies peppered in, "and... I wanted to speak to you on behalf of Loki Laufeyjarson. You know. The god your ancestor imprisoned for all eternity."

Helga shot to her feet, but I darted in front of her before she could hoof it toward the door. She raised her hands defensively, and I flinched, half expecting a bolt of lightning to fly from her fingertips.

"No, no, wait," I panic-babbled, hands also up as I took a step back to give her space. And continue to block the door, of course. "I'm not going to hurt you—"

"I doubt you could, human."

*Human.* Was that supposed to be a burn? I rolled my shoulders back and forced a smile, nodding. "Yeah, exactly. Look, I just want to talk. Hear me out to the end, and I'll make it worth your while."

The goal was to empty my entire bank account into hers, or at the very least promise that, but if it took a few visits that cost me a grand or two each time, I could swing that as well. Opa had left me some wiggle room, thank fuck.

We lingered in a tense standoff for ages, just sizing each other up. I had an extra inch on Helga, but she had magic at her disposal—hardly a fair fight. When it seemed like she wasn't about to charge through me like a Norwegian battering ram, I lowered my hands and told her everything. *Everything.* From the kidnapping to the villagers to the crate with a loaf of bread in it. The dress I'd worn for weeks, Loki's healing abilities and how much I initially loathed him. About our games, the crushing loneliness, the ache in both of us as we faced each new day inside that goddamn mountain.

How he helped me escape in the end, putting my happiness and safety above all else—*me*, just a human.

I carried into my escape, two weeks camping in the woods in October, avoiding everyone and anyone, not making eye contact until I reached a hotel in Oslo—paranoid as fuck, spending another week locked inside my room out of fear that Oskar and his dad had realized I was gone. Searching for her, determined to fulfill my promise. Right up to now, to the knot in my stomach and the lump in my throat. I was just an ordinary girl in love, desperate to free a man who didn't belong in a cage anymore.

Helga said nothing throughout all of it. She just stood there, staring, waiting for it to be over, her expression seldom veering away from suspicious. When I'd finally vomited out the whole story, I grabbed at the kitchenette peninsula again, needing the support to stay standing. My knees threatened to buckle, but I held firm, waiting, the truth out in the open now—shared with someone for the first time since I'd escaped. Even my few friends and family that I'd reached out to in November still thought I was just frolicking around Scandinavia, quarter-life crisis fully engaged.

At long last, Helga turned her back on me and drifted over to the futon. She sat at the edge, elbows on her knees, staring at the faux fire program I had going on the TV.

"Nora," she said with a sigh, the electronic flames catching in her eyes. "You know why he's there."

"He started the apocalypse centuries ago," I said flatly, icy relief flooding my veins that I could finally *talk* to someone about this—someone who wasn't Loki. "But, he didn't, you know, push everybody over the edge. There were three—" I held up my fingers to emphasize the point. "—necessary acts to kick-start Ragnarok. He was in prison, you know, *again*, when the others performed the following two. He just joined in on a war that was already happening."

She shot me an incredulous look. "And that excuses him —for the death of Baldur, for all the atrocities that followed?"

"Fuck no." I pushed off the peninsula and drifted to the other side of the pull-out couch, settling on the flimsy armrest. "Look, I get it. He deserved to serve time. He can be a huge asshole—I'm not oblivious to his flaws. But eight hundred years is enough, don't you think?"

"Are you one of his acolytes?"

"I..." My cheeks warmed. Was I some Loki fanatic? Not exactly. "Uh. No. Look, he has amazing powers. Healing, luck, prosperity... He could help *so* many people around the world, and he's finally ready to do good. Change the narrative. Make a fresh start—"

"And did the father of lies tell you that himself?" Helga

interjected, the question followed by a cold, humorless laugh. She then plopped her hat back on her head, stood, and zipped up her coat. Every step closer to her leaving made my chest tighter and tighter, to the point that when she finally marched toward the door, I felt like I couldn't breathe.

"No," the witch said decidedly, her tone final, her stride confident. "No, I won't—"

"Eighty grand," I choked out, flying off the futon after her. She stopped suddenly, and I drew a pathetic, stuttering half breath, still stuck in panic's clutches. At least that had gotten her attention. Slowly, Helga faced me again; I did my best to compose myself, flipping my braid over my shoulder and squaring off with her like I really meant business. "Look, I hate that I know this, but you're in debt. A *lot* of debt. I know your ex took your credit cards and bled you dry while you were together... And fuck him. My ex is a piece of shit, too. I'm sorry. But I know you're struggling financially, and I can pay you eighty thousand dollars if you break the curse for us. It's literally all I have to my name, but it can be yours tomorrow if you do this."

Helga's confidence faltered, her cheeks turning bright red as soon as we made eye contact. The PI had included details of all her finances in his report, including screenshots of cryptic tweets that suggested she was still struggling nearly a year after her shitbag ex-boyfriend ran up her credit cards. I hated to take advantage of that, but obviously it was a trigger point—and if this was the button I needed to push to get Loki out, then so be it.

"After the eighty grand, you'll get a yearly stipend for the rest of your life," I told her, hoping the promise of financial security until she died was enough to sweeten the pot. Loki and I hadn't exactly discussed it, but he had found a way to make that fucking village thrive; he could do the same for Helga, at the very least, once he stopped bankrolling all those assholes.

Slowly, Helga unzipped her coat, then pulled off her hat. She shook her head, fidgeting with her nails, and sighed.

"Nora, we've all heard about his curse. It's like... our coven's legacy," she admitted softly. "The story passes from mother to daughter, witch to witch, just so we *know*. And..." Her cheeks hollowed like she was biting at them, and when she finally met my eye again, something unreadable glinted back at me—something that made my heart skip a beat and my blood run cold. "And to break a curse like that, the process is as violent as it was to *make* the curse. Do you understand? Are you prepared for that?"

I straightened, adding a bit of steel to my spine. "Whatever it takes."

The rewards outweighed the risk, surely. Loki could literally *save* people. He could put an end to famines and droughts. Persuade warlords to back the fuck off. Heal the unhealable with nothing but a touch. There was so much he had to offer the world, and my heart insisted that after eight centuries of penance, he was ready for that.

"His powers will benefit the world," I added. "He can heal people and—"

"I know what a god can do," Helga said curtly. Of course she did. Was it common knowledge in the supernatural community, or were the women in her family just experts on the god I loved? From the muddled look on her face, there was no telling either way, but she continued to fidget and sigh, pacing between the door and my tiny kitchen, until finally she just stopped, the air around us stilling. "So, eighty thousand... American dollars?"

I nodded, desperation making my mouth dry, the lump in my throat swelling. *Just say yes. Just say yes.* Time slowed as she considered the offer, and a few minutes later, her leaning against the peninsula, me standing in the middle of this miniscule apartment literally shaking, Helga's gaze slid to me, her eyes more gold than brown now, and it felt like she could see right through me.

"Do you love him, Nora Olsen?"

"Yes," I whispered—*choked*, my first time admitting it out loud. The witch gnawed at her lower lip for a moment, then cleared her throat.

"Would you die for him?"

I blinked back at her, mouth opening but no words falling out. Because what the fuck was I supposed to say to that? Would I *end* my life for Loki? I... I had no fucking clue.

My brain was just static, but my heart suddenly raced, a fire sparking in my gut. Helga took my silence as answer enough.

"That's what I thought," she muttered, turning on the spot and marching for the door.

"*Yes.*" I stumbled after her, spitting out the word in a panic, terrified she might walk away for good if I didn't. Slowly, Helga rounded back to me, her eyes wide, eyebrows inching up her forehead. I took a few deep breaths, my fingers tingly and numb but my head unnervingly clear, my heartbeat strong. "Yes, I will."

I loved him, and he deserved to be free. In the grand scheme of the universe, Loki's life added so much more depth than mine. Mine was fleeting, over in a flash, while he had an eternity to make the world a better place, to right wrongs and fix the mess Ragnarok had left for *his* people. He'd fight it, but... I could be just another piece in the tragic backstory that turned him into a superhero. They all needed that push, right? In the comics, the movies, the books—the hero needed a reason to fight.

Holy fuck.

I hadn't woken up this morning thinking I'd sign my life away for him, but what other choice did we have? If the supernatural existed, then maybe there was an afterlife, too. Maybe it wouldn't be so bad, floating around on puffy clouds and playing harps without a worry or care.

So, why did I feel like throwing up?

Like screaming bloody murder and hightailing it out of Norway for good?

*Fuck.*

*What the actual* fuck *am I doing?*

"Are you sure you love him? That's the only way it works." Helga cracked her knuckles on one hand, then the other. "Or you die for nothing."

I swallowed thickly, staring down at her hands with a wary frown. Was she gearing up to murder me right here and now? Loki would have prepped me for this if he knew, right?

"Yes," I told her, voice hoarse and soft. "I love him."

And I was fucking petrified to admit it suddenly, but that didn't change the fact that it was true. Helga and I fell into another stare-off, both refusing to blink first, until she finally tossed her hat on the counter, then shrugged off her coat.

"I want forty today," she remarked, confident now—like she had officially made up her mind, "then forty when the job is done. After, I want eighty thousand US dollars a year for the rest of my life."

"That's, uhm..." I found myself nodding, mind full of

static again. Was this really happening? Had I just set something in motion that I would live to regret?

Or, you know, die with regret?

No.

I took a calming breath, then held out my hand. No, this was the way it *had* to be to get him out. No one said it would be easy, and freedom was never *free*—there was always a price.

After all this time, after falling for my dark god, I was ready to pay it.

"Deal," I said, and we both shook on it. Helga held on for a few seconds longer than necessary, like she was offering me one last out, but I just gripped harder, shook firmer.

"Okay then." The witch pulled away, then dragged one of the barstools out from under my peninsula and hopped on. "Let's discuss the specifics of the spell, then." She set her phone on the counter and swiped her finger across the screen, tapping in the four-digit code to unlock it. "But first, let me pull up my bank account for the transfer..."

"It seems a shame to destroy such a beautiful village."

Cloaked under Helga's camouflage spell, making us not quite invisible but completely indiscernible from the surrounding environment, I stopped my slow, careful creeping through the snowy pines to face her. "Are you *fucking* kidding me?"

The witch shrugged, jostling the huge bag hanging off her shoulders, overloaded with supplies for the spell to break Loki's curse. Pretty easy to go overboard on all the herbs and stones and crystals and ceremonial blades with half my net worth in her bank account, but whatever.

"I'm just saying," she said with a nod to the village nestled in the valley to our right. "I've never seen anything like it—a true blend of old Norway and the new. It could be a nice tourist destination—"

"Helga."

"I know, I know. I'm only half-serious, I promise." She held up her hands innocently, which were covered in ancient symbols drawn in henna by a crone from a friendly Oslo coven. Protection, apparently, from Loki's influence, while a few of the other runes enhanced Helga's innate power. I, meanwhile, had been carrying all our fucking supplies for the last week as we hiked the exact route I'd taken when I first escaped, all the way back to Ravndal, with a few shortcuts suggested by my witchy companion along the way. No runes. No protection symbols. I relied entirely on her to ensure none of the villagers saw me again; the day before we left Oslo, I could have sworn someone was following me around the grocery store.

Hello, intense paranoia. Welcome back.

In the last week, I'd wondered more times than I cared to admit if Helga was in league with those assholes, and here she was, just bringing me back, taking half my money and serving me up for them like a fucking sociopath. We got along fine enough, both knowing when to chat about anything *but* our current situation and when to give each other space. I'd hauled two tents out here, allowing us time apart each night, and so far she felt... trustworthy.

But when it came to Loki, I trusted no one. *Every* human out here had screwed him over, and Helga was descended from the very witch who had started this nightmare. Until the deed was done, there was always time for a little grisly betrayal.

Speaking of grisly...

My gaze flitted to her belt, from which hung a wonky silver blade. Braided leather wrapped loosely around her hips, and this morning she had emerged from her tent wearing a long green dress and a fur that she said was wolf skin, her blonde locks woven into a crown around her head. I felt like I'd been hiking the final leg with an extra from some historical drama, but hey, whatever she needed to do to perform the ritual, I was game. Want to look like you just strolled off the set of *Vikings*? Be my fucking guest.

The March snows didn't seem to faze her one bit. Meanwhile, even though I had been through what I hoped was the worst of Norway's long, dark winter, I still wasn't used to the biting cold. My cheeks burned as we stood at the tree line, peering down into the valley of Ravndal. Up here, the snow climbed to my knees and soaked the bottom of Helga's dress, her animal-skin boots. All those pretty houses below, the plowed fields, the lawns—green. Lush. Like winter hadn't touched them. Hell, it was somehow a smidgen brighter out here than it was everywhere else, the sun seeming to last longer, the air warmer. Loki gave these people *so* much, and in return they fed him lies, denied him modern tech, and held his consorts captive for the rest of their lives.

To the right of the village, that mountain soared. Snowcapped and ominous, it loomed over everything. Overshadowed *everything*. Torches illuminated the path from Ravndal up to Loki's tomb, each one connected by chains from the base of the hill to the mouth of the cave. Almost a year ago, men in masks and robes had shoved me in a box and dragged me up that exact path, the rocky grit making the crate bounce, making my stomach churn. When I climbed it today, it would be for the last time.

"Are you ready, Nora?"

A burst of adrenaline left me light-headed, and I grabbed at a nearby pine to steady myself. Climbing that hill would be the last of *anything* I ever did, really, and the thought had my heart racing, my knees weak. Once we started, there was no going back. Not that I *wanted* to, but I'd be lying if I said I wasn't scared of the ritual, about what would happen to me at the end of it, *right* before the curse broke.

But it was for the greater good. And... for him. I missed

him. In the five months since I'd last seen Loki, I missed his smile, his laughter—the patronizing and the authentic. I missed his sourdough loaves and the sex. I missed his mouth on my skin, his hands in my hair. I missed the way I caught him looking at me in the quiet times, thoughtful and affectionate and *real*.

Yes, I was fucking terrified of what was to come—but I would make this sacrifice for him, for his freedom, and for the good of mankind.

Not that I saw myself as a martyr, but—

"Yeah," I said softly when Helga nudged at my arm, the touch forcing me out of my head. Swallowing hard, I readjusted my ten-ton backpack, then sighed. "Yeah, let's do this."

Wordlessly, Helga raised her hands, the sigils darker than the world around us. Seconds later, a raging fire broke out in the main building down in the village—where they had forced me, sobbing and begging and fighting on a bum ankle, into a crate. Flames exploded from the rooftop and licked the dark horizon. Below, tiny figures raced from their homes, alarms ringing, when suddenly another fire erupted, this time on the opposite end of the valley. The witch at my side moved her hands gracefully, like a conductor gently guiding her musicians, and before long, six fires raged throughout the village.

"That should keep them busy," she mused, taking in her handiwork with a slight frown. I had no clue how Helga personally felt about this, about freeing a damned god and turning on the villagers who had kept him docile in his cage all these centuries, but I also didn't give a fuck about her opinion. She wasn't doing this out of the goodness of her heart or because she thought Loki should be free. She was doing this because I offered to pay her, to lift her out of her crushing debt, and that meant she didn't *get* an opinion.

"Let's go." I slid my night-vision goggles back on, then grabbed her sleeve and started down the steep slant out of the forest, mindful of rocks and roots. No need to sprain another ankle out here.

Not that it really... mattered.

It wasn't like I'd be walking away from this.

Once we were out of the snow, we moved at a steady clip, jogging over landscape that smoothed the nearer we came to the village limits. The raw, wild beauty of Norway's woodlands had been tamed here, the ground level, the grass frozen but thick and green. As fires burned, smoke billowing into the sky, more alarms sounding from the village, we veered right, headed onto the gentle hill to the cave's opening. Halfway up, I glanced over my shoulder, then stopped when I spotted a familiar face.

Oskar.

Limp-running with a cast still wrapped around the calf Loki had snapped all those months back. Of *course* the bastard suspected something.

Before I could point him out, Helga set a fire across the base of the path, one that stretched from one side to the other, then blazed up all the chains around us. I hissed, the fire brutal on the infrared, and yanked off my goggles.

"They definitely know something's up now," I muttered, blinking the flashing lights out of my field of vision, mildly annoyed that she hadn't given me any warning. Heat engulfed us from either side, blanketing Helga and me in a brilliant orange glow. She said nothing, her jaw set, the breeze toying with wisps of her hair, with the wolf pelt wrapped around her shoulders. For a moment, she looked so ancient, so worldly, the fire sparking brightest in her golden eyes.

Until she shook her head, a twenty-one-year-old woman of this day and age once more, and then started up the hill again. I followed, goggles hanging off my gloved fingertips, and ditched the huge backpack as soon as the cave's opening was close enough. Free of the burden, I sprinted the rest of the way, bypassing a crouched Helga. She loitered at the moss-shrouded mouth, digging into her bag and preparing for the ritual, while I blitzed into familiar territory, heart in my throat.

I stopped as soon as I passed inside. Being back in here, even on the other side of those fucking bars, knocked the wind out of me. So dark. So depressing. Memories came flooding back, emotional reminders of what I'd suffered in here, how Loki continued to suffer while I was gone. The gate stood tall and proud like always, caging in the beast, and I bit the insides of my cheeks, *hating* the sight of them. To my left, a red light blinked from a nook in the wall. Scowling, I faced it head-on and flipped the camera off. *Fuck you. Fuck all of you.*

"Loki?" My call echoed into nothingness, and I padded closer to the bars, heart lurching when everything suddenly lit up from the inside. Soft white light spilled up to the landing, followed by swift footsteps, bare feet on stone. I wrenched off my gloves and tossed them aside, waiting, shaking, staring hard at the figure that rose into view.

He had let his hair grow out. Auburn waves, messy and unkept, trundled down to his shoulders, and he stopped a few feet from the bars, face in shadow—but even that couldn't hide the scruff. Shirtless, beautiful, he appeared to be wearing the same black pants I'd last seen him in, only they were rolled up his calves.

We stared at each other for a beat, and then Loki strode right up to the bars, blinking tired eyes like he wasn't sure if he was awake or dreaming. I just stood there, rooted, knowing that if I approached the bars, I'd probably electrocute myself before the ritual even started trying to get ahold of him.

"What are you doing?" he rasped, voice thick and strained—unused. He looked me over hurriedly, top to bottom and back again, and then reached through the bars. "What...?"

Loki took it, the electricity's warning, flesh sizzling red as his fingers groped out for me.

And then his arm fell. His mouth tightened. He retreated a few paces, shaking his head.

"Go *home*, firebird."

I sniffled, not bothering to keep the tears at bay, not fighting the smile that stretched my mouth too wide. Excitement made me shiver, the cold a thing of the past, my heart whole again. "No, I promised." Sniffing again, I gestured back to Helga without looking to her, just listening to the clink and clatter of her ritual tools. "I did it. I found her, and we're going to get you the fuck out of here."

Loki gawked at me, the slight twitch in his cheek the only tell that he had heard a word I'd said. Dragging off my wool cap, I tossed it aside and smoothed my staticky hair. I had kept it loose—just for him. Maybe after, he could... run his fingers through it like he used to, like he did when he thought I was asleep.

"What, cat got your tongue?" I babbled, my words tainted by the shitstorm inside. They quivered, same as me, with excitement, relief, nerves, and gut-wrenching fear. But I forced out a watery laugh, wanting to keep the mood light and happy—or I'd crumble. Only it sounded fake, even to my ears, and made Loki's frown deepen. He stalked back to the bars, glowering at the witch behind me, and just as he drew a breath, lips parted, *something* on the tip of his tongue, Helga called my name.

"We can start," she announced when I glanced over my shoulder. Situated some fifteen feet from the bars, a huge shallow obsidian bowl sat at her feet, incense burning around it, surrounded by black sigils painted on the floor that mirrored those on her hands. Even all the way over here, I could smell the herb concoction in that bowl, earthy and piney and reminiscent of the Norwegian woods I'd spent so much time in—too long for my liking.

"What are you...?" Loki glared down at the bowl for a moment, then looked back to me, shaking his head fiercely. "No, firebird. *No*. What's happening?"

Helga's hurried whispers tickled my ears, an old and foreign chant falling from her lips as she brought the ceremonial blade to her palm, then dragged it across her skin. Blood dribbled and pooled, and she deposited it into the bowl, dousing the herbs. So. It had begun, then. Swallowing thickly, I turned my back on her and focused on Loki. The plan had been for him to keep up the charade, to trick the villagers into thinking I was still here after I'd left, but he had let himself go. The long hair. The coarse scruff. He'd lost weight, seeming paler, sadder, and thinner than I remembered.

I hated to see it now, hated to imagine him wasting away to nothing while I, what, carried on living my life like he didn't exist? *No*. A tear cut down my cheek, and my sniffle dragged his furious green gaze back to mine.

"It's time to get out, Loki."

"But at what *cost*?" he hissed, pressing up to the bars, hands wrapped around them, chest taking their crackling sting like it was nothing. Obviously he suspected something was up. He knew my moods, my expressions—knew the sound of my voice when I was on the verge of breaking apart in his arms.

"Nora."

With a small smile, I drifted back to Helga, never once taking my eyes off him. Loki stiffened as the witch helped peel away my outer layers—the winter jacket, the scarf, the double sweaters that had kept out the Norwegian chill during the last week. Right down to the interior thermal wear, which I shed as well, leaving me in just my bra and underwear. To him, I must have looked so much *better*: fuller, thicker, healthier. We had gone in opposite directions the last five months, and that wasn't about to change anytime soon.

"Firebird, *stop*," he growled as I braced against the cold, skin littered with goose bumps, my teeth starting to chatter. Taking a deep breath, I quieted them, quieted my hammering heart and my racing mind.

"I love you," I told him, wishing I had said it sooner— that we had more time to be in love with each other. Loki's arms dropped, hands limp and scorched at his sides. After a beat, the shock passed, replaced by a tightness around his mouth, his hands in fists. I licked my lips, all the pieces of our story falling into place before me, resolve warming in my belly. "I love you, and you should be free—"

"Only a fool loves a god," he argued, his tone harsh, bitter—unnecessarily cruel. "It always ends in..."

*Disaster. Heartache. Death.* Yeah. I knew that. Our eyes met, and realization sparked between us, his suspicions proven correct.

"It's okay," I whispered. He ought to know that—I had

chosen this, agreed to it, walked in here with my eyes as open as my heart.

"No, it's not," Loki snarled, grabbing at the bars again, yanking, tugging, the corded muscle up his arms going taut. Slowly, the metal warped, but it didn't matter. Those weren't keeping him trapped in here. He pulled harder, more frantic as I unclasped my bra and let the straps slide down my arms. "Firebird, go home. I'll stay here. You don't have to... Go *home*."

Bra on the floor with the rest of my gear, I raised my hand, hating the way it shook even as things started to settle inside, an unnerving calm sweeping through my veins. "Quiet and dignified, remember? You told me some deaths can be—"

"*Fuck* what I said!" Loki wrenched one bar out completely, his fingers blistered, electricity in the air as he hurled it aside. "Get the *fuck* away from her!"

I had never seen him so animated, so *powerful* as he bellowed at Helga in rapid-fire Norwegian. A few words sunk in, but the rest flew right over my head, devolving from a modern dialect to something else entirely. The witch behind me fell silent, and when I glanced back, I found her shaking.

"Don't stop," I murmured, hooking my thumbs around my underwear's waistline and tugging the cotton down. As soon as I stepped out of it, I shuffled closer to her, and my heart skipped a beat when she brought the knife to my throat. Just hovering. Not close enough to do any damage yet, but we were there—one final step away from breaking Loki's chains.

The death of a loved one.

Sacrifice in its highest form.

Willingly given.

"I love you," I said, our eyes locked and my voice thick. Loki shook his head at me, gritted his teeth, wrenched another bar out and tossed it aside, but I kept going. "When I'm gone, please do good. I know you can. You can *save* people. Please. Don't waste your freedom."

"This is absurd," he snarled as he tried to shoulder through the opening that was still too small. "Put the fucking blade down, witch."

"Are you sure, Nora?" Helga whispered to me. This was my chance—the moment that could change *everything*. He didn't want me to do it. Helga was willing to walk away at any point, my bank transfer pending into her accounts.

But looking at him, thinking back on all he had done, all he could still do, the fear dried up. The tide inside ebbed, leaving nothing but smooth sand clear on to the horizon. This was the right thing to do for everyone.

Loki deserved to be free and whole again.

And I loved him enough to give him that.

"I'm sure," I murmured. Loki cracked a third bar, splitting it down the middle, electricity dancing up his arm.

"No!" His roar made the mountain shudder, made the ground quake. "*No!*"

"Be good," I told him, stiffening when the silver dagger found my throat. Lips wobbling, I sought out his eyes, even as mine flooded with tears. "Be good for your firebird."

Helga struck, slashing the blade across my throat. Blood spurted like a bright red firework. Pain exploded through my every cell.

And as I collapsed to my knees, numb with shock, a god screamed my name.

## 30

## LOKI

*"Nora!"*

She wasn't supposed to come back.

She was supposed to go *home*. Escape while she had the chance. Live a normal life. Marry some fucking human who would never *quite* satisfy her like I could—not sexually or emotionally, not able to challenge her or open her mind, but that was just the way of the world. I would rather her endure that than this. This was madness.

This was—

"Nora!" I tore into the bars of my cell, ripping them out root and stem, hurling the charged metal aside. I so rarely uttered her name aloud. Always firebird. *My* firebird. But now I couldn't stop, as if screaming her name for all the realms to hear would bring her back—would stop her pain. The witch held her up by her hair, spilling her life into that bowl. My sacrificial lamb. My darling girl who had fought so hard to survive... dying. For me. For my life to go on.

*Fuck* that.

I didn't want that.

I had never wanted that.

300

She wasn't supposed to love me this much.

No one had ever loved me this much.

When I'd wrenched the last of the bars away, finally able to pass through, I ran. I used my legs as I hadn't in her absence, power humming through me, dormant strength rousing as I charged forward.

And as always, the invisible barrier stopped me. I pounded against it, even as it shred my hands and painted the ground with golden blood. I screamed. Roared. Descended into madness as the witch cut Nora's throat again, just to bleed her faster, her beautiful red life force filling the bowl, spilling over the side. She spoke hurriedly, this witch dressed like her ancestor, a vision of an age gone by. Not once did she dare meet my eyes, nor did she flinch at my rage. She did her duty, performed the rite.

Killed my firebird.

I pounded and pounded against the ward, against the unseen bastard that had been my gatekeeper, my warden, these last eight centuries—until suddenly, I fell through.

Gone was the wall made of steel, iron, and stone. Just air now. It hit me all at once as I tumbled to the ground, the surge of my power, the return of every last ability I had been gifted with upon the day of my birth. When I pushed up, the mountain stone cracked beneath my palms, strength beyond measure at my fingertips again. The runes littered across the ground faded, each one briefly catching fire before burning out, all turning to ash and blowing away in the evening breeze.

Centuries ago, I would have stilled. I would have sat back and reveled in all the divine glory flowing through my veins once more.

Tonight, I lurched forward, scrambling for Nora's limp body, her eyes half-closed, her beautiful lips parted—her

throat slashed open. Knocking the ceremonial bowl aside—
it slammed into the wall, obsidian shattering in an instant—I
rolled her corpse onto her back, planted a hand over her
neck, and sealed the wound. For so long, I'd really needed to
dig deep to heal, concentrate, *give* a bit of myself to my
victim. It came so effortlessly now; just a touch and her skin
wove itself back together, smooth and pristine, like there
had never been trauma.

Teeth gritted, I tipped her head back by the chin, then
breathed a lungful of godly air into her mouth. Watched
her chest rise out of the corner of my eye. Listened—so
frantically straining—for the tepid beat of her heart.
Nothing. The last eight centuries had taught me patience
beyond measure; I did it again, and again, and again,
willing her to fucking *live*, all the while knowing three
other entities controlled that. Had they severed her lifeline
yet? Cut clear through the strands of Nora Olsen's
destiny?

Had they even survived Ragnarok?

Maybe there was a chance—

*Thump.*

*Thump-thump.*

A heartbeat. Slow and failing—but *there*.

"There you are," I whispered, cupping her cheeks and
wishing she would flutter back to me. "There you are,
firebird."

Only she wouldn't. This mortal girl who loved me
enough to die for me—she clung to life so tenuously that
perhaps even a slight jostle would kill her all over again. If I
wanted her back, there was no time to waste. Vengeance for
all those who had wronged me, for the village of false
worshippers beyond the mouth of this cave, would have to
wait.

When had that ever been the case—putting the needs of another over my own?

Never.

Only for her.

Only for my—

"I'm sorry that I had to do that." I slowly lifted my gaze from Nora's perfect, lifeless face to the witch towering over us. Sigils tattooed her hands, symbols I barely recognized anymore. Protection, probably. Like little marks and letters would keep her safe from my influence, from my profound ability to worm into a human's mind and extract what I needed. It was fucking laughable. As I placed a hand on Nora's chest, tracking the barely there rise and fall of her breath, the witch fiddled with her nails and cleared her throat. Bolstered herself. Attempted to sound *strong* as she said, "I didn't make the spell... didn't set the requirements. But I know it. And you need to remember that if you *don't* do good like she said, I know exactly how to put you back in here."

Modern creatures had become so bold as to threaten a god—a god in possession of his full abilities, at that. Fire scorched up my throat, clouded my vision and tinged it with red, and I rose swiftly, too swiftly for her to track if the shock in her eyes suggested anything. Words failed me, as they tended to do around Nora, and I lashed out childishly.

Shoved her.

As if that proved a point.

The witch sailed back and crashed into the wall, her skull cracking on impact.

A little tendril of satisfaction unfurled inside me but was quickly quashed by guilt.

For I had failed her already, my darling firebird. That wasn't *good*.

Sneering, I stalked across the cave and pressed a finger to the witch's forehead, healing her just enough to close her split skull, mend the swollen brain inside. Not enough to bring her back to consciousness; she could wake up on her own, alone in this dreadful place, just as I had for eight hundred years.

I forgot her the second I turned away, wholly fixed on Nora, on her fragile, naked form lying there amidst ritual incense and scattered herbs. Snatching her jacket along the way, I wrapped her up, then gently cradled her in my arms and stood. No time to waste. Her heartbeat had slowed down again; perhaps her lifeline hadn't been fully severed, perhaps I had mended it just enough to keep her a few moments more, but that strand was fragile and tenuous.

*Move, you fucker.*

I charged out of the mountain for the first time in eight centuries, and despite my best intentions, I floundered in the free air. So crisp and clear and *cold*. All that I had imagined it would be—but tainted by the smoke rising from the village. Nora and the witch had set fires to keep them busy. I grinned down at her, at the way the breeze rustled her hair, at the gentle snowflakes descending upon her pale flesh. Clever girl, my firebird.

Dead ahead, a figure stuttered to a halt in my line of sight.

Oskar.

Oskar and the leg bone that would never fully heal. All the color drained from his face when our eyes met, and he stumbled backward, the gun in his hand useless. The affectionate lift of my lips that I reserved for Nora twisted into something cruel and jaded, and I exhaled a curt breath at him, as if extinguishing a candle. A gale-force wind dragged him off and over the elevated path, and he cried out for his father, for me—*Lord Loki, please!*—as he pitched into the rocky greenery below. The snow might cushion his fall; I certainly didn't give a fuck about his fate.

My eyes drifted to Ravndal, to the few buildings in need of repair after the witch's flames. With another breath, the fires reignited, blazing bright blue and ripping into previously unscathed structures. All but one.

Lucille.

*I feel you, sweet crone.* Her presence was a familiar one, and I spared her house in the center of the village, vowing to return when my firebird was well.

Carefully, cautiously, I set Nora down, mindful of her head, her delicate human bones. And for the first time in eight hundred years, I shifted. Simple as breathing, I transformed from half-jötunn god to a giant hawk. So many times, in the dead of night, I'd feared that if I ever got my powers back, I would have forgotten how to use them. But they were a part of me, and they came forth with ease, simple and comforting, like I was finally *home*.

I owed it all to her.

To the little human who had kicked me in the face when we first met, called me every name in the book, *screamed* herself hoarse at me.

Loved me.

Gently, I coiled my talons around her, cradling her, and then took flight.

All the while hoping the trio I sought, the women I *needed*, had survived the apocalypse that I, Loki Laufeyjarson, most certainly didn't start.

Not in its entirety, anyway.

31

# LOKI

Yggdrasil had seen better days, but the fact that the world tree still had the odd green leaf here and there clinging to its charred branches told me the Norns were alive and well. They were, after all, tasked with caring for the great tree. Each day they watered its roots, taking from Urðarbrunnr, the Well of Fate, to keep the tree satiated. During Ragnarok, I'd no clue what had become of the mistresses of fate, the trio of wise women who wove the tapestries of life for *all* living things, but having left Midgard behind with a very human woman in my clutches, the occasional rustling leaf suggested they had survived.

That they still maintained their sacred duty.

There were three such wells scattered across the roots of this great tree. On its branches sat the nine realms, from Asgard, land of the godly Aesir, right down to Hel, domain of the dead—ruled over by my darling daughter, Hel.

Who...

Had survived the apocalypse?

No idea, really. We hadn't exactly kept in touch, even before the end of days.

306

Urðarbrunnr nestled within the roots that fed Asgard, situated on what had once been a great green plain, the well a sprawling sapphire-blue spring. The Norns—Urd, Verdandi, and Skuld—dwelled within that territory, playing with fate and weaving lives together.

Tearing them apart, too.

Humans had a great deal of respect for those three. I, on the other hand, had once been accused of meddling too much in their tapestries.

Our relationship had always been... tensely cordial at best.

Yet now it needed to be something more, something *deeper*. For without them, my firebird would perish for good.

After traversing the celestial paths that wound along the trunk of the world tree, guided by starlight, by the colorful swirl of distant galaxies, I veered hard to the left, tucked Nora into my underbelly, and dove into the root in question. All the realms had doors. All the roots had passages. All the branches had an interior full of riches and dangers that few dared trod.

You just needed to know where to find them.

Fortunately, I'd had plenty of experience stabbing at the world tree all by my lonesome until *something* finally opened.

A gust of damp, musty air greeted me on the other side. Leaving the ether behind, I crossed into *the* root—and found the realm untouched. Asgard had suffered greatly during Ragnarok, the ancient halls in smoldering heaps, the meadows scorched, the earth dead, the Aesir gone and scattered.

Here, the Norns had maintained their little patch of territory well, hoarded it as one does the most sacred treasure. I landed upon lush grassland, soft and pliant as it had been when I'd last visited centuries before Ragnarok even entered anyone's mind. The thick green blades cushioned Nora's failing body and tickled my feet after I changed back into my normal form. Hoisting her into my arms, I headed straight for the glittering sapphire in the distance, with its cluster of primordial rowan trees in which the women built their hall. The plain stretched out to the horizon and beyond, empty but fertile beneath a hazy hickory sky.

With Nora in my arms, limp and wrapped in her Midgardian coat, I marched the rest of the way. There was something to be said about approaching the Norns with humility, and if I touched down in my hawk form, enormous and imposing, I might send them scattering on the wind. So I approached on their terms, shirtless, barefoot, tromping through the long grasses and clutching a human. Nora's chest rose and fell in uneven, stuttering beats, her heart rate way down by the time I reached the edge of the glittering spring.

The trio of women gathered at the shoreline, filling their buckets, eyeing me warily in silence as I slowed my march to a cautious stroll, head slightly dipped. They never aged, these three, though occasionally they altered their appearance—all for dramatics. Bearing the same olive-skinned complexion, they wore identical black gowns and sported dark blonde hair, though they had each styled it to their liking.

Urd sat nearest to me, her hair in a tight bun on top of her head, her feet in the spring, her violet eyes on Nora. Said to be the eldest of the trio, she controlled the past—what once was. Beside her crouched her sister Verdandi, her hair in a long braid down her back. Controller of the now, decider of human fate, she studied my figure with only mild interest.

Skuld rose to her feet when I finally stopped before them, seeming to look right through me and Nora—but of course. With her hair wild and free, her skin lightly freckled in comparison to her sisters, she wove the future, crafted tapestries for what was to come.

She was usually the most upset with my meddling.

Today would undoubtedly be no different.

Mouth stretched into a warm smile, I dipped down, about to spew some formal greeting that would have appeased the Norns centuries ago, when Urd sighed and pulled her feet from the spring.

"Loki." She crooned my name like a chastisement. "You cannot escape fate."

"It was hers to die for you," Verdandi added. Her gaze dropped to Nora, neither pitying nor apologetic—frank, matter-of-fact as always. Death rarely moved these three, not when they saw *every* death coming long before it ever happened.

"Yes, well..." I stood taller, sensing a groveling approach wasn't the way to go about this. "Change of plans, ladies, oh wise ones, sisters of *fate*." Carefully, I set Nora at the edge of the well, wishing that it was a healing spring instead, that one sip would cure her of every ailment, including death. Her head lolled to the side when I stepped back, her eyes closed, expression peaceful. It pained me not to touch her, to monitor her fading heart, her cooling flesh, but I couldn't give myself away—couldn't let them see how desperately I needed this favor, how desperately I needed *her*. Hands clasped behind my back, I faced the sisters again with a slight arch of my brows. "I've a deal to make."

Urd and Verdandi exchanged fleeting glances, their

mouths quirked as if to say *Of course you do, liesmith.* I'd been known for my deals across all the realms, little tricks and ploys to wriggle my way out of trouble. Not today. This wasn't for me.

And it wasn't for the sisters of the past and present to decide, but for the mistress of the future. I looked to Skuld, the supposed maiden of the bunch, but resisted the urge to really *push.* No gentle nudging of my influence would sway her—or any of them, for that matter. These three were primordial beings, separate from gods and infinitely more powerful. My wheedling would be like a fly pestering a bear.

As always, I'd have to rely on my words.

Some things never changed.

"It cannot be done, Loki, son of Laufey," Skuld remarked, her hair ruffling in the soft winds, her tone annoyingly final. I gritted my teeth, a flash of anger sparking in my gut.

"You haven't even heard my proposal in its entirety—"

"We do not bring humans back from the dead," Urd rasped. She shook her head, like she felt *sorry* for me, and I gnashed my teeth further, pain rippling through my jaw.

"Not for you," Verdandi added.

"Not for anyone," Skuld concluded. I rolled my eyes. Dramatic creatures, the Norns.

"Weave her strand with mine." Kindred spirits, we four, for I too had a flair for the dramatic. A stunned silence panged between us, and I looked to the rowan trees. Instead of leaves through their many branches, tapestries of every color hung, woven together to create the fabric of humanity, of all living things. Slowly, the strings would thin and eventually snap, thus ending a human's life. Rumors ran wild through Asgard that there were strings dedicated to the gods, too—that no one could escape fate. Studying the patterns now, the frayed strings spindling away from the others, the variety of color and depth, I still didn't know the answer to that one.

But I was taking a risk.

For I had been touched by fate, just like Nora, and these three wenches were responsible.

"Weave her strand with mine," I said again, firmer this time, taking a step toward the harbingers of destiny and doom. "I've enough life to share with her. She isn't dead yet."

"She isn't alive either," Verdandi fired back. Panic skittered down my spine, cold and painfully present, but I pressed on, ignoring it.

"It's not difficult—"

"What you propose is to craft another god," Urd remarked, her thick brows knitted. "It cannot be done."

"Weaken me, then." I offered it without hesitation. "Make me human, just like her."

Nora had sacrificed everything for me—for the chance that I might walk out of that fucking mountain. For all we knew, the spell could have failed. The witch could have betrayed us. But she loved me. She gave all that she had for my happiness, my life. She had such faith in me, such trust, and I owed her the same.

If it meant I lost everything, became average and ordinary, powerless after just a taste of all that I possessed... So be it. For love, trust, respect, honor—I would do the right thing.

For once.

Urd and Verdandi exchanged hurried glances, while their sister Skuld appeared very faraway, her eyes glossed over, the white swallowing the purple iris, the black pupil.

Studying the future, what impact my downgrade from god to mortal might have on me—on the greater plans for the nine realms.

"You are needed, son of Laufey," she deduced after a dreadfully long time. Blinking away the fog of the future, her eyes returned to normal, to the violet she shared with her sisters. I cocked my head to the side, holding her gaze and smirking. Well then. Now I had *leverage*.

"Whatever it is, I won't do it without her."

Skuld's lips twitched, as if fighting back a grin of her own. "I know."

Her sisters huffed and muttered to one another, their ire for Skuld bending the rules for *me*, of all creatures, abundantly clear. But the master of all our futures said nothing to them. Instead, she drifted toward the towering rowans, toward the intricate tapestries, and crouched at one tree's base. I watched her, arms crossed, as she picked through the dirt, through the few exposed roots, until she plucked a black string from the ground. Thinner than a strand of hair, the slightest touch could destroy it. I stiffened. Nora's strand. Her lifeline, *there*, in Skuld's delicate fingers. The Norn pinched it between her thumb and forefinger as she ambled back to the group, holding it up for me to see, forcing me to squint at it.

With a snap of her fingers, a golden strand materialized in her other hand. In contrast to Nora's, the string I assumed belonged to me pulsed with vitality. Gold and thick, long enough to pool and spiral at Skuld's feet, it seemed impervious to harm.

"She will live, son of Laufey," Skuld announced. She then licked the ends of each strand and began twining Nora's around mine. "But she will live with no extraordinary gifts or powers. She is fragile. Nora Olsen is *human.* Ageless from this moment on, her life will be tied to yours, and yours to hers. Should something kill her—disease, destruction, injury—then you too shall perish."

Doubt whispered across my skin, made the hairs on the back of my neck rise. Humans were so painfully delicate; an accidental fall could kill them. *Her.* It could kill her—and then me.

Well. That simply couldn't happen. She had a god to protect her, to care for her, to cherish her in her prime. From me, she would experience immortality, and even without all the bells and whistles, that was pretty fucking great. Never would she fall ill. I'd mend every broken bone, dry every tear.

For I had a debt to pay that would take an eternity to fulfill.

"Agreeable, wise ones," I croaked.

With that, Urd and Verdandi joined their sister, assisting her with the sensitive work, and I drifted back to Nora. Settling on the well's edge, I gathered her to me and tossed her jacket aside. Skin to skin, I held her, her forehead tucked under my chin, then patted her face down with the cool waters of the sapphire spring.

And there, where no one else could see, a god wept when a human moaned and finally drew a deep breath, her pulse quickening, the color returning to her cheeks.

Our fates entwined.

For the good times and the bad—we belonged to each other.

Bound together forever, my firebird and me.

# NORA

Rain on a metal roof.

Rain on the windows.

I came to surrounded by a soft and serene pitter-patter, but somehow I was totally dry. Dragging in a deep breath, I shifted about in a bed saturated with linens and cushy pillows, a little too hot beneath it all. Before I even opened my eyes, however, I felt refreshed. An ease flowed through my limbs, each one relaxed, cozy, nowhere near stiff. Not sore. Not aching. No pain. Just—me in bed, listening to the rain.

Swallowing hard, I frowned and opened my eyes.

Easily—too easily. No struggling to lift my lids, no fighting to stay conscious. Dimness greeted me. Not quite darkness, but shadows and warm wood instead. A steeped roof overhead, exposed beams as far as the eye could see. Wood walls, reminiscent of the stacked logs used in frontier cabins that I'd once seen in a history textbook.

It should have hurt to swallow. Helga had...

She...

Slit my throat.

The pain of it—that was my last memory. Heart racing, I shot up in a huge square bed, nothing like Loki's strange round one from the mountain. So... normal. Ordinary. The linens were a mishmash of soft pastels, while a white-and-blue checkered duvet topped it all off. The pillows stacked three deep. My chest heaved as I chased my breath, tried to slow the frantic drumbeat behind my ribs. To my left, a plain, curtainless window overlooked a forest.

My frown deepened. Maples?

Leafless maples and oaks and aspens...

No pines.

I rubbed at my forehead, then crawled out of bed, which nestled in the corner of what appeared to be the upper floor in a small log cabin. Without a stitch of clothing to be found, I dragged one of the baby pink sheets off with me, then padded to the open edge of the loft, peering over at what was maybe a nine-foot drop to the first level. Below, a potbelly stove worked hard, fire crackling inside and warming the space. Beside it stretched a kitchen reminiscent of Loki's creation in the main hall, only pared down to accommodate the essentials: a fridge, an oven crowned with two electric burners, and then a few counters, one with a deep farmhouse sink. Near the plump woodburning stove was a two-seater couch, its cushions fat and inviting.

"Where the fuck am I?" My voice came out all gruff and strained, and I cleared my throat as I tiptoed to the thin iron ladder at the far right of the loft. Unsure if I was alive or dead, whether it would even matter if I fell, I took the rungs one at a time, mindful of the sheet draped over me, slow and steady until I touched down on a polished hardwood floor. It had a rustic charm to it, dark knots and deep whorls in the planks, and much to my surprise was pleasantly warm to the touch.

Heated floors. I nudged open a door next to the ladder, revealing a four-piece bathroom. Then I tiptoed into the dining area—look at that, a fully stocked fridge.

Three huge jugs of mango juice.

I poked at the lids. Felt... real. All of it felt a little *too* real, actually.

Seriously. Where the *fuck* was I?

Was this my afterlife? Alone in a cabin?

Had I come back as a ghost to haunt this place? You know—the wailing lady of the woods, a spirit who made the shutters shake, whose otherworldly screams sounded like the wind screeching through the rafters...

Yikes.

Depressing thought.

Sheet hanging over my shoulders, I speared my hands through my hair. It was loose. Fluffy. *Clean?* Like someone —not me, obviously—had taken the time to shampoo and condition it while I was out. Because it didn't normally feel this glossy, but maybe this was just a perk of being dead.

Great hair.

Still accompanied by the dulcet beat of falling rain, I headed past the bathroom and down a short corridor to a door. Painted green, a windowpane up top, little white curtains obscuring the view—idyllic, all of this. While I found the door locked, it was easy to undo the dead bolt, to tap the little push button on the knob. As soon as I cracked it open, a rush of cool air flooded in, and I embraced it, stepping out and filling my lungs with a fresh crispness—no humidity, no thick wet in the air, like it *wasn't* pouring rain.

Outside, a covered porch stretched the width of the cabin, two wood chairs arranged in front of what I guessed was the window into that bathroom. Ahead, a muddy clearing surrounded the building, the grass straddling the line between green and brown—like it was in the throes of early spring. Clumps of melting snow dotted the landscape, both in the clearing and the sparsely wooded area beyond. Maples. Aspens. Oaks. Teeny, tiny, fragile buds clung to the thin branches. Not a pine tree to be found.

It reminded me of upstate New York, not Norway.

Seriously.

What the fuck?

Was this where we went when we died?

Wrapping the sheet tighter around me, hoisting it up so it wouldn't touch the mud, I crept down the front porch steps. As soon as I cleared the overhang, a dumping of rain hit, cold and so painfully *real*. I gasped, blinking the water out of my eyes and gazing up at a dreary grey sky.

Soaked to the bone in seconds, I should have gone back inside to the heated floors and the full fridge. Instead, I drifted around the clearing, memorizing every detail of the quaint log cabin with its silvery roof and its green door. A perfect circle enclosed the structure, cleared and flat and muddy, broken up only by a stack of wood at the rear. By the time I made it back around to the front of the cabin, I had a fairly clear picture of it all—rustic, pastoral, comfortable. Something from a time gone by. Not at all what I imagined my afterlife to be, but it wasn't so bad.

*Crack.*

I whipped around when something snapped in the woods, heart in my throat, drenched pink sheet fitted snug to my body like a glove. A figure emerged from between the trees, a hood drawn over his face—that figure *had* to be a man, so tall and imposing, broad and *strong*. I licked the

317

rainwater from my lips when he too came to a halt just at the tree line.

Slowly, he tugged his hood down.

My knees almost gave out.

*Loki.*

He looked so... normal. Dark jeans. Brown hiking boots. A white tee poking over the top of his zipped black rain jacket. Shorter hair than the last time I'd seen him, trimmed and maintained, styled almost, so that his dark auburn waves had a bit of volume even slicked back over his head. Clean-shaven. Strong jaw. Dimpled chin. That *mouth*. All those months apart—I had *missed* his mouth, for all that came out of it, for all he could do with it.

In his huge hands was a crinkly blue tarp, the splintered ends of collected wood poking out on either side.

His eyes—were at peace.

My lower lip wobbled.

This *had* to be the afterlife. He looked so good, so healthy and vibrant. So calm.

*It's not real, you idiot. It's a trick.*

"Hello, firebird." *Fuck*, that sounded real. His voice, so gravelly and deep, husky masculine perfection that tingled pleasantly between my thighs... It was just how I remembered. "Good to see you awake—"

"Am I dead?" I hated the way my voice cracked, but I didn't *want* to be dead. Sure, I'd chosen it, but that didn't make me feel any better now.

The sizable bulge in his throat bobbed, like he'd swallowed hard.

"No, you're not dead," Loki rumbled, stepping out of the trees and into the clearing, mud squishing under his boots. "You're *mine*."

All the butterflies in my chest rustled to life, shaking off

TO LOVE A GOD

the sleep and the quiet before taking flight. *You're mine.* A year ago I would have dreaded the declaration. Now I welcomed it, felt it in my bones, in my racing heart.

He took a few noisy steps toward me, then stopped when I brought my hand to my throat. Nothing out of the ordinary there, the skin smooth beneath my fingertips. No scar, even though I *vividly* recalled the tinny, bitter agony of that dagger sailing across my throat. Slicing the flesh open, my blood spilling and spilling until there was nothing left. I'd gone numb at the time, but I had still been... aware.

Back then, that had been the worst part: the awareness. I'd thought I would have blacked out, but nope. I felt the rivulets of red oozing out of me. Heard Loki screaming my name. Cursing and bellowing and shaking the mountain.

No mountain here.

I glanced around, just to be sure. "Are we... out? Is this real?"

"Yes." Loki tossed the armful of wood aside, the tarp splayed open as soon as it hit the ground. "To both." He reached out for me briefly, then let his arms fall back to his sides, hands flexing in and out of fists. Vulnerability rippled across his features, exposed and raw, hesitant even, as he cleared his throat and burned a hole into my forehead rather than my eyes. "Thank you, Nora... for loving me."

Warmth spilled down my face, tears intermingling with the rainwater, hot and cold colliding. I *loved* him back then —and that hadn't changed. Wiping at my cheeks, I marched forward, and then a few long steps later broke into a run, crashing into him as he swept me up and hugged me tight.

So warm... Loki's once chilled skin had such a delectable heat to it now, like freedom breathed *life* back into him. I couldn't get enough of it, especially as my teeth chattered against the chilly rain, but I had no desire to head

319

back inside—to be anywhere but here, in the arms of a god. Our mouths quickly found each other, and I cupped his face, lips parted, eyes shut, savoring the familiarity of a kiss I thought I'd never taste again.

When we tentatively broke apart, Loki did so with a soft chuckle, his forehead to mine, his arms locked snugly around my waist. His smile was *everything*, and my lips peeled back, mirroring it, feeling it in my heart.

"Come now," he whispered. "Let's get you inside."

A quick grip adjustment had me draped over his arms, legs dangling, toes curled, my arm hooked around his neck. I stole a lingering kiss, nails raking up his cheek, desire soft and hot as liquid gold flaring in my core.

"Can't have you catching our deaths out here," Loki murmured against my lips as he carried me toward the cabin. I frowned, waiting for him to correct that—*our* deaths —and when he didn't, I let out an incredulous laugh.

"Uh, *what* was that?"

"I'll explain it all, I promise," he told me, shoving open the cabin's green door and whisking me inside. He kicked it shut without looking back, eyes locked on mine, a fire igniting between us that threatened to steal my breath away. Loki set me down and wrenched the soaked sheet from my body. Tossed it aside. Pressed me up against the wall. Boxed me in with his hands on either side of my face, his cock nudging at my center. His affectionate smile turned predatory, dangerous, and he cocked his head to the side. "I'll tell you everything... *after*."

My hands dropped to his jeans, undoing them with shaky fingers, and when he kissed me again, it was like he kissed clear through to my soul. He consumed every inch of me, hungry and harsh and *mine*.

*You're mine.*

If I was his, then he was mine, too. Out of that mountain, we belonged to each other.

He could tell me his secrets later. *After.*

I knew he would. With great relish, Loki would talk and talk and talk, smug and proud and full of tall tales that I would call bullshit on.

And out here, together and free, wrapped in his arms as the rain pitter-pattered on the roof, as the fire crackled in the stove—I'd love every second of it.

## THE END

# EPILOGUE: NORA

*Five Years Later*

"And now we're fairies!" I trilled dramatically, arms up, smile wide as I watched twenty little ballet dancers in their leggings, their baby pointe shoes, their delicate flouncy skirts, whirl around Studio C like a tornado. We always ended the Tiny Tots classes with free movement, allowing them to just do what kids did: run free. They had had forty minutes of keeping themselves in check, going through the motions, learning the most basic steps and positions, when all they *really* wanted to do—at least the majority—was lose their shit to music and bounce around the room.

I loved watching them let loose. Our two junior instructors were lost in the storm, taking some time to be silly alongside chubby-cheeked five-year-olds in tutus. Next week, we would put together a routine for the final show of the year, the one where most would choke on stage and barely do the movements they'd spent a month learning. But it was all worth it for their parents to take photos, to film their little darlings—*sometimes* little terrors—doing what they loved. From this batch, I estimated eight would carry

322

on for more intensive work at the next level. From those, maybe five had the drive, the focus, and the desire to compete.

But who knew, really. In the three years that I had been running this place alongside Annabelle, a fellow former New York dancer who'd had enough of the competitive scene, kids had a way of surprising you.

Which meant my life would *never* be dull or routine again.

A wave of exhaustion suddenly pounded into me, and I caught Gwen's eye, the senior of the two instructors helping run the Tiny Tots lessons. A slight quirk of my eyebrow was all she needed, and as I glided out of the eye of the hurricane, headed for my chair next to the unmanned piano, she took over.

"Okay, now we're *tigers*," she cried, and all twenty little ones dropped to the ground, their faces warping from beautiful to primal, roaring and growling as they crawled around. As soon as I cleared the chaos, my elegant, straight-backed saunter turned into a waddle, and with one hand on my enormous belly and the other on my lower back, I sidled over to the chair that I'd been sitting on more and more these days, then plopped down.

*Fuck* my feet hurt.

So did my back, my knees, and my head, but that was nothing unusual after a Tiny Tots lesson. Cute little things, our youngest dancers, but holy *shit* could they ever get distracted over nothing. My condolences to kindergarten teachers.

Unfortunately, the aches and pains throughout my body were a given at this stage of my pregnancy. According to my doctor, I was healthy as a horse, progressing well and on track for my estimated due date in three months.

But carrying a demigod came with a lot of unknowns, and I was under the impression that things would only get worse before they got better.

Fun stuff.

It was totally manageable, however: being the co-owner of a thriving dance studio, surrounded by women day in and day out, meant everyone catered to my first-time pregnancy fears and needs.

And having a divine husband with power beyond measure helped a bit, too, I suppose.

The end of class song finally tapered off, and the littlest ballerinas erupted into our customary round of applause. First it was directed at me, then Gwen and Ericka, then to each other. With that, the door opened at the far end of the studio, and in poured the moms who had been watching class from the observation deck nearby, hidden behind a two-way mirror so the students didn't get distracted.

Because as soon as Mom appeared, distracted they were, an explosion of screeches and laughter bouncing off the walls and amplifying my headache to the point that it was *just* sharp enough to make me wince. Normally I was in the thick of things, chatting with parents as the other instructors set up for the next class in about twenty minutes. Today, however, I hadn't the strength to get off this fucking chair, so I waved instead, catching the eye of a few moms with sons and daughters in our more advanced classes. They flashed me sympathetic smiles, and I fired back an apologetic one of my own, genuinely upset that I couldn't talk shop from all the way over here.

"Loki! Loki! Loki!"

Uncapping my water bottle, I sat up straighter and watched as the crowd of five-year-olds abandoned their moms for someone *far* more interesting. Every Tiny Tot

class for the last three years absolutely *adored* my husband;
he was the biggest distraction of all, and no matter where I
was in the building, no matter which studio, I always knew
when he turned up from the shouting. Little alarm bells, my
girls.

He sauntered into the room with his shoes off—having
been shouted at about hard-soled shoes countless times in
the beginning by *all* the dancers, he finally knew better—
then crouched low to greet the girls. Moms chatting nearby,
the class swarmed, and I could barely get a look at him
beyond the crop of neatly swept-back dark auburn hair on
the top of his head. There was a brief snap of silence, then
another explosion of laughter and shrieks, and I shook my
head with a sigh.

He was doing something he shouldn't.

Some trick, with legit magic or just a sleight of hand,
that would only endear him further to this generation of
tots.

It happened every time, and not once had he ever
revealed his trade secrets.

The show only lasted a few minutes this time, before he
finally stood and waded through the battalion of tiny
ballerinas. He flashed the moms a smile in passing, which
had them all whispering behind his back as he carried on
toward me. Not that I could blame them: Loki was the
subject of all the hot gossip around the studio. They thought
I didn't know, but it was so fucking *obvious* the way they
looked at my husband—the way men and women
*everywhere* looked at him, utterly infatuated with this
ridiculously handsome creature. Outside of the cave, he
gave off an aura of power and influence, easily charming
and beguiling all who came into contact with him.

But he only had eyes for me.

I knew that now.

Me—and the occasional third we let into our bedroom here and there, just to keep things interesting. But he never looked at our casual friends-with-benefits the way he looked at me. Even now, after two weeks in Italy, he stalked across the studio with a hunger in his eyes, like he wanted to devour me whole over and over again despite the fact that I had ballooned up—that my ankles and feet were just big balls of swollen nonsense.

He never had to pretend that he desired me, wanted me, *needed* me.

And neither did I. Just the sight of him walking toward me now made my heart so fucking happy, made my belly loop at the thought of his mouth on mine. He looked sun-kissed and refreshed, but two weeks on the Amalfi Coast would do that to you. Dressed in a pair of dark slacks and a plaid green crewneck sweater—Loki was partial to Armani these days—with sleeves scrunched up to his elbows, forearms corded with muscle, my man looked good enough to eat.

Two weeks apart, surging with baby hormones, I was fucking *starving*.

Thankfully, this was his last trip abroad for the remainder of my pregnancy. Loki was and forever would be a wanderer, and after relocating his old consort Lucille from Ravndal to a stunning cottage in Italy, he liked to pop over every so often to make sure she was surviving well on her own.

To all her coastal neighbors, Loki was her rich, breathtaking son who doted endlessly on his aging mother. Her seaside home was a classic for the region and stocked with every modern amenity. Her garden was lush but manageable, with a few olive and lemon trees that were always in season, always bearing fruit. After living out most of her life in that fucking village, both Loki and I agreed that she deserved the best, and he had charmed—bewitched—everyone on her street into taking care of her when we weren't visiting. That poor woman wanted for nothing, surrounded by her countrymen, reconnecting with lost family, covered financially by a god who gifted her with infinite luck, and it would be like that until she drew her last breath.

"Hello, firebird," he rumbled, swooping down to kiss my forehead, then my lips. His natural scent—woodsy, earthy, masculine, and intoxicating—was the only one that didn't make my stomach turn. Lately, every other cologne or perfume had me running for the bathroom. Today, I inhaled deep, eyes fluttering shut as I breathed him in, welcomed him home to my body, and when I opened my eyes again, I found him crouched in front of me, both hands on my bump beneath the flimsy maternity workout top. "*Why* are you still working?"

"Because I'm fine," I insisted, this quick back-and-forth a conversation we'd had almost weekly from the day we found out I was pregnant. It hadn't exactly been planned, but five years in, two officially as husband and wife, it felt right. Loki had wanted me off my feet from the beginning, but I'd stood my ground: absolutely not. No fucking way. I planned to be here, with my dancers, with my business partner Annabelle, until they forced me on leave.

All my protesting didn't exactly wipe away the skeptical look that flickered across his features every time I said it—*I'm fine*. He wore it out in the open until I gave him a chastising tap on the nose, which then had him grinning.

"Well, I'm home now—for good."

My eyebrows shot up, and I let out a scoff. *My* turn to be skeptical. "Uh-huh. Sure."

Loki went here, there, and everywhere in a flash. He had always been on the go before Ragnarok, and after eight hundred years of confinement, it didn't feel right for me to stand in the way of his true nature. He liked to roam, and for the first two years, he had taken me with him. We roamed together: every country, every continent, every uninhabited island. The far reaches of the globe were new to the both of us, and we had explored them together. When it came time to settle, we chose California.

No more bitter cold for us. Not for a while, anyway.

Over the last three years, he occasionally took me on weekend trips to different realms, but those were few and far between. Cool as it was to see other supernatural creatures, to meet elves and dwarves and the few surviving Norse gods scattered around Asgard, I was still painfully human. Immortal, sure, but immune to literally nothing. Loki feared for me out there, and while I knew he went into hard-core protective mode off Earth because he loved me, there was also a sliver of self-preservation to his behavior.

If I died, he died. No coming back for either of us. That was the deal he'd struck to save me from death after I freed him from that curse. After sacrificing for the life and happiness of each other, we faced eternity together.

Which was still a lot to process. The full weight of it hadn't hit me yet, but it would in maybe a decade or so—when our kid had aged but I hadn't. When friends and family noted that I looked the same then as I had in my twenties ten years prior. Then we would have to move on. Start fresh. Keep everyone at a distance, if only to maintain our secret. After all, if Loki picked up an enemy or two along the way—and his personality had always suggested he would—it would be a disaster if they learned that killing his very human wife would kill *him*, too.

But for now, we had settled into relative normalcy. I'd opened a dance studio in Malibu a few miles from our secluded beachfront home with an old ballet friend from New York. Annabelle was sick of the Manhattan scene, unable to move up in her company and looking for change. Loki and I were majority owners of the business, but she was a great partner all the same. Our studio had blossomed since it opened three years ago, and many of our senior dancers joined competitive companies. One even danced in London now, while we had a few championship titles from competitions. There was a waitlist to enroll, and our students enjoyed themselves.

After all the shit I'd gone through *before* Loki, things were actually... good.

Great.

Fan-fucking-tastic.

*Especially* when Loki upheld his end of the bargain. We hadn't heard from Helga since we left Norway, but my man did good when he could. He had healed people around the world, always in secret, their memories altered so their sudden recovery was a medical marvel, a miracle, rather than the work of a god. Locally, he worked as a consulting investigator specializing in missing women and children cases. His solve rate was one hundred percent, which was suspicious, but it wasn't like I could ask him to, hey, maybe *don't* find the little girl stolen by some disgusting pedophile. Maybe *don't* split his skull in half when you find them.

No way in hell.

Occasionally he slipped. Loki enjoyed gambling and fucking with humans—and other supernatural creatures— who deserved it. He had a standing relationship with crime families in LA, Chicago, Tokyo, Rome, and New York that I didn't approve of, but one step at a time. For the most part, he did more good than harm, and that was a vast improvement on his past life.

"Are you done for the day?" he asked, our baby kicking at his hands and then my bladder in the span of about ten seconds. Wincing, I sat up straighter to adjust, while Loki just peered down at my belly like he could see the little gremlin inside.

Loved the kid already, of course, but if he could leave my bladder alone, that would be fucking swell.

"I have one more class—"

"Firebird," Loki purred, flicking that seductive gaze up at me and tipping his head to the side, "I think you're done. Annabelle can handle it."

Ever the charmer, his influence didn't work on me like it did the others. Maybe because we were bound together, he couldn't *make* me do something if he tried.

Well, no. That was a lie. His tongue, fingers, and cock were still all very persuasive tools at his disposal.

"Is that so?" I shot back, eyes narrowed. Of course Annabelle and all our instructors could handle the studio without me, but—

"Hmm, yes, I think so." My husband sidled closer, skimming his hands down my legs and wrapping around pointe shoes that were really just pretend pointe shoes, all looks and no substance anymore to accommodate for my grumpy feet. "*I* think you could use a hot bath and a very *long* massage..."

I sucked in my cheeks to hide a smile, every muscle *begging* me to concede. Because, yes, I could absolutely do with one of Loki's massages—best in all the realms. Drumming my fingers on my bump, soothing our shifty boy inside, I pursed my lips and fluttered my lashes, as if really taking the time to consider his offer.

"Yeah," I admitted finally, making him wait as long as I could. "You're right." Before he could ease away and help me up, I caught Loki by the chin, keeping him at my knees. "Hot bath. Massage. Pint of cookie dough ice cream." I squeezed when his lips parted and he drew a breath, stopping whatever was about to come out of his smiling mouth. "The *good* kind of cookie dough—from that shop in Brussels."

He could travel across the globe with the snap of his fingers, which meant he could—and frequently did—appease the cravings monster inside me in a heartbeat. One of the many perks of marrying a god, apparently.

Ducking his chin down, Loki pressed a hand kiss to my palm, then grinned at me, the twist of his lips both impishly and unabashedly affectionate. "Your wish is my command, firebird."

"Damn straight," I said with a giggle. He then heaved his pregnant wife onto her swollen feet. We said goodbye to the dancers, to the instructors, to Annabelle, to Roslyn at reception. Loki brought the car around to the front door, and I sidled into the mint-green 1962 Mercedes-Benz that Loki babied in our garage on weekends, secretly *very* glad to be off my feet, and popped my sunglasses down beneath the beaming four-o'clock California sunshine. Then stole a quick, fiery kiss from my man and let my hair down as we drove off into our very own sunset, a hot bath, a massage, and a pint of the world's best ice cream on the horizon...

I mean...

What more could a girl want in her happily-ever-after?

## ACKNOWLEDGMENTS

Thank you to Amanda, my editorial GODDESS, who is always ready to read my latest concoction. You know just how to punch my first draft fears in the face, and that's a valuable skill. Props to Sandra, my phenomenal proofreader at One Love Editing. You may specialize in contemporary, but I'll bring you over to the dark side yet. And lastly, to Linda. Thank you. You catch typos better than anyone out there, and I'm so grateful for your help on every single manuscript.

Thank you to all my many Liz Meldon readers who followed me on this dark romance adventure. I'm so grateful for your continued support and excitement about all my new projects. You make this easy. You make this fun. Here's to all the dark and beautiful HEAs in the future.

Much love to my friends, my family, and my sun and stars for always supporting my author dream.

And finally, thank you *you*, dear reader, for taking this journey with me. *To Love a God* was an emotional book for me to write. I drew a lot of inspiration from my own experiences with isolation and depression with my chronic brain injury situation, and Loki and Nora both experienced many of the exact same emotions in that fucking cave that I did in my own life over the last four and a half years. Finding a way out of the darkness is really important to me, so writing their happy ending has been oddly cathartic. This book really was a passion project, and I hope the strength of these characters touches you in some way. It did for me.

Don't forget to leave a little review, either on Amazon, Goodreads, or your social media. As an indie author, I rely on reader squees to help spread the word about my work, and I appreciate every word you write!

See you in **2021** for my next dark paranormal romance standalone novel: ***In the Demon's Debt***!!

xoxoxo

Evie

# ABOUT THE AUTHOR

**Evie Kent** is a dark paranormal romance author who loves a possessive anti-hero and a strong-willed heroine. She has been #teamvillain for as long as she can remember, and thinks the dark side definitely has more fun.

Her work errs toward soft dark, and features soulmate-level romances with dubious beginnings, along with a dash of angst and a dollop of kink.

WEBSITE
FACEBOOK READER GROUP

**More from Evie:**

**LILY OF THE VALLEY SERIES**
*(Dark-ish M/F Paranormal Romances, Same World Standalones)*
To Love a God
Surrender: A Lily of the Valley Novella

*Smoke and Mirrors: A Dark Space Standalone*
*(November 2021)*

---

RHEA WATSON & EVIE KENT

*(One author, two pen names — darker content with multiple heroes)*

### SERIES LAUNCH 2022

---

**EVIE KENT writing non-dark paranormal romance reverse harem romances as RHEA WATSON:**

### ALL THE QUEEN'S MEN SERIES
*(Paranormal Romance RH Standalones, Same Universe)*
Reaper's Pack
Caged Kitten
Root Rot Academy: The Complete Trilogy
*Bloodline: The Complete Trilogy (September 2021)*

---

### RHEA WATSON TRILOGIES & DUETS:

### ROOT ROT
*(Professors-Only Academy Reverse Harem)*
Term 1
Term 2
Term 3

### BLOODLINE TRILOGY
*(Wolf Shifters & Fated Mates)*
Raised by Wolves (#1)

Hunted by Wolves (#2)
Loved by Wolves (#3)

Made in the USA
Monee, IL
22 October 2022

16385401R00204